HERE BE MONSTERS

HERE BE MONSTERS

Anthony Price

THE MYSTERIOUS PRESS • New York

For Shirley and John Kasik

First published in Great Britain 1985
by Victor Gollancz Ltd,
14 Henrietta Street, London WC2E 8QJ

Copyright © 1985 by Anthony Price
All rights reserved.
The Mysterious Press, 129 West 56th Street, New York, N.Y. 10019

Printed in the United States of America
First Printing: May 1986
10 9 8 7 6 5 4 3 2 1

Library of Congress Cataloging-in-Publication Data

Price, Anthony.
  Here be monsters.

  I. Title.
PR6066.R5H4   1986   823'.914   85-63085
ISBN 0-89296-154-6

PROLOGUE:

The Pointe du Hoc, 1944–1984

HE HAD BEEN there before, but that other time he had arrived under the protection of darkness, and had departed fearfully in the half-light, with the dawn at his heels. So he had never seen the place before in his life.

What surprised him most was the grass. Somehow he hadn't expected the grass, although it must have been there then—some of it at least must have survived the *Texas* and the *Satterlee* and the bombers. But all he could remember from the darkness was a dreadful confusion of shell-holes and bomb-craters, occasionally and inadequately illuminated by dim torchlight and the distant flash of battle flickering from Omaha and Utah.

So the grass had surprised him, not the silence—not the silence, even though the sounds of that other time were what he chiefly remembered, far more than the fear and the excitement: the natural sound of the sea on the beach below, the crunch of boots on the pebbles . . . and the human sounds, of whole men whispering and cursing, and wounded men crying and cursing; and the inhuman noises, of the guns far away on the beaches, and far too close from the undefined Ranger perimeter just up ahead.

But those sounds, although he could still remember them rationally, no longer echoed in his head. They were part of a fading past, unlike the surprising grass.

And it was treacherous grass, too: it had been scuffed and trampled by yesterday's crowds, so that when he had been tempted away from the path to take an unwise look into one of the larger craters—a foolish, irrational temptation to see just what sort of hole one of those 14-inch shells from the *Texas* had made—he had slipped on the edge, and had sat down painfully on his bottom and slid half-way into the crater, scrabbling with heels and fingers.

7

Then the boy had appeared from nowhere—of all people, a nice solicitous American boy, just like Ronnie at the same age —just like Ronnie, coming to him down by the lake in front of the cabin, when he had hooked himself carelessly, and cried out, angry with his carelessness—just like Ronnie, just as helpful and vulnerable.

The boy had insisted on helping him out of the crater. And then he had shrugged him off angrily, just as he had pushed Ronnie away, all those years ago by the lake, with the hook still embedded in his flesh.

Ronnie! he thought. And with that thought all the doubts and the realities—and the unrealities—of the past fell away from him, leaving only his raw determination of the last forty-eight hours.

Ronnie had a good life, with Mary and the children—children who were almost indistinguishable from Ronnie himself now, already dating their High School sweethearts, and not at all awed by Grandpa!

And—

And he had done everything that they—They—had asked of him, so very carefully, over the years—

The path (*there had been no path then, never mind the grass!*)— the path was taking him close to the cliff-edge now, even offering him some sort of wooden stairway to the beach below (*By God! That would have been damn useful, back in '44!*).

But he had to leave the path here, to make their rendezvous.

He looked back. The boy was still there, watching him doubtfully, but he couldn't bring himself to acknowledge that concern, which would surely increase when he set off along the cliff-edge, instead of descending to the beach—

(*He could remember the beach in the dark well enough, anyway: all the wreckage of the assault, and the wounded still waiting for evacuation, before his hair-raising rope-ladder climb up the cliff: he had no desire to see that beach again!*)

And there was a man picking up litter around the nearest pill-box, too. And he wasn't at all sure that he hadn't been followed; although such matters were outside his remit; besides which, it might be they themselves who were watching over him; and, in any case, it was their business now; and, in the last case of all, it didn't matter now, anyway—

8

He had done everything they had asked of him, so carefully, so very carefully, over all the years—and, until now, so successfully . . . First, out of conviction; then in doubt, then out of necessity (even then to protect Ronnie, maybe?); and finally almost out of habit—? But he had done it, anyway!

But now, when it mattered most or least (he honestly didn't know which now), *he had given himself this last instruction of all, which would save everyone a great deal of trouble—Them, him, the Central Intelligence Agency, and Ronnie—and Ronnie and the grandchildren most of all!*

He just had to find the right place, that was all.

And it had to be out of the boy's sight—and the pill-box-poking Frenchman's . . . and there was someone else, further away, also scavenging among the debris of yesterday's anniversary celebration . . .

It had to be the right place: the beach below, memory reminded him, was of pebbles and fallen rocks. But he must get the maximum height, to do it right—

It wasn't as simple as he'd thought it would be, from the recollection of that original climb, and the dark descent, when he'd had a young Ranger to shepherd him, making light of the hazards which had left him in a hot-and-cold sweat. And the grass was still treacherous and slippery.

But now he was almost out of sight of the boy. And the slipperiness of the grass was in a way a bonus: they would say *"Silly old fool! He ought to have known better than to have gone so close to the edge!"* And the boy could testify that he had slipped once, already—another bonus!

Here, then? He advanced cautiously towards the edge. Beyond it, the empty sea crawled towards the invisible beach far below, from an equally invisible horizon where it joined the grey evening sky. But there wasn't a sheer drop: the edge had been gouged and smashed by the bombardment of long ago, presenting him with an unsatisfactory descent.

Further along, then. At this rate he would soon reach the place where the actual meeting was scheduled. But that was not for another quarter of an hour (and of course they would be on time; although that was a purely academic virtue now).

It had been a cutting of some kind up which he had originally scrambled finally, and down which he had descended later, so far as he could remember; it might even be the same cutting. There had been a dead German in it, halfway up, on whom he had nearly trodden, and a row of dead Rangers at the top. He could have joined them that night, quite easily: it had happened to a good many of them that day, and probably more than half those who had survived had died in a thousand other ways in the thousands of days since then; he was really doing no more now than joining that majority, bowing to their vote.

And here was that cutting, surely. But, most annoyingly, there was a young French couple tightly embracing each other at the head of it, the girl's long legs pale in the grass, the man's hand on her breast. That wouldn't suit his contact at all! But, then, that hardly mattered.

Rather than disturb the couple, even though the climb-down taxed his strength considerably, he negotiated the steep side of the cutting, until he came breathlessly to the bottom of it, close to the edge of the cliff again. Only when he reached it, he felt a stab of pain under his ribs as he saw the steepness of the other side, which he now had to ascend; and as he tried to catch his breath the thought came to him: *Why not here, then?*

Once again he explored the cliff edge. There was, at last, a perfectly clean drop: the pebbles and boulders were perhaps fifty feet below him.

But was that enough?

He stared down, suddenly fascinated by what he had never seen in daylight, remembering the torchlight glimpses of wrecked equipment and dead men's boots protruding from under blankets on that same margin between the cliff and the sea.

Did he really want to die? It had seemed so easy and so logical, these past few days—why did it seem so difficult now?

He looked out towards the darkening horizon. He had done everything that they had asked of him, even down to that meeting with the Englishman. They would keep their promise now—of that he was sure. So why not—

He heard a shout behind him, and turned towards it in surprise.

The young Frenchman was running down the cutting towards him—

"M'sieur! M'sieur!"

The old man glimpsed the girl higher up, smoothing down her rumpled skirt as she looked around her. The skirt had a floral pattern, and she was wearing a white sleeveless blouse. And she was dark-haired, and although he couldn't see her face clearly he was sure that she was pretty. And he was suddenly overwhelmingly glad that the young man was coming to rescue him.

He opened his mouth to say something, without quite knowing what he was going to say. But the young man caught his arm fiercely before he could speak, and swung him round so that he was facing the grey blankness of the sky. Then he had no more time at all as the young man broke his back expertly and propelled him outwards over the cliff.

I

ELIZABETH EXAMINED HERSELF dispassionately, first close-up in the large mirror over the washbasin, and then cap-à-pie in the full-length mirror on the wall to her left, beside the window.

As usual, the splendid view from the window diverted her attention away from herself. It was so much better than the forbiddingly administrative outlook from her own office, which was on what Paul referred to as "the Lubianka side". In fact, the ladies' room as a whole was better than her office, in view and size and furniture, as well as in the fragrant cleanliness which Mrs Harlin required. The very existence of such a palatial ladies' room, catering for the needs of only two ladies, had to have originated in some architectural accident or plumbing exigency. But it nevertheless also inhibited her from complaining about her own broom-cupboard office: no one could accuse a department with a ladies' room like this of sexism.

She returned to the consideration of herself. No one, either, could quarrel with that hair or that figure, or the clothes. It was the face which was the problem.

The door opened behind her, and she caught a glimpse of Mrs Harlin's head and shoulders in the mirror before she turned.

"Oh—there you are, Miss Loftus!" Mrs Harlin always addressed her formally, even in the sanctuary of the ladies' room, as though they were on camera there too.

Elizabeth smiled gratefully, almost honestly, as to an important ally in the game of life. "Oh, Mrs Harlin—" she touched her hips lightly "—is this really right for me? What do you think?"

The question sucked Mrs Harlin fully into the ladies' room, her duty momentarily forgotten. Instead, her official face became sisterly-motherly, as it always did on appeal. "Is it washable?"

"So they say. But it was a tremendous bargain," lied Elizabeth, sorting her real questions into the right order, but holding back from them.

"It's a beautiful dress—quite beautiful." With her widow's pension as well as her salary, Mrs Harlin wasn't short of a buck (as Paul was wont to observe so coarsely), but she also had a natural dress-sense almost as infallible as Madame Irene's. So what gave this ploy substance was that her advice was always genuinely worth having.

"But the colour, Mrs Harlin—this shade of green?" Elizabeth held steady. "For me?"

"Oh . . . yes, Miss Loftus—" Mrs Harlin's eye swept upwards inexorably "—with your hair. And that sculptured style is *so* becoming."

She had almost managed to miss the face, thought Elizabeth, turning back to the mirror. That face—that damned hereditary face, which had somehow contrived to jump back more than two centuries on the maternal side, skipping women who had usually been handsome and recently even beautiful, to reproduce exactly the features of the eighteenth century Varney who had been an Admiral of the Blue in the West Indies and whose oil-painted features—brutal chin, buck-teeth and arrogant nose—no doubt off-put visitors to the National Portrait Gallery now as much as they had once done his crew, and probably his Franco-Spanish enemies too.

"Do you really think so?" Well, all that money and art could do—her money and the combined art and advice of Madame Irene and Monsieur Pierre—had been done, and would have to do.

She leaned forward, pretending to check her eye make-up (*"The Eyes—they are Mademoiselle's best feature"*). "Is the Deputy-Director in yet, Mrs Harlin?" she inquired casually.

"Yes, Miss Loftus." The nuance of disapproval was because of the eye make-up: Mrs Harlin was old-fashioned there. "I was about to say—to remind you—that your appointment with him is due now, and that he's already asking for you."

"Oh yes?" Elizabeth transferred her attention to her cheekbones. The object of Madame Irene's strategy, so far as she could decipher from the euphemisms, was to draw attention away from Admiral Varney's salient features. Some hope! "Is he?" She knew Latimer was in the building, having observed his well-scraped Vauxhall in the underground car park and squeezed her beloved Morgan in as far away as possible from the area in which he might manoeuvre it subsequently. But that hadn't been the car which really worried her, nevertheless. "Is anyone else in?"

"Anyone else?" It wasn't quite an improper question, yet Mrs Harlin knew that Elizabeth's present assignment did not involve direct liaison with anyone else in Research and Development other than Chief Superintendent Andrew, who (as they both knew) was up on some embattled miners' picket line in Yorkshire until Saturday, pretending to throw rocks at his fascist colleagues. But when it came to business Mrs Harlin was properly close-mouthed.

So she had better improve on that, thought Elizabeth. "I take it Dr Mitchell isn't in?"

"Ah!" Mrs Harlin sighed sympathetically. "As a matter of fact he is in this morning, Miss Loftus."

Elizabeth stopped looking into her own eyes (*"They are Mademoiselle's best feature"* was at least partially true, because she had missed Admiral Varney's little piggy eyes, if the National Portrait Gallery picture was to be trusted), and turned to Mrs Harlin in surprise. For Paul's car hadn't been there when she arrived, and Paul should have been safe in Cheltenham at the moment. "He is?"

"He arrived just after you." Mrs Harlin could hardly know the full extent of the problem. But she knew that there was one.

"I thought he was at GCHQ." Hopelessness engulfed Elizabeth. Paul was so clever in every other way; not simply— *un*simply—intellectually clever, but·shrewd in such a Byzantine, Machiavellian, self-interestedly way that it would have been embarrassing to watch him bare an Achilles heel of stupidity at the best of times; but actually to be his blind spot, his weakness, herself—to be *his* Achilles heel, when she admired him so much—was almost more than she could bear.

"He was." Sympathetic understanding warred with departmental protocol, if not with security, in Mrs Harlin. "But the Deputy-Director sent him an SG yesterday, Miss Loftus, to be here this morning without fail."

"Oh," said Elizabeth. "Where is he at the moment?"

"Dr Mitchell is . . . well, he's hovering in my office at the moment, Miss Loftus," admitted Mrs Harlin, Elizabeth's tortured silence weakening her normal circumspection. "He's talking with Commander Cable. Or . . . he was when I left, after Commander Cable had been with the Deputy-Director and with Major Turnbull. And Dr Audley is also here."

"Oh!" She repeated the *oh* knowing that Mrs Harlin would relate it only to Paul, and not to this suspicious gathering of the clans. "Well, let's get it over with, Mrs Harlin, then."

"Don't you worry, Miss Loftus." Whatever it was which accompanied the words, it wasn't a smile, and it boded no good for Paul, even though Mrs Harlin had a motherly soft spot for him. "You have an appointment with the Deputy-Director—remember?"

"Elizabeth!" James Cable saw her second, but welcomed her first, with his own special mixture of gentleness and good manners, which together always put him ill at ease in the presence of an ugly woman. "It *is* good to see you again— and you look like a million dollars, too—don't you agree, Mitchell?"

"I don't know about a million dollars." An edge of unrequited love sharpened Paul's answer quite unnecessarily, in spite of his lack of embarrassment. "But she certainly looks expensive, I grant you that, Commander."

"Expensive?" Dear, very dear James—how father would have loved James, with all his naval ancestors striding back across their quarter-decks, from Trafalgar to San Carlos Bay! It was a bitter thought that in a year or two some wretched, mindless, suitable girl, who knew the Princess of Wales and was approved by his bone-headed mother, would get Commander James Cable for sure. "Expensive?" In his own way, James was just as smart as Paul, or he wouldn't be here. Indeed, he might not be pretending stupidity now, for he was not burdened with Paul's weakness where she was concerned. "What d'you mean—'expensive'?"

Mrs Harlin loomed from behind Elizabeth. "The Deputy-Director will see you now, Miss Loftus," she said blandly.

"I mean, just look at her, Jim-boy," said Paul. "Apart from coiffure and the paintwork—and God only knows what that cost—look at the dress, which is probably a little French something from Welbeck Street, or that new place round the corner there, where she gets her trousers and those other things —is it *culottes* or *sans-culottes*? Or maybe it's German, because Faith Audley's also on a German jag of some sort at the moment, so I'm told."

"He has been asking for you, Miss Loftus." Mrs Harlin cut through Paul's unlikely fashion intelligence. "*If* you'll excuse me, Dr Mitchell?"

"Of course, Mrs Harlin." Paul shrivelled slightly, well aware that he was over-matched. "I'm sorry—"

"Thank you, Dr Mitchell." Because she had a soft spot for him, Mrs Harlin accepted his surrender gracefully, with one of her thin smiles.

"But—" Paul drew a breath "—but I must talk to Miss Loftus nevertheless."

"Tripod masts," murmured James Cable, swaying slightly towards Paul. "Tripod masts—remember?"

"What's that, Commander?" said Mrs Harlin dangerously.

It wasn't in the least surprising that they both knew what a tripod mast was, the naval officer and the military historian —the sometime-sailor and othertime-scholar. But what the devil did those masts signify here and now?

"Tripod masts—yes." Paul nodded to his friend, then braced himself in Mrs Harlin's direction. "Nonetheless . . . and in spite of the Deputy-Director . . . I will speak with Miss Loftus now, Mrs Harlin. On a purely professional matter. And an urgent one." He turned towards Elizabeth, and pointed at the entrance door behind her. "Just two minutes, Elizabeth —outside."

"Dr Mitchell!" snapped Mrs Harlin.

"Professional business, Elizabeth. Flag of truce on other matters—that's a promise. Scouts' honour."

17

"Dr Mitchell!"

"It's all right, Mrs Harlin." Elizabeth could see that Paul was genuinely worried, and that he didn't care about hiding his real feelings. So that was perhaps the right moment for her to start worrying too. "Very well, Paul. Two minutes."

"Hmm . . ." The sound indicated that Elizabeth had gone down a snake in Mrs Harlin's estimation. "Very well, Miss Loftus. But I shall inform the Deputy-Director that you are on your way."

"Well, Paul?"

"I'm sorry I fluffed it out there, Elizabeth—with the fashion bit. But I always do, you know me . . . Just, I prefer you unadorned."

Naked and unadorned? remembered Elizabeth. He was still fluffing it. "Two professional minutes, you said."

His face set, almost expressionless. "We haven't seen each other for an age, Elizabeth. We've both been busy."

She felt absurdly disappointed with his breach of trust. "Paul—you *promised*—" She broke off.

"I'm not breaking any promise. We've all been busy."

"Then get to the point."

"That is the point. I know what you've been doing here: you've been co-ordinating the Cheltenham inquiry—Audley's big job."

Elizabeth stared at him. There was no reason that he should know who was on the computer at this end. No reason, except that he was Paul Mitchell.

"I know because I've been not only supplying you with some of your information, but also answering some of your questions, Elizabeth." He seemed to be able to read some of her mind. "Has it ever occurred to you that everyone has an individual style of mind—mind, as distinct from literary style? And once you know the person, it's almost as good as a fingerprint. Like a mind-print . . . But, anyway, I know— okay?"

That was really quite interesting, and not least because it warned her how much she still had to learn. "So what?"

"So it's quite important, in its way, what you've been doing.

18

And you're asking the right questions. You're good, Elizabeth
—I hate to have to admit it, but you *are* good. You sit here,
in that little nunnery cell of yours, and you actually *think*. And
you think to some purpose."

"Now you're being patronizing—that's what I'm thinking
at this moment."

His eyes clouded. "Of course. Don't you realize that that's
my doom, Elizabeth—the one gift the Good Fairy denied me?
If I love someone I always say the wrong thing to her, no
matter what I mean to say. But we're talking business now."

"I've yet to hear any." She couldn't afford to weaken.
"Come to the point."

"I'm still there, I haven't left it. I—" He stopped suddenly,
and shook his head, though more at himself than at her,
Elizabeth thought. And, in spite of his redoubled promise,
that suggested that he still wasn't talking business. "Look,
Elizabeth, I obviously haven't got a lot of time, so I can't
explain in any detail how I know what I know, so what I *think*
may not seem very convincing to you. But I want you to listen
—and to bear with me, please. *Please?*"

"For about thirty seconds." She didn't look at her watch.
"You heard what Mrs Harlin said?"

"Oh—the hell with her!" He gestured. "And bugger Oliver
—*Fatso!* Blame me, if you like."

"It's easy for you to say that. You're old establishment. I'm
hardly fledged."

He stared at her. "Not so easy, actually. I'm on a bloody
knife-edge with our Deputy-Director. But . . . not that I care.
Just trust me this once, enough to listen to me, Elizabeth—
Miss Loftus, if you like." The stare became fixed. "In fact, if
you listen to me now, you can be *Miss Loftus* for ever after.
And that's another promise—until the Sun stands still, and
the Moon ceases to rise. Okay?"

The offer took her aback. He was offering her . . . he was
offering her too much, in terms of what he had to offer. Or
perhaps he was offering enough to frighten her, on those terms.

She had to devalue it, to make a jest of it. "Okay, Paul. But
only if you'll tell me what 'tripod masts' means, between you
and James—?"

Again that clouded, defenceless look. Then it vanished. "That's easy—James was just warning me to lay off. To run for my life, before Mrs Harlin sank me without a trace." He almost smiled. "*Tripod masts*—you ought to have got that one, *Miss* Loftus, with all those naval histories of your father's that you copy-typed for him."

The reminder of past drudgery hardened her heart finally: he knew altogether too much about that past of hers, and by recalling it he merely encouraged her to hold him to his latest promise. "I know what tripod masts are, Dr Mitchell."

He took the point: she could see him reading the full meaning of the smallest print of the agreement he had proposed. "Not what they *are*, but what they *meant*." The fixed emotionless stare was back. "Perhaps not inappropriately on this occasion, more than Commander Cable meant himself."

There was no percentage in trying to read his riddles. "And what did they mean?"

"Death, Miss Loftus, just death." He let the word sink in. "The battle of the Falklands—not the recent unpleasantness, but the original one in 1914. James and I both read it up when he got back from there, just for curiosity. Before he closed in on Port Stanley in 1914, von Spee sent in a light cruiser to have a look. And the poor devil in the crow's nest spotted tripod masts in the harbour. And he knew in that second that he was a dead man, because they meant *battle-cruisers*—too big to fight, and too fast to out-run—I'm sure you remember that, Miss Loftus."

Elizabeth did remember that, from Father's cold comparison of the customs of naval warfare in the good old days of wooden ships, when a man could surrender to superior force without losing his honour, and the rules of the supposedly more-civilized twentieth century, in which no quarter was asked or granted—"the logical requirement of democratic warfare, which was of course conducted not for vulgar profit, but for noble causes."

"I see." And on a quite juvenile level she could see—that James had warned Paul not to tangle with Mrs Harlin, who certainly had tripod masts. But, on a more serious level, Paul had seen the masts, yet had stayed to fight. "So what is it that you have to tell me, that's so important it can't wait?"

"Okay." While she had been thinking, so had he been. "I think we have all the ingredients of a panic. And, as we don't have them very often here, they always scare the pants off me."

"What sort of panic?" The *why* could come later.

"I don't know, exactly. But all the signs are there."

Better to let him have his way. She must be late already, but she could handle the Deputy-Director, at a pinch. "What signs?"

"We've all been taken off what we were doing. And I know what I was doing—and what you were doing, close enough. And I know what Major Turnbull was doing, for other reasons, which I don't intend to bore you with . . . And I've a pretty damn good idea what old James was up to, come to that."

As usual, he knew too much for his own good.

"All right." He misread her silence and her expression, nevertheless: with people, and perhaps with her in particular, he was fallible. "They took me off. And they took David Audley off. And they took *you* off. Which I know because I have this access to the computer, to pick its brains, and they haven't cancelled it. So I tried to pick *yours* a couple of days ago. And you just weren't available. See?"

Even with her limited experience, Elizabeth saw. Anyone armed with those rights of access and his knowledge of how the department worked (never mind his insatiable curiosity) could probably elicit a great deal of information. For a start it might be mostly negative, but he would surely have more sophisticated methods than counting the cars in the car park to find out more.

The very thought made her cautious. "And what did you conclude from that, Dr Mitchell?"

"It didn't start with you." He shook his head. "I was engaged in something quite interesting, not to say important." The shake became almost an apologetic shrug. "I thought maybe I could find a substitute."

Again, Elizabeth saw—and saw also how he had reached this pass: he had cast around for someone else to do the job he'd been given—someone engaged on less important matters —before making a fuss. And, naturally enough, he'd tried to hang the albatross on her neck first—the most junior, if not the newest, recruit.

Oh, *typical* Paul! "And came up with a dusty answer?"

The corridor door behind them *swished*, and she saw his eyes flick past her, and then come back to her almost pleadingly.

"Miss Loftus—" She just caught the last of Mrs Harlin's frown at Paul as she turned "—the Deputy-Director has asked for you again. I cannot reasonably invent another excuse, unless you actually wish to be indisposed. At the moment he insists that either you are here, or you aren't." She gave Elizabeth the benefit of the doubt, just. "I do think you ought to come now."

Tripod masts! thought Elizabeth. Or, to get away from their ridiculous naval code, from a past which she preferred to forget, here was a *snake* or a *ladder*, and she could choose whether to go up or down.

"Thank you, Mrs Harlin. Please tell the Deputy-Director that I'll be with him as soon as I'm free."

Mrs Harlin very nearly replied. But then she didn't, and Elizabeth watched the door *swish*, and lock.

"This had better be good, Paul—Dr Mitchell." That he was regarding her with that ridiculous expression only irritated her more, sharpening her voice: on his face it was a positively unnatural look, quite alien to his character. "And it had better be quick, too."

"Oh—it's good." Far too late, he erased the expression. "That is, it's good intelligence. But it's bad news for you. Because I think Fatso is going to send you into the field."

"Why—" She just caught the wrong question in time—the *Why do you think that's bad news?* question. "*How* d'you know I'm going into the field?" Besides, damn it, it wasn't bad news at all—it was good news!

"Because Jim Cable is taking your job, as of now. And you've got an appointment with Fatso in minus five minutes. And because I can read the signs when they're in big flashing neon lights."

He knew more than he was saying. All that stuff about using

his SG rights might be true, but that also was window-dressing, concealing some other source of information which he was not about to reveal. So she must push him.

"You haven't really told me anything I couldn't deduce from the cars down below." She gave him Admiral Varney's down-the-nose look.

"Is that so?" She got a Mitchell-ancestor look in return —maybe from his 1918 grandfather, of whom he was so inordinately proud, who had died on the far side of the Hindenburg Line. "And you counted David Audley's car too, did you? And that didn't worry you, then?"

"Why should that worry me?" But it did now, all the same.

"Oh—come on, Elizabeth! Jack Butler's on leave, because he has to take *some* leave, *some* time . . . So he made bloody sure that David wasn't around when Fatso Latimer was running the shop. And Fatso wouldn't have summoned David back if there wasn't an emergency—he may be a basket-hanger, but he isn't an idiot." He glowered at her. "And I'm being sent back to Cheltenham. Though there's precious little I can do there in David's absence."

When he delivered the final emphasis she knew that he wasn't going to tell her any more. But, because of his weakness (and however badly that made her feel, for pressing that unfair advantage), it was worth one more push—even if she had to lead in with that wrong question, which she had managed to avoid.

"All right. So maybe there is some sort of emergency. And maybe the Deputy-Director is going to give it to me."

"No 'maybe'—"

"All right—no 'maybe'." She concealed her pleasure, but thought that he was a fool not to allow for it. But then, where she was concerned he was quite often foolish, they were agreed on that. "And I'll even grant you the field-work hypothesis— though you haven't supported it with a single hard fact." That was the first element of the push. Now for the second. "But why should that be bad for me?"

He pursed his lips. But, of course, he wasn't *that* foolish: he knew when he was being pushed.

"For heaven's sake!" She acted out a pretence of irritation by settling her handbag under her arm and swaying towards the door. "I've had practically two years here—even allowing for the instruction courses, and the information seminars, and all the rest of it . . . I know we are 'Research and Development', and not an active department. But we do undertake field-work on occasion—I do know *that* too."

What she also knew was that she didn't need to elaborate on that. He had been engaged in field-work when they had first met. And she had been the field in which he had been working.

"Yes." He couldn't escape from his own memories. "We do field-work."

"So what are you complaining about?" The truth about Paul was that although he was reputedly very good in the field, he had several very bad experiences among those memories, which were probably warping his judgement now. Nevertheless, the more he agonized, the more certain she was that he had something more than hypothesis to go on.

A tiny muscle twitched in his cheek, betraying the clenched teeth beneath.

Field-work, thought Elizabeth happily. "You're just wasting my time." She settled her handbag under her arm, and started to make the beginning of her turn towards the door.

"Elizabeth—!"

So much for the running of the Sun and the rising of the Moon! thought Elizabeth. But this wasn't the moment to remind him of their already-forgotten treaty—not when he was cracking.

"Well?"

"I can't tell you what I think you're going to do. But you mustn't do it." For a moment he was lost for words. "Field-work is always a matter of choice—we're not contracted to do it."

Those were the wrong words, even though accurate. Because they both knew that she couldn't refuse, even if she had wanted to. Which she didn't.

"Why can't you tell me?"

"Because . . . if I'm right—" He damn well knew he was

right! "—it's a secure classification. And I can't buck that. Not even for you." He shook his head.

God! No wonder he'd been treading like a cat on hot bricks! And—if he was on a knife-edge with the Deputy-Director, as he well might be, being Paul—those bricks would have been more like red-hot if he'd accidentally stumbled on a secure classification! Because—because, if he even *mentioned* it to her (having once been cleared for it himself), and then she let it slip, she would have to account exactly where and how she'd got it. And that would be all nine lives at one go for the cat.

Poor old Paul! she thought, with all the tolerance of pleasure: to be admitted to such a classification was a mark of professional confidence—not a snake, but a ladder. So he couldn't have told her in advance anything better calculated to encourage her to accept whatever was offered—he'd got it all dead-wrong again!

"Ah!" Now she could afford to be merciful. "Yes—of course." Nod to him—she owed him that, at least: he'd come in far too close for safety already, knowing already that those tripod masts were there in harbour, waiting for him.

But now he was fumbling in one pocket after another, to find something. "But I suppose there's no reason why you shouldn't have read the newspapers." He was fiddling with a tiny fragment of newsprint, to prise it out from his wallet. "David always says that half our work starts in print somewhere, long before we get a tip-off. So you could have read this, from last week's *Telegraph*." He looked at her as he offered it. "And that will establish whether I'm right, anyway."

Elizabeth took the fragment. It must have filled a hole somewhere, at the bottom of a column: just one small paragraph, with a little two-line heading. It was, she remembered from the Newspaper Course, what they called a "filler". And the *Telegraph* liked fillers—those tiny bits of news which might, or might not, see the light of day, according to the space left by more important stories above.

Just a matter of chance, in fact—

25

And chance, and Paul (who had been trained by David Audley, and who was cleared for this particular *secure classification*), had rescued this fragment from oblivion.

"I'd like it back, please." After the half-minute he generously allowed, he reached for the evidence of his indiscretion. "Have you ever heard of the Pointe du Hoc, Miss Loftus?"

He had remembered the Sun and the Moon. Perhaps the indiscretion had sharpened up his memory.

"No," she lied, with false innocence. "It's in Normandy, somewhere—?"

"Or Thaddeus Parker?"

"Who?" She had maybe been a shade too innocent with that "Normandy, somewhere?", when it was obvious from the text where the Pointe du Hoc was. But she didn't have to pretend this reaction: that wasn't the name in the test. "Who?"

"They got it wrong—'Edward Parker'." He held up the cutting for an instant, before slotting it back among his credit cards. "He ought to have been 'Tad', but for some reason he was always 'Ed'. So they made him 'Edward' somewhere along the line." As he replaced the plastic folder in his pocket, "You've never heard of Thaddeus Parker—Major 'Ed' Parker?"

"No."

D-DAY VETERAN
IN DEATH FALL

A 70-year-old American veteran of the D-Day landings, Edward Parker, fell to his death from the 100-foot cliffs of Pointe du Hoc yesterday—

"—never."

The door clicked again behind her, and then *swished*, as they stared at each other.

"Miss Loftus," said Mrs Harlin.

"Well, if I'm right, you will in about two minutes, Miss Loftus," said Paul.

Elizabeth hardly had time to think, as Mrs Harlin swept her on, tripod masts erect and guns trained, doors clicking and *swishing* at her touch.

"I don't think he's very pleased with you—" Click-*swish* "—Miss Loftus, Deputy-Director."

"Ah!" At least he didn't look too displeased. "Thank you, Mrs Harlin."

Swish-click.

"Please do sit down, Miss Loftus—Elizabeth." At the moment he wasn't looking at her at all—he was studying the display on his screen, which she couldn't see. But that was her first time as "Elizabeth" with him. So did that make him "Oliver" with her?

On balance *no*, she decided. Because . . . he might be "Fatso" to Paul, and something more polite, but even ruder, to David Audley . . . But he was God's viceroy to her at this moment, and if he ordered her to jump over the cliff at Pointe du Hoc she would at least think about doing so.

Also, if Paul was right, she was about ten seconds away from Thaddeus Parker, *alias* Major Ed. And close to a secure classification thereafter.

"You've been rather elusive this morning. Have a chocolate?"

The only object on the desk itself was a large box of Thornton's chocolates, which had already been extensively plundered. What they said about Oliver St John Latimer was that when he was unhappy he went on a diet to make himself even more miserable. So he must be very happy now.

"Thank you, Mr Latimer." The truth or a lie?

"Yes?" He looked at her, and waited.

Mrs Harlin had been angry, so Mrs Harlin might have sneaked, Elizabeth decided. "I was delayed by Dr Mitchell. I'm sorry."

"Oh yes?" He still didn't look displeased—and he certainly didn't seem surprised. In fact, he looked almost sympathetic. "Is Dr Mitchell being difficult, Elizabeth?"

So he knew about Dr Mitchell and Miss Loftus, and their little difficulty. But then, it was his business to know about such things, because he was the Deputy-Director—indeed, at this moment, the *Acting* Director, wearing Colonel Butler's metaphorical red coat, even if it was a size too large for him.

"No, Mr Latimer." It occurred to Elizabeth almost simultaneously that he *might* actually be trying to be sympathetic, but also—and for sure—that he was enjoying the feel of that metaphorical coat across his shoulders. So now a lie with icing on it was indicated. "I appreciate your—concern." *Look grateful but embarrassed, Elizabeth!* "But that problem is . . . contained now." It wasn't difficult to look embarrassed, particularly with a chocolate in her mouth.

He nodded, and reached across to the box himself. "So what did he want, then?" He gave the box a little push. "Have another one?"

Did a weakness for chocolates suggest truthfulness in other matters? she wondered. "I shouldn't—but I will." But she also had to remember that he was an extremely clever man. "It seems that he sent me an SG after I was detached from the daily movements analysis. And he wasn't happy with the answer he received." She would have to brief Paul about this.

He munched for a moment. "How did he know you were on analysis?"

She wasn't there ahead of him, but at least she was ready for anything. "Oh—" *This had better be good, Elizabeth!* "—I asked him about that . . ."

"And what did he say?"

Only the truth would do. "He seems to know my style. He calls it a 'mind-print'." She shrugged, a little disbelieving, a little irritated.

"He does?" Another nod, and another reach towards the box. But there were so few left now that he had to lean forward to search among the empty paper containers. "Like the radio-operators . . . But to do it with SGs is really quite ingenious . . . He's no fool, is your Dr Mitchell, Elizabeth."

That was one crack too many. "Not *my* Dr Mitchell, Mr Latimer."

"No. Forgive me." He found his chocolate, and then turned towards the screen as he fed it to himself. "You know, the results of your Civil Service interview a couple of years ago, and all that . . . they were quite good, you know." He had got a chewy one this time, and it was giving him problems. "And your other fitness tests."

Patronizing chauvinist *pig*! thought Elizabeth. But then she

28

checked her own prejudice, and reassessed her judgement. What he was doing was prudently clearing her for what Paul plainly believed was beyond her capability.

Prudent level-headed Deputy-Director! "Colonel Butler said my results were satisfactory."

"More than satisfactory. They said you were a late developer, and they'd probably have failed you if you'd come to them straight from Oxford, in spite of your first-class degree and your hockey Blue ... It seems that they are presently indulging—or trying to indulge—some sort of positive discrimination in that regard." He shook his head at the screen. "It won't do, you know—it won't do at all! Though I suppose they *might* have passed you ... because you were female ..."

Patronizing chauvinist *pig*! "I'm still female, Mr Latimer." Not even a secure classification was worth this! "I may have developed, but I haven't changed in that respect."

"Oh—" He left the screen instantly, to blink at her in surprise, almost as though he was seeing her for the first time "—yes—?"

"You sent for me, Mr Latimer. I'm sorry I was late." She often—too often!—saw Admiral Varney's face, but it was only very rarely that she heard his voice.

"Yes ... Miss Loftus." Suddenly he really did see her. And suddenly he wasn't a little fat man with an almost empty box of chocolates in front of him on an empty desk.

Tripod masts!

Then he relaxed, and the masts faded into her imagination, and he was a little fat man again.

"How's your Latin, Miss Loftus—Elizabeth?"

"My—what?" She couldn't have heard correctly.

"Your Latin. *Veni, vidi, vici?*" He stared at her, and she had heard correctly. "*Hic, haec, hoc*—and *Gallia est omnis divisa in partes tres?*"

She had heard correctly—but she didn't know how to answer.

Elizabeth could only think *Paul had been wrong!*

"No matter!" He didn't seem to expect an answer. He seemed to know all the answers to his own questions. "No matter, Elizabeth. You just tell me now about the Pointe du Hoc in 1944 instead."

29

II

TEN YEARS AS a school-teacher had taught Elizabeth how to deal with the clever-awkward girls, who had simultaneously known too much for their own good, yet not half enough. But what she had somehow forgotten was how such girls resisted The Enemy.

"The Pointe du Hoc is a headland on the coast of Normandy, between Grandcamp and Vierville—"

"Spare me the geography, Elizabeth." Oliver St John Latimer munched his chocolate. "Waterloo is a village near Brussels, and Gettysburg is a small town in Pennsylvania, and neither of them has moved an inch on the map since 1815, or 1863. So the Pointe du Hoc is still where it was in 1944—shall we take that as read?" He munched contentedly. "Just tell me something I don't know—eh?"

Dawn, 6 June 1944, Companies D, E and F, 5th Battalion, US Rangers—

"*Rangers*, the Americans called them, Liza—like our *Commandos*." Major Birkenshawe locked a bushy white eyebrow at her. "You know what they are? Real cut-throats is what they are, Liza!"

Elizabeth tried not to wince. Long, long ago, when she had been in pig-tails and short skirts—when Father had first brought Major Birkenshawe to the house—the Major had told her that "Elizabeth" was far too big a name for such a very little girl, and that he proposed to abbreviate it.

(*"You see, you're a lucky little girl, to have such a name. Liz, Lizzie, Elisa—and Betty, and Bet, and Beth . . . Bessie, too. And when our Queen was a little girl like you, she was called 'Lilibet'—shall I call you that, eh?"*)

"Yes, Major. Like the Paras and the SAS?" What really bugged her was that, in the kindest and most helpful way, he always took her ignorance for granted still, just as he had done over twenty years ago.

"Funny thing, that," said Colonel Sharpe.

"Funny, Colonel?"

"'Rangers', Miss Loftus."

Now, Colonel Sharpe was different, and she was genuinely grateful to the dear old Major for producing him on demand, once she had given him the specification. But then the thing about the Major was that he knew how to obey orders. His wife had taught him that, if not the army.

(*"If you want a clever fella, that knows his stuff, I've just the man for you, Liza. Served on Monty's staff, saw it all—probably planned half of it himself, I shouldn't wonder—house full of books, head full of knowledge—resigned to run the family business—would have run the Army otherwise. Retired now—Sharpe by name, and sharp by nature —never got on with your father—funny thing, that—"*)

That last wasn't really "funny", because Father had never got on with masterful equals who had made successes of their lives. But everything else was undoubtedly "funny" (but not very funny), about the Deputy-Director's very specific orders. And that not only because any one of the men in the department could have done this job more quickly, if not better, but also (and more) because he had instructed her neither to use any of the department's immense facilities, human or otherwise, nor to go straight round to the Americans in Grosvenor Square and use any of her professional contacts. And although he must have his reason for this, none was as yet readily apparent to her.

Sharpe was looking at her, and she had the uncomfortable feeling that he had already smelt a rat, while she could only smell the Major's fierce tobacco.

(*"Hugh's girl—Hugh Loftus—remember him, Sharpe? Used to teach the wife's nieces at the High—works for the Government now— Civil Servant—waste of a good teacher—better paid though, eh Liza?"*)

Elizabeth waited. Colonel Sharpe didn't know what to make of her. But that was no reason why she should feed his suspicions.

"Though perhaps not more so than our choice of 'Commando' as a name for our special forces," he said at length. "You know its origin?"

It was a small innocent challenge to an ex-history teacher. "We took that from the Boers, who fought us in South Africa, didn't we?" He would appreciate a counter-challenge. "And we gave them 'Concentration Camp' in return?"

"What's that?" Major Birkenshawe bristled slightly. "I think you've got that wrong, Liza. 'Concentration Camp' was a Hun invention."

"I'm sure you're right, Major." Elizabeth smiled at him. "But 'Rangers', Colonel?"

He studied her for a few more seconds. "The original of the name is obscure. But it seems most likely that they derived from Rogers' Rangers in the eighteenth century. And they were a corps of frontiersmen who were recruited to assist the regulars. There was a film about them—I rather think it starred Spencer Tracy."

Major Birkenshawe grunted approvingly. "Damn good actor—and the delightful woman he used to appear with—cheekbones and hair—your hair looks particularly nice today, Liza—suits you, like that—Sorry, Sharpe—Rangers, you were saying?"

Colonel Sharpe gave the Major a nod, more affectionate than condescending, and Elizabeth wondered how such an acquaintance had become more than nodding, they were such an unlikely pair. But then Father and the dear old Major had been equally unlikely friends.

Then the Colonel came back to her. "A curious fact, which they must have overlooked, is that the Rangers fought for the British during the American War of Independence. And that would make them not just enemies—'Loyalists' to us, of course —but actually traitors. And 'traitor' is always a pejorative word."

The Major nodded, even though he looked as though he wasn't at all sure what "pejorative" meant. "But they were good, though—those fellas . . . Saw 'em training once, in '43, before I had my little misfortune." He had raised the stump of his right arm quite unselfconsciously. "*Training*, they called it—" Major Birkenshawe pushed his stump back into place "—looked *damn* dangerous to me—if you'll pardon my language, Liza. They were shooting at each other, and blowing each other up, and climbing up cliffs—I remember thinking that the real thing couldn't be a lot more dangerous than what they were doing."

"That was the Isle of Wight manoeuvres, was it?" Sharpe turned towards him, away from Elizabeth. "On the cliffs?"

The stump moved, as though it had a life of its own, and was remembering. "Must have been '44. Isle of Wight—you're right there. Shot grapnels up, with lines attached—" He stopped suddenly, massaging the stump and staring midway between them. "That's right! Remember thinking 'Sheer madness! Not a hope, if Jerry's on the top—glad it's not me!'" He grinned ancient nicotine-stained fangs at Elizabeth. "Amazing how it comes back! Killed a lot of men training, did the Americans. Had a lot of men to kill, of course—big country . . . But these were good men—very keen—could see that."

"And that must have been when you were involved on the Merville planning, Maurice?" Colonel Sharpe interrupted him gently.

"Probably was. Another piece of lunacy! 'Never drop half the men within twenty miles', I told 'em. They wanted to land gliders right *on* the battery! 'Not a chance', I said. 'Only chance you've got—Jerry won't believe what's happening—probably give him heart-failure'."

"But you said 'Go' all the same." The Colonel paused. "And weren't you scheming to go with them?"

"Of course." The Major retired for a moment behind a foul-smelling smoke-screen. "Just curiosity—wanted to see what sort of b—— *mess*-up they made of it." He applied another match to his pipe one-handed. "And they did." He stabbed the pipe-stem towards Elizabeth. "Took the battery, though—got to give them that—bloody massacre all round— sorry to have missed it. But that's the luck of the game, Liza."

Elizabeth stared at Major Birkenshawe. When he had talked with Father there had of course been no place for her, even if she'd wanted to stay. So, in all these years, she'd regarded him as an old buffer—to a pig-tailed child he'd seemed an old buffer from the beginning, and as they'd both aged he'd become one. But once upon a time there'd been a *young* Major Birkenshawe, happily and bloodthirstily engaged in planning daring deeds. And (what was perhaps more eloquent) he could still dismiss the ruin of his military hopes and his mutilation as "the luck of the game", as Father had never been able to do.

"Boring you—or shocking you?" He might not be the same to her now, but she was evidently the same helpless female to him. "Besides—Americans, what you want—Rangers, too— Omaha, for them. And the right of the line—always the place of honour, eh Sharpe?"

"Yes." Colonel Sharpe zeroed in on Elizabeth again, with that too-knowing eye of his. "But it's all in the books and the records, Miss Loftus."

"So it is, Colonel. But is it all correct?" She didn't really know what she wanted.

"What d'you mean—correct?"

"Well—" How could she explain that whatever she wanted, whatever it was, could hardly be in the public library, if Oliver St John Latimer wanted it? "For example, the Rangers landed at a place called 'Pointe du Hoc'."

"That's right. That was the place Maurice saw them practising cliff-climbing for. There was supposed to be a German battery there, which had to be taken out somehow—like the Major's battery at Merville, which was beyond the eastern flank of the British landing beaches. They both flanked the landing areas. In fact, I think the Pointe du Hoc guns could have taken in the Utah beaches as well, actually. They couldn't be left to get on with the job, Miss Loftus."

"But there weren't any guns on Pointe du Hoc, Colonel."

He nodded cautiously. "No . . . as it happened, there weren't. The Germans had prudently pulled them back to a new position."

"Which wasn't manned?" But if there was a mystery here, why should it interest the Deputy-Director?

"True. But things always go wrong in battle." He shrugged. "That whole area was heavily bombed—and bombarded. But, in any case, a Ranger patrol still found the guns and disabled

34

them. And that was even before they'd finished with the garrison at Pointe du Hoc, if I remember correctly."

Major Birkenshawe nodded agreement. "They were good men—I told you, eh? Proper desperadoes—gangsters, I shouldn't wonder—probably all enlisted in Chicago!"

The Colonel cast a sardonic glance at his friend. "I rather think the Rangers were more like the old frontiersmen, with their fieldcraft and initiative—" He caught himself, as though he suspected that he had been sidetracked. "—what exactly is it that you want, Miss Loftus?"

They were back to that, thought Elizabeth. "You know that in Chester Wilmot's book—and in another one I've looked at —the name isn't spelt correctly: it says 'Pointe du *Hoe*', not Pointe du *Hoc*'?"

"Is it the Pointe du Hoc you're interested in?" The Colonel's voice was too casual.

"Isn't that where they've just been junketing?" the Major intervened. "One of the places, anyway—read about it recently—Her Majesty the Queen and the President—that actor chappie—and the Frogs. Kept the Germans out, for some reason—?" He frowned. "Read something else, too. Just yesterday—in the *Telegraph*—" He became aware that the Colonel was quelling him with a look. "Sorry! Pointe du Hoc, you were saying—?"

If the Colonel was close to anything, he was too close, decided Elizabeth. "The Rangers landed elsewhere, did they?"

"Yes." The Colonel was only slightly diverted from his suspicions. "There were two battalions of them."

"Yes?" Elizabeth could see professional memories weakening him.

"They took heavy casualties. Fifty-per-cent or more in some companies." He drew a breath. "Lack of specialized armour, that was largely due to . . . and a predilection for frontal attacks on strong points—not the way to use elite troops. They should have been infiltrated through the weak points." He caught himself again. "The main force was supposed to swing west, and link up with their comrades on the Pointe du Hoc, you see, Miss Loftus."

"Hah!" exclaimed Major Birkenshawe. "Now *that* was a

35

strong-point, guns or no guns!" Then he shook his head. "She doesn't understand, y'know!"

"That was the correct use of Rangers, actually." Colonel Sharpe watched Elizabeth, and ignored the Major. "Only the best troops could have got up there—and then caused all the trouble they did. I was attached to that American division, and we were expecting a strong counter-attack that first evening—or the next morning. The Germans had a good division in that sector—better than the one our chaps had to deal with on the British beaches, actually. Though of course their tanks were closer to us. If there'd been armour close to Omaha on D-Day as well, God only knows what would have happened . . . Anyway, we'd been arguing about the position of that good division before D-Day, but we didn't get confirmation until far too late. And there were several battalions in reserve—so, with the way things were on the beaches, we were expecting to get hit any moment. But there weren't any tanks. And the Americans had made a pretty amazing recovery, actually."

The Major started to cough politely, but inadvertently took in too much of his own bonfire, and choked frighteningly for the best part of a minute, to everyone's embarrassment.

"Sorry about that, Liza." He wiped his face with what appeared to be a square of torn sheet. "But do you understand a word of all that?" He cocked a huge eyebrow at her. "Divisions and battalions—all that stuff?"

"Yes, Major." For one fraction of a second Elizabeth began to hit back, irritated alike by his pipe and his assumptions, and sickened by the torn sheeting; but then she remembered that she actually loved the Major, who had always treated her with courtesy and who had now unearthed Colonel Sharpe for her, when everyone else had failed her. "Yes, I *think* I do, that is." She smiled at him, then at the Colonel, as though she was stretching her knowledge to its limits. "So what did these Rangers do on the Pointe du Hoc—or whatever it's called?"

"Hah! I rather suspect they did what they were originally recruited and formed to do, Miss Loftus. Which happened far too rarely with the American Rangers—and with other elite formations I could mention."

Elizabeth waited. When a man wanted to give distilled

wisdom to the world, it was better to let him have his way without side-tracking him with too many intelligent un-womanly questions.

"Half the time they were squandered on conventional war-fare. They threw away a whole Ranger battalion after the Anzio landing." The Colonel drew a reminiscent breath, and gave the Major a nod. In another moment he'd be fairly launched.

"Huh!" This could have been the right moment for the Major to cough usefully. But instead he nodded back wisely. "Half the time they should never have been formed in the first place." He blinked at Elizabeth, as though surprised that he had formulated a complete sentence. "Stripped the rest of the army of good men—ours as well as the Yanks. Never enough good line NCOs—off swanning around on hair-brained schemes in private armies. Could tell you a tale or two about *that!*"

"Yes." The Major's threat concentrated the Colonel's mind wonderfully, so that he re-focused on Elizabeth. "Pointe du Hoc—as I was saying . . . When they'd finished their business there, there weren't many of them left. But then, being Rangers, I rather suspect they got up to all sorts of mischief, which probably pulled the Germans away from the right flank of Omaha. God knows what they did—*we* certainly didn't know exactly, in the Command Post, even though they sent a staff officer off, to try and find out. But I never saw *him* again —they probably shot him, because the Rangers hated staff officers." He smiled at Elizabeth. "But then I had to go back to report to Monty—I was his spy, you see."

The Deputy-Director sat up, one podgy hand still fumbling in the wreckage of his chocolate box. "How's that again, Miss Loftus—Elizabeth?"

"How's . . . what?" He waved the hand vaguely—insult-ingly—as though he hadn't really been listening, but then she had said something of unexpected interest, against the odds. "This fellow you talked to—?"

She had to reel back. What she had just said had come just before Colonel Sharpe had discoursed at length on Field

Marshal Montgomery, and then on the use (and misuse) of elite soldiers, which had ranged all the way from the Rangers on the Pointe du Hoc, forward to the Green Berets in Vietnam (and the Paras in the Falklands), and back to the Spartans at Thermopylae, almost two-and-a-half thousand years earlier.

"Well . . . I think he was attached to the Americans so that he could report back to the British—"

"Who?" He was concentrating on her.

"Colonel Sharpe. The man I told you about—who told me about the Pointe du Hoc."

"Yes, yes—" He waved away the obvious fact that he hadn't been listening, quite unembarrassed "—but *how* was it that you got on to him—tell me again—?"

Cool it, Elizabeth! "You told me not to consult the records, or anyone in the department." Paul would have given her all this in ten seconds flat, even though he was a 1914–18 man. "Or the Americans." The nice young CIA man at Grosvenor Square, who was ex-US Navy and knew all about Father's war record, would have done the same, only better, over an agreeable lunch. "So . . . there's this friend of my father's, who had this friend who was on the planning staff before D-Day, and was seconded to the American army as an observer. But he wasn't really an observer. Or . . . I mean, he was . . . but his real job—"

"What's his name?" snapped Latimer. "*Name*, Elizabeth—*name*—?"

"Sharpe." Elizabeth floundered. "Colonel Sharpe—with an 'e'. I don't know his Christian name. But his family had an electrical firm in Hampshire, near Portsmouth. And they went into electronics—computers, I think."

Latimer punched the keys of his machine, while Elizabeth tried to conscript any other morsel Major Birkenshawe had let slip. "I think they had a new factory just near Havant."

Latimer fed *Havant* into the Beast. "Next time, Elizabeth, if you talk to anyone, get his full name and address. What is the name of the firm at Havant?"

And his Credit Rating? And his next-of-kin? And the Beast wasn't helping her, she could see that reflected on the Deputy-Director's face. "I don't know, Mr Latimer." Damn them both—the Beast and the Deputy-Director! "He's—he must be nearly seventy years old."

"Yes." He prodded the Beast again, but only received another dusty answer, probably *Search continuing*, if not *Insufficient data*; to track down the Colonel, it would have to talk to other beasts, and such linkages took time. "Yes." He looked up at last. "If he was on D-Day planning then he would be, wouldn't he?"

He was saying *Don't be silly, Miss Loftus*. And, most annoyingly, with some justification.

"But never mind him, for the moment. Continue, Elizabeth."

Continue? But after two slaps she was not about to invite a third. It hadn't been Colonel Sharpe he had been after, when he'd suddenly stopped pigging his chocolates. So she hadn't reeled back quite far enough.

"The Americans sent a staff officer to find out what was happening—?" She repeated the words tentatively.

"Yes?" He found the last of his chocolates. "Name?"

She had half-feared as much. "I don't know, sir." It was no good pretending. "Colonel Sharpe didn't say. And I didn't think to ask." All the same, it wasn't quite fair. "I didn't think it was important. But then, I didn't know what was—or is—important." The truth was that Paul, or any of the others, might well have done better on *this* job. But she couldn't bring herself to suggest that. "I'm sorry."

"No need to be." He popped the last chocolate into his mouth and examined his finger-ends. "Not bad at all."

He looked positively smug. But he must be referring to the chocolates.

"Colonel Sharpe didn't know what came of that, because he had to report back to General—" Elizabeth frowned. Had it been "General" or "Field Marshal" then? "—to Montgomery. But in fact they broke through from Omaha to the Pointe du Hoc within the next thirty-six hours."

"Parker." He finished chomping and swallowed. "Major Thaddeus E. Parker."

Elizabeth stared at him in genuine and unfeigned astonishment.

"The name of the American staff officer." He attended to the last remnants of the chocolate in his mouth. "His name was Major Thaddeus E. Parker."

Elizabeth thought, first, that she had been quite incredibly lucky—thanks to Paul. Indeed, doubly and even trebly lucky: because, thanks to Paul and dear old Major Birkenshawe and Colonel Sharpe, she had actually touched upon the man in whom the Deputy-Director was interested, and was now aware of him, however belatedly and inadequately. Or even quadruply lucky—because she had accidentally left the Deputy-Director scope to demonstrate his superior knowledge, the exercise of which pleased him as much as his chocolates.

But then, when she thought about the possible uses of her luck, she remembered that he had quite justifiably slapped her down twice, and she had been close to admitting that inadequacy. So, if she wanted to hold on to a possible chance of field work, she had better assert herself quickly now.

"'E' for 'Edward', of course," she nodded. It was a guess, but it was a fair extrapolation from what Paul had said. All she had to be careful of was not to admit the special knowledge of "Ed" which Paul had given her.

"What?" His frown cancelled out the first slap. "*Edward*—?"

Now for the second slip—with acknowledgement to Dr Paul Mitchell, that she owed him a favour. "The late Major Thaddeus E-for-Edward Parker, sir." But she had better cover the guess, just in case. "Presumably."

"*Presumably?*" All his earlier patronizing smugness was instantly consumed by the anger of the Deputy-Director, red in tooth and claw. "Just what the hell have you been playing at, Miss Loftus?"

The anger frightened her. "Nothing, sir—"

"You were specifically limited to 1944." The anger became cold, and all the more frightening. "You were *specifically* instructed not to question the computer." He flashed the frown at the Beast's blank screen, and then shook his head, half at the Beast, and then half at her, in incomprehension; and she knew exactly what that meant—that he had already debarred her from anything the Beast knew about *Parker, Thaddeus E., Major, United States Army*, if not also *Hoc, Pointe du*, and *American*

Rangers, and even *D-Day* itself; and then, if she'd even tried to get any of them thereafter, the treacherous Beast would have signalled her attempt to him. "Nor talk to anyone in the department." The frown became accusing. "But you've talked to Audley, Miss Loftus, haven't you?"

So that was why she'd been kept out of the building! "No, Mr Latimer. I have *not* talked to Dr Audley. I haven't even set eyes on him for—for at least a month." The truth of that lent outrage to it, even while she was preparing herself for what might be the next accusation—because Paul would be his next victim.

"No?" The Deputy-Director was just not quite so confident with recalcitrant women as he might have been with men, and that gave her the extra half-second she needed, to protect herself and Paul, by defending them both with a counter-attack.

"I was only guessing." She had to get the mix exactly right, to make this cake rise. "I don't think . . . I don't seem to recall . . . that I was *specifically* forbidden to read the newspapers, was I?"

"What newspapers?"

He hadn't seen Paul's cutting. So someone had blundered, somewhere. But her half-truth—and total lie—was alive, and unquestionable.

"It was an item in the *Daily Telegraph* that I saw." That, at least, was the absolute truth—even if the item had been culled from among Paul's credit cards. But she mustn't give him time to ask *when*! "An *Edward Parker* fell to his death from the cliffs of the Pointe du Hoc just recently."

He stabbed the Beast's keys angrily. "Damn!" And then, almost as though it was David Audley addressing the Beast, "Bloody thing!"

Brothers under the skin! thought Elizabeth. Because, in the end, they both mistrusted it.

Oliver St John Latimer abandoned the computer, and snatched up the telephone, which lay hidden behind it, and punched numbers into it.

"Records?" He looked at Elizabeth quickly. "Which day was it in?"

41

She had had enough time. "I'm not quite sure." He would be a *Times* and *Guardian* reader. So neither of them had found space for this unimportant filler. "The past few days—I've been away from my flat, so I bought the *Times* . . . there was a pile of *Telegraphs* on the mat, when I got back—"

"*Telegraph* cuttings—the last week—*Parker* and Pointe du Hoc." Latimer addressed the receiver. "What d'you mean, you're short-handed?"

The receiver squawked back at him, less inhibited than the inhuman Beast: the Librarian was a genuine librarian, of independent character and impeccable provenance, as well as vast experience and devoted loyalty.

Oliver St John Latimer deflated visibly, overawed by Miss Russell's reply. "Yes—yes, I quite understand—yes, I do appreciate that, Miss Russell—with the holidays . . . I do see that . . . But if you *can*—*Parker*—yes—*Major Thaddeus E. Parker—Pointe du Hoc*—?"

He looked at Elizabeth, and through her, as he waited. And, on her own account, she ran back everything she knew, to extract anything of importance from it.

They had all been there, in Normandy, for the remembrance D-Day: the Queen, the President of the United States, and the President of France (had he been there? She couldn't remember! Major Birkenshawe had said "the Frogs", anyway!).

But Major Thaddeus E-for-Edward Parker hadn't "fallen to his death" then, when they were there—otherwise it would have been a bigger story, not a filler (that was what they had emphasized on the newspaper course: that circumstances and timing were an integral part of newspaper "tasting"; David Audley, himself an inveterate and compulsive scanner of newspapers, and their Fleet Street expert, had said as much; and David in his time had reputedly managed to suppress—or at least to emasculate —certain highly inconvenient items, usually in exchange for leaking more conveniently attractive ones).

"Yes, Miss Russell?" The Deputy-Director continued to look through her. "*Edward* Parker—*Edward?*" He focused momentarily on Elizabeth. "Yes, do that, please." Now he was looking at his screen, and she could guess what was on it.

Anyway . . . the "death fall" could not have happened

42

during what Major Birkenshawe had dismissed as the "junket-ings" of June 6th. And, by the same token, it must have been a genuine accident: if there had been any suspicion of foul play it would also have made bigger headlines in more papers—

"Yes, Miss Russell—the same classification. Thank you." Latimer replaced the receiver.

That was the contradiction to all her conclusions: an aged American had accidentally fallen over a French cliff forty years after he had once presumably climbed it, to rate six lines in a British newspaper. But now he rated a *Secure classification*.

Elizabeth readied herself for the first service in the second net. And, knowing Latimer even a little, it would be hard and fast—and most likely *"Why didn't you mention this before, Miss Loftus?"*

"Well, now . . ." His hand moved towards the chocolate box, but then gestured vaguely at her instead ". . . what was it you discussed with Dr Mitchell, Elizabeth?"

Ouch! But she was sufficiently on her toes not only to get behind the question, but also to decide how she was going to return it.

"Dr Mitchell?" She would demonstrate her innocence by misconstruing his drift. "Dr Mitchell is no problem, Mr Latimer." That would suggest to him that Dr Mitchell *was* a problem, and that she had not been entirely honest for the first time. But it would also suggest that the problem was purely personal, and that she had nothing professional to hide. "I thought we'd dealt with that. So far as I'm concerned . . . we have." She gave him an Admiral Varney look. "And I really don't see what Dr Mitchell has to do with Edward Parker—or Major Parker—?"

"No—" The chocolate-seeking hand retreated "—of course . . . But I didn't really mean that, Elizabeth, I do assure you—"

But she didn't want him to explain what he had meant. "I presume Major Parker and Edward Parker are one and the same?" She didn't want to go too far, either. But the further she got away from Paul, the better. "But obviously they are." She was on the edge of prudence now, but she couldn't stop herself. "In which case . . . I would like to know what I've really been doing. Because it hasn't made very much sense to me so far."

"What you've been doing?" He drew in a breath. "You have been doing what you were instructed to do, Elizabeth. You have been obeying orders."

She had gone too far. Because Oliver St John Latimer didn't lose his temper, he simply became silkier. And he was very silky now.

"Yes, sir." She must sound contrite, but not craven. Now that they were far enough away from Paul she must think of her own interests exclusively. "I wasn't questioning that."

"Of course not!" He smiled at her suddenly, and scooped up the Thornton's box, and cast it into his waste-paper basket. And then reached into one of the drawers of his desk, and produced another one. "I quite understand how you feel— I've felt the same way myself, on occasion." He tore off the wrapping of the box like a child with a Christmas present. "And it isn't as though you're an expert on military history—"

God! That was turning back towards Paul! "I found that quite interesting, actually!" *How could she have found it interesting?* "Colonel Sharpe's theories on the role of special forces— military elites . . ." She could just about sustain a few minutes' interrogation on that now.

"Hah!" Latimer appeared to be giving all his attention to the contents of the box. "Now *that*, I do agree, is interesting . . . though more sociologically and politically than in the 'bang-bang-you're-dead' sense . . . And, of course, *we* are an elite too, Elizabeth—" He looked up suddenly at her "—you realize that." He thrust the box at her. "Have one?"

She had better have one. "I don't feel particularly elite at the moment."

"Because you didn't get some elderly ex-soldier's Christian name?" He made his own choice, and wolfed it. "No matter . . . Although he *does* seem . . . not uninteresting, in his way, I agree." He selected another of his favourites. "No . . . the trick, with elites, is that they should be used precisely—almost surgically—for whatever is required, and for nothing else."

44

Chocolates notwithstanding, he went up a ladder on Elizabeth's board. For that was almost exactly what Colonel Sharpe had said.

"So I am going to use you *precisely*—and even perhaps *surgically*—now, Elizabeth." He looked at her, and she could see that he was happy in his work, as well as with what he was chomping. "You did teach Latin in that girls' school of yours, didn't you?"

It didn't quite shatter her confidence, because it wasn't the first time he'd hit her with *Latin*. But, of course, he had her *curriculum vitae* at his finger-tips, so she couldn't deny the truth. "Yes."

"Up to O-level? For two years?"

"Yes." Mrs Hartford had become pregnant; and then she had decided that her new baby was more rewarding than a teacher's derisory salary. "With difficulty."

"You obtained good results, nevertheless?"

That was also true—although it was not what she had entered into the record: she had certainly not revealed that she had typed the manuscript of Father's *Dover Patrol* from nine to half-past eleven, and then prepared next day's lesson from half-past eleven to one o'clock, five nights a week. "I kept one jump ahead of the class. On Mondays I was sometimes three jumps ahead. But there was one particularly clever girl in the class, with slave-driving parents, so it was usually touch-and-go by Friday." The memory still made her squirm inwardly—and frown outwardly. "I trust you are not about to order me to teach anyone Latin, Mr Latimer."

"Eh?" For a moment he seemed slightly abstracted.

"I said—" It had sounded ridiculous the first time. But then so had the Pointe du Hoc "—it doesn't matter."

"Good gracious, no!" His answer exploded as though by delayed action. "I was about to tell you what happened to Major Parker. The *late* Major Parker—as you quite rightly pointed out, Elizabeth."

On balance, that was an improvement, decided Elizabeth.

"And he was late back in 1944—that is, he was late extricating himself from the Pointe du Hoc, to report back to his commander. There was a motor-boat, or some such craft, waiting for him under the cliff there. But it was almost getting light, so they headed directly out to sea, because there were still Germans on the cliffs on either side of the headland, they thought. And that was extremely fortunate for the RAF pilot they found as a result, about four miles out. He'd been shot down the previous evening—a certain Squadron Leader T. E. C. Thomas. Aged twenty-eight." Latimer waved a hand at his screen. "All the details we have about him will be available to you, Elizabeth. And David Audley will also be available to you."

It was Elizabeth's turn to think *Good Gracious!*, even if she didn't say it. "What do you mean—'available'?"

"Exactly that. He knows all about Squadron Leader Thomas, and he should by now be able to advise you on your best course of action." He made a cathedral spire with his fingers and gazed at her across it. "Be advised by him—I'm sure he will be extremely useful to you. He's waiting for you now, and he's entirely at your disposal."

"At . . . my disposal?" It was the wrong way round—was this what Paul had guessed at when he'd tied himself in knots. "David Audley?"

"Yes . . . Have you any objections, Elizabeth?"

Objections, rising up like tripod masts, presented themselves to her. David Audley was so vastly senior to her that what he was blandly proposing was not so much like one of Father's little beardless midshipmen commanding a grizzled petty officer—it was more like a barely-qualified able seaman having his captain at his disposal. Indeed, it had been David who had been chiefly responsible for her recruitment. Apart from all of which, David was notoriously difficult to control and very much a law unto himself: giving him to her as subordinate adviser was like being asked to take a rhinoceros for a walk. And—perhaps above all—he was about to bring his Cheltenham investigation to its climax.

"Objections, Mr Latimer?" Of course, he knew all that as well as she did; yet, against all those objections—and the ones which had not yet occurred to her—there was Father's old adage about the unwisdom of rejecting opportunity when it knocked, no matter how risky; but she still needed to know one thing, nevertheless. "Has Dr Audley agreed to this?"

"Agreed? Of course he has! He's quite enthusiastic, even." The cathedral fingers intertwined, to become a double fist. "He is a brilliant man, with an unrivalled experience of events going back . . . many years. So it's your good fortune that I can let you have him for a day or two, Elizabeth."

More tripod masts—a whole forest of them! Because Latimer had to be lying when he claimed that David was leaving Cheltenham "enthusiastically", never mind that he was "happy" to advise a raw recruit on her first field assignment. And, even supposing that he had a soft spot for his own recruit, he was notoriously at odds with Oliver St John Latimer, and would never willingly dance to Latimer's tune. Never, never, *never*!

"He will help you." Latimer raised a finger. "But the final decision in this matter will be yours, Elizabeth."

So, in spite of all that, Audley *was* dancing. And the world was turned upside-down, thought Elizabeth, as all her half-connected and inadequate pieces of information arranged themselves on the board, to make little sense.

Forty years ago the American Rangers had stormed the Pointe du Hoc, and Major Thaddeus "Ed" Parker had subsequently picked up an RAF pilot from the sea, as an accidental result. And now, forty years later, "Edward Parker" had fallen to his death from that same Pointe du Hoc, and all the alarm bells in Research and Development were ringing to mark his passing!

Also, she remembered suddenly, David Audley had *unrivalled experience of events going back . . . many years*? Even, remembering what Paul had once said about David, there had once been a tank commander by the name of Audley (although it was hard to imagine the man she knew as a fresh-faced boy with one pip on his shoulder!), who had actually been there in Normandy when "Ed" Parker was fishing his RAF pilot out of the drink. But that was stretching coincidence too far, surely—surely?

"I understand." She didn't understand. But she damn well wasn't going to beg him to tell her what he actually wanted her to do. "But—you were saying—?"

"Yes." He frowned at her, and obviously couldn't remember

what he had been saying before David Audley had intruded, to divert them both. Instead, he reached for another chocolate. "What was I saying?"

"Major Parker rescued this RAF pilot." But she mustn't underestimate him. "On June 7th, 1944. Four miles off the Pointe du Hoc."

"Yes." He munched again. "About Parker—talk to Major Turnbull first, Elizabeth. Let Dr Audley cool his heels for a few minutes. Just listen to what Turnbull has to say. Then you'll know we're not wasting our time."

Elizabeth's heart sank even more at the mention of Major Turnbull, remembering her one and only meeting with him. "Major Turnbull?"

Latimer nodded, manipulating his chocolate. "He's waiting for you, too. And you may need him for extra leg-work." He nodded again. "He's got a job on, but we can hire some extra help for that—" He swallowed "—so if you want him, just tell him what you want him to do. But he's been looking into the Parker accident—he'll tell you all about that, anyway."

David Audley *and* Major Turnbull? If he had given her Paul . . . well, she could handle Paul. And dear James would have been easy, and maybe a labour of love. And Del Andrew would always have told her the truth, the straight unvarnished truth: the bonus of Del's preference for pretty Page Three girls was that he treated Plain Janes (and even plainer Elizabeth) as *mates*, and not *playmates*, with no bourgeois sexual hang-ups. But giving her David and Major Turnbull, who were each inscrutably old-fashioned, suggested that this was either a cruel test of her ability or a high mark of confidence.

Meanwhile . . . meanwhile, Dr Audley could cool his heels, and Major Turnbull could wait, because they were both waiting her pleasure. And her pleasure awaited that of the Deputy-Director—that was her pleasure now, anyway.

He reached out towards the box again. But this time he thought better of his greed, closing the lid on it and pushing the box to one side.

She waited. Because, although he might know from records that she had 140-words-a-minute shorthand, which was a skill Father had required of her for his voluminous correspondence, she knew how to wait. Compared with Father, who had thought that he had all the time in the world and didn't have to be polite, the rest of the world was a push-over.

He played with the box, wanting to open it again. "I must say . . . you're demonstrating a remarkable lack of curiosity, Elizabeth."

"Am I?" There was a difference between the Deputy-Director and Father, of course: with David Audley and Major Turnbull waiting, he had time at his back, if not politeness. But it would be foolish to go down a snake merely to revenge herself on Father. "I'm sorry. I was only waiting for you to bring Major Parker up-to-date. With . . . with Squadron Leader Thomas, was it?" She swallowed her pride. "Has he fallen off a cliff too?"

"No." Her obeisance mollified him. "Not as far as I know—not yet. But I'm sure Audley will tell you all about that."

"Indeed?" After that crack about "lack of curiosity" she must assert herself. "So Dr Audley will tell me all about Squadron Leader Thomas. And Major Turnbull will tell me all about Major Parker." She smiled. "And they are both at my disposal—Dr Audley and Major Turnbull."

"That's right, Elizabeth." He smiled back, and nodded. And then waited for her to protest.

"But you don't want me to teach them Latin grammar?"

"What?" He stopped smiling.

"Or lecture them on the use of Special Forces?" She gave him a Varney face. "But if Major Turnbull knows all about Major Parker he probably knows more about the Pointe du Hoc than I do. So it can't be that . . . and Dr Audley's Latin is certainly better than mine." She pretended to think. "Although his Latin would be more the medieval variety, wouldn't it? Not the classical sort—*arma virumque cano*, and all that—?"

He stared at her for a moment. Then, somewhat to her surprise, a slow and very different smile spread across his face, crinkling its lines with what might be genuine pleasure—she had never seen him smile like that, with face and eyes as well as mouth betraying satisfaction. It was almost a conspiratorial

49

smile, admitting her to a club for which she had not put herself up as a member.

"They don't worry you, then?" He tested her gently, as though he couldn't quite believe his luck.

"Worry me?" If she'd ever been of a mind to protest, she couldn't do so now. "Dr Audley and Major Turnbull? Why should they worry me?"

"No reason—no reason at all, Miss Loftus." He raised one hand defensively. "It was merely a thought."

And an insulting one. "They have their orders, presumably."

"They have indeed." The smile had vanished, but the glint-in-the-eye remained. "They have indeed."

"Yes? So if the worst comes to the worst I can always order them to tell me what I am supposed to be doing. Which at this moment I still don't know."

"Ah . . ." But he was quite unabashed, of course. "Now . . . where were we—?"

It didn't really matter what she said, because nothing would deflate his self-esteem. "I think we were in the sea, four miles off the Pointe du Hoc. And was that the start of a beautiful friendship?"

"What? Between Parker and Thomas? Good heavens, no!" He sat back. "Does that surprise you?"

It did surprise her. Because there had to be a relationship between these two men, if David Audley and Major Turnbull had not been wasting their time. And it had to start with that heroic rescue.

"It does, a bit." But then suddenly it didn't. Because it hadn't really been an heroic rescue at all, merely an accident of war, albeit a happy one: simply, among the thousands of random chances which had decreed life or death that morning, the vagaries of wind and tide had drifted one half-drowned British pilot into the arms of a handful of weary Americans who were themselves beating a delayed retreat from a hostile shore. In the midst of greater events and more pressing business the pilot would have been just a lucky survivor.

"Yes?" He waited for her to finish thinking.

"Maybe not." She frowned. "But they did meet."

50

"They did. June 7th, 1944—that was the first time. And the second time was last week."

"Last week?" Well, it certainly hadn't been a friendship, beautiful or otherwise, Elizabeth agreed silently; the forty years' interval precluded that.

Latimer nodded. "So far as we have been able to establish. Just the two meetings. Although they did exchange Christmas cards for a few years, apparently. But even that stopped after a time. So . . . just those two meetings, Miss Loftus. 1944, 1984. The first, pure chance—the second, quite deliberate."

Elizabeth remembered the Parker cutting. "On the cliffs at the Pointe du Hoc, would that be?"

"No." He gazed at her almost blankly. "Major Turnbull will tell you about the Pointe du Hoc. But . . . no, Miss Loftus—Elizabeth . . . Thomas was nowhere near there at the material time, as our constabulary would say."

It had hardly been likely, for they must both be old men now. Yet he must be giving her the co-ordinate of the latitude of truth, if not its longitude.

"So why are we interested in them?" *Parker* and *Thomas*? she wondered. Or was it Parker *or* Thomas? Or, since Parker was dead—Thomas?

"Thomas, Elizabeth." He forestalled her. "Squadron Leader Thomas, pilot that once was—Dr Thomas, retired schoolmaster, that is. A most distinguished teacher of the classics—Officer of the Order of the British Empire, no less. Plus a couple of honorary fellowships and the Gold Medal of the British Classical Association, awarded for leading many a likely young lad into the realms of gold." He gave her a hopeful look. "You haven't heard of him by any happy chance? From your teaching days?"

Elizabeth shook her head mutely.

"No? Well, you're not really a classicist—I appreciate that." He smiled his non-smile at her again. "But, anyway, our Dr Thomas wasn't always a classical teacher. He was a civil servant in the Foreign Office for ten years, after he came down from Oxford the second time, with his doctorate, after the war. A little eccentric for the embassy lot—he might have done better in the Treasury . . . *Anyway*, he was there, and one day

51

his name turned up on this list of ours, you see, Elizabeth."

She nearly said "What list?". But it was a redundant question, because there was really only one sort of list that ever got as far as R and D. "He was a security risk, you mean?"

"No." His hand strayed towards the Thornton's box. "No. Not exactly."

"Not exactly?" It occurred to her that all this had to be a long time ago, "this list of ours", if since then Dr Thomas had not only changed horses in mid-stream, but had had time to ride his new mount to a very different winning post. "When was this?"

"1958."

Twenty-six years ago. He had called it "our list", but it must almost have been before his time. And, indeed, almost before Audley's time too, since both he and Latimer had also changed horses themselves to come into this thankless service —just as she herself had done, come to that!

"He was forty-two then." Latimer supplied the answer to a question she had not yet reached; she had been about to think *and I was in pigtails then, learning about Old Lob the Farmer and Mrs Cuddy the Cow in kindergarten*. "Came down in '37—First in Greats—from Jesus, of course."

Of course?

"Two years' teaching. Then the war. Then Oxford again."

Elizabeth kicked herself. "Thomas" was a Welsh name, and Jesus College, Oxford, had still been full of Welshmen in the years before and after the war.

"They offered him a fellowship. But he'd had enough of that, apparently."

She wrenched herself away from Oxford—away from Turl Street, full of Welshmen from Jesus, and West Countrymen from rival Exeter, and the Taj Mahal restaurant, and the sun slanting down towards All Saints' and the High, so long ago, so long ago . . . and, but for Father, a fellowship for Elizabeth Loftus?

But—*damn that!* "Tell me about this list." That was one past she didn't have to think about: that was the might-have-been past which existed only in her imagination. "It wasn't an SR list—?"

"No." He stirred, as though Colonel Butler's chair was becoming uncomfortable. "It was a rather odd business altogether. It might be better for you to read about it for yourself—" He gestured towards the empty screen beside him "—you're cleared for it. All you have to do is punch 'Debrecen' into the computer—D-E-B-R-E-C-E-N. It's all there—what there is of it."

The name meant nothing to her. But then codenames never did mean anything—*Overlord, Cobra, Horserace, Ajax, Warsaw, Peeler*—they were all nonsense unless—or until—you were cleared. And even then, now that the Beast-computer ruled, every punched-in inquiry was recorded for posterity. It was easy to understand why they all hated the machine which used them while they used it.

"In fact, there were two lists, Elizabeth." Latimer squirmed again, and she realized that she'd been staring him out of conscience. "We had one, and the Americans had one. And the Americans eventually shared theirs with the West Germans, against our advice. And we only tipped them off—the Americans—because we needed to curry favour with them, after Suez . . . If *they*'d got it first they'd never have trusted us . . . Not that it did us any good, in the end. More like the opposite, in fact."

The two "in facts" bracketed far more information than she'd expected, even though she still didn't know what it meant. But as there was a chance that he might actually be giving her more than was in the official record in those asides of his, it was worth pushing her luck. (There were times to push, and times to hold back, and the trick was judging the right time, was what David Audley always preached. And one right time was when your contact was pleased with himself.)

"Two lists?" But how to push? "Major Parker was on the American list, presumably?"

"He was." He rewarded her initiative with a tiny flash of approval. "But we didn't know that at first—" He waved his hand in a jerky disclaimer "—when I say 'we', Elizabeth, I don't mean *me*, of course—I had no part in the affair . . . It wasn't *known*, let us say, until we compared lists in detail, the Americans and ourselves. And by that time both Thomas and

53

Parker had been completely cleared, you see. Among others."

"Cleared of what?"

"Ah . . . well, let's just say cleared of being in the wrong place at the wrong time, for the present? Audley will tell you." His hand hovered over the Thorntons' box, as though it had a life of its own and was trying to assert itself. "Suffice it to say that until that comparison, nothing even remotely suspicious had been established against either of them."

"How good was the vetting?"

Latimer bridled slightly. "It was . . . it was good enough, as far as it went." He frowned. "No—it *was* good—let's be fair." He nodded. "If it had been me, I might have cleared them, too—shall we say that?" The effort of "being fair" taxed him sorely, she could see: he didn't want to be fair.

But that was not what she wanted right now. "So they compared the two lists?" She had to keep him moving. "And came up with the Pointe du Hoc?"

"Not immediately, no. That came later. What they came up with first was Parker's name in Thomas's address book and vice-versa. So *then* they started to double-check." He stared at her. "And, you know, that really is the one *absolutely* curious thing about this whole wretched business, when you think about it."

"What is?"

He shifted in his chair. "The Pointe du Hoc—or that particular point in the sea midway between the two American landing beaches anyway, where Parker picked Thomas up. Because that really was the only connecting link between them which anyone could come up with. They were each on their own respective list in '58, and they'd met just that once in '44 —and they gave exactly the same account of it, near enough. Apart from those few cards . . . which they'd stopped exchanging long since . . . there was nothing else. They both worked for their governments—they were both civil servants. But Thomas had no American connections of any significance, his work was strictly European. And Parker's was strictly South American . . . or maybe Central American." He blinked irritably. "'Hemispherical', the State Department called it. But it doesn't matter. What matters is that they checked Parker again too, and pronounced him pristine. He remembered Thomas from '44, but that was all. Their paths hadn't crossed again."

"And we cleared Thomas?"

"He was cleared also." Traces of irritation remained in Latimer's expression. "And we were duly reminded that he was a D-Day hero who deserved better of his country than to be hounded by inquisitive little men in dirty raincoats."

"So he was cleared." The point had to be pressed. "So what happened then?"

"He resigned . . . not long afterwards." Latimer waved his Thorntons' hand vaguely.

"Why?" The point still had to be pressed. "If he'd been cleared—?"

"He had been cleared. And by that time the whole Debrecen investigation had been aborted." Another vague gesture. "He said he wanted to go back to teaching. The Foreign Office blamed us. You must ask Dr Audley—he blamed the Foreign Office."

That at least sounded like David Audley, whose instinct in adversity was never defensive. But, as Latimer kept saying, she could ask David about everything in due course. What mattered now was that Latimer expected her to ask *him*, judging by his expectant expression.

In fact she had a Wimbledon Centre Court queue of questions, all pushing and shoving. But now a new one had just jostled its way to the very front.

"Yes, Elizabeth?" He played not so idly with the lid of his box.

"One thing, you said— *two* things, actually—I don't understand."

He rubbed the tip of his nose. "Only two things?"

Supercilious pig! "You cleared Squadron Leader Thomas. Back in 1958."

He worked on his nose for a moment. "He was cleared, certainly. Twice, actually. But not by me."

That re-emphasized minor matter, in passing: that whatever had gone wrong in "this wretched business", Oliver St John Latimer was not going to take any past blame.

55

"And Major Parker was cleared."

"So he was." He agreed cautiously. "By the Americans."

"Yes." That was another straw in the wind. Or a bale of straw. "So how do we know they never met again, before last week?" She sought wisdom as politely as a Fourth Former catching out her teacher in a spelling mistake. "They were both cleared—but we've been watching them for twenty-six years? Or have I missed something?"

"Ah . . ." He opened the box. "Will you have a chocolate?"

"Thank you." As she selected one he watched her so intently that she wished she knew which was his favourite.

"And I'll have one too." His smile mortified her as he pounced on his preference gratefully, greedily. "No . . . no . . . No, there, I must admit, I am relying on the Americans, Elizabeth."

"The Americans didn't abort their original investigation?"

"Uh-uh." He shook his head, unwilling to swallow his chocolate prematurely. "It was . . . it was a joint decision, back in '58. The whole affair had become very messy politically. Indeed, counter-productive." He disposed of the chocolate at last. "There have been faint echoes of Debrecen down the years since then, but never loud enough to justify a reactivation. Until last year, when a rather unpleasant episode occurred in America, involving one of the names on the American list." The pudgy hand, which had been toying with a brighty-coloured sweet-paper, clenched it. "A very nasty affair."

Elizabeth pretended innocent interest. When Latimer had been in America last year there had been a minor panic one evening while she had been duty officer. But she had never been privy to the details, which had been swiftly taken out of her half-trained hands by Paul Mitchell.

"Involving Major Parker?" She reinforced her pretence with the question.

"No." Latimer relaxed. "No. But his name was at the top of the list when they decided on reactivation."

"Although he'd been cleared?"

"Cleared in 1958." He reached for another chocolate. "What

they did, Elizabeth, was to programme his whole career into that computer of theirs in Fort Dobson. Every decision he'd had a hand in, every advisory committee he'd served on—what it achieved, or didn't achieve. And they came up with some altogether damning conclusions."

"He's a traitor, you mean?"

"No. That is *exactly* what he isn't—or *wasn't* rather, seeing that he retired five years ago. All the evidence points to him having been a one-hundred-per-cent red-blooded American. And also a one-hundred-per-cent loser, you see." Latimer smiled evilly at her. "The New Model Traitor, Elizabeth, is the one you can't call a traitor to his face without risking an action for slander."

Elizabeth shook her head. "Now you've lost me."

"It's quite simple. He backed losing causes—the Bay of Pigs, Batista, Somoza—all the equivocal fire-fighting decisions which ended up with the whole house going up in flames. Even with Allende—he helped to overthrow Allende in a way which made him a martyr, not an exile." Latimer nodded. "So far as they can establish, no secret he had was ever betrayed to anyone, least of all the Russians. He just helped to make all the wrong decisions. Which, when you think about it, is a much more efficient treason than the conventional variety."

But there was a flaw in this argument, thought Elizabeth. "So there's no evidence that he was a traitor?"

"None at all." Latimer nodded. "No evidence."

"So . . . he could just have been stupid, Mr Latimer—surely?"

He nodded again. "Or unlucky—quite so! And we could make traitors of half our governments since the war—and before it—on the same basis. I agree, Miss Loftus—Elizabeth. But they thought of that too, you see." Another beastly smile. "So they leaned on him—they asked him questions, and they let him know he was being followed. And they bugged his phone, and burgled his house—they did all the things which are considered to be the unacceptable face of security, to suggest to him that they knew more than they actually did." He looked at her sidelong. "Why?"

57

She knew that answer, anyway. "To make him run?"

"To make him run. And, of course, he did run."

But that wasn't strictly accurate. "But he was a D-Day veteran, Mr Latimer. How was that 'running'?"

"He didn't attend the D-Day celebrations, Elizabeth."

"But—"

"He came back to Europe—for the first time since 1945." Latimer cut her off. "He wasn't interested in D-Day."

"But he did go to the Pointe du Hoc, Mr Latimer."

"Yes. But you'd better talk to Major Turnbull about that." Latimer toyed with his box of chocolates. "It's what he did before that which matters to us now. And *why*, even more than *what*."

It wasn't difficult to read between those lines: if the CIA had been *leaning* on the poor devil, then they would have leaned all the way to France, with their usual enthusiasm.

"Before he went to the Pointe du Hoc, Elizabeth, he visited Squadron Leader Thomas, at a place called St Servan, where Thomas lives now, in France. It is his retirement home." He pushed the Thornton's box to one side. "So far as we are aware, that was the first time they'd met again since Parker deposited Thomas on the beach—Omaha Beach—on June 7th, 1944. And two days later he was dead. And I do not *particularly* like being told all that by their Head of Station in London, as a friendly piece of information. Because it rather suggests to me that they know their business better than we know ours."

Well, that at least accounted for the urgency, thought Elizabeth: they could hardly allow such "friendly" intelligence to lie in the pending tray—not even David Audley could argue with that; and Latimer himself would be doubly sensitive about their efficiency in Colonel Butler's absence, of course.

But all that, and not least the American interest, made her own leading role even more odd. "So the CIA is helping us, then?"

"No." He made another cathedral spire with his fingers. "They regard Squadron Leader Thomas as our affair now. Though we shall have to tell them the outcome, in the circumstances, naturally."

A knot of anxiety twisted inside her suddenly. The outcome was what was expected of her. "But if Squadron Leader Thomas is a traitor, Mr Latimer—"

"Was, Miss Loftus," he interrupted her. "He's retired now. He's an old man sitting happily in the sun—happily and blamelessly."

That made it nastier. "But if he *was* a traitor, like Major Parker . . ."

"There won't be any concrete evidence?" He adjusted the angle of the spire slightly. "No, I don't expect there will be. Or nothing we could ever hope to proceed with, anyway. But we shall be able to re-assess everything he's done in a new light. *If* he was a traitor, that is." He closed his eyes for an instant. "The initial assessment must be largely subjective in the first place. And perhaps even in the last place."

"Unless he runs—like Major Parker." No wonder Audley hadn't complained about her preferment! thought Elizabeth grimly. "Or falls over a convenient cliff."

"He hasn't done either of those things yet." He seemed to catch a glimpse of her disenchantment. "We do have him under surveillance now, Elizabeth—however belatedly. Dale, from Paris, is superintending it. And Dr Audley has the details for you. And Major Turnbull has other information for you, as I said."

"Oh yes?" He had been going about things in a curiously back-handed way, she thought irritably: while she had been researching an obscure episode of the Second World War, other people had been doing real work. "So . . . why have I been doing what I've been doing?"

"My dear Miss Loftus—Elizabeth!" He opened the ca- thedral roof. "All that was mere spade-work, what others have been doing. There was no need for you to be burdened with it. And I wanted you here, to hear what I have told you, without any pre-conditions."

He hadn't wanted her to talk to anyone. But why? "So I'm an expert on the American Rangers, Mr Latimer?" *Big deal!*

"So perhaps you will have something to tell Squadron Leader Thomas that he doesn't know about?" He inclined his head almost apologetically. "When you talk to him?"

"Talk to him?" But at least that was a clue as to what he expected of her.

"Why not?" He spread his hands again.

Why not? thought Elizabeth.

"What I am asking you to do is . . . not easy, Elizabeth—I know that." He squirmed in Colonel Butler's big chair. "But that is the particular nature of this section's work. And you were chosen for it because you had particular aptitudes—not simply policeman's aptitudes, for pursuing facts without emotions, but something more than that, and much more rare . . . Which I do not propose to define, because there are some things which cannot be put together again after they have been taken to pieces." He smiled suddenly. "And because we do not have the time now for such esoteric discussion."

Was he complimenting her with his trust? wondered Elizabeth. *Or was he bull-shitting her—as Paul would say?*

"You've got to get to know this man Thomas." Latimer leaned towards her. "You've got to know *about* him first—and Audley will help you there. But I don't think you'll get the answer I need without meeting him face-to-face, in the end."

That was telling her. "And if he runs then—?"

"Then our problem's solved." He sat back. "But if he was going to run, I think he would have done so by now, for what it's worth."

So Thomas was a harder nut to crack than Parker, was what he thought. Perhaps even an uncrackable nut.

"Did we make a mistake in '58?" The cathedral reformed momentarily, then collapsed as he reached for the chocolates. "Because if we did, then we re-activate our whole Debrecen list. And it's up to you to tell me, Miss Loftus."

III

"UNSATISFACTORY, MISS LOFTUS." Major Turnbull answered the question without hesitation. "My investigation was unsatisfactory."

Elizabeth felt the word envelop her, as though he intended that it should apply to her also. It was only the second time that she had spoken face-to-face to the department's newest recruit, but her recollection of the first encounter was all too vivid.

"Unsatisfactory, Major?" The repetition of his rank (if it really was his rank) recalled Major Birkenshawe to mind, but only for an instant, since her own dear old major resembled this one in nothing except that. "In what way unsatisfactory?"

"It is evident that you have not read my report, Miss Loftus." His unnerving immobility, not only of body and features but also of eye, began to work on her again.

"No, Major." She fought the urge to explain her failure, and finally settled on saying nothing at all, remembering the last time—

"What a dreadful-sounding place!" (Superintendent Andrew, secure in his impeccable and genuine working-class accent, had been lodged in the tiny village of Grimeby, the better to find out why one of their Known Agents was presently fishing in the troubled waters of the Great Miners' Strike.) *"Grimeby!"*

But Major Turnbull had waited for her to elaborate on her stupidity.

"You can see how people living in a place like that might want to throw stones at the police—'Grimeby'!"

Only then had Major Turnbull pounced.

"Had you visited it, Miss Loftus, you would know that Grimeby is a not unattractive hamlet on the edge of Baldersby Dale. And had you cared to research it further, you would know that 'grime' has nothing

whatsoever to do with coal-mining. It refers, in fact, to a standing stone of great antiquity nearby, dating from Viking times and sacred to the Norse god Odin, 'Grim', or 'Grimar', being a colloquial rendering of his fierce expression. The god of war and battle, Miss Loftus, as well as the patron of wise men and heroes. And also the god of hanged men riding the gallows as his steed."

But not this time, by God! He could look at her as grim-faced as Odin himself riding his gallows. But whatever his objection to her might be—whether it was professional, against women in this line of work, or Father's simple old-fashioned misogynism—whatever it was, it would cut no ice with her this time. This time he was going to do the talking.

Finally he looked at his watch. But then his hand returned to his lap, the fingers loosely clenched, alongside the other hand, which hadn't moved. If he had a train to catch he was evidently prepared to miss it rather than forgo the satisfaction of making her speak.

Elizabeth weakened. "Go on, Major." She forced herself to smile. "Yes?"

"Very well, Miss Loftus." He didn't bat an eyelid, but she could feel his satisfied prejudice like an aura, now that he had asserted his superiority. "What is it that you want to know?"

That was a superficially reasonable question, thought Elizabeth. But, as David Audley always maintained, questions usually give you answers about the questioner. So in this instance, since he knew she hadn't read his report, he was also fishing—and probably for anything the Deputy-Director had told her, for a start.

Well, that other time she'd been easy meat. But this time she must simply remember that his brief had been Major Parker's death.

"Everything, Major." Another smile. "Why was your investigation unsatisfactory?" He'd know a false smile when he saw one. "A tragic accident, the newspapers said?"

"Yes." The eyelids still didn't bat as he realized that she had learnt her lesson. "The French were waiting for me, Miss Loftus."

"Waiting for you?" Innocent and genuine surprise. "On the Pointe du Hoc?"

"Nearby." There was perhaps the faintest suggestion of Lowland Scottish, perhaps from the hard land of the Border, in his voice. "The local paper suggested that he had come to Normandy for the D-Day gathering, on June 6th. But that was not so. He did not arrive until the afternoon of June 7th. The day of his tragic accident." He repeated her words without commitment to them.

"Yes, Major?" She must not jump to conclusions. But tragic accidents in this line of country were generally neither tragic nor accidental; and it was only on the very cliff-edge of possibility that this elderly American had come half-way across the world to do alternatively what he could have done much more easily at home, on his own account.

"The newspaper reported him as staying at Bayeux. I traced him to a hotel there. I gave the clerk twenty francs, and he was on the phone before my back was properly turned. I went directly to the Pointe du Hoc. They took me as I was on my way back to Bayeux."

"Took you?"

"With the utmost courtesy, Miss Loftus. But without argument."

She mustn't waste time trying to imagine that scene. "What did they want?"

"They wanted to know what I was doing."

Another silly question then. "And what were you doing?" A hard man like Major Turnbull would have had a cover-story. "You were stringing for PA? Or Agence-News Angleterre?"

"No, Miss Loftus. There was a DST man in attendance, so they already knew exactly who I was. A simple lie would only have invited trouble."

That was interesting, though logical—that the Major had a European reputation before Colonel Butler had recruited him, and long before Mr Latimer had sent him back to France. "So what was your complicated lie?"

He gave her Odin's stone face again, looking down on Grimeby from Baldersby Dale. "In any period before or after Her Majesty the Queen has been invited to a foreign celebration, if there is a suspicious death we investigate it as a matter of routine, Miss Loftus."

Phew! "And what did they say to that?"

"There was nothing they could say. They could not deny that Her Majesty was there on June 6th, in Normandy. And they knew they couldn't question such a story without making an issue of it. Especially not after I'd reminded them of the *Vive le IRA* slogans they had failed to erase."

Not bad at all, thought Elizabeth. When the safety of the Royal Family was involved, all foreigners expected John Bull to be at his most truculent. "And they believed that?"

"No, Miss Loftus. If they had believed that I would have said so." He paused, and as the pause lengthened she felt herself sucked into it.

"So what did—"

"If you will let me finish, Miss Loftus." He cut her off smoothly. "They pretended to believe me. And then they were uncommonly helpful and co-operative. They allowed me to interview three witnesses—two Frenchmen and an American youth. The Frenchman had been engaged in clearing up the area, after the previous day's ceremonies. The American youth was the grandson of an officer in one of their destroyers, which gave close support to the American troops who stormed the position in 1944." He paused again. "I take it that you are aware of what happened on the Pointe du Hoc, Miss Loftus?"

"Yes, Major." It might be smarter to feign female ignorance, but there was a limit to what female flesh-and-blood could endure. "That would be D, E and F Companies of the 5th Rangers. And the destroyer was presumably the *Satterlee*."

"Yes." Not a nod, much less a smile—not even a bloody *blink*! Even Father had more grace on the rare occasions when she produced the right answer! "The boy had been delayed by an accident involving the truck in which he'd been hitch-hiking. But he was an excellent witness, observant and intelligent. I have no reservations about him."

Elizabeth frowned, and plunged over her own cliff before she could stop herself. "He saw Parker fall?"

"No, Miss Loftus. I did not say that. I neither said it, nor implied it. I said the boy was an excellent witness. If he had

64

seen the man fall then my investigation would not have been unsatisfactory. None of these witnesses saw the man fall. Neither did two adult Americans who were also on the headland at the time. I was shown transcripts of their evidence. All five of them arrived on the scene after he had allegedly fallen —the boy, one of the Americans and one of the Frenchmen almost immediately, within sight of each other, the other two shortly after." He paused. "Altogether there were seven people in the vicinity."

Seven?

"Indeed?" She was not going to be caught so easily again: the as-yet-unaccounted two must wait until the Major chose to summon them. "Why were you not able to interview the Americans—the adult ones?"

He stared at her in silence for a moment. "I was told that they had returned to America. Their evidence was certainly of no significance in transcript. They merely confirmed what the boy and the Frenchman said, but in less detail."

"Who were they? Why were they there?"

"I was told that they were tourists."

It was like playing a game—a game of snakes-without-ladders, from which he evidently derived some secret ego-inflating pleasure. But she was at least beginning to get the hang of his rules. "And is their transcript to be relied on?"

"No, Miss Loftus. I did not say that. But so far as it went it was factually accurate, I believe."

Whatever he stated as a fact was a fact, and "I believe" prefixed a genuine opinion. But "I was told" indicated an untruth. Those were his rules. But since she was boss it was about time she started making the rules. "Why were the French so helpful?"

"The fact that I was there at all meant that I'd been tracking him. They didn't know how much I knew already. Perhaps they thought I might give them something."

Some hope! thought Elizabeth. "And the missing eye-witnesses?"

"Eye-witnesses?" He produced no reaction, of course.

"Seven people, you said, Major." Now for her rules. "You may have all the time in the world, but I've got Dr Audley cooling his heels down the passage. So I don't have time to play games."

"Hmm . . ." His lips compressed. "I did not say all their evidence was useless. It was not. The boy's evidence was in reality of greater significance than the French police suggested —or pretended to suggest. He was able to testify that Parker was unsteady on his feet—how he lost his balance and fell while crossing the rough ground near the edge of the cliff."

That suggested a genuine accident, thought Elizabeth. But she was done with questions now. "Seven people, Major. Tell me about the other two."

"The two other persons present were a man and a woman. Both young . . . both French. They had been observed earlier by the American boy, and also by one of the French refuse-collectors. The boy said that they were 'necking', and the Frenchman described what they were doing more colourfully. But from where they were lying in the grass they would certainly have had a clear view of the point at which Parker went over the edge."

Eye-witnesses. But then why was he playing so hard to get.

"All the witnesses agreed that there was at least one shout, or cry. The boy thought that there were two. When they came within sight of the place . . . which is in a gully, or possibly a stretch of heavily bombed or bombarded cliff-edge . . . they also agreed that the young Frenchman was kneeling on the grass, with his female companion close by. The boy says that they were both very emotional—'all het-up, and crying'—but his grasp of the French language is limited. The refuse-collector's recollection is that the man said 'he fell—he jumped —I do not know'. And then perhaps 'I ran—I was too late— he is gone'. But he is uncertain about either the exact words, or their exact sequence."

Eye-witnesses, Elizabeth thought again. If they had been making love just above him, maybe their eye-witnessing had not been exact. But it was now reduced to one thing or the other, whatever the sequence.

"The first of the other two Americans arrived then, followed by the other one shortly afterwards. They both then proceeded to the bottom of the cliff by the wooden staircase, together with one of the Frenchmen—you are conversant with the geography of the Pointe du Hoc, Miss Loftus?"

Not in 1984, Major Turnbull—only in 1944; and there was certainly no easy way down then, never mind up! "Of course."

He gave her one of his blank looks. "The evidence is unsatisfactory after that. The American boy says that the young man spoke to his girl-friend. He doesn't know what he said—only that the girl burst into tears, and became hysterical. The refuse-man *thinks* he said something like 'What shall we do?' But then the young man turned to him and said that he must take his *fiancée* from the scene of the tragedy—that he would take her back to the car, so that she could recover there."

That was par for the course, thought Elizabeth: men expected women to become hysterical on such occasions. And, in her educational experience, men were often inadequate on such occasions, and unwilling to deliver the necessary slap, which she had always found easy. And, in this case, the Frenchman and the American boy would no doubt have been relieved to have an hysterical *fiancée* led away out of their sight by a protective *fiancé*.

But Major Turnbull's lack of expression as he waited for her to react to this reasonable sequence of events, combined with what he had already said and left unsaid, suggested that there was more and better—or more and *worse*—to come. And, for choice, *worse*.

"I see." So the two adult Americans (*let's say the two CIA men, for a guess, Major*) had gone rushing off, in the faint hope that their subject had survived the fall; and that had been a mistake. "And that was the last anyone saw or heard of the *fiancé* and the *fiancée*, Major?"

"No, Miss Loftus." He managed to look pleased without moving a muscle.

Now she was stumped. Either she had missed something, or she was reduced to a tragic but boring accident again. And that made no sense.

"Yes, Major?" Instead of attempting nonsense, she simulated intelligent expectation of whatever he had in store for her.

"The young man phoned the Gendarmerie at Bayeux next

day. He told them that he had seen it all. But the lady with whom he had been at the time was not his *fiancée*. So he was not about to come forward to testify what he had seen, in person."

Not his fiancée, thought Elizabeth. Therefore someone else's *fianceé*—or someone else's wife, more like: that went without saying in France, or anywhere else, but in France particularly, for such matters were *bien entendu* there, even in the Gendarmerie at Bayeux.

But they were evidently not *bien entendu* by Major Turnbull. "What else did he say?"

"After he had indicated the delicacy of his situation he became disappointingly inexact, I was told. He saw an elderly gentleman, whom he took to be a foreigner by his dress, and who appeared to have strayed from the path. But he neither saw anyone fall nor jump. The old man was there—he heard a cry, which made him look up—and the old man was no longer there. Then he reacted as anyone might have done, rushing to the spot, on the edge of the cliff. And then other persons ran to join him. But it was useless—there was nothing he could do, or could have done, to avert the tragedy. He deeply regretted his inability to come forward in person, but the reputation of the young lady was at stake. And nothing would bring the elderly gentleman back to life."

"And you believe—" No, that was the start of a foolish and unnecessary question "—I mean, did *they* pretend to believe that, Major?"

"For my benefit they did. It is on the face of it a plausible enough story. And I could hardly question it without raising difficulties for myself."

That wasn't the complete story, decided Elizabeth. "Did they explain why they picked you up?"

"They did not. I had given them a sufficient reason for being there, asking questions. But their reason for keeping an eye on the place was if anything rather better than mine for being there."

She was getting closer. "They didn't believe the man's story?"

"Please let me finish, Miss Loftus. I detected a certain

68

embarrassment. Because they were a little late in picking me up. Consequently I was able to examine the ground at leisure." He paused deliberately, and continued only when he was sure of her. "In my considered opinion, the two adult Americans were watchers, not bodyguards. And they did not anticipate any danger, since they allowed him out of their actual vision in a potentially hazardous area." This time the pause was longer. "But I do not know anything about the dead man. I presume you know more about *him*, Miss Loftus?"

Elizabeth held her tongue. It would have been satisfying to have teased him, but it would have served no useful purpose. All she had to do was to season her impatience and let him speak without interruption.

If he was disappointed, he didn't show it. "I do not know whether you have had occasion to visit the place, Miss Loftus—?"

He was actually fishing! But then, perhaps it was her special knowledge of the Ranger units of 1944 which had tickled his curiosity. "Please do go on, Major."

"The site is cordoned off, and marked. And it is certainly the same site which the American boy described to me. And I had an opportunity to examine it, as I have said."

Curiously, he was about to echo something Paul had once said to her about his battlefields: he was talking about the actual place now, which he had seen; and Paul had said: *"People can lie, Elizabeth, or they can be wrong. But the ground never lies, and it's never wrong!"*

"People fall over cliffs, Miss Loftus, for three reasons. They go over by accident, because they venture too close and they slip. Or they choose to jump, and they do jump. Or someone pushes them. And, for any reasonable assumption to be made, each possibility requires different criteria."

Apart from expertise on Anglo-Danish place-names and Norse gods, Major Turnbull evidently had a coroner's experience of death, thought Elizabeth.

"He was an old man, and he was none too steady on his feet. We know that because he slipped on the grass earlier. And if he had wanted to jump, then there are several stretches

69

of cliff which make jumping easy, where the drop is quick and inviting."

So jumping was eliminated.

"The whole of that area was heavily bombed and bombarded, but there is a perfectly adequate path across the site. In spite of his physical infirmity he left that path, and negotiated a most difficult terrain in order to reach a gully. It is not only a much less promising place from which to jump —it is not simply lower, but the actual cliff there is something less than sheer for a further distance—there is something of an overhang, which makes it very difficult, if not impossible, to ascertain whether the drop is either clean or sufficient."

Elizabeth nodded. "So he didn't jump."

"It is a reasonable assumption that he did not. But, by the same token, it seems unlikely that he fell from such a place, Miss Loftus. It is exactly the sort of place from which an adventurous child might have fallen, while peering over the edge of the overhang. But the man whom the American boy described would have found that far too difficult. Such a descent would require a quite unreasonable degree of imprudence."

"But he could have slipped. He had already done that once."

"Then he would still not have fallen over the actual cliff edge, in my estimation. To fall there he would have required outward velocity—a downwards slither would have been insufficient."

Elizabeth thought for a moment. It was really no wonder that he had described his investigation as "unsatisfactory": he had been ordered to verify a tragic accident, only to find conflicting evidence, and then French Security waiting for him. All of which would not have endeared the assignment to anyone, least of all someone like Major Turnbull.

She stared at him, and wondered what she meant by "someone like Major Turnbull", when she really knew absolutely nothing about him except that he had passed Colonel Butler's scrutiny six months ago.

"Yes, Miss Loftus." He stared back at her. "I am well aware that I am offering you a card-house of unsupported hypotheses.

The man *may* have fallen. The French *may* have traced the young man and his woman. It is even remotely possible that the American boy had been rehearsed, and that he is a natural-born liar. You might even be entitled to assume that the man Parker did not fall—or jump—or was pushed . . . from the place I observed. All that is possible. And I warned you of my dissatisfaction—had you read my report you would have saved yourself time which you may well have wasted."

Yes. But the Deputy-Director had rated this meeting as more valuable than reading words on the screen, and what did that count for?

"Yes, Major," she heard herself say meekly. Simply, if the card-house was good enough for the Deputy-Director, it had better be good enough for her—at least until she had talked to David Audley. "But please continue, nevertheless."

"You wish for more of my theories, Miss Loftus?"

That, of course, was what was really so painful to him, although he showed no sign of pain (or anything else, for that matter!): the nearer he was to facts, the happier he was, the further away, the unhappier. So the odds were that his report had been much more severely factual than this, and much less a card-house. "Yes, Major."

"Very well. If we assume that he did go over the cliff from that gully, we need a reason for him making the descent into it. And if the American boy was telling the truth about him, then there is at least one good reason. Which would also account for the presence of the two adult Americans, who were covering him at a discreet distance."

If he was making this painful effort, then it was only fair to meet him half-way this time—especially as he had already committed himself on the likely identity of the Americans. "He was making a contact."

"That is correct." He looked at her. "You may know better, Miss Loftus . . . but the manner of my assignment to him suggests that to me."

"Yes." Elizabeth hid behind a sympathetic nod of agreement. "Yes, Major?"

"The gully is not an ideal place for a contact, Miss Loftus. It has the advantage of being dead ground unless you actually overlook it—and the man and the woman were well-placed both to do that, and to observe the approaches from all directions. But all those approaches are wide open to observation—it has no covered approach, or exit. If I am right, he went there because that was where he was told to go. But also, if I am right, it was never a contact point. It was a killing ground—that is the sum of my opinion, Miss Loftus."

The card-house was complete. But she couldn't leave it quite there. "What was the actual cause of death?"

"Multiple injuries, consistent with old bones falling a vertical distance of nineteen metres. The beach at that point is composed of fallen chalk and large pebbles. You could find a similar beach westward from Eastbourne, past Beachy Head, Miss Loftus. Somewhere towards Birling Gap, where I used to go shrimping when I was a boy." He showed no sign of being stirred by that far-off memory. "They made free with the medical report. He had a fractured skull and a number of broken bones, and serious injuries to internal organs—quite enough to kill him without the broken neck which I believe was the actual cause of death before he hit the beach—"

There were plenty of reference books and atlases and maps in the library, but Mrs Harlin had her own private shelf closer to hand.

"May I have a look at your French Michelin, Mrs Harlin?"

"Of course, Miss Loftus." From the expression on Mrs Harlin's face, Elizabeth judged that she was still in the doghouse for keeping the Deputy-Director waiting while supposedly transacting her sex-life with Paul Mitchell. Even, when she had taken the Michelin from its slot between the *Good Hotel Guide* and *Success With House Plants*, she seemed momentarily unwilling to surrender it. "I'm afraid that you have missed Dr Audley, Miss Loftus. He had an appointment which he was unable to delay any further."

"Oh?" So that was the way the wind blew. But then Mrs Harlin notoriously had a soft spot for David Audley, who cultivated her as lovingly as she did the line of exotic pot-plants on the window-sill behind her, with which he suborned her at regular intervals. Keeping David cooling his heels unnecessarily probably rated almost as badly in Mrs Harlin's book as ignoring the Deputy-Director.

"Oh?" But as she reached for the delayed Michelin, smiling sweetly, she thought *Huh!* to herself grimly. It was easy enough for the Deputy-Director to say—and to repeat finally and blandly—*Dr Audley will be at your disposal, as I have said, Elizabeth. He knows what I want, and he will brief you and assist you accordingly. He has been relieved of all his other urgent duties.* But the reality of dealing with David Audley was going to be very different— and here was the first proof of that. Because, on a scale of difficulty from one to ten, Major Turnbull was suddenly reduced to one, with Audley at nine-point-five, for all his superficial charm—and that was Paul's experienced opinion equally with her limited experience.

"Indeed?" Her hand closed on the Michelin. Well, maybe Paul was no push-over when it came to the crunch. But she was not about to go running back to the Deputy-Director at the first check. If she could handle a recalcitrant fifth form whose parents had paid in advance for exam results, and type Father's illegible manuscripts while running his house for him with the smoothness of a Royal Navy First-Lieutenant, then David Audley maybe didn't rate nine-point-five after all. Com- pared with Father (never mind the fifth form) he bloody-well didn't move the needle!

She pulled the Michelin out of Mrs Harlin's hand. "Then I presume he left a number where he can be contacted, Mrs Harlin?"

St Servan—and it would be well to the back—

"No, Miss Loftus."

She would not look up. Compared with the British Michelin, with *St Albans*, and *St David's*, and . . . *St David's*, and *St Helen's* and *St Ives*, and whatever else, there were pages and pages of *saints* in France, recording the ancient triumph of Christianity over paganism—*Ste-Affrique*, and *Ste-Agrève*, and *St Beat* and *St Brieuc*—*St Étienne, St Dizier*—tiny places, remembering out- landish, forgotten saints—who had been *St Fulgent?* Or *St Lo*, where so many Americans had died in 1944 (but not Major Ed Parker!)—and *St Nazaire* (where so many of Father's friends had distinguished themselves, and died too)—and, and, and

73

—St Quentin, where Paul's 1914–18 heroes had gone over the top into the German barbed-wire . . . but—*almost there—*

"Miss Loftus—"

St Servan—that looked like it—*Ile et Vilaine*, not far from *St Malo*—therefore not too far from the Normandy battlefields, and the Pointe du Hoc—

"Miss Loftus!" A white envelope was thrust into the outside edge of her vision.

Elizabeth revenged herself by ignoring the envelope, with an effort. For there were other St Servans—or Saint-Servans: there was one far to the east, in Haute-Marne, and another, far to the south-east, in the Vaucluse—*St Servan-les-Ruines—*

"Miss Loftus—" The envelope intruded even further "— Dr Audley has marked this message 'Urgent'. So if you could *perhaps* spare the time to look at its contents—?" Mrs Harlin's voice was tight as a eunuch's bow-string in old Constantinople.

Elizabeth accepted the envelope, which was addressed and privatized to her in Audley's own untidy hand.

Those examiners had been good, thought Elizabeth critically. *Those Cambridge examiners—they had been good at deciphering calligraphy, as well as taking up his historical scholarship, who had once awarded David Audley his double-first at Cambridge! For not even dear James Cable's illegible scrawl was worse than this—*

Elizabeth—If you want to know more about Haddock Thomas, put your skates on, and get on down double-quick to the Abyssinian War memorial, on the Embankment, where I shall meet you—

Abyssinian War?

Which Abyssinian War was that—?

"And Dr Mitchell, Miss Loftus," said Mrs Harlin, as though both names were now equally distasteful to her.

"Dr Mitchell, Mrs Harlin?"

"He'd like you to lunch with him in the Marshal Ney public house, Miss Loftus. If you can spare the time from other duties." Mrs Harlin pursed her lips. "Strictly a business lunch, he said."

IV

AFTER FIVE MINUTES Elizabeth realized that she ought to
have known better, and after ten she knew better: it should
have been obvious from the start that David Audley would
never cool his heels for her, and even more obvious that he
would try to run the show. In his place she would have done
the same.

She looked up and down the road again in vain, and then
across it, towards the gleaming green-glass Xenophon Oil
tower on the far corner; and then turned back to her continued
half-contemplation of the Roll of Honour of the Abyssinian
War of 1867–8, which listed the officers, NCOs and other
ranks who had "perished in battle, or died of wounds or
disease" for Queen and Empire—

Particularly, she ought to have known better than to have
come running at Audley's first command, when she could have
let him wait while she punched *Debrecen* into the Beast. She
had only herself to blame.

And what sort of name was *Haddock* Thomas for God's sake!

Whatever long-forgotten imperial requirements had launched
the power and the glory of the British Empire in Abyssinia—
Marxist Ethiopia now, but Christian Abyssinia then presumably—the brevity of the casualty list identified it as one of
Queen Victoria's smallest and healthiest wars—

The big complication was the presence of the Americans—of
the CIA—on the Pointe du Hoc. But then, if Parker was an
undoubted traitor, he was their traitor, so they had a right to
be there, watching him. And, by the same token, *Haddock*
Thomas was hers—was he?

75

It had certainly been an imperial war. For, in addition to names from the 4th, 33rd and 45th Regiments (judging by the Donovans and the Kellys, the 33rd must have been an Irish regiment), there were officers *"attached"* to the Punjabi Pioneers, the Bengal Lancers and the 27th Baluchis . . . plus (which would have gladdened Father's heart) a little midshipman from the Naval Rocket Brigade, poor child!

But it was not simply a memorial to the Abyssinian War: the bronze tablet on which the names were inscribed was supported by two elephants, carved in a high relief, facing each other across a trophy of cannon, drums, spears and battle-flags; but one elephant had half its backside chipped away and one face of the obelisk was scarred and gouged, in memory of the German bomb which must have fallen nearby, maybe forty years before—

Forty years? That took her back to the Pointe du Hoc again—

"Miss!"

The taxi seemed to come from nowhere. Or, since it hadn't cruised gently along the kerb into the edge of her vision, it must have executed a quick U-turn across the traffic, from the opposite direction.

Elizabeth peered into the cab. But the cabbie, who must have leaned across to his nearside to shout at her, had already straightened up and sat waiting for her to get in. And the meter flag was already down.

She almost got in, but then she didn't. Instead, she took a step back, to the safety of the Abyssinian War memorial.

The cabbie turned towards her again. "Well, Miss—you comin' or en'tcha?"

"Coming where?" She had the elephant at her back now.

He gave her a questioning look, as though she'd just changed her mind. "Dr Audley's fare, en'tcha?"

If this was the field, thought Elizabeth, it was not at all how she had imagined it—going blindly into it. But then nothing in R & D had ever been as she imagined it, all these months.

But then no doubt the little midshipman had never imagined himself on an Abyssinian mountainside, with his rockets.

She hadn't time to arrange herself comfortably before he lurched her sideways with another fierce U-turn, to get himself back *en route*—whatever the route might be.

"Can y'sit yerself one side or the other, Miss . . . so I can see?"

Elizabeth slid obediently into one corner of the cab. "May I ask where we are going?"

"Yus—you may." He twisted the cab up a narrow street behind the Xenophon tower, cutting ahead of a CD-registered Mercedes full of Arabs which had just pulled away from the oil company's entrance. "Dont'cha know, then?"

"No. I do not know."

The taxi raced up the narrow street, then turned into an even narrower one, which looked like a cul-de-sac.

Elizabeth waited, unwilling to weaken his concentration while their lives were at stake. Then, when there was only a blank wall ahead, he swung into what appeared to be a loading bay, turned narrowly past a line of vans, and came into daylight again, in another street.

"Where are we going?" Wherever they were going, it would cost the British tax-payer. "Is it far?"

"No." He jumped the lights at a crossing, ahead of a terrified old lady in a Metro. "Nothin' followin' us now—'e's backin' out of Napier Lane by now, f'r all the good it'll do 'im. Silver MG Maestro, EUD 909Y?"

Paul drove a silver MG Maestro, of which he was inordinately proud; but she'd never thought to look at its number-plate. "No."

"No?" He cocked his head. "Well, 'e was the one—an' not bad, neither, 'cause he remembered me when I went round the second time, past 'im, an' went like the clappers after us, into Pict Street . . . not that it did 'im any good, like I said—but we're comin' up now, Miss—"

Elizabeth looked around. They were back beside the river now—on the Embankment, somewhere—?

"Only 'e *was* good—so just in case, it might be as well for you to get out quick-like—right? An' that'll be two-fifteen, wiv any small token of your esteem, Miss, for my time an' trouble —like, silver MG Maestro EUD 909Y?"

Elizabeth stared at the Abyssinian War Memorial, just across the road from where they were drawing into the kerb, under the canopy of Xenophon Oil's entrance.

"Quick now, Miss!" He held out his hand. "Say a tenner?"

"A tenner?" Just in time she remembered whose fare she was. "I'll tell Dr Audley that."

Up three—four—five marble steps—after the fifth, as she stepped on the huge Xenophon mat, the dark-green glass doors bearing the same oil-rich-gold colophon hissed open automatically, drawing her inside and then cutting off the sound of London behind her as they hissed shut again.

Too much information jostled momentarily in her brain, coming from too many directions. There was visual information all around—the overwhelming green-and-gold assault of the entrance hall of Xenophon's Aladdin's cave: not only the green-and-gold of marble and mosaic, but a jungle hothouse profusion of growing things which would have made Mrs Harlin's mouth water.

Then memory sorted out the driving theme of Xenophon's public relations, on television and in the colour supplements and across innumerable billboards: "*Xenophon grows*" was a slogan carefully divorced from the growth of Xenophon's profits, and there were green leaves entwined round the Green *X* symbolizing the company's well-publicized concern for the environment of its operations—*There is no acid rain in our rain forest!*

But where did Squadron Leader Thomas—*Haddock* Thomas —peep through those leaves?

And if EUD 909Y was Paul, why was Paul sticking his neck out beyond common sense—

"Elizabeth!" Audley brushed aside a trailing piece of jungle. "Where on earth have you been?"

"David." She stifled the temptation to say "Dr Audley, I presume?" The field was already too much like a jungle for such flippancy.

"You're late." Audley tugged at the sweaty striped knot of his rugby club tie. "Come on!" He gestured towards the lift doors.

She stood her ground. David Audley was much younger than Father was—than Father *would have been*: it still required an effort to think of Father in the past tense—but he was quite old enough to be her father, nevertheless. But if she weakened now, she would be lost.

He abandoned the dreadful tie. "Come on, Elizabeth—*please!*"

"You owe some taxi-driver two-pounds-and-fifteen-pence, plus tip. And he makes that ten pounds exactly."

"What?" He blinked at her. "Why didn't you pay him?"

"I thought ten pounds was too much for just crossing the road. Which was where I was. As you well know." In spite of herself, she weakened. "The Abyssinian War memorial, David—remember?"

"Yes . . . Yes, I'm sorry about that, Elizabeth. Just a little old-fashioned precaution. But in this case just to annoy Paul Mitchell."

"Paul?"

"I said I was sorry. And I know I should have chosen somewhere farther away, for form's sake." He raised one massive shoulder apologetically, and then grinned at her. "It's an interesting memorial, though—don't you think?"

"Quite riveting." That was one pitfall which she knew how to avoid: the study of war memorials was Colonel Butler's only known hobby, and the rest of the department indulged this macabre taste almost out of habit now. But that didn't mean she had to reward his grin. "If you think it was necessary to encourage Paul to make a fool of himself, then it achieved your objective, anyway."

"It was Paul?" He smiled at his own question, as though amused by it.

"It was EUD 909Y, according to your taxi-driver. But why, David?"

"Why indeed!" He shrugged diplomatically. "He should be back in Cheltenham. But he's still foolishly protective where you're concerned—is that not true, Elizabeth?"

"He thinks I'm not up to . . . whatever this is." If he was fishing, then she could fish also. "He showed me a cutting from the *Daily Telegraph*."

"God bless my soul!" But his surprise wasn't quite genuine. "Well . . . I must admit that I taught him to read his newspapers thoroughly . . ."

On second thoughts, she had no need to fish. He was supposed to be helping her, not vice-versa. "Why are we here, David?"

He raised an eyebrow. "Didn't you read my note? What have you been doing, Elizabeth?"

"I was told to speak to Major Turnbull first. About the man Parker—the man in the *Daily Telegraph*."

"*Ah!*" The eyebrow dropped. "And getting information out of the equivocal Major was like squeezing blood out of that proverbial stone?" He nodded sympathetically. "So what did he have to say, then?"

"He said—" Elizabeth stopped suddenly, first because she realized that she couldn't afford to let *vice-versa* work like this, with her answering all the questions, and then because someone was heading directly towards them across the foyer.

"Dr Audley?" It was one of the two beautifully-tailored and coiffured receptionists from the marble desk. "Dr Audley, Sir Peter will see you now." The woman smiled her practised reception-smile at him, simultaneously taking in Elizabeth, pricing her from head to toe, and adding a nuance of apology to her smile on the basis of her combined estimation of their importance.

"Eh?" Audley frowned into her politeness. "What?"

"Sir Peter, Dr Audley—" She faltered under his frown "—Sir Peter will see you now."

"Ah—hmm . . ." Audley's face became a mask of vague intransigence, for which his somewhat battered features were well-suited. "Right. Then you just tell Sir Peter that we'll see him in five minutes—right?"

The woman's own face, at least above the pasted smile, registered something like consternation. It was as though, as a junior archangel at the Gates of Heaven, she had said *Saint Peter will see you now*, only to discover that she had been addressing some Old Testament prophet who rated her master as just another newcomer.

But then she rallied. "Sir Peter is a very busy man, Dr Audley."

"And so am I." The intransigence was not so much vague as blandly and brutally confident. "Five minutes, tell him—right?"

The hate above the woman's smile was almost tangible. "Yes, Dr Audley. If—if you would take the left-hand lift . . . when you are ready?"

"Thank you." Audley turned back to Elizabeth. "Now, Miss Loftus—as you were saying—?"

Elizabeth watched the receptionist's retreating back, outwardly stiffened, but inwardly slumped. He would never have dared to treat Mrs Harlin like that.

"I was going to say . . . I was going to say that you are a pig sometimes, David—to quote your wife."

"Only when it is necessary—to quote Tsar Alexander, Elizabeth."

"But I was late, you said. So it wasn't her fault."

"You were late—and she's paid to handle awkward bastards like me. And we're paid to do what I'm doing now, actually."

"Which is not telling me a damn thing?"

"We haven't time for that now—which is tactics, Elizabeth." He glanced towards the lifts, and so did she. There were three of them, and there were people waiting outside two of them, on the right. But no one was waiting outside the left-hand one, which was open and empty.

"What tactics?"

"What tactics?" He came back to her. "Getting an interview with Sir Peter Barrie was a slice of luck to start with, because he probably spends half his life jetting somewhere, first-class. Like this morning, for instance, Elizabeth."

"This morning?"

"He was booked to Cairo this morning, top security. Because Xenophon's got a deal going with the Egyptians, so my Israeli friends tell me. But when his old friend—his *very* old friend— who, quite surprisingly, is *me* . . . when his old friend phones him up this morning, first his secretary says he's a busy man, and hard luck . . . But then she phones me back and says he has got maybe a few spare minutes, between one pressing

81

matter and another. And that begins to interest his old friend, Elizabeth. And then you're quite unconscionably late. But he's still got time to spare. And that might also be luck. But I think I've had all the luck I can reasonably expect already. So that interests me even more. So I'm just pushing my luck for another five minutes, do you see?" He smiled hideously at her. "Besides which I really would like to know what Major Turnbull said about Mr Edward Parker, Elizabeth."

"And I'd like to know what Squadron Leader Thomas has to do with Xenophon Oil, David."

He nodded. "Fair enough. And the answer is—absolutely nothing, so far as I know." He looked at her. "So now I get my answer—fair?"

It wasn't in the least fair. But, unfair or not, she needed Audley more than he needed her. "He thinks Parker was murdered."

This time the look was elongated. "Yes . . ." Then he nodded again. "Yes . . . although he didn't say quite as much in his report. But then he has this thing—this psychological block, would it be?—about unveiling his opinions in print." He cocked an eye at her. "But if he says that was the way of it, then we had both better believe it . . . And that justified dear Oliver St John Latimer taking me away from more important matters, I suppose."

More important matters? There was a display of time spanning Xenophon's international, intercontinental, world-wide operations, electronically illustrated over a huge spinning globe in the middle of the foyer, continuously red for this minute of British Summertime, and green for Xenophon's own communications satellite, as it fulfilled its function from the North Slope of Alaska to the China Sea. But Elizabeth felt only the pressure of the red numbers adjusting their verticals and horizontals as her own lifespan was counted.

"Good God!" exclaimed Audley, looking past her. "*Razzak!*"

The emphasis twisted her towards the direction of his attention. "What?"

"Razzak!" This time he only murmured the name, but took a half-step sideways as he did so. "Well, well! *Hullo there!*"

There had been people there, in the doorway, where the

doors had been hissing them in and out all the time as they had been talking. But now there was a large Arab there, transfixed by Audley's glance.

"Hah!" The man's hesitation was lost in his slight change of direction. "David—of all people! What black mischief are you up to here?"

"My dear fellow—not the same as yours, I hope!" Audley completed the step. "I didn't even know you were in London —" He broke off as the same receptionist whom he had bullied came out of nowhere to intercept the Arab.

"General?" The same welcoming smile was there, but it was a desperate smile, bereft of both hope and confidence. "General Razzak?"

The Arab turned towards the woman. "Madame . . . I have an appointment with Colonel Saunders. But it was made very recently, by telephone, so I quite appreciate any delay. So I will wait here—" He flicked a glance towards the entrance, which was now partially obscured by two large men who were patrolling the steps at different levels, admiring the view "—until the Colonel is free?"

"Ah—" began Audley.

"A moment, David—" The Arab held up a mutilated hand. "—I am at your service, Madame."

"Oh—yes, General." The effort of not looking at Audley embarrassed the woman. "Colonel Saunders will see you now. If you will go to the right-hand lift, General. Level Six."

"Thank you, Madame." The Arab bowed. "That is most kind of you. After I have transacted the common courtesies with this gentleman I will go directly to Level Six. And meanwhile, if you could report my arrival to my embassy? Would that be possible?"

"Of course, General. Immediately."

"Thank you." The Arab smiled sweetly at her, and then cased the foyer for a second time as she returned to the desk. "The Libyans have put a price on my head, so I have to take these boring precautions, David—please forgive me."

"And the Iranians too, presumably?" Audley was quite matter-of-fact.

"And them too!" The Arab completed his scrutiny, and

grinned at Audley. "You have your cross to bear—and I have my crescent. The irony of which is that I shall go to Paradise, while you will find yourself rubbing shoulders with them in Hell."

"But you'll put in a good word for me? For old time's sake?"

"I will not." The Arab had already observed Elizabeth surreptitiously, but now he studied her with frank curiosity. "Until you remember your manners, David."

General *who?* Elizabeth racked her brains. Audley had once been a Middle Eastern expert, as well as the author of a scholarly work on the Crusader Kingdom of Jerusalem, until he had blotted his copybook. And he was still very thick with the Israelis. But that somehow made this friendship more unlikely.

"I beg your pardon, Miss Loftus." Audley sounded slightly distant. "May I present my old and dear friend, General Muhammed Razzak, late of the Egyptian Army?"

Razzak, of course! She had once heard David say, *à propos* the Sadat assassination, *it wouldn't have happened if old Razzak hadn't been in Washington at the time.*

"*Enchanté*, Miss Loftus," The General carried her hand to his lips with what was left of his hand—there was no index finger at all, and the palm was dreadfully scarred. "But of course! You are the daughter of the gallant naval captain who once sank all those German torpedo-boats when his own ship was itself sinking—I remember reading of his death in *The Times*. You have my sympathy, Mademoiselle, for your loss."

"Thank you, General." In spite of the hand, and the fact that he was just beginning to run to fat and was also old enough to be her father, he was an attractive man still, Elizabeth decided. But why should he remember a three-year-old *Times* obituary?

"Belated sympathy," murmured Audley dryly. But then David also knew the real score, which lay between herself and Father.

"Belated only because I have not had the pleasure of meeting Miss Loftus until now." The General held her hand just a second too long, as though he derived information from it. "And he was an historian also—a most distinguished naval historian."

"That's what good intelligence is all about, Elizabeth," said Audley. "He didn't really need an introduction—any more than he's a real Egyptian. He's really an Albanian-Turk—one of Mehemet Ali's imports, by descent . . . And definitely not to be trusted with the week's housekeeping money."

General Razzak cocked an eye at Audley. "Just as *Audley* is . . . what is it? Anglo-Norman? And would that be *Norseman?* And are the Norsemen not the sea-raiders who burnt all the Christian churches and monasteries—and nunneries, and made free with the holy ladies therein?" He smiled at Elizabeth. "You would not have to trust the housekeeping money to such terrorists, Miss Loftus—they would also take it from you." He nodded. "And as for your gallant and distinguished father, as it happens I have read his account of Admiral Lord Nelson's campaign, which ended with the Battle of the Nile. General Bonaparte's Egyptian expedition is my hobby, and I hope to publish my researches one day . . . Did you assist your father with his researches, Mademoiselle?"

"What he means, Elizabeth," said Audley quickly, "is, are you helping me with my researches now? And what I meant, when I said he was an 'old and dear' friend, was that we've known each other for a few years, and we've both cost each other dear. And I've paid more than he has."

Elizabeth blanked out her memories of transcribing Father's anti-Nelson prose, word for word, not daring to object to it while suspecting that Father's severity with Nelson's human frailties was due either to his knowledge of his own defects or to his blindness to them—even now she could not decide which.

"I did, General." She wasn't attractive enough to coquette with General Muhammed Razzak, so it had to be an intellectual, blue-stocking, response. "If you'd like to see Father's notes . . . will you be in London long?"

He shook his head. "Alas no, Mademoiselle. " He didn't look at Audley. "As I'm sure you both know, I have business with Xenophon. Although I am not a businessman."

"You're here because Barrie didn't fly out this morning?" Audley looked quickly towards the red time-fingers over the revolving Xenophon globe. "And so he's screwed up all your security precautions? So you're here to sort things out with his Head of Security?"

General Razzak spread his amusement between them, with a wicked glint for Audley and pretended regret for Elizabeth, as though he knew quite well what they were about. "And if I said 'yes' to that—" He zeroed in on Audley "—would you answer me truthfully in return?" He shifted his glance to Elizabeth, but then swung away from them both, towards the reappearing receptionist who had brushed past the cascade of foliage to hover on the edge of their game. "Madame?"

"General . . . please forgive me for interrupting you." This time the reception-smile illustrated a confusion of unreconciled priorities with which Elizabeth could readily sympathize: did the Egyptian general, who was booked in with Xenophon's security chief, rate above the horrible Dr Audley, who behaved as though he out-ranked Saint Peter himself, whose special lift still gaped open?

"Dr Audley—" Faced with an absolute decision, the woman came to it bravely "—Sir Peter is asking for you. And I really cannot put him off any longer, Dr Audley."

"No?" Anglo-Normans, secure in the Battle of Hastings, lacked the grace of Mehemet Ali's Albanian-Turks. "Oh, very well, then—tell him we're just coming." Audley cold-shouldered her, coming back to General Muhammed Razzak. "And if I assured you on my honour that this has got nothing to do with you, as far as I know—that it's purely domestic? Would you believe that?"

"On your honour—I would." Razzak nodded. "And it would make me happier, too."

"Then we can both be happier." Audley returned the nod, and then transferred it to the receptionist, and finally gave it to Elizabeth. "Let's try the left-hand lift then, Miss Loftus—" He spread an arm and a hand for her, to shepherd her towards the open lift-doors. "—Razzak, I'll phone you tomorrow evening maybe—okay?"

"You can phone me. But you won't get me."

"Okay." Audley shrugged. "I'll just give Jake Shapiro your kind regards." The hand urged her irritably.

"Of course!" Razzak bowed to her. "Another time, Miss

Loftus? I am particularly interested in the landing of the British army in 1799—relatively speaking, as an opposed landing, it was remarkably efficient—I would be very grateful for anything you have on that, from contemporary records and diaries—" He bowed again "—Miss Loftus—"

"For Christ's sake! Come on, Elizabeth!" Audley grimaced at her as he started to move. "The only really smart thing we ever did in Egypt was when Disraeli borrowed the money from Rothschild's to buy those Suez Canal shares. But then we should have handed the bloody place over to the Australians in 1918—they were the only Anglo-Saxons the Egyptians ever respected—*come on, Elizabeth!*"

Elizabeth came on, towards the left-hand lift, with its welcoming open doors, not daring to look farewell at General Razzak after that.

"David—who is Sir Peter? Sir Peter Barrie?" She entered the lift, and swivelled towards him. "What has he got to do with Squadron Leader Thomas?"

He made a face. "Don't keep calling him 'Squadron Leader', for God's sake, woman!"

"Why not?"

"How much do you know about him?" Audley searched the lift for controls. "You know . . . I wonder which floor we want—?"

"Hold on, David! I know practically nothing about him—and absolutely nothing about Sir Peter Barrie. So don't press the button yet."

"You don't? Well, the presence of General Razzak should tell you something." He scratched his head. "There don't seem to be any buttons—just this one marked 'Emergency'. It must be controlled from the desk, by that woman." He took a step back towards the doors, but they started to close and he was forced to retreat.

The lift began to move, and Elizabeth began to panic.

Audley grinned at her. "She nearly got me. She was just waiting for that, I'll bet! Not that I blame her . . . You were saying—?"

Mustn't panic. "Where is that emergency button, David?"

"Just here—the red button—*Christ, Elizabeth*—!"

The lift stopped.

"For God's sake woman! What did you do that for?" exclaimed Audley.

"Because I have an emergency, David. I know practically nothing about Squadron Leader Thomas—whom I must not call 'Squadron Leader'—except that he was shot down on June 6th 1944, and rescued by the late Major Thaddeus E. Parker on June 7th." Elizabeth decided that she would hold on to the Deputy-Director's other revelations for the time being.

Somewhere in the distance there was a bell ringing. Presumably it was an emergency bell.

"And I know nothing at all about Sir Peter Barrie, whom I am about to meet." She faced him. "And that is my emergency."

He stared at her for a moment. Then his mouth opened.

"Executive floor lift?" The voice came out of a small speaker alongside the red button. *"You have a problem? Please speak into this receiver, alongside the emergency stop."*

Elizabeth pressed her bag tightly over the speaker. "Solve my problem, David."

He stared at her for another, much longer moment. "I don't think you have any problem at all, young woman." He shook his head. "The problem is all mine."

The speaker mumbled again, muffled by her bag.

"All right, Elizabeth—I give you best." The shake became a nod. "We vetted both of them, back in 1958. And cleared them both—Peter Barrie was a wronged man, and a victim . . . old Haddock was also a wronged man. But also a philanderer. It was a cross between a Feydeau comedy—or a Whitehall farce, or maybe a 'Carry On' film—and a James Bond novel. Everyone got egg on their faces."

"What about Major Parker?"

Audley shook his head. "What about him?"

"He was on the list too."

His face hardened. "You know what list you're talking about?"

Audley was usually so friendly that when he wasn't he was

at once rather frightening. "Mr Latimer has cleared me for it, David."

"Oh, he has, has he?" She could almost feel the heat under his look. "Well, we haven't the time—and this isn't the place —for Mr Oliver St John Latimer's list. And you can lean on your red button until hell freezes over, Miss Loftus."

Elizabeth summoned her last reserves. "So what is Sir Peter Barrie's connection with—with Thomas—"

"That's easy. He was Thomas's best friend, or near enough, back in '58. Until Barrie shopped him." He relaxed slightly. "So I thought you should begin with him. But I wouldn't advise you to delay him any longer. He's a busy man, as that woman said."

She lowered her bag. "Hullo? Hullo? Who is that?"

"Executive floor lift?" The voice seemed relieved. *"Please speak into the receiver, alongside the emergency stop—the red button!"*

"The red button?" She made herself sound flustered. And when she thought about David Audley and Sir Peter Barrie that wasn't too difficult. "I think I pressed the button by mistake—the lift just stopped."

Audley leaned forward. "She pressed the red button by mistake," he repeated grimly. "So what do we do now?"

"You have a problem, caller?"

Audley gave Elizabeth an old-fashioned look. "Our only problem is that the lift has stopped."

"Please press the red button again, caller. The lift will proceed."

Audley continued to look at her as he pressed the button. "Don't bother to apologize. I'd hate that."

Thirty years with Father, who had been a fully paid-up life member of the Never Apologize Society, had at least inured her to that weakness. "I wasn't going to."

He relaxed, and became almost his old self again. "I'm glad to hear it. I am seldom wrong, but it's always good to have one's judgement vindicated by events."

To the extent that he had recommended her recruitment, she was his invention. But if he was reminding her of that he still had a lot to learn, in spite of his seniority and experience, she decided as the lift-doors opened.

89

"Dr Audley—Madam." A Mrs Harlin-class battle-cruiser was waiting for them in what must be Xenophon's Holy of Holies. "I'm so sorry about the lift, Dr Audley." She gave Elizabeth a tripod-masted look. "Sir Peter will see you now." She indicated their route, through another of Xenophon's exotic jungles. Except that those couldn't be *real* flowers surely, could they? "Shall I lead the way?"

"By all means." Audley bowed slightly to Elizabeth as the woman moved ahead. "After you, Miss Loftus," he murmured.

"Thank you, Dr Audley."

"And God help us—" As she passed him she heard the rest of his murmur "—Peter Barrie and David Audley, both."

V

ELIZABETH LOOKED ABOUT her in surprise.

"Home from home, maybe?" Audley had been looking round too. And he was also surprised.

That was just about exactly right, thought Elizabeth. Or, anyway, it didn't look like a Xenophon room: no company symbol, no green-and-gold colour scheme, no expensive furniture—and, above all, no vegetation, apart from a spindly Busy Lizzy plant on the window-sill. The books in the shelves were mostly paperbacks, and many of them looked as though they had been well-read. In fact, the whole place looked lived-in, as nowhere else in the great tower had been, or ever could be. It was like a suburban flat—almost tatty, even.

Audley picked up the paperback which lay on the coffee-table, with a slip of paper in it marking the reader's place.

"Henry Williamson—*A Fox Under My Cloak.*" He made a thoughtful face. "Paul would approve of that. Ypres 1915, is it, this one?"

"Among other places."

Elizabeth turned towards the voice.

"I've only just discovered him properly. I thought he was merely the author of *Tarka the Otter*, who ruined himself by backing the Fascists in the Thirties. It makes me ashamed, how ill-read and ill-informed I am. Hullo again, David Audley."

He was as tall as David, but thin, almost gaunt, where David was proportionately big. He reminded her slightly of pictures she had seen of George Orwell.

"And hullo again, Peter Barrie." Audley replaced the book where he had found it, taking care to keep the marker in position. "Though, in the circumstances, that hardly seems adequate, after all these years—don't you think?" He bent down and adjusted the book. "1958—was that a good year for claret?"

Sir Peter shook his head. "I don't think I bought much wine that year. I was in somewhat straitened circumstances—remember?"

There was something between them which was too big to be communicated except in small talk. So that was why Audley had been . . . the way he had been, perhaps?

"So you were. Although you wouldn't have bought any '58 in '58, anyway. I bought some '49 in that year. It cost me a fortune—I should have bought it before and kept it longer. One so often does things too late. My wife's into early English water-colours at the moment." He shook his head sadly. "Far too late."

Sir Peter was looking at her. "Introduce me, David."

Audley gave her a vaguely apologetic look. "There! I've done it again—or *not* done it." He turned the look back to Sir Peter. "I got bawled out by General Razzak in your front office not five minutes ago for just the same thing—would you believe it?"

Sir Peter continued to study her. "General Razzak?"

"None other. And as he's here to see your Colonel Saunders he's probably rather miffed with you, as well. For upsetting his security arrangements in Cairo at the last moment—would that be it?"

Sir Peter smiled at her suddenly. "Probably." The smile had an oddly conspiratorial quality, as though he wanted to share it with her. "You know, he's not going to introduce us. But I believe you are . . . Miss Loftus? And I am Peter Barrie."

His hand was gentle. "Sir Peter."

"And you are a colleague of David's?"

"A junior colleague, Sir Peter." Just as suddenly as he had smiled, she knew why he had done so. "His manners were always bad, were they? Even back in 1958?"

"Always bad." He nodded agreement. "But one must not be offended by them." He glanced at Audley. "I have some dealings with a man who thinks very highly of you, David. You have had dealings with him a few years ago. Eugenio Narva."

"Oh, yes?" Audley ran his eye along the bookshelf idly. "I seem to recall meeting him once, yes."

They weren't just name dropping, decided Elizabeth. They were sending messages to each other in code.

"He certainly remembers you. He asked me if I knew you."

"And what did you say?" Audley moved down the bookshelf.

"I recalled meeting you once, long ago." Sir Peter paused. "You'd vetted me, I told him."

"Yes." Audley nodded to the bookshelf. "Since he probably knew that already . . . that would have been the right thing to say." He came to the end of the shelf, and looked round the room again before finally coming back to Sir Peter. "Nice place you've got here, Peter."

"I think so." Sir Peter nodded happily.

"Homely." Audley gestured towards the books. "I remember some of those, from when I searched your flat in Tavistock Road, back in '58."

"Yes?" The man didn't seem in the least surprised, unlike Elizabeth herself. "You have a good memory, then."

Twenty-six years? She had been at primary school, among her picture-books and crayons, reading about Old Lob, and Mrs Cuddy the Cow, and Mr Grumps the Goat—or had Mr Grumps been a donkey?

"Uh-huh." Audley observed her astonishment, and stretched out to tap one—two—of the larger books. "Powicke —*Henry III and the Lord Edward.* Two school prizes, with embossed school crests on front, and *P. W. Barrie, Upper Sixth, Bishop* . . . Bishop Somebody—*Bishop Somebody History Prize* . . . See for yourself, Elizabeth." He pulled one of the faded green volumes from the shelf, and handed it to her.

The crest was that of a once-famous direct grant school, now a successfully independent public school, which was presently and quite infamously poaching sixth formers from girls' public schools. And not at all to the girls' advantage, thought Elizabeth bitterly.

"Bishop Creighton, David."

"*Creighton*—of course! A boring Victorian historian—I should have remembered." He sniffed derisively, and then gestured towards the other books. "And all the rest—the early Penguins with the advertisements in 'em—see that old yellow Penguin, Elizabeth—and those Bernard Shaws. The reason I remember 'em is because I bought the same books at the same time—1940s, 1950s—and they're still in my shelves too." He jerked his head in a different direction, towards a corner of the room. "But that desk . . . we had one hell of a job getting into that, without damaging it . . . That was there, too."

"Quite right. And I'm very glad you were so careful. Because that was my grandmother's desk—not very valuable, but valuable to me." Sir Peter smiled at Elizabeth again. "I used to have a flat in Tavistock Road, Miss Loftus."

"We didn't damage it," growled Audley defensively.

"I didn't say you did. I didn't even know you'd searched the place, David." Sir Peter's mouth twisted. "Or I guessed you must have done, eventually. But there never was any sign of it that I could see, anyway." He came back to Elizabeth. "I lived there until quite recently. But I was away so often, and particularly during the last few years . . ." He shrugged. "And there were a couple of burglaries—" He switched to Audley "—ordinary burglaries, David: they just stole the silver and the hi-fi . . . At least I presume it wasn't you, after all these years, was it?"

Audley was still looking round. "Not as far as I know."

"No?" Sir Peter stared at him thoughtfully for a second or two. Then he turned to Elizabeth again. "Well, so I thought . . . I had this dreadful ecological penthouse here, where I lived more than half the time, but I couldn't relax . . . So I thought—it was Mother's old flat, and I'd lived in it off and on since I was a child. But it was only things, really—and shapes."

"Home from home," snapped Audley. "And RHIP—*Rank Has Its Privileges*—eh?"

"What?"

Audley nodded. "I wondered why this place was bugging me so much—apart from its lack of plant life."

Peter Barrie smiled. "Yes, David—?"

Audley nodded again. "This is the *same* room I searched, back in '58—just a couple of miles away, and a couple of hundred feet up—right?" He ran a quick glance round the room. "Same furniture, same *dimensions* . . . same books, plus another twenty-six years' shopping—only the windows are different: we came in through the door, but you had sash-windows in Tavistock Street, naturally—right?"

"Right, David." Peter Barrie beamed at him. "The windows were really too expensive here. But I've got a sash in my bedroom—would you like to see?" He included Elizabeth in his pleasure. "Moving the walls was no problem —they were only partitions up here, nothing structural. And the builders loved it: they'd never had to do anything like it before—they just added ten per cent for a lunacy factor, I rather think."

Elizabeth felt herself absorbed by them both—by what they were saying to each other, and what they were both saying about each other: two old men—or old-young men, old enough to be her father, each of them, but young enough still to take pleasure from deliberate irresponsibility, as Father had never been able to do, because he had never been reconciled with the unfair cards fate had dealt him.

"Elizabeth—I'm sorry." All the time, Audley had kept half an eye on her, at intervals. "I do apologize, for all this chat."

"And so do I," agreed Peter Barrie. "But after twenty-six years this is something of an old boys' reunion, you might say."

"I don't mind." She could even forgive Audley now for leaving her high and dry. "All this is very—" What was it, apart from fascinating? "—educational, Sir Peter."

They looked at each other, each slightly off-put by her choice of adjectives.

"How—'educational', Elizabeth?" Audley got in first.

He was no longer an ally, she thought. When they'd entered this strange room, which was suspended in time as well as space, it had been two-against-an-absent-one. But now, with the way David remembered Peter Barrie after twenty-six years, it was two-against-one—and she was in the minority.

"More than that." Two-against-one, then! "If this room is vintage 1958—" At least that was an improvement on 1944, which was before she'd been born! "—then tell me about 1958, for a start, please."

The allies consulted each other again.

"How much does she know, David?"

95

"Practically, sod-all, Peter. I'm just her minder—I'm not a bloody KBE-tycoon, like you."

"Yes. But I received your message."

"And cancelled your trip to Egypt, Sir Peter?"

"Yes, Miss Loftus. But that's what comes of having a bad conscience—even after twenty-six years." He cocked his eye at his ally. "Who was it said no one could afford to buy back his past?"

Audley grimaced at him. "God knows. It's certainly not Kipling."

What had Audley put in his message, to stop Sir Peter Barrie's Egyptian trip, and bring General Muhammed Razzak hot-foot to the Xenophon Tower? It was obvious that neither of them was going to tell her—they were waiting for her to tell them.

So she had to hit them with what she had. "Squadron Leader Thomas, Sir Peter?"

"'Squadron Leader'?" He reproduced Audley's reaction.

This time, she would wait for an explanation.

He was looking at David. "How many planes did Haddock destroy?"

"Six." Audley raised his huge shoulders interrogatively. "Or ten if you include the Luftwaffe."

"Eleven—if you include the Tiger Moth during training." Sir Peter held up one hand, with its fingers spread wide. "He lost seven British and hit four Germans. But they were only probables, weren't they?"

Audley shook his head. "I think you've got to count them. Allowing for the number of missions he flew—to be fair."

"Very well. Four of them."

"He may have hit others."

"Possibly." The five fingers bunched into a fist, and then sprang open again. "Shot down twice—once over France, and walked home—once by the Americans—right?" He grasped two fingers with his other hand.

"That was bad luck—the second time, Peter."

"Bad luck—good luck—" The three remaining fingers remained standing "—if you ask me, he was born lucky, was Haddock."

"You could say that," agreed Audley. "Compared with some."

"With most." Two fingers and a thumb, actually. "Came down hard twice—once, battle damage . . . once, engine failure—*four*—right? Plus the Tiger Moth."

Audley rocked uncertainly. "By the same token, I lost four tanks—if you count two which broke down in England, during exercises on Salisbury Plain, Peter."

"Four." There was only one finger left. "Ditched twice—once off Eastbourne Pier—or Brighton Pier, or somewhere—" The thumb disappeared, but a new finger came up instead ". . . and once on D-Day, when the British shot him down—and the Americans picked him up, which cancelled out the previous offence, he used to maintain . . . which makes seven all told, agreed?"

"Sir Peter—" For Elizabeth, that was enough of Haddock Thomas's wartime career for the time being "—I was referring to . . . to later on, after the war."

"You never told me about those four tanks of yours, David." Sir Peter addressed Audley, ignoring her.

"Losing tanks is boring." Audley took the first volume of Powicke's *Henry III and the Lord Edward* from her, and replaced it beside its comrade. "Tell her about 1958, Peter."

"But you know more about that."

Audley adjusted the books in the shelf. "I can tell her my version any time. But mine is the official record. And who believes the official record?" He trued-up the line of books, until they were like guardsmen on the Horse Guards, waiting for the Queen to inspect them. "Yours is how it really was."

Sir Peter Barrie presented a suddenly-different face to her —not his remembered Tavistock Street face, but his Xenophon Oil one. "Why d'you want to know, Miss Loftus?" He blinked, and the friendly Tavistock Street face was back again. "After all these years—?"

"Because it's her job, Peter," said Audley.

"Let her answer for herself then. Always assuming that I can recall such far-off events—why, Miss Loftus?"

"You can remember," said Audley.

"Not if I don't choose to." Sir Peter Barrie pronounced the

threat mildly, but he knew that he had let her see through the gap in this curtain. "You know, I do seem to recollect some of the questions *he*—" Without taking his eyes off her he indicated Audley "—*he* once asked me. Do you want the same answers—if I can remember them?"

She had to get away from their old games. "I'd much rather you told me why you've got a bad conscience about Squadron Leader Thomas than David did. Then I can draw my own conclusion."

"I see. So I must believe him, when he said you knew 'sod-all' about old Haddock, must I?"

She was in there with a chance. "Not quite 'sod-all'. But I would rather like to know why you both keep calling him 'Haddock', for a start. Is that really his name?"

"Indeed?" It was a hit—a palpable hit, she could see that from the way he suddenly shifted to Audley at last. "Why was he called 'Haddock', David? It wasn't because he kept being shot down into the sea, and then swam ashore—was it? Because I don't think it was—because he was 'Haddock' long before that, wasn't he?"

Audley was back among the books. "You know why. And you want to talk to her, not me—so you answer her then."

Sir Peter Barrie frowned. "I know about 'Caradog'—or 'Caradoc', or whatever it was . . . And even *Caractacus*—is that it? But how did it—metamorphose—'metamorphose'—? Was it at school?"

"God Almighty!" Audley slammed back the book he'd half-removed from the shelf. "He was your friend—*ex*-friend —not mine! And you ask me?"

"Oh yes . . . he was my friend." It was neither the Tavistock Street face nor the Xenophon Oil one now, but a painfully-assumed mask which was perhaps midway between the two. "Or *ex*-friend, as you are so pleased to remind me—"

"Not 'pleased'." Audley chose another book. "Pleasure doesn't come into it. Just fact."

"But you investigated him. I never did that."

"I investigated you too." Audley looked up from his book. "Did you have a nickname? I never established that!"

"Where is he now?" Sir Peter Barrie brushed the question aside. "What's he doing now?"

Audley switched to Elizabeth. "*Thomas—Squadron Leader,* —*T. E. C.—RAFVR—OBE, DFC, MA*—'Royal Air Force Volunteer Reserve, Order of the British Empire, Distinguished Flying Cross, Master of Arts, Jesus College, Oxford'—*Thomas, T. E. C.*—'Thomas, Tegid Edeyrn Caradog'—and you can't get more bloody Welsh than that, short of scoring a try at Cardiff Arms Park, against England. And the funny thing about that, Elizabeth, is that he never did score a try, and he hasn't really got a Welsh accent. And he accounted for more British planes than German . . . and for a lot more women in his time than either British or German planes, if he ever bothered to log his score." He appraised her momentarily. "Though you should be safe there, because he must be rising seventy now, nearly. But I wouldn't bet on it, all the same, because he had a weakness for brains as well as blondes—and brunettes, and red-heads, and whatever came to hand." He nodded. "Like the man says—I investigated him."

Whether it was deliberate 'tactics', or whether it was because he was fed up with proceedings which he wasn't supposed to be running, Elizabeth didn't know. But what she did remember now, which was much more comforting, was why the Deputy-Director had summoned Audley of all people to help her unravel Tegid Edeyrn Caradog Thomas. Who better than Audley?

"Then answer the question," Sir Peter pressed him. "Why 'Haddock'?"

Except—*who better than Audley?* thought Elizabeth. *So why Elizabeth Loftus?* That wasn't nearly so comforting.

Audley misread her expression. "I can only give you a partial answer to that, Elizabeth. Because nicknames are often only partly amenable to logical explanation."

"That's true." Sir Peter nodded. "When I was in the RAF —" he half-turned to Elizabeth "—which was after the war, and I was a wingless wonder in the engineering branch, so I didn't destroy any aircraft, British or German . . . But I remember this very distinguished Group Captain who was always known as 'Padre', not because he'd once had to say

99

grace in the mess at dinner, but because the only grace he knew was his school grace, and that was in Latin, Elizabeth."

Latin! remembered Elizabeth. *Ugh!*

And—*why hadn't the Deputy-Director chosen Audley?*

But she would think about that later. "Why 'Haddock', David?"

"It was when he was at Oxford, before the war. He was at Jesus from 1936 to 1939—scholarship from Waltham School, then First in Greats." He continued to misread her. "It's all to do with the way 'Caradog' is pronounced, more or less, in Welsh, and then anglicized—it comes out as 'Craddock'. So he was 'Crad' at school. But at Oxford, which has always been more flippant than Cambridge and the rest of the civilized world, it somehow became 'Haddock'. And that followed him ever after—to the RAF, and back to Oxford after the war, and then into the Civil Service. And finally back to Waltham, where it displaced the original 'Crad' immediately."

That was more of an answer than she'd expected. And, cutting away the irrelevant fat of the nickname, it left her with a curious circular odyssey, beginning and ending with Waltham—and with one strong prejudice she shared with her late headmistress.

"Of course!" exclaimed Sir Peter. "He went back to teach at the old school, didn't he!" He caught Elizabeth's expression. "You've heard of Waltham?"

"I have." This, at least, was something she didn't have to think twice about, to pretend ignorance or any bland non-committal knowledge.

"You don't approve of it?" He read her face accurately. "I thought it was a very good school. In fact—in fact, I believe we took two Old Walthamites in our last graduate-trainee intake. A bio-chemist from Cambridge, and an economist from Bristol University—both high-flyers."

That figured, thought Elizabeth grimly. "It's a very good school."

And that was the unarguable truth: Waltham had always been a first-class public school, disgustingly well-endowed with money.

"And the present headmaster is a brilliant man. We've had him to lunch here—and we bought him an IBM computer, for his computer studies centre, Miss Loftus."

That also figured. Not the least of Waltham's unfair advantages was that it was blessed with a Board of Governors who knew their business, and had both the prestige and the money to tempt and buy the best—the best staff, from the headmaster downwards, and the best pupils, with their generous scholarships, picking and choosing their elites.

Sir Peter was beginning to look a little lost. "And one of our trainees was a girl—I beg your pardon, if that sounds male-chauvinist . . . but we have had difficulty, recruiting high-flying women into Xenophon. And we're rather pleased with this one."

She didn't doubt it—that was the final insult, added to the injury: it was not so much that Waltham was among the boys' public schools which had jumped on the band-waggon of poaching sixth formers from girls' schools; it was that, where most of them did the girls very little good, but merely stole their fees and decimated their old sixth forms, Waltham probably *did* actually sharpen them up, with its celebrated university-entrance expertise. Because Waltham did everything well— all too bloody well!

But that had nothing to do with this, she admonished herself. "Tell me about Haddock Thomas, Sir Peter."

"I will—in a moment, in just a moment." He saw that he wasn't going to get anywhere with her. "Where did Haddock go, after Waltham, David?"

"He didn't go anywhere. He stayed on there until he retired. That was two or three years ago."

"Oh." Sir Peter drew a long, slow breath. "I see."

"You didn't know he went to Waltham?"

"I knew he went there. I didn't know he stayed." Sir Peter stared at Audley. "He wrote to me from there. Twice."

"But you didn't reply." It was a question.

"I did, actually." For a moment he stood on the edge of continuing, then he drew back from it.

"Yes?" Audley pushed him with uncharacteristic gentleness. "The second time being . . . ?"

"Yes." Sir Peter nodded, but left the second time equally unelaborated. "Was he . . . happy? Eventually?"

This time Audley was slow to reply. "It would seem so, by all accounts." Still the same gentle voice.

"Yes?" For the first time Sir Peter's voice was without colour, as carefully neutral as Switzerland. "No, I didn't know." Sir Peter's face weakened very slightly. "No, it wouldn't have done. And I take it that his work . . . he taught the Classics—Latin and Greek—?"

Audley nodded. "Very successfully. I'm reliably informed that Waltham took more of the top scholarships to Oxbridge—and Bristol and Durham—than Winchester, proportionately. And as for university entrance . . . they say that just being in his Classical Sixth was like being given the key to the door." Another nod, with a cynical smile. "He used to make the rounds, keeping up his contacts—with his old pupils, as well as the professors and the dons . . . And with a girl in tow, somewhere, very often. But always discreetly, of course." The smile vanished.

Sir Peter frowned. "Where did he get them? Waltham's a bit out of the way, surely?"

Elizabeth heard herself sniff. "Waltham has girls in its sixth form now—" She caught Audley's eye "—bright girls."

Audley grinned wickedly. "But Haddock himself was dead against that, Elizabeth. In fact, my reliable informant says he damn nearly resigned prematurely when he was out-voted."

"Oh yes?" She fought her prejudices.

"He let himself be out-voted?" Sir Peter was less unhappy now. "But he was always rather against democracy—ever since the Athenians voted for the death of Socrates."

"They stopped his mouth with gold, was what he's alleged to have said afterwards." Audley was happier too. "They gave him a grant to entertain his sixth formers in his house in the South of France. And they increased his salary."

Sir Peter cocked his head. "I didn't think the Classics had so much clout these days?"

"They don't, my dear chap," agreed Audley. "But your old friend had a lot of influence—not just on account of his university results . . . or even because he was an ex-president of the Imperial Classical Association . . . which has a few rather well-placed fellows and members in the higher reaches of power, even now." He shook his head suddenly. "Come on, Peter—I can tell Miss Loftus about Haddock any time. It's that twenty-six-year-old bad conscience of yours she's interested in. Or would you prefer my version of events?"

"Isn't that in your record—your version of them, David?" Sir Peter switched to Elizabeth without waiting for an answer. "Very well, Miss Loftus. I suppose I should be glad of the opportunity of speaking for myself, even though I'm not particularly proud of what I did." He paused. "Is that what you wanted to hear, David?"

But Audley didn't seem to have heard him: he seemed to be concentrating on the books he had last seen in 1958, to the exclusion of everything else now.

"What did you do, Sir Peter?" Since the Master of Xenophon Oil was waiting for comfort which Audley was clearly not about to give him, she had no choice but to push him forwards.

"I destroyed his career." He accepted Audley's refusal, coming back to her, to meet her eyes without blinking.

"Squadron Leader Thomas's career?"

"Squadron Leader?" In spite of all their talk about aeroplanes—planes British and German, crashed or shot down or "ditched"—the rank was meaningless to him. "Yes, if you like, Miss Loftus—Squadron Leader Thomas—Caradog Thomas—*Haddock* Thomas—" He shrugged "—whoever you like, it's the same man. And it's the same thing: *I shot him down*, Miss Loftus. And he didn't bale out, or walk away . . . or swim ashore . . . not after I'd got him in my sights." He almost looked at Audley again, but held himself steady in the end, on her. "Or maybe he did—I don't know now, Miss Loftus."

"What did you do?"

"What did I do?" He drew a breath. "We were both career civil servants. Or . . . I was in the process of resigning, actually. Because . . . it was after Suez. Because it was different, after Suez—" another breath, taken in slowly "—or, that was my excuse anyway, at the time, to myself. But you could interpret it quite differently: you could say that I was a second-class honours man, with second-class prospects . . . But with the prospects in oil, after Suez—that's in '56, that was—and with what I knew . . . I suppose you could say that I knew where the first-class prospects might be. What I was doing in the Civil Service suddenly seemed . . . unprofitable to me, in more senses than one, at any rate."

"And Mr Thomas?" It didn't seem right to refer to the man by his nickname when she'd never met him. "How did you—?"

"Destroy his career?" He half-looked at Audley again, as though for confirmation. But the big man was still pretending to browse among the books. "I did—didn't I David?"

"If you think you did . . . tell her." Audley didn't look up. "After all this time it's a bit late to agonize. If that's what you're doing."

"Yes." Sir Peter gave Audley a Xenophon look. "All right, Miss Loftus. He wants me to remember, so I will." He stared at her, sorting his memories into separate columns, adding and subtracting to prepare his balance sheet. "I wasn't in the process of resigning—I had already resigned. And I wasn't buying claret. By then I was clerking for this Greek, who had cornered a piece of the tanker tonnage, and was cashing in on it. And I was learning Arabic at evening classes . . . When *he* came out of the woodwork." He nodded towards Audley. "1958?"

"Uh-huh." Audley turned the page of his book.

"1958—I was beginning to think I'd made a mistake, somewhere down the line: that I should have read Arabic at Cambridge, or stayed in the Foreign Office." A trace of lingering bitterness still showed in his voice. "And then he turned up, with what seemed like a fool question. Except he had a Special Branch man in tow—or a secret policeman of some heavier variety. So it didn't seem like a silly question at the time." He gave Audley another look. "You scared me, David."

"I wasn't after you." Audley turned another page. "Not particularly."

"It didn't seem like that." Sir Peter came back to her. "He wanted to know where I'd been on holiday, the summer before."

"And you didn't appear too scared, actually," murmured Audley.

"But I was."

"It didn't stop you telling me—to go bowl my hoop elsewhere," said Audley mildly. "The first time, anyway." He raised his eyes to Elizabeth. "He wasn't helpful the first time."

"But he came back a second time—in working hours, with the same policeman in attendance—right there in the middle of the Greek's office!" The recollection of the second time, even in this customized room on the pinnacle of the power and glory of Xenophon Oil, made Sir Peter wince. "The Greek damn near sacked me on the spot . . . Which, with what he was doing—the way he was sailing his tankers close to the wind —you could hardly blame him . . . To have one of Sir Frederick Clinton's bright young men interrogating one of his clerks—" For a fraction of a second the Master of Xenophon became the Greek's clerk again in his memory "—which was what saved me, I suppose."

"Huh!" Audley closed the book. "Stavros didn't quite know how much *you* knew, eh?"

Sir Peter nodded. "He told me he'd see me right if I kept my mouth shut about his business."

"And you could continue to date his daughter?" Audley cocked a knowing eye.

"That too," agreed Sir Peter evenly. "But if it didn't concern his business I'd better tell you what you wanted to know, or go and register at the nearest Labour Exchange."

"And not continue to date his daughter?" Audley matched agreements. "I was rather depending on that to open you up."

It was exactly as David Audley's wife always said—had said from their very first meeting: *When David plays, if you want to play with him, you had better learn to play dirty. Because that's the way he plays!*

Sir Peter looked as though he was beginning to remember how much he had once disliked Audley: the two men studied each other in silence, each estimating and re-estimating what they observed, each aware that the other had put on weight and muscle since 1958, but neither quite sure now who had the edge on the other if it came to trouble-making.

"Your new boss is that military fellow—Butler, is it?" Sir Peter changed the subject casually. "Looks a bit stupid, but isn't, by all accounts?"

"That's right." Audley accepted the change mildly. "Right both times. Do you know him?"

"Not really. I knew old Sir Frederick much better." Sir Peter smiled. "And your economics fellow better still—Neville Macready . . . Do you see much of him?"

"As little as possible." Audley returned the smile.

Elizabeth had been halfway to thinking *the tortoise and the armadillo*, but those two smiles amended the image. It was more like *the elderly shark and the middle-aged tiger*—and each was showing its teeth.

"A slightly surprising appointment, wasn't it?" The tiger tested the depth of the water with a provocative paw. "Butler, I mean—?"

"Very surprising, more like." Audley nodded, but then looked away towards the unfinished line of books as though the subject was beginning to bore him. "It should have been Oliver St John Latimer, if some bastard hadn't queered his pitch. He was the obvious choice."

"Is that a fact?" Fascination got the better of Sir Peter. "Was that Macready?"

"No-oo . . ." Audley pounced on a tattered paperback. "*Europe and the Czechs!* That's a very early Penguin!" He handled the antique paperback reverently. "Macready hates Latimer, but it certainly wasn't Mac."

"No?" Sir Peter echoed the rejection of his first candidate doubtfully.

"No." Audley replaced the fragile heirloom. "That was one of your '58 library. I remember now. And as you never throw books out there should be a copy of *If Hitler Comes* somewhere along here—" Audley moved further along "—*ah!*"

Elizabeth began to understand the nature of the exchange. If Sir Peter Barrie knew so much about the byzantine internal politics of the department then he was not just name-dropping to warn Audley of his influence in high places. For, if he knew that much, he must also know that Audley himself had been the other front runner—indeed, the odds-on favourite, if Paul's assessment had been correct. So that "slightly surprising appointment" guess had been cruelly barbed.

Audley looked up. "Come on, Peter!"

Sir Peter frowned. "It can't have been that RAF fellow—the one who married the Ryle woman, after Ryle divorced her—?"

"Hugh? Good God, no!" Audley grunted contemptuously. "But I didn't mean that, my dear chap . . . it was *me*, of course, if you must know—I was the bastard—I can't abide the egregious Oliver, so I put in the boot much the same way as you did with old Haddock. Or maybe not in *exactly* the same way. But I did queer his pitch sufficiently. And Jack Butler is my daughter's godfather, you know—" He gave the tiger a huge shark-grin "—or perhaps you didn't know? But it doesn't matter anyway, because that isn't what I mean." The shark-grin vanished. "What I meant was for you to stop pissing around, Peter, and start telling our Miss Loftus about your eternal triangle—you and old Haddock and the fair Philadelphia, eh?"

Elizabeth just caught the dying glow of the flash of hate, beyond that old unforgotten dislike, which momentarily illuminated Sir Peter's face, as she turned towards him. Or was it pain—it was gone so quickly that she couldn't be sure.

"The fair Delphi—'*Delphi*', was it?" Audley's voice came from outside her range of vision, casually seeking confirmation on the surface, but evil with certainty underneath. "They both worshipped at the same shrine, Elizabeth. So they both asked for an answer from the Delphic oracle: 'Who loves me?'—*Philadelphia Marsh*, only and beloved daughter of Abe Marsh, *ci-devant* Abraham Marx, no relative of either Karl or Groucho or Spencer."

Whatever it had been, it was pain now.

"But they each received an equivocal answer." Audley only continued when it was evident that Sir Peter had nothing to say. "Only . . . Haddock was a classicist, so he knew that when the oracle at Delphi said 'No', that didn't necessarily mean the same thing. But poor old Peter Barrie wasn't a classicist, so he thought 'Yes' meant 'Yes'."

"*No!*" Interrogation would never have wrung that pain from

the man, not with the whole of Xenophon's green-and-gold tower beneath him, thought Elizabeth. And Audley hadn't tried to interrogate him.

"That was the way it was." Audley knew when he was on a winner. "They were both after the same girl. And Haddock won." He paused, but not long enough to allow any objection. "So his good friend shopped him."

"That was *not* the way it was—and you know it." Sir Peter registered his objection too late. "You've already said as much yourself."

"Oh—sure! The first time I twisted your arm you wouldn't talk. But when the Greek twisted your arm . . . then you gave me Haddock. So you'd sorted out your priorities by then—right?"

Sir Peter Barrie looked at her for a long moment, which she realized was the moment Audley had been working towards from the beginning.

"Miss Loftus . . . in a perverse way he's right—the truth, the whole truth . . . and everything but the truth . . . that's how he's right."

She felt for him, recalling the same division of truth which Father's mourners had delivered and withheld at his funeral, as they had briefly held her hand, with the rain dripping from their caps, or their hats, or their umbrellas—those who knew him, some of them old shipmates, and those who only knew him from his medals and the naval annals and afterwards: all of them had possessed a piece of that truth, and perhaps she herself only knew a part of it, after all.

The truth was that the truth always had one more dimension than even the most complete profile imagined. "Yes, Sir Peter?"

"I don't really know what you want. But if you want me to shop him now, I'm afraid I can't help you. Because I think I loved them both, Miss Loftus."

Past tense—*loved*? But Haddock Thomas was still alive, so what did *loved* mean?

"Delphi was younger than I was—ten years younger." He dismissed Audley with a half glance. "And Haddock was almost exactly eleven years older than I was . . . I know that, because he used to say that he was conceived after the battle of Loos and born during the battle of the Somme—and that's 1916. So I was midway between them. And . . . it wasn't just 'Yes' and 'No'. I thought he was too old for her, as a matter of fact, Miss Loftus."

Elizabeth struggled with the mathematics of what he was trying to tell her, which somehow added up to the dreadful arithmetic of the whole blood-stained Twentieth Century: Haddock Thomas had been a pilot in Father's war—but Sir Peter had been just too young for that . . . and *Delphi—Philadelphia Marsh*—?

"He introduced me to her. It was at a party in the American Embassy—Dr Marsh was one of their economic advisers, commuting between Bonn and London and Washington . . . Haddock had worked with him, off and on, ever since he'd joined the service, after he'd come down from Oxford the second time, after the war."

"Where—when did you meet . . . Haddock?"

"At Oxford, in '48. He was a post-graduate—a Farnsworth scholar. If you want to address him correctly he's *Doctor* Caradog Thomas. I was a mere undergraduate."

"But you were friends."

"Not then. I seconded a motion he proposed in a debate. 'This house does not believe all cats are grey at night'. After that we were friendly acquaintances. I didn't meet him again until . . . '53—no, '54. He was Foreign Office, I was an economic dogsbody. It was in Paris."

"And that was when you became friends? But he was older than you."

"Oh yes. Eleven years *and* a war older, Miss Loftus. But he always maintained the war didn't count—those were his lost years, he said, so they were struck off. And that made the difference only five years." He thought for a moment, then shrugged. "I didn't think of him as being older, anyway. Not then."

He stopped, and Elizabeth knew she would have to jog him again to make him go on. "He introduced you—?"

"Yes. To Delphi Marsh. He knew a lot of people—a lot of girls. I didn't." He was slowing again. "It was a long time ago."

"Yes, Sir Peter. She was his girl?"

"No. She was no one's girl when he introduced her." He took his memory by the throat suddenly. "Then she was my girl—very much my girl, Miss Loftus. We had an understanding. We went on holiday to Italy together. Then she went on holiday again, but without me. And then she was Mrs Caradog Thomas." He drew a single breath. "And then she was pregnant, and then she was dead, Miss Loftus," he expelled the words with the same breath, as though to clear them finally from his chest, once and for all.

"Dead?" The sudden ending to an otherwise familiar story took Elizabeth by surprise. "She died—?"

"In childbirth?" He shook his head. "She was knocked down by a car."

"A lorry, actually," murmured Audley.

"A lorry, then." He continued to look at her as he half-turned his head towards Audley. "If you want to know all the details I'm sure he has them on file somewhere. But it was no one's fault. At least . . . at least that was what Haddock wrote in his letter."

Elizabeth frowned from Sir Peter to Audley. It was as though they had assembled a jigsaw for her, carefully sorting the straight edges and the surrounding pieces, but leaving the centre blank. "But how did—? You said . . . he was 'shopped' —how was he shopped?"

"Quite simply, Elizabeth dear. As simply as 'B' comes before 'T', to start with. Meaning that I came to 'Barrie' on my little list before I came to 'Thomas'. Because they'd both been on holiday in foreign parts, but one tends to work alphabetically."

"But—" Elizabeth came within a tyro's breath of adding *why*, only just catching herself in time: for whatever original reason, Audley had only been doing then what she was doing now, all those years ago "—but Sir Peter had left the service —the Board of Trade, or the Treasury, or whatever—by then, surely?" It was lame, but it was better than nothing.

"Very true," agreed Sir Peter. "But then, even if I had still been employed in Whitehall, it was still a great nonsense."

Elizabeth looked at him. "Why was it a great nonsense?"

"For three reasons, Miss Loftus. You yourself have supplied the first: I had quit the Queen's service—I had, as it were, privatized myself. And although the Greek had some fairly hot little secrets of his own, they were hardly the sort which should have interested British Intelligence. Besides which, I was never really privy to any of his secrets, I only suspected things here and there. But the second reason is more to the point, though actually not dissimilar. Because, when I *was* in the service, what I was doing was hardly top secret. It was sensitive, of course—some of it. But none of it was really in the least important. What I had in my head was of far more use to the Greek's oil deals than to any foreign power, actually. So if they were after a traitor, I was a very poor candidate."

Audley shook his head. "I told you, Peter—I wasn't particularly after you."

"So you said. Although it didn't seem like that at the time. And you *were* certainly after that Italian holiday of mine—" He came back to Elizabeth "—which is my third point. Because there was no mystery about that, you see." The corner of his mouth dropped slightly. "It's rather ironic—I'd guess that's the only time I've been properly vetted, with expense no object—would that be correct, David?"

Audley puffed his cheeks. "It was the only time *I* vetted you. *That* would be correct."

"Uh-huh? Well, the other times wouldn't have amounted to much, compared with *your* time, I would guess."

"Why was it ironic, Sir Peter?"

"Ironic *and* expensive." He smiled at her with his mouth, but not with his eyes. "It was a rather special holiday. I was with the girl I expected to marry. And she was beautiful—I suppose I was rather proud of myself: I'd never expected to capture such a beauty, and . . . partly because I loved her, and—but perhaps partly to impress her, and make sure of her . . . I drew most of my savings out of the bank—I hoped to make more from the Greek, one way or another—and I splashed it around, Miss Loftus." He added. "We flew to Rome, and stayed at a good hotel—she was used to good hotels. And I hired a car, and we progressed by slow stages—

and more good hotels—to Florence. And then to Venice . . . I knew what to show her, because I'd slummed that same route long before, mostly hitch-hiking and sleeping semi-rough. But this time it was all first-class and over-tipping." For a fraction of a second he looked clear through her. Then he focused again, and shrugged sadly. "And if you want another irony . . . obviously I didn't impress her at all. I only put her off, it would seem, judging by what happened afterwards. Though it didn't seem so to me, at the time." He thought for a moment. "No . . . but I must have left a trail a mile wide—" He nodded to Audley "—for *him* to follow—what was it, David: '*Where did you go?*', and '*Who can vouch for you, that you were there?*', and '*Which day was that?*'—I couldn't remember which day it was, exactly . . . but I'll bet you found enough over-tipped waiters and chamber-maids and hotel managers who recalled the silly young Englishman and his *bellissima signora*, eh?"

Audley made one of his extra-ugly faces. "I wasn't after you, Peter."

"Yes you were. And you checked." The old bitterness lay beneath very thin ice. "And you pushed me."

"And you were scared." The ugly face became brutal. "If you had such a bloody-clear conscience—why were you so scared?"

"Has it never occurred to you why?" The ice cracked. But now it was anger which showed. "My God, man—it was *because* I had a bloody-clear conscience that I was scared! I knew it couldn't be the holiday, so it had to be something else. So I thought it was the Greek, don't you see. I thought he'd been up to something really nasty that I didn't know about. In which case I was out of a job again—*and* compromised— *and* with hardly any money, too!" All the vivid memories of 1958 suddenly animated Sir Peter Barrie's face, melting its ice to reveal both anger and bitterness. "You're absolutely right —I *was* scared! I was scared stiff, if you must know."

"Ah . . ." Audley came as close to embarrassment as he was capable of doing when caught in an error. But then he shrugged it off quite easily, as he always did. "So that was why you served up the Haddock?"

Sir Peter's mouth tightened. "Which I have regretted ever

after. And never more so than now, I think." He looked at Elizabeth suddenly.

"He was on the list," snapped Audley. "I would have come to him without your help, sooner or later."

"Would you?" Sir Peter ignored him. "What are you up to, Miss Loftus?"

"What did you say about him, Sir Peter?"

"Huh!" Audley sniffed. "Actually, he said very little, as I recall."

"But also too much. I said—" Sir Peter's features contorted "—or, something like, I said . . . *'If you're looking for holidays abroad—mysterious holidays—why don't you try Dr Caradog Thomas? He's always going on holiday abroad. And his last holiday was the most mysterious one of all, you'll find—ask him about his Romanesque churches—ask him how he liked Cluny.'*" He controlled his face with an effort. "I was frightened, Miss Loftus. So I cracked. And I said, in effect . . . 'Do it to my friend Haddock—not to me!'" He paused. "And now I am justly served, with my own treachery. Which is how the past always serves us, I suspect."

He really loved the man Thomas, his ex-friend, thought Elizabeth. Even after Thomas's betrayal of their friendship—or the combined and ultimate betrayal of it by Thomas and the beautiful Miss Philadelphia Marsh—even after that, he still loved the man, his once-upon-a-time friend. Because, in spite of all that, he counted his betrayal the greater one.

She looked at Audley, and guessed that he had known all this too.

"I don't know what you're up to now." Sir Peter pulled her back to him, but then stopped suddenly. "No—I know you can't tell me that—can't or won't—I know that. But I still have two things to tell you, neither of which you may find very much to your taste, perhaps. But there it is."

Audley surely knew all this. But whether he had or not, his instinct had been right, to drop everything in order to make sure of catching Sir Peter Barrie to start her off on Dr Caradog Thomas.

"Yes, Sir Peter?" she stepped meekly into his silence.

The silence continued for several long seconds. "He forgave me, you know, Miss Loftus. Naturally."

"Fff—" It was the last thing she'd expected until she heard it. Then it was . . . natural, of course. "*He* forgave *you?*"

"I still have this letter—his second letter, which he wrote after Delphi's death . . . Quite a long time after, because I was away, and I didn't hear about it at the time." Another silence. "I have both his letters still. But I will not show them to you. But . . . he very carefully explained why he left the service—that it really had nothing at all to do with the Intelligence badgering. Nothing to do with me, in fact: '*Like you, I am mine own executioner, mine own liberator*'—I'll give you that much."

Another silence set in. But this time she must let it live out its natural life.

"And the other thing is—" Once again he turned to Audley "—that you're wrong, David Audley. Because if it's Haddock you're after now, then you're just as wrong now as you were back in—back in whenever it was, when you persecuted us both. Check me again, if you like—you can have a free run. But leave Haddock alone—it's simply not in him to be a traitor. I'd stake my life—or Xenophon's profits for the year, whichever you reckon the more valuable—on that. Because he worships different gods."

It wasn't until they were in the lift that Audley spoke again, beyond the minimal grunts and required pleasantries of farewell.

"A remarkable man, Elizabeth. And not a second-class man, either. But he was quite right to leave the civil service. He was a man of action—a born money-maker, not a spender. The Greek understood that. Whereas . . . whereas Haddock Thomas was something else again."

"What else, David?"

Audley stared at the red button. "A man of different action. A better man, too."

"Better?" She had to remember that Audley had cleared both of them. "Even though he seduced his friend's girl?"

The lift stopped.

"Seduced . . . and married, Elizabeth. And I rather think she was his one true love." He looked at her as the lift-doors opened. "Or is that too sentimental for you to swallow?"

Audley had married a much younger woman too: that was something else she had to remember. "So you still think he's innocent?" She met his gaze. "In spite of Major Parker?"

"I think . . . I think you are supposed to make your own mind up about that, my dear." He gestured for her to leave the lift. "So what do you want to do next? Or can I return to my more important work at Cheltenham? You can always use Major Turnbull for your leg-work—his legs are younger than mine."

She stepped out of the lift, and the decisive click of her high heels on the Xenophon mosaic floor mocked her irresolution.

"Well, Elizabeth?"

If he had wanted to go back to his Cheltenham investigation nothing either she or the Deputy-Director could have done would have stopped him, decided Elizabeth: Cheltenham was important enough for him to have appealed over both their heads. Therefore he did not want to go back. And that meant he was more concerned with Haddock Thomas than he pretended to be.

Paul, she thought suddenly. If Paul meant business, then this must be the business he meant—

"Well, Elizabeth?" The question was repeated just a little too casually, confirming her suspicion.

"I need to know more about Thomas before I go to see him, David." She needed to talk to Paul. "I'd like to have a look at the Debrecen records."

"I can tell you all about that." He relaxed slightly. "Most of it is what I put into it myself."

"Who else can tell me about Thomas?" She didn't want him around when she met Paul. "Who would you recommend? That we can rely on?"

He stared at her for a moment, as though in doubt. "There is someone I can perhaps lay on for you. But it'll need a phone-call or two. And we'll have to go to him."

She smiled. "Okay—will you do that, David?" But she must give him more than that to do. "And will you brief Major Turnbull for me, while you're about it?"

His doubt increased. "Brief him about what?"

About what? She needed something quite complicated and time-consuming, yet reasonable.

"About what, Elizabeth?"

She found herself staring past the nearest bank of Xenophon jungle, towards the reception desk and at the beautiful receptionist he had bullied, who was watching them uneasily.

She was beautiful—

"I'd like to know a lot more about Thomas's wife, David. Sir Peter Barrie's ex-fiancée?" The idea expanded as the two sudden deaths telescoped over the many years which separated them. "Particularly the circumstances of her death."

He frowned. "It was an accident, Elizabeth. We did look at it carefully, you know—?" But he knew he couldn't really question the request. "All right, if it will put your mind at rest, we'll see what Turnbull can turn up. But he'll be wasting his time."

Time was what she needed. There was something going on which she didn't understand, but which relegated Cheltenham to the second division. And if anyone knew what it was, Paul would know enough to guess at it. And she could always handle Paul, at a pinch.

"I'll meet you back at the office after lunch, David," she concluded.

VI

IT WAS ALL according to what you were used to, thought
Elizabeth as she paid the taxi-driver.

They were all accustomed to meet in pubs up and down the
river, as well as in more respectable places—to meet, and to
meet people whom they did not wish to be seen meeting in those
too well-frequented respectable places: that was apparently the
way David Audley had always operated, and Paul emulated
him in this, as in other things. But, although she liked to
regard herself as entirely liberated and equal to all occasions,
there were still pubs and pubs. And the Marshal Ney was quite
evidently one of those in the "and pubs" category.

She could see that the taxi-driver agreed with her as she
tipped him. He had been doubtful when she had named the
place and specified its location; but now that they were here,
surrounded by urban decay and the smell of the river (or of
something worse), he was certain that it was not really the
sort of destination for a well-dressed lady from Whitehall—
or, at least, a lady whose face precluded any romantic or illicit
intention.

"Right, love?" He watched her study the pub sign above
the door of the saloon bar. "The Marshal Ney—right?"

There was no name on the sign, only a representation of
what might be the bravest of Napoleon's marshals, although
it looked more like a pirate brandishing a cutlass from astride
a kangaroo.

Elizabeth's heart faltered. There wasn't a soul in sight, only
a lean black cat which paused in its unhurried crossing of the
road to eye her. Then she remembered something Paul had
once said. "Do they call it 'The Frenchman'?"

He nodded, and engaged the gears, and gave her up for lost.
"That's right, love—'The Frenchman' it is."

She watched the taxi move slowly away—slowly, because

the cat itself was in no hurry to give it right of way on its own territory—and then pushed at the door. It yielded unwillingly, with an unoiled screech.

If anything, the smell inside was more insistent. But there, to her enormous relief, was Paul, elbow-on-bar, nursing his Guinness, with his ear inclined to a shrivelled little man on the other side.

"Elizabeth!" He straightened up—almost stood to attention. "What a delightful surprise!"

Her relief, which had almost graduated to gratitude, instantly evaporated. But she could hardly say "What a dreadful place! Why did you bring me here?" with the possible owner of the dreadful place staring open-mouthed at her.

"Met my friend Tom." Paul indicated the little man. "Tom —Elizabeth."

"Lizbuff." The little man climbed on something behind his bar, raising himself to her level, and offered her his monkey's paw, the fingers of which were stained bright nicotine-brown.

"Tom." She shook the paw.

"You don't wanta believe 'im, though." The little man half-glanced at Paul, screwing up his face, which he was able to do the more expressively because he seemed to have no teeth.

"In what way shouldn't I believe him?" Elizabeth questioned this sound advice innocently.

"I ain't 's friend, for starters." Tom emitted a curious sucking noise. "An' 'e ain't surprised, neither. 'E was expectin' you."

"Oh yes?" He had only confirmed her most recent conclusion, but it was still irritating to be computed so accurately. "And what made you so sure, Paul?"

"I wasn't sure—not quite." He was unabashed by Tom's betrayal. "Tom—why don't you just push off to your other bar, like a good chap, eh?"

"Oh yus?" The little man didn't move. "Lady's teetotal, is she? Ain'tcha got no manners, then?"

"Will you have a drink, Elizabeth?"

"It's a little early for me." She smiled at Tom. "If you don't mind."

"Suit yourself, Miss." Tom stepped down off his box and shuffled towards a faded curtain at the other end of the bar. But then he stopped and turned back, with his hand on the curtain. "Prob'ly jus' as well. You wanta 'ave yer wits about yer wiv 'im, Miss. 'Cause 'e's artful." He nodded. "Artful—like the other one." He watched her with sharp little eyes. "The big fella—okay?"

"Okay." She wondered how much he knew—or guessed—about their business. "Thank you, Tom."

"And thank you too, Tom," Paul called after the little man as he disappeared through the curtain. "I'll do the same for you some time."

Elizabeth studied him. "Why were you so sure I'd come?"

He returned the scrutiny. "I wasn't sure. It depended on . . . oh, several things."

"Such as?"

"Does it matter—now you're here?"

Artful. It was a curiously archaic word, but nonetheless accurate. "Let me guess. You thought maybe I wouldn't get away from David Audley? 'For starters', as Tom would say?"

"That was certainly a consideration." He drank again. "Let's say, Elizabeth, that I did you the compliment of assuming that you would. And that you would then do what I would do, if I were in your dainty shoes."

She had to clear this matter first. "But you're not, are you."

"No. More's the pity."

"So what has all this got to do with you?"

He thought for a moment. "If I was to say that what happens to you does concern me—" He held up his hand quickly to forestall her "—no, let me finish—that would not be good enough, I know! So I'll give you a choice: either I'm insatiably inquisitive, and when something rather extremely interesting is happening I like to know about it—especially when I've been written out of it." He smiled. "Curiosity and sour grapes, maybe?"

Some truth might be there, but nowhere near all of it. "Or?"

"Or . . ." He took another moment. "You know, the way our revered department works, Elizabeth, is never in straight lines. We circle round problems, in different dimensions, looking for openings. We behave eccentrically, even amateurishly, and certainly unpredictably." He squinted at her suddenly. "How *did* you get away from David?"

Whatever it was that he didn't want to say, it must be closer to the truth. But she would come back to it from a different direction. "I'll tell you how, Paul—if you'll tell me why you tried to follow me this morning."

"To the Xenophon building?"

She stared at him. "What? I started from outside there. But—?"

"You thought you'd lost me? You did. But I've seen David use that silly trick before. And the coincidence of Xenophon was worth a try, so I went back and lurked behind the Magdala obelisk. And back you came."

"What coincidence?"

"Oh—come on, Elizabeth!" He cocked his head at her knowingly, but also with a suggestion of anger. "Stop buggering around, for God's sake!"

"What do you mean?" She hated to be sworn at like that, and he knew it.

"What do I mean?" The anger increased. "I mean . . . I mean that I stuck my neck out for you this morning, to the edge of blowing a secure classification, when I gave you Ed Parker. Because you weren't cleared then for the material in which his name comes up—I know, because I punched it up on the computer not ten minutes before, and your name wasn't on it. There were only four names there: Jack Butler's, of course. And then *Latimer, Oliver St John* and *Audley, David Longsdon,* and finally poor bloody *Mitchell, Paul Lefevre.* And the computer duly registered that I'd made that particular inquiry, so any moment now I shall be in trouble, for sure."

"Paul—"

"No. I haven't finished. So then you went in for your little session with Fatso, and did your Joan of Arc bit, letting yourself be summoned by your voices. Which I also know, because I waited for a bit, and then I punched the Beast again. And low and behold! There was a new name on the clearance! Which was—would you believe it—none other than *Loftus, Elizabeth Jane.* Recognize that name?"

"Paul—"

"I still haven't finished, dear Elizabeth Jane." He bulldozed forwards. "Which inquiry the computer also duly registered. But you can only die once, so they say . . . So what did Elizabeth Jane do then, I ask you? Or, what did she eventually do? Why, she went and stood outside the London headquarters of Xenophon Oil Incorporated, did she not? Which are presided over by none other than *Barrie, Sir Peter William, KBE*, whose name also rang a bell, because it figured in a certain list, from long ago, to which Elizabeth Jane now has free access. Correct?"

As a small boy, he must have been objectionable, she decided. Indeed, she had known girls at school like him, whose power lay in their precocious understanding of how systems worked, and who never scrupled to use their knowledge. But, on the other hand, he *had* stuck his neck out—for that last and as-yet-unrevealed reason.

He nodded. "But that was all of two hours since." He looked at his watch. "What *have* you done with David, Elizabeth Jane?"

He had never called her "Elizabeth Jane" before. But there was an edge of bitterness in that additional "Jane" which could mean that he was going off her at last, thank heavens!

"I gave him a job to do. Or two jobs, actually." When she thought about it, she didn't really want him to go off her in bitterness: she wanted so very much for him still to be a friend, but even more than that she needed him as a colleague, to pick his brains.

"Two jobs?" He grinned. "I'll bet he didn't like that!" The grin vanished. "Was one of them—" The rattle of the curtain-runners stopped him. "What is it, Tom?"

The strange sucking-noise was repeated. "Thought you might like a re-fill, *Doctor* Mitchell. An' maybe it's not too early for the lady now?"

"Go away, Tom," said Paul.

"I only *arsked*—"

"And I only said 'Go away'." Paul addressed the curtain, which had closed again, and then caught Elizabeth's eye, which had just taken in the emptiness of the saloon bar of the

Marshal Ney public house. "You don't need to worry, Elizabeth Jane: he's nipped out and put a 'Closed' sign on the door, so we shan't be disturbed. And his standard charge is pound a minute, or double-or-quits. But he won't play with me, because he says I cheat when we cut the cards." He shrugged. "Which isn't true, actually—I'm just lucky at cards. But half the burglaries in this part of London are probably planned here anyway at the same rate—a pound a minute, tax-free. Or double-or-quits."

It was all according to what you were used to, remembered Elizabeth. "'One of them', you were saying?"

"Yes. Was one of those jobs to talk to Neville Macready? About Sir Peter Barrie?"

Neville Macready was their economic intelligence specialist, so that would have been a sensible move, thought Elizabeth. So she would not deny it. "And if it was?"

"I've already asked him." He accepted her question as an admission all too easily because it suited him. "Xenophon's money is Texas money, ultimately. So Barrie's loyalties are American, in the final analysis. Macready says he's buddy-buddy with the State Department at a high level when it comes to global decisions. He advises the Americans, and then they tell him what to do. And then he does it, more or less—sometimes more, and sometimes less, but always thereabouts."

"Indeed?" She tried to sound more knowledgeable than she was. "But Xenophon's big in the North Sea."

"Oh, sure. And Barrie was one of the driving forces there early on. That's how he got his 'K'. In fact, Mac rates him a pretty sound chap, all in all—I think he must have tipped us off now and then, about American intentions, for Mac to be so protective." He cocked an eyebrow. "I hope you haven't been nasty to him—you or David? I don't think Mac would like that very much."

"No." She shook her head hastily. Maybe she should have seen Neville Macready herself. But after that one look at the Haddock Thomas material on screen—and only on screen, because no print-out was allowed—it had seemed even more urgent to pick Paul's brains further.

"I should bloody-well hope so!" He pulled a face. "Barrie

can probably pull strings all the way to the Cabinet Office. You're messing with the top brass now, Elizabeth Jane. And don't say that I didn't warn you, either!"

He was patronizing her again, but this time she had to be nice to him, no matter what he said. "You did warn me." Why was it so hard to smile at him? "I'm grateful for that." The smile came at last, even though she was ashamed of it. "So now I really would like to know what the hell's going on, Paul dear."

"Uh-huh?" The smile weakened him, but insufficiently. "What d'you think is going on?"

That was fair enough really. He had given her what he thought was good advice, and she hadn't taken it. And he had also given her information, which she had used, and he could yet be in deep trouble for that. So now he wasn't going to give her anything she didn't deserve.

"I think two quite separate things are going on, actually— related in one respect, but quite separate in another. Am I right?"

"Could be." He waited shamelessly.

"How did you know I'd have to get away from David Audley to keep this illicit rendezvous?"

He shrugged. "Simple Sherlock Holmes deduction, from known facts and soundly-based assumptions." He grinned. "And I also asked him what he was doing."

"And he told you? Just like that?"

Another shrug. "It was while you were playing Joan of Arc. And he was there, like Mount Everest waiting for Mallory. Or was it Irvine?" He pretended to frown. "No matter. All you have to remember is what happened to both of them: they were never seen again." He nodded.

The thought of Audley cooling his heels at the office a second time inhibited her from playing his game. And if that meant seeming prissy, then so be it! "You know that David has been told off to help me? And Major Turnbull too?"

"The Major? Phew!" He sketched surprise. "I didn't know *that* . . . I did know about David . . . from David. Better you than me, Elizabeth Jane—that's what I know. Better you than me."

It was time to play dirty. "Perhaps I'll ask for you next—seeing as you know so much already, Paul. And you're so keen to help."

Mock horror. "*Oh no*! Perish the thought!" Then he was suddenly serious. "Someone's got to mind the shop in Cheltenham. Though without David there isn't much I can do except cross my fingers and hope for the best." He weakened even as he spoke. "What do you want?"

"If you want to help me, then just tell me about the Debrecen List."

"The Debrecen List?" His face closed up. "But you know all about that now—?"

"Only what's in the record."

"Well, you'd do better to ask David." He was himself again. "I was . . . God! Was I at prep school then?" He scratched his head. "I was in short grey trousers and long socks, anyway —long socks with elastic garters under the turn-overs . . . No —you'd better ask David. He was right there—in the middle of it all!"

"But I'm asking you. Because you're on the 'Need to know' list."

"That was pure accident. It was only because of something which came up last year, when Fatso was in America—you remember the flap there was then, last summer? When we were all on holiday relief as acting duty-officers? You were on the edge of it, I seem to recall. I put through a call to you one evening—which you handled with your customary efficiency." He smiled. "You remember?"

"Yes." She nodded cautiously.

"Well, that was Fatso. He'd got himself into all sorts of trouble over there, asking the wrong people the right questions."

"But there was nothing about . . . about Mr Latimer in the file, Paul."

He gave her a sly wink. "Yes . . . well, there wouldn't be, would there? Old Fatso doesn't wash his dirty linen in private —he buries it deep, so no one can get wind of it." He thought for a moment. "But . . . let's see now . . . if you compare the date of entry of that item about the death of a man named

Robinson, and the CIA maybe reactivating their Debrecen operation because of it, then I think you'll find that it coincides with the absence of one Oliver St John Latimer on a private and unofficial visit to foreign parts. Which I take to be cause and effect."

Elizabeth stared at him, desperately trying to recall the tantalizing ingredients of the Debrecen material from her one quick—too quick—reading of it: from those very strangely hot-and-cold beginnings in 1958 which had been equally strangely terminated the following year, through the long, empty silence afterwards, over one whole quarter of a century.

"But that wasn't the start of it." It didn't need any stretch-of-memory to produce the one other Debrecen entry, which had preceded Oliver St John Latimer's trouble by a year. "Or the re-start?"

Paul stared back at her. "The Irishman, you mean? The also-deceased Irishman?" The stare became blandly cynical. "I had nothing to do with that—that was all David Audley's work. I wasn't even in England then."

"But the Irishman was going to tell us about Debrecen."

"Maybe." He shrugged. "Whatever he was going to tell us, he was killed before he could talk. And it wasn't David's fault. He seems to have behaved fairly heroically, reading between the unwritten lines."

"Yes." She had never thought of loyalty as being one of Paul's few virtues, so the temptation to press him was irresistible. "But then David needs to be heroic where Debrecen is concerned, doesn't he?"

"What—?" He covered up whatever it was—could it really be that virtue?—by leaning over the bar and staring at the curtain "—what I need is another drink, Elizabeth Jane—Tom!"

"And what I need is for someone to tell me the true story of the whole Debrecen episode, Dr Mitchell."

"You don't want much, do you!" He still concentrated on the curtain. "Drat the man! Tom!" But the curtain still refused to open. "But you've looked at the Beast, anyway."

"The computer has been edited."

"What d'you expect?" He gave up. "Look, Elizabeth Jane—

Miss Loftus—everyone has a skeleton in the closet somewhere. You have, I'll bet . . . I know I have . . . and so has Research and Development. And you never know who'll come poking in the closet some day. So what d'you expect?"

"Who edited the computer?" She somehow couldn't imagine Colonel Butler breaking the rules. And although rules meant nothing to David Audley, he lacked the seniority to doctor securely classified material. "Was it Latimer?"

"No. It was already neutered when Fatso became Deputy-Director last year." He shook his head quickly. "It must have been old Fred Clinton. He made the original decision to abort the operation. So he had over twenty years to think about it." He shook his head again, but slowly this time. "You'd better ask David, my dear."

"So you keep saying. So *everyone* keeps saying."

"So maybe it's good advice." He looked at her almost desperately. "No one knows more about Debrecen than he does. At least . . . no one on our side—no one who's still alive, that is. All I know, beyond what's in the file, is hearsay from him, what he's let slip. And that's worth nothing."

He was suddenly so miserable that she decided to chance a straight question. "What d'you want to tell me, Paul?"

He swallowed. "Can't you guess? I'd rather you did, if only to set my mind at rest a little." He attempted a Paul Mitchell smile, but achieved only a painful grimace. "I think you have guessed, actually."

She had to put him out of his misery, she owed him that. "You mean, why Latimer put me in charge, and not David?"

The grimace improved slightly. "That's my girl! And—?"

"It's really David's skeleton—isn't it?" She didn't need to wait for confirmation. "He was in charge of the original operation. And he always had a lot of influence with Sir Frederick Clinton. So if there was a bad mistake it was his—right?"

"Right." He looked at her expectantly.

"And Latimer is gunning for David." That didn't need confirmation either. But the next statement did. "But he reckons David might be—no, David *is* . . . clever enough to muddy the waters if he was in charge—?"

126

"Right again." He nodded. "Fatso wants David out. But with David in charge . . . anything could happen." He stopped suddenly. "Look, Elizabeth . . . I know David pretty well. He recruited me—"

"He recruited me, too," Elizabeth heard herself snap.

"So he did. But you're the '82 vintage. I'm the '74, and *I* know how his mind works. Everyone thinks he's devious— that he's a meticulous planner. And it just isn't true. Because what David likes, and what he does best and enjoys most, is working from hand-to-mouth in an emergency, improvising and botching up and making good." He frowned at her. "It's like . . . he's like—have you ever heard of the Sopwith Camel, Elizabeth—Miss Loftus?"

"The—what?" It took her a second to adjust from David Audley's idiosyncrasies to Paul Mitchell's. "It was—it was a First World War aeroplane, wasn't it?" She was only doubtful for another half-second: with Paul it had to be *that* war. "It was. But what—"

"It was. And it wasn't very fast. And it had no rate-of-climb worth talking about. And it was a little bugger to fly, spinning pilots into the ground if they gave it half a chance." He leered at her ghoulishly. "But in combat it could turn on a ha'penny. And when the Hun bounced it . . . if a Camel pilot got one second, to pull his stick, no one on God's earth—or in God's sky—knew where the Camel was going. The Camel pilot came down on *his* tail, out of nowhere." He stared at her. "And *that*'s David—to the bloody life!"

It wasn't loyalty, thought Elizabeth. And it wasn't admiration, either: it was something much more complicated, which she didn't have time now to explore.

She didn't have time! "But I'm not a Sopwith Camel, Paul. And David will still have time to—to pull his stick, or whatever—" She floundered in the midst of a metaphor she didn't fully understand.

"That's right—exactly right." He evidently understood his own imagery. "But *he*'s escorting *you*, don't you see? If anything goes wrong—if you fail abysmally, or if you get shot down . . . and you are his recruit—his pupil—as well as his responsibility . . . Christ! If there's one thing Jack Butler would never forgive

—one thing that would discredit David finally and for all time—it would be that. And Oliver St John Latimer knows it. Because he's an Audley-watcher too. And he's watched him longer than I have. And he knows what he wants. *And . . .* he's not stupid, is our Fatso—he's bloody good." He gave her another dreadful smile. "And that's half the trouble, of course."

Half the truble? If that was *half . . .* ? But that was another thing to think about tomorrow.

"So he's done everything right, you see." Paul had the bit between his teeth now. "Jack Butler won't be able to fault him when he gets back from his leave, whatever he may suspect privately. Because—*Item One*—that American was on the De-brecen List—the Americans' list, which is in the file . . . and I've been busy checking off some of the English names, so I know. And I don't doubt he's acquired some evidence that that 'tragic fall' was—" He gave her an innocently-raised eyebrow "—an efficient shove, maybe?"

So that had been Major Turnbull's function, she understood: to confirm legitimate suspicion and justify further action—

"Yes." He read her face too easily. "So—*Item Two*—take appropriate action?" The eyebrow remained raised. "One dead Debrecen American. But two recent entries in the Debrecen file. So let *Loftus, Elizabeth Jane* win her spurs. It's time she did a bit of field-work, to get experience and earn her keep. But give her David Audley, who is elderly and should be responsible, and who was her recruiting-sergeant . . . *and* who knows all about Debrecen—*Good thinking, Mr Deputy-Director*: Defence of the Realm properly secured, essential training of promising staff advanced, and duty well and truly discharged." The eyebrow lowered. "And Fatso's back well and truly protected while he inserts his poniard into David Audley's back—see how it works, Elizabeth Jane? *Because David can't refuse to help you*—see?"

What she saw was a Paul she hadn't seen before—not so much cynical as strangely bitter. But then the curtain scraped on its runners again.

"Right, then!" Tom sucked his toothless gums noisily.

"Buzz off, Tom." Paul continued to stare at her. "You're too late. You're too late and I'm too late. We have to go."

"Oh yus?" Tom advanced nevertheless, until Elizabeth couldn't ignore him. "Got 'is measure, 'ave you, Miss?" He flashed an irreverent eye at Paul Mitchell. "Looks like 'e's lost 's sixpence, an' found a dud shillin'."

"If you don't buzz off this minute, Tom—" Paul spoke with quite uncharacteristic malevolence "—I'll have the Old Bill object to the renewal of your licence next time, if it's the last thing I do on this earth."

He was so obviously serious that she found herself looking at him again compulsively, and the scrape of the curtains closing was a distant sound in a much larger silence.

"I'll tell you one thing about David, that I do know . . . when he really gets himself into trouble." He fixed the malevolent look on her. "And one thing about the Debrecen file—the thing he has in common with it."

She had read the file, but it was suddenly a blank in her mind as she thought about David Audley, with whom she had only worked once. Only that had been—

"They both kill people, Elizabeth—Elizabeth Jane . . . *Miss Loftus*." He stumbled over the confusion of names. "Or . . . people end up *dead*, one way or another, when they get together. And I have a very strong presentiment that they're going to do it again, this time, between them."

It was really very strange, very strange indeed, this almost fastidious abhorrence he had about violent death, thought Elizabeth. And it was strange not because this time she herself might be involved on the edges of it—that really wasn't strange at all—but rather because his whole ten-year civilian academic career, and his devoted hobby over the last ten years, involved the concentrated study of that 1914–18 bloodbath in the trenches of France and Flanders.

"But it doesn't worry you, does it?" Calculation, only half-masked by curiosity, had replaced honest passion. "Not one bit, eh?"

"Of course it does." Normally she could lie more readily, and much more convincingly. But this time he caught her off-balance, in the middle of remembering another reason why his hatred of violence was so odd—

"No, it doesn't." Calculation had taken over. "Old Fatso's not so stupid—I'm the stupid one. He's got your number right to the last decimal point, naturally: fitness reports, psychological profile, and all the little—*nasty* little—small print . . . all those bloody-minded, cold-blooded naval ancestors of yours, of the flog 'em and hang 'em brigade, from the Nore and Spithead."

What she remembered was that, when the chips were down, Paul himself had a natural talent for violence, instinctive and efficient. "I really don't know. But then I don't really know what you're talking about, either."

"No, you wouldn't." He nodded mild agreement. "And your old man, too—that's the special beauty of it, from Fatso's point of view: not just the chance to up-anchor, and make sail, and put to sea . . . But a bloody-marvellous father-figure target to sink as well—right, Elizabeth Jane?"

The passion was back. It was deep-layered now, under that false mildness, and then under mocking calculation and curiosity. But it was there all the same, and she half-wished that it worried her more, instead of merely irritating her.

But then it was anger, rather than irritation. "I don't see what my father has to do with this." The anger flared. "Or with you."

"Nothing to do with me." He felt the heat. "As of this minute I was never here, and we never met." He straightened up, and gestured towards the door. "And seeing as we haven't met, and I shall have to buy an alibi to prove that I was somewhere else—that I *am* somewhere else . . . or at least half-way there—" He frowned suddenly, and made a silly face. "When you gave David those jobs . . . what did you say *you* were doing? I mean . . . just curiosity—?"

This time she wasn't off-balance, by one guilty half-second. But she couldn't tell him. "You can take me with you, and put me off in Bond Street. I'll take a taxi from there." But she mustn't leave him time to work that out. "Only . . . you said, Paul, that when David and Debrecen got together—that when they came together—?"

"People end up dead?" He nodded. "And so they do."
Another nod. "Back in '58—there were two—*two*, if you count
one in America, as well as one over here." Pause. "And in '83
. . . well, there was one a few years before that, when the KGB
hit someone up in Yorkshire." Pause. "But then there was '83,
down in Dorset. About which I know no more than you do,
because all I know is what is in the record." Pause. "And then
there's '84 . . . which was also in America. And which is also
in the record, more or less." This time the pause was so long
that she had almost decided that he had finished. But then he
nodded. "But mostly less, rather than more. Because, for a
secure file, it's still bloody non-committal, don't you think?
What David calls 'half-arsed'—whatever that means . . .
'Half-arsed', would you say, Miss Loftus?"

"What else does David say about it—about Debrecen?"

"Ah . . . now, as everyone keeps telling you, you'd better
ask *him*, I think. And then draw your own conclusions. Because
in my experience he never says quite the same thing twice. So
we should maybe compare notes some time—over dinner,
say?"

She had to remember that he was still Paul. And not getting
what he wanted only made him want it more: for Paul, failure
was a beginning, not an end. "He won't tell me the truth?"

"That depends." He pointed at the door again. "I have to
establish my alibi."

"Depends on what?"

"On lots of things." He swivelled on his heel, away from
her, then towards her. "David knows his duty. Do you know
yours, Miss Loftus?"

"I know what I've got to do, Dr Mitchell."

"Do you, Miss Loftus? And does it include scuppering David
Audley to please Oliver St John *Fatso*-Latimer, pray?"

"No, it does not—"

"But are you sure of that, Miss Loftus? And is David Audley
sure of it?" He held the pub door open for her. "What you
both want to ask yourselves is . . . do either of you really know
what you are doing? As opposed to what you *think* you're
doing?"

131

VII

"GORBATOV—THAT IS absolutely correct, Elizabeth." Audley shifted his long legs in the Morgan's confined space. "It all starts with him. Before Gorbatov, Debrecen was without light, and void, so far as we were concerned."

For a man hypothetically cast as a prosecutor at his own court-martial, if not commander of the firing squad afterwards, David Audley had been just a little too relaxed, Elizabeth had thought.

True, he had protested briefly when she'd insisted on driving. But that had been more for form's sake than genuine desire, since they both knew that he was a bad driver, unable to keep his mind on the road at the best of times, and that this time she wanted his mind on other matters.

And true, he had been momentarily querulous at the sight of the little Morgan, into which he would not fit easily. But then, again, he had quickly adjusted himself to the imposition, mentally as well as physically, launching instead into a long anecdote about a hot-shot USAF pilot he'd once known, who had once owned just such a car—

"Flew Voodoos, out of Upper Heyford in Oxfordshire—photographic reconnaissance—took some very pretty snapshots for us on one occasion too, much to the annoyance of a certain ally across the Channel . . . Bought himself one of these—same colour, British Racing Green, naturally. And you know what tickled him most, Elizabeth?"

Too relaxed, she thought. But no, she didn't know, she had said.

"Bought it from the factory (he'd been on the waiting list for years, of course), and paid for it in cash . . . some of which we'd just given him, for services rendered . . . but most of which was gambling profits —he was a mean poker player . . . But, anyway, he paid in cash, and there was seventeen shillings and fourpence change to come from his

*money. And they only had pound notes, so they sent an apprentice lad
across the road to a pub to get him his seventeen-and-four, down to the
last penny. Tickled him pink, that did.*"

Much too relaxed. It hadn't tickled her at all.

"What was his provenance?" Although they weren't quite out
of London proper the traffic was already thinning in the brief
gap between closing time and early departure home. "Was he
ever in the real army—Red Army?"

"So he maintained. One of the heroes of the Patriotic War,
who ran up the red flag over the Reichstag, or the Brandenburg
Gate, or some such place, in '45. But I have my doubts,
although he had his army stuff off pat, certainly. So they say."

She was meant to pick that up. "You never interrogated
him?"

"No." He gazed ahead sightlessly. "He came across just
about the time I came into the Service. So I was doing my
homework while they were taking him apart. And I suppose
you could say he was out of my league."

Elizabeth drove in silence for a time, beckoned by the
motorway signs. Paul had warned her that she would be out
of her league in this affair, but that wasn't a bad way of
improving one's game. All the same, the idea of an age of the
world when David Audley had not been in the Blues' team
overawed her somewhat: it was a defect in her powers of
imagination that she could not readily enough accept that
those who were old had once been young—that dear old Major
Birkenshawe had once been a dashing subaltern, and even
Father had been a dewy-eyed little midshipman—*even Father!*

"There were three of them, who assessed him—all Fred
Clinton's trusted cronies. One was a don from Cambridge,
who'd been a Doublecross consultant; one was ex-SOE—one
of the few Fred had been really thick with, and had kept an
eye on; and there was a soldier, an ex-regular who'd watched
Fred's back during the war. And he was the one who didn't
reckon Gorbatov as a front line warrior: 'In the army, but not
of it' . . . meaning that he'd been NKVD from the cradle,
keeping watch on the lads as they carried the red banners
westwards."

133

The West, the final blue sign ahead proclaimed, echoing him and inviting her into the fast lane.

"His version—*Gorbatov*'s version—was that he'd been talent-spotted by one of Ignatiev's lieutenants in 1950, as a politically reliable career soldier. A very tough egg by the name of Okolovich—Anatoli Okolovich. And we knew all about *him* . . . In fact, he was an up-and-coming man at that time, and an invitation from him to join the happy band certainly wouldn't have admitted refusal: it would have been either the Communist Party or the farewell party."

That was one of Paul's little black jokes, so maybe it had started as one of Audley's. Elizabeth took a quick sidelong look at the big man beside her. He was so utterly unlike Paul in so many ways that the ways in which they *were* like each other—ways which were sometimes no more than similar phrases and jokes trivializing unpalatable truths—emphasized their underlying similarity. So, allowing physically for Paul's age and much better looks, and mentally for his admiration of Audley, was this the shape of Paul Mitchell to come?

"So he did the sensible thing, and ended up in '56 as General Okolovich's leg-man in eastern Hungary, when the balloon went up there. Except that, according to him, he'd been feeding the General with soldierly warnings about trouble in store . . . which Okolovich had unwisely bowdlerized before passing on to his ambassador, one Yuri Vladimirovich Andropov—you remember him, Elizabeth?" He turned towards her. "What's the matter, Elizabeth?"

She glanced at her mirror again. "There's a police car about three hundred yards behind us. He's waiting for me to put my foot down."

"Ah!" He nodded, and then hunched himself to view her speedometer. "72–73? Young woman in British Racing Green sports car? Do you always play with policemen like this? It's very naughty."

"I just don't want to get stopped, that's all."

"No? But you could show him your card then—and make him hate you. And then put your foot right down again, and make him hate you even more. Paul—your own Paul—does that all the time, so I'm told."

134

"I'm not Paul." She decided not to rise to "your own Paul". "Is there any reason why I should be hurrying? When are we meeting Major Turnbull at this pub of yours?" She studied her mirror again. The police car would drop her at the next junction. "Would that be about 5.30? You know more about opening times than I do."

"I suppose so." He looked at her innocently. "I take it that you've had lunch? You couldn't have spent half the morning at that *salon* of yours—?"

They both knew that she had ostentatiously placed a distinctively-labelled *Rochard Frères* bag in the car, so he couldn't deny her cover-story. "I snatched a sandwich." But, on second thoughts, that casual reference to Paul might be a hint that he guessed—or, being David, somehow *knew*—where she'd been. "I hope you had something, David—I'm sorry, if I kept you hanging around, waiting for me. That was thoughtless of me."

"Not at all! I like your style, young woman." Audley chuckled. "Putting the Defence of the Realm second to Jimmy Rochard's summer frocks is like old Macmillan sitting on the Front Bench when he was Prime Minister, ostentatiously reading letters from his gamekeeper before his official bumpf." Another chuckle. "Same with your Paul—or *our* Paul, if you prefer . . . First thing every morning, he should be reading his overnight SGs. And what does he do?" He gave her a knowing look, as though wishing to share an answer known to them both; which reminded her oddly of the object of their journey, since in Latin he could have actually worded the question to convey their shared certainty.

"What does he do?" She was certain that he did know about Paul and herself now, but she decided to play hard to get. "I'm sure I don't know—?"

"Why, he reads his morning post from all those 1914–18 veterans with whom he zealously corresponds, before they finally fade away." He cocked his head, half smiling, half frowning. "What is he into at the moment—the battle of Loos, is it?"

Elizabeth shrugged. "I've really no idea." But Paul was right: *once a Sopwith Camel pilot pulls his stick, no one knows where the Camel is going!* "But I do remember your Mr Andropov. He wasn't very nice to the Hungarians, was he?"

"Correct." A minute, and slightly more than a mile, passed while Audley consulted his own memories. "So you can appreciate why General Okolovich was scared in '56, having given the egregious Andropov demonstrably incorrect information about the state of the Hungarian nation before the rising. Because when the dust had settled, and they'd buried the 30,000 dead—including all the good Russian soldiers who'd turned their tanks over to the Hungarians, and offered to fight for them . . . when *they* had been shot too, if they were lucky—Comrade Ambassador Andropov was after blood. So Okolovich was very scared indeed. And while Okolovich was scared, poor old Gorbatov was comprehensively *terrified*. Because he hadn't got anyone worth a damn to shop. So he knew he was for Siberia, if he was very lucky—or the chop, if he wasn't. And he knew enough to know which was more likely." Audley waved a huge hand across the windscreen. "Actually, if he had reckoned on Siberia he wouldn't have minded, because he was born there—his parents had been shunted off there in the twenties, because his grandfather had a Tsarist commission, but hadn't annoyed his other ranks sufficiently to be lynched out of hand when the Red Revolution reached his regiment—he *liked* Siberia, did Andrei Afanaseevich Gorbatov." Audley nodded at the windscreen. "But then he remembered this colleague of his—or nodding KGB acquaintance—who'd done a tour in Canada during the war, and gone off to the North-West Territory of Canada, to tell the Canadians what a splendid fellow Uncle Joe Stalin was. And this fellow had told him about all the endless trees and snow, just like Siberia, but with the birds and the booze, and no questions asked afterwards. And Gorbatov then conceived the idea that if he followed the yellow-brick road to the West there was a land over the rainbow—with trees and snow, and women and drink, and no questions asked, like home only better." He nodded again. "So when he came over to our side he offered all he had in exchange for the North-West Territory. He thought he might be safe there, too, as well as happy."

The police car had fallen away, out of sight if not quite out of mind, baulked of its prey. But she wasn't sure, now that there was nothing behind her, whether they hadn't passed the word on. So she would just have to keep her eye on the rear-view mirror.

"So our people said 'Maybe'. Only at first they were disappointed, because he gave them the usual chicken-feed about Hungary. Which they knew already, because of all the Hungarians who had come over—not just the ex-communist patriots, but the AVRM secret police types, who were afraid of both sides . . . But then he gave them Debrecen, and that was something new."

Elizabeth steadied her foot on 70. It was a curious international idiosyncrasy that the Americans, who worshipped the individual, supplied cars which were equipped to adhere to speed limits, while the regimented Europeans let their drivers take their choice, and pay accordingly.

"Something new." Audley agreed with himself. "That's what concentrated their minds: they'd never had a smell of it before—and, according to Gorbatov, it had been functioning for at least three years, before he nerved himself to run. Which was when Okolovich took possession of his records, so the warnings he'd sent could be doctored out—then he knew he was being measured for a necktie."

Elizabeth nodded at the road ahead. That was a fairly ordinary scenario for defection, anyway. In the West it was often much more complicated, because life itself was more complex, with all its secret guilts and its multiple moral choices. But KGB colonels were not the type to experience sudden blinding lights accompanied by divine voices telling them to change course: with them it was usually naked self-preservation which dictated action.

"He was quite frank about it. Although our Wise Men didn't altogether believe him. They were inclined to think that he wasn't so clever as he pretended to be—that he might well have given Okolovich dud information, and was about to get his just deserts. *And* he had a fairly sizeable drink problem, which he said had been caused by worry . . . But they reckoned it might have been the chicken which laid his egg for him—

the drink problem. And what also made 'em think he wasn't too bright was that he didn't rate what he had about Debrecen as being the jewel in his crown. Because he hadn't had anything directly to do with it, it was way above his clearance as well as being outside his jurisdiction. It just happened to be something he knew the bare minimum abut in general, but two specific things about by pure accident. He actually thought we knew about it already—took it for granted, even. Huh!"

Now, at last, they were getting to the lean meat of the official record, which had dismissed Colonel Andrei Afanaseevich Gorbatov in one short paragraph. "What did he say about it . . . Debrecen?"

"In general? Huh!" Audley sniffed. "'That place where they process the foreigners—you know'. Which they didn't. So they left it for a few days, and then worked back to it one evening when his vodka gauge was into the red. Only to discover that that was all he *did* know—not his directorate, big-time stuff for First Fifteen players while he had to scrum-down with the Hungarians." Audley paused. "But there were these *two* times when someone was off sick, and he had to sub for them. It was just on the transport arrangements—picking people up from an airfield, who'd come in by light plane cleared from somewhere in the west, or south-west—picking 'em up and delivering 'em, secret VIP treatment, semi-disguised subjects—hats, dark glasses, raincoats. All he knew was that they were Anglo-Saxon—or Anglo-American—mostly youngish, or even young. And he knew the dates, near enough, over these two three-week periods in the summer. That was *all*." He nodded to emphasize the last word. "In the end they took him apart —leaned hard on him. But that was all he had."

But that wasn't all that was in the record, thought Elizabeth. "All?"

"They didn't like it, of course." Audley breathed in deeply, and expelled a sigh of remembrance. "Most particularly, they didn't like the bit about the semi-disguised VIPs being *youngish* or *young*. Because that smelt too much like laying down new claret, for drinking in the seventies. Like the Cambridge thirties vintages were laid down." Audley spoke off-handedly now, reminding Elizabeth that if there was one thing he hated, and invariably referred to in his most casual voice, it was the infamous Cambridge gang. For he was a Cambridge man himself, and desperately proud of it.

"So what did they do?"

"They went for Debrecen, of course." Audley's voice harshened again. "This was '57—Hungary was still wide-open to us then, after '56, in the sense that the Hungarians all loathed the Russians so much that they'd do anything for us." The harshness was almost gravelly. "And we had any number of Hungarians who were prepared to go back, if they knew we wanted something." He drew another breath. "That was when we got all the physical data—pictures, measurements, the lot."

That had certainly been precise: the long-disused Imperial Hapsburg hunting-lodge in the forest, well away from the city and effectively in the middle of nowhere; which the Nazis had reanimated and uglified with military perimeter and buildings as a training centre for their Brandenburg elites, which had operated far beyond the battle lines in Russia, which lay only a few miles away; and which, when the wheel had turned full circle, the Russians had in turn occupied, to train a very different elite to fight a very different war in the opposite direction, so it seemed.

All the physical data. "But they'd gone by then?" She spurred him.

"Uh-huh. The birds had flown." She just caught him twitch under her spur. "The eggs had hatched, and the fledglings had departed for warmer climes, never to return." He looked at her suddenly. "That was the difference: *never to return.*"

"Why did they close it down?"

"Ah . . . well, at first the Three Wise Men thought it was because of the Rising in '56, simply. And they were half-right, anyway."

"How—half-right?"

"Because there were Hungarians who'd seen too much, in the nature of things, Elizabeth." He made a face at her. "Because there were AVRM Hungarians—most of them were bastards, and some of them got lynched in '56." He looked at her again suddenly. But this time he really saw her, as he had not done before. "Jesus Christ, Elizabeth! You don't really remember '56, do you? When the Iron Curtain was split open wide for a time, and you could drive all the way to Budapest, and the people in the villages would cheer you on, and offer you drinks? And Suez—when Radio Cairo went off the air after our Canberras had hit it? You were just a baby then, of course."

Momentarily his guard was down: *Hot heart, cool head* was what he preached, which was the old KGB–NKVD axiom. But the recollection of long ago—and perhaps of a mistake he had made in that far-off time—was animating him now, and betraying him as it did so.

"I'm not quite with you, David—?"

"It was the Age of Innocence, love. Or relative innocence, anyway—when I was young . . . or, if not quite young, not *senile*, anyway." He grinned at her hideously. "Old memories —senile reminiscences, no more." He flexed a leg, and massaged its constricted knee. "The fact of it was that he wasn't the only defector. Because there was this Hungarian AVRM who came over at about the same time—probably for much the same reasons as Gorbatov. Only he went over to the Americans, not our people. But he'd run all the rackets in the Debrecen district, and he was nobody's fool. So it transpired."

So that was what had happened, Elizabeth realized in a flash: the British had stumbled on something, more or less by accident. But, when it had gone cold on them, they had naturally offered it to the Americans—*naturally*, because after Suez they must have been hell-bent on ingratiating themselves with their former allies, and Comrade Colonel Gorbatov had said "*or Anglo-American*", so they had something to offer.

"And what did he say?" And that, to clinch the matter, helped to account for those two lists—one British, but the other American.

"He'd got the other half of the sweepstake ticket." Audley nodded. "Which he shouldn't have had. But he was a lot smarter than old Gorbatov, anyway. Because, when he came across, it was Debrecen that he reckoned was his ticket to the good life—the bit printed in Russian, which the Americans would want to read, do you see?"

Elizabeth saw, but didn't quite see. Because the record was inexact here, to say the least, and what Paul had told her about David confirmed its equivocation about the exact nature of Debrecen: *"he never quite says the same thing twice"*.

But she had to cut through all that now, after the Pointe du Hoc and their Xenophon interview, and all the miles which were slipping away now, at more than one for each minute, towards Major Turnbull and the one-time Squadron Leader Thomas.

"What *was* Debrecen, David?" If he'd never said the same thing twice he probably wouldn't say the same thing now, when his neck was on the block. But even the difference between what he said now, and what he had once said, was something she had to establish. "Really?"

He took the point of the question, judging by the mile-or-more he used to think about it, at 70 mph, while estimating both ends against the middle.

"Uh-huh." He took another half-mile. "Well, that's the million pound bingo question, Elizabeth." He tried to stretch a leg again. "It used to be the sixty-four-thousand dollar question, but we've had inflation since then."

Another mile, tenth by tenth, almost empty and featureless, and boring now that there was nothing sniffing her British Racing Green tail across the Wessex countryside, which was opening up on either side. But she could still afford to wait for her answer.

"Our Three Wise Men were never 100 per cent convinced —just about 80 per cent." About half a mile. "And neither were the Americans."

"Why not?"

"Why not?" Four-fifths of a mile. "Deep down, they didn't want to believe that young Americans could betray 1950s America—even though they put a man on it who believed that *everyone* was guilty, until proved innocent. And even then probably not. He was a hard man—in some ways a monster."

That led straight to the next question, but he continued before she could get it out. "Our people had fewer illusions. Not because they were smarter, but because they had bitter recent memories. And also we'd just come down in the world

—and down with a bump, after Suez. So we weren't just the poor relations—we were maybe the baddies. So what was there to betray? A British Dream, like the American Dream? What dream?" He glanced at her. "So what was Debrecen? Our people weren't sure—but they knew they were on to *something*. And they reckoned there might be an American angle, and they needed to get in with the Americans again, after Suez. So they decided to offer them what they'd got as a present, in the hope of re-establishing co-operation." He tossed his head. "That was my first big job: carrying tribute to Caesar." Then he shook his head sadly. "I had no idea what I was getting into—no idea, poor innocent youth that I was!"

Elizabeth noticed that her speed had crept up to 85, but mercifully there was nothing behind her. And there was nothing of the truth in his last words, either: he had been a rich bachelor in his thirties in '58, and the reverse of innocent for sure, then as well as now. She dropped back to 70. "What went wrong?"

"Hah!" He brightened perversely at the memory. "Absolutely nothing—at first. In fact, when they knew what I'd got with me, it was all roses and violets. Because it was exactly what they wanted, so they thought—because they had their appalling Hungarian, you see. About whom we didn't know, but who had given his half-ticket to them, so they had a much better idea of what Debrecen might have been than we did. They knew more—*and* they'd also had a look at the place, just like us. But with the same result. And they really didn't know what to do next, or even where to start." The brightness remained, but it was as frosty as a short winter's day. "And then in flew Sir Frederick Clinton's new star, with a warm Special Relationship smile on his face and the rest of the ticket in his briefcase. Roses and violets, Elizabeth."

But dust and ashes to come, thought Elizabeth grimly. "You had the dates Colonel Gorbatov gave you. But what exactly were these people doing in Debrecen? Why were they there?"

Audley gazed out of the car window at his side, as though he had suddenly found the rural view more interesting. "You've read the record, haven't you?"

"Yes." She waited for him to continue, but instead he

went on admiring the Hampshire countryside. " 'Hand-picked subjects, with good career prospects, psychologically equipped for deep-sleeping'."

"Yes." Audley nodded at a cow which, from its melancholy expression, looked as though it had heard all about the new EEC milk quotas. "So?"

"So what was so particularly important about Debrecen?"

Audley turned towards her. "Isn't that enough?"

It ought to be enough, thought Elizabeth with a deep-down shiver: the idea of long-term treachery, waiting to mature like wine, but cellared instead in the dark recesses of certain human souls. But somehow it wasn't. "No, David."

He smiled a sudden genuine smile, which cruelly reminded her of that smile of Latimer's. "Quite right, Elizabeth. But how do you know?"

Elizabeth was torn between the two smiles. Because if Paul was right and Latimer was gunning for David . . . if it came to the crunch—whose side was she on? *Whose side?* The answer confused her horribly, it was so immediate. And she knew she must cover her confusion. "Don't ask me how. I don't really know."

"Of course! Who ever does, when it comes to instinct? Don't worry, my dear—be glad that you've got it, that's all." He nodded. "Everyone thinks they have it, but it's atrophied in most people—like the hunting instinct. I knew a troop-sergeant in Normandy who'd never fired a shot in anger until we landed, but he always knew when there was an 88 waiting for us." Nod. "Your Paul hasn't got it—with him it's mostly reason and logic, plus a little experience and a lot of knowledge . . . all topped off by low cunning and an eye for the main chance. But most women have more of it than most men, anyway. So just be thankful."

Her Paul, again. Yet, for another inexplicable reason, she felt impelled to defend him now. "You do *my* Paul less than justice, I rather think. He's very loyal to you, for a start, David."

"Loyal?" He half-spluttered. "*Loyal?*"

"Or . . . or protective, let's say."

He said nothing for another mile, digesting her indiscretion;

which must either have confirmed his guess or confused his certainty; and that seemed to be enough for him, too, for the time being.

"Debrecen—" He rubbed both his knees simultaneously "—what the unspeakable Hungarian had given them, among other things, was names, Elizabeth. Not the traitors' names, which he didn't know . . . the names of the Russian top-brass he'd welcomed, on behalf of Rakosi—he was one of Rakosi's front men. Rakosi was the Hungarian top man, Elizabeth." He half-apologized for assuming her ignorance of mid-20th century history. "Because the Russians couldn't ship in their top brass, to Debrecen, without going through the motions of trusting Rakosi, who was *their* front-man. Uh-huh?" Pause. "So he was there with the red carpet, first for Shelepin, and then for Zhurkin, and also for Semichastny—all future KGB bosses, but also all top *Komsomol* youth leaders. And two of them genuine war heroes—Shelepin was a Hero of the Soviet Union, for his partisan work behind the German lines, and Zhurkin had flown Russian fighters all the way from the Spanish Civil War to Korea—he was a sort of 'Red Douglas Bader', with his tin legs . . . But they were all real heroes of the people's revolution—even Semichastny, who was trained as a chemical engineer in the Ukraine—son of an illiterate mill worker, pre-revolutionary, whose umpteen children had all made the grade under the new regime: getting a hand-shake from them, and a pat on the back, and a 'Right trusty and well-beloved' commission—which was to be filed in the archives of Dzerinsky Street, never to see the light of day—all that would have been like being tapped on the shoulder by Her Majesty, and blessed by the Archbishop of Canterbury . . . Or by the President of the United States—or bussed on each cheek by the President of the Republic—do you see, Elizabeth?"

Or touched lightly by the Chancellor of the University, and gowned colourfully for excellence? Touched in the remote hope that the twin evils of ignorance and intellectual arrogance might forever be expelled?

"You mean, it was just a morale-raiser?" She heard her incredulity. "All that trouble? And the risk—?"

"Ah . . ." The long legs bent again, and the knees came up for massage. "There was another reason—or two reasons . . . Because there was another name. And, if the Wise Men of Research and Development and the Pentagon had it right, it was the big name—the Name of Power, Elizabeth. Although you'll never even have heard of it. Because if you punch the name on that wretched Beast of ours the thing will perform its two favourite actions: first, it will not answer your question, but will request your authorization instead; and second, it will sneak on you to the head teacher and master-at-arms, whether you have clearance or not." He let go of his knees and smiled at her. "But I am a different sort of beast. A human beast, am I. And I spit on the new beast—may it be visited with sudden extreme variations of temperature and floods of water from the sewers, and electronic illnesses hitherto unknown. And, most especially, I spit on the memory of its prophet and servant, Comrade Professor Kryzhanovsky—*Kryzhanovsky*." He pronounced the Name of Power without benefit of Russian sound, syllable by syllable, much as a Russian might have attempted *Worcestershire*. "*Vladimir Ivanovitch Kryzhanovsky*, Elizabeth."

This, again, was the authentic Audley: the Audley whom Paul loved to imagine as casting himself as one character after another out of his beloved Rudyard Kipling.

"I've never heard of him, David," she said meekly.

"No, you wouldn't have done. He's long dead, thank God. And . . . *hmm* . . . and since it *was* natural causes maybe we should thank Him, blasphemy or not—" He stopped suddenly.

"Yes, David?"

"*Hmm* . . ." He growled the sound from the back of his throat. "I was just thinking that maybe the blighter's had the laugh over us after all these years. Or, if he hasn't, he has *now*, anyway."

If this was the authentic Audley, she might get more by letting him simply think aloud than by prodding him with questions. But the miles were slipping away towards their destination, and time with them. "Who was he, David?"

"He was a psychologist, and by all accounts a damn good one. Moscow-trained, but cut his teeth in the Ukraine. Which was where he got to know Semichastny—and that was where Semichastny got in with Khrushchev, of course. But we didn't get a line on him until '54, when the Petrovs defected—at least, not a line that put him right in the heart of the KGB reorganization, anyway . . . But he wasn't *just* a psychologist, he was big on the whole new technology scene. Like, he was in on the beginning of the personnel selection in the space programme. One of the first papers of his we got was entitled *The Symbiosis of Man and Machine: Future Trends*—or something like that.''

Elizabeth's chuckle was only half forced. "I can see why you don't—or didn't—like him, David. If he was a computer psychologist—''

"Ah—now that's just where you're wrong, Miss Clever-Clogs," Audley interrupted her quickly. "Or . . . not quite right, anyway. Because I think he was even more shit-scared of the computer than I am—or of its Fifth Generation, which he foresaw thirty years ago. Although he called it 'The Fourth Evolution'—'evolution' was his codename for *revolution*, which caused him to skate very gingerly and obtusely round its edges, with impenetrable clouds of jargon.''

A road sign arrested her attention momentarily. They were off the motorway now. The miles had flown, and time had flown with them.

"When the machines start thinking for themselves—what a brave new world it will be," murmured Audley. "All the right answers supplied without asking! Our old capitalism will be in serious trouble—but *his* old Marxist–Leninist–Communism will be a ridiculous, incompetent, irrelevant joke . . . that's what he foresaw, I shouldn't wonder. But he didn't say so. He was sitting much too pretty for that.''

The turn-off was only a few miles away. "What did he do at Debrecen, this . . . Kryzhanovsky, David?''

"Season your impatience, Elizabeth. The one thing leads to the other. What Comrade Professor *Kry*-zan-*off*-sky saw was the rise of information technology. He was one of their experts on Bletchley Park, he made a study of it. Knew all about Ultra, he did—and said what idiots we were, not to build on it. He'd have made them all Heroes of the British Empire, with special perks and privileges. And kept 'em all behind the wire for the rest of their lives."

"David—"

"Just let me finish, love. What he said—or is reputed to have said, because we've never had a sight of the document in which it was said, if there is one—was that as the machines were improved, so human intelligence-gathering of the old-fashioned variety would inevitably be down-graded. And, at the same time, methods of vetting would become more efficient." He sniffed. "Which is something I've yet to see, I must say—but you can't be right all the time . . . *Anyway*, his blueprint for the future was technology at one end of the spectrum—satellites and computers and listening devices, plus a sort of super-GCHQ. Then a much-reduced conventional intelligence force in the field, mostly engaged in surveillance of the homeland—keeping that nice and tidy . . . with only a minimum of conventional foreign-based agents. But then, right at the other end, the new generation of *Kry*-zan-*off*-ski boys and girls, hand-picked in their own countries."

She was going to miss the turning for sure. "The deep-sleepers, you mean?"

Audley didn't answer immediately. "Well . . . that's what some people thought. But that was pretty much old-hat." He fell silent again. "It's possible he had a variation on the old theme."

There was a sign way ahead, at the bottom of the long hill they were descending. "A variation, David?"

"Yes." Another silence. "How would you go about catching a traitor who never betrayed any secrets, Elizabeth?"

"Who never—?" It wasn't the right name on the sign. She accelerated angrily. "Never betrayed anything?"

"And never communicated with any control. He has no contacts, no drops—nothing. No connection at all, for years. And then only the very occasional, unscheduled, one-sided, one-off word from on-high. And then not to give information, but to do something—or to try not to do something—in the future." He looked at her. "Like, not being a spy in 10 Downing Street, reporting on the Prime Minister, but being one of her top advisers *not* reporting on her—just advising her." He

shrugged slightly. "Or, better still, *being* the Prime Minister."
Another shrug. "Or, say, being Oliver St John Latimer putting
David Audley out of business—*that* would be a famous victory
for the other side now, wouldn't it?"

There was another sign ahead.

"That's our turning up ahead, Elizabeth," said Audley
conversationally. "'*Fordingwell 5—Little Balscote 8*'—we want
Fordingwell, the King's Arms, okay?"

"You don't mean it—" She was surprised at the steadiness
of her voice "—do you?"

"Huh!" Audley *harumphed* scornfully. "Tut-tut, Miss Loftus
—such lack of confidence in our admirable Deputy-Director!
No, of course I don't mean it. Oliver St John Latimer is a fat,
self-satisfied, pen-pushing, button-pressing *paperhanger*. But,
on the one hand, he's a Clinton appointment from way back,
and old Fred never erred. Meaning that he's done more
damage to the KGB in Britain over the years—and *real* damage, too—than . . . oh, than almost anyone." He grinned at
her mischievously. "It was merely an illustration. Not that he
may not be doing the devil's work now, no matter how good
his intentions. But that's a minor problem."

He knew. But of course he knew. Only now, compared with
Debrecen, that certainly was a minor matter. "An illustration
of Debrecen?"

"Uh-huh. At least, according to the Americans." He nodded. "Catch 'em young—choose 'em well. See 'em just that
once, on the home ground—one by one, with the full treatment,
VIP treatment, to reassure 'em that they'll always be loved
and honoured, even if only in secret—that was rated very
important psychologically, since they'd be on their own ever
after, right to the grave." He craned forward to study the road
ahead, which had narrowed almost to single-track as they
climbed away from the main road. "The Americans were
very hot on the psychological aspect of it, once the Comrade
Professor's name had been dropped—whispered in their ear by
the Hungarian. Because they'd had their eye on the Comrade
Professor for some time."

There was something not quite right about what he was
saying. "The Americans? So what did you think?"

"Oh . . . I never really went for it. Or not hook, line and sinker, anyway." He sat back. "Not far now. And I could do with a nice cup of tea and a big plate of sandwiches. It's a splendid old place, the King's Arms—you'll like it, Elizabeth. Good meals, soft beds—good cellar. It's an old coaching inn. And this evening we'll meet our contact, who lives a few miles away, just the other side of Balscote." He smiled at her. "You'll like him, my dear. He's a sharp old swine."

Damn him! "Why didn't you go for it?"

"Too neat and tidy, in the first place. All the bits fitted too well—in theory. And there was no bloody way of confirming them."

"You mean, Debrecen had already been closed down—the place?" As the car breasted the ridge she saw roofs ahead, down below in the next valley, where the coaches had once presumably forded Fordingwell's stream. "Was that because of the Hungarian Rising?"

"No. It was because of the Hungarian's defection, more like. Plus old Gorbatov." He made a face. "But all neat and tidy, like I said."

Elizabeth frowned. "But didn't that compromise the whole operation—their defection?"

"You think so?" He sounded a little scornful. "So where should we start our counter-operation, just in case?"

She slowed down to pass a farm tractor, which had courteously pulled on the verge for her. "You had those dates."

"That's right—clever Elizabeth!" He waved at the tractor driver. "Two years before, certain persons—*mostly young, or youngish, age not known exactly*—certain persons—*Anglo-Saxon, or maybe Anglo-American, nationality not known exactly*—spent some days abroad in high summer, when half the likely lads in the Western World were stretching their wings: '*There's the haystack, Audley, my lad*', says old Fred Clinton. '*Find me some needles*'. Phooey!"

They were among the first houses.

"No computers, remember, Elizabeth. Just one temporary secretary and two researchers was all we could run to. Apart from which, it wasn't at all the sort of job I'd expected to be doing—sweating over lists of names, and generally having to behave like a grubby divorce investigator." He sighed. "Delusions of grandeur."

"But—" She had to keep an eye open for the King's Arms now "—it was important, surely—?"

"Ah! Now *was* it?" He gestured ahead. "It's a bit further on . . . The Americans thought so. They had a whole team working on it. But I didn't—I wasn't so sure."

"Why not. If Kryzhanovsky was top brass, David. And Shelepin and the others?"

"Oh yes—all big time stuff." He nodded. "But we only had the Hungarian's word for it. Plus old Gorbatov's dates. *But suppose they weren't on the level*—what then, Elizabeth?"

The road widened suddenly, into a miniature village square, with straggling uneven terraces of houses set back on three sides, and the church on her right, away beyond the church-yard and inevitable war memorial.

"It could have been all pure disinformation, designed to divert us from more important things—as it damn well did, in fact, whatever it was. Over there—" He pointed across the square "—see the sign?"

A coaching inn it certainly was, complete with an arched gateway to admit its coaches into a cobbled yard beyond. But there was another farm tractor labouring across her bows, towing a waggonload of baled straw.

"Go under the arch," ordered Audley. "Or suppose it was *half* genuine, eh? Like . . . if the Hungarian was *kosher*, so they'd thrown old Gorbatov at us, like a bit of over-ripe beef—strictly expendable, *with the wrong dates*—how's that for size?"

Elizabeth stared at the King's Arms, computing both ends of the puzzle against its middle. The trouble was, though, it had more than two ends: because, although David was an expert on disinformation tactics, both Eastern and Western (and it was even his contention that every operation should have a disinformation cover built into it as its first line of defence), it was also the case that David was defending himself now against Oliver St John Latimer. So he had a vested interest in debunking Debrecen in 1984, even more than in 1958.

"Go on, Elizabeth—" He pointed ahead again "—I'm

dying for my cup of tea. And my sandwiches. *And* my pint. In that order, but with very short intervals between."

Wisps of straw from the bales lay in the street, and as she stared a faint breath of wind animated them as though they still had life in them.

Delusions of grandeur, she thought: Audley's then, back in the 1950s, but perhaps hers now, in the 1980s—and Paul had warned her about that, in so many words, risking his own professional skin in doing so.

And . . . all those great names which Audley had casually dropped—great Russian *Names of Power* from the past, about which she had read during the last two years—*Andropov* and *Ignatiev, Shelepin, Zhurkin* and *Semichastny*—names not really so very different from those ruthless English Elizabethans about whom she had taught her history scholarship sixth-formers, almost only the day before yesterday: *William Cecil* for *Yuri Andropov*, and *Francis Walsingham* for *Alexander Shelepin*—and *Sir Thomas Gresham* and *Archbishop Bancroft*, and all the rest of the Tudor sixteenth-century espionage *apparat*.

But now she, little stupid Elizabeth Loftus, who had thought herself so clever, was here in her green Morgan outside the King's Arms, Fordingwell, beside her own private *Francis Walsingham*, trying to out-think him—what foolishness was this?

But then Father nodded at her, agreeing with her at last for once!

"Come on!" said Audley irritably, almost old-maidishly. "When you get to my age, young woman—then the creature-comforts begin to matter."

She looked at him. "If all that's true—or any of it—then why did Major Parker go to see Squadron Leader Thomas—Dr Thomas? And why did someone push Parker off the Pointe du Hoc?"

"What?" He hadn't expected her to bite back. But he was still her own Francis Walsingham, and didn't like being bitten. "Jesus Christ, Elizabeth—you tell me! Or, better still, you ask Major Turnbull—our mysterious, equivocal galloping major —you ask him about the late Mrs Squadron Leader Dr Thomas—" He looked at his watch "—you ask him that in

151

about fifteen minutes' time, young woman . . . And *then* you ask me the same question—right?''

She put the Morgan in gear. The square was wide-open, and there was nothing coming left-and-right, so she went through the archway trailing an angry, irresponsible *zroom*, to halt one yard short of a trough of geraniums inside the yard with a jerk which would have put Francis Walsingham through the windscreen if he had not been wearing his seat-belt.

"We're booked in, I take it?" If it had been Paul she might have added '*And in two single rooms?*' But that was one thing she didn't have to worry about with David Audley, because of his dearly-beloved Faith.

"Yes—" He struggled with his safety-belt "—how d'you get this damn thing off?"

She almost helped him, but then didn't. If he was so clever he could get himself out of the car, she thought savagely.

The square of the old coaching yard was a mixture of English hostelry styles, from what might be half-timbered seventeenth century—or more like eighteenth century, because Fordingwell would have been nowhere until the coaching age—to Dickensian brick and mock-Tudor additions—

But then she thought as she headed for the hotel entrance . . . *in fifteen minutes—how the hell am I going to handle Major Turnbull, with David Audley beside me?*

Horse-brasses, post-horns, old prints (or not-so-old) of hunting and coaching—reception desk ahead, unoccupied—dining room on the right, tables laid for dinner, nice-and-cosy, beams overhead and candles on the tables, ready for the inevitable *pâté maison* and *prawn cocktail* and *whitebait*—

Bar, or maybe lounge, on the left—

Broken teacup on the floor, with spreading spilt tea across the dark-red Cardinal-polished tiles—

There was a small crowd of people in the bar, but they were not drinking. And now a waitress from her right, blank-faced and unseeing and unwelcoming, crossing ahead of her, into the lounge—

Elizabeth stopped, partly because she was uncertain, but mostly because the waitress was quite obviously not going to give way to her—was pushing past her even now, even before she had decided to stop—so that her attention was pulled in the girl's wake.

The crowd split apart as the waitress reached it, allowing Elizabeth to take a split-second memory-photograph of it: the ruddy-faced young man in shirt-sleeves, the archetypal young farmer on his knees—the man in well-cut tweeds—the man in an ordinary shapeless suit—the youth in sweat-shirt-and-jeans —grouped around a man lying flat on his back on the glistening tiles.

"What did the doctor say?" The young farmer half-shouted at the waitress urgently, on the edge of panic.

"Is 'e breathing?" The waitress joined him on the same edge, breathlessly.

"God Almighty—*what did 'e say?*" The young man stared at the girl for an instant, then switched back to Major Turnbull irresolutely, and then looked up to the girl again. "Sandra— for God's sake—*what*-the-'ell did 'e say?"

The man-in-tweeds blocked off Elizabeth's view momentarily, as he knelt beside the Major. "I think he's stopped breathing," he announced.

Adrenalin flowed in Elizabeth as she pushed forward. "Can I help?"

They all looked at her.

"Are you a nurse?" asked the man-in-tweeds.

"The doctor said, is 'e breathing?" said Sandra. "Because—"

Elizabeth knelt beside the Major, feeling for his carotid pulse.

"Give her room!" commanded the man-in-tweeds. "Is he alive?"

Four minutes to brain-damage—but how long had they been arguing over him?

Her own brain was trying to work. She put down her bag and chopped him hard on the sternum—once, twice—as she remembered the St John Ambulance man do to the dummy in the sixth-form First Aid class.

"Get him flat." The Major's false teeth were awry: she had seen them a few hours ago, unsmiling at her, but now she had to get them out of the way, to do what must be done, however hopelessly. "Help me get him flat!"

Hands everywhere flattened the Major. "Arch his back—support his neck." The hands continued to obey her unquestioningly, as she remembered how the girls had tittered when plain Miss Loftus had kissed the dummy, mouth-to-mouth. But no one was tittering now.

Someone took the teeth from her. He had looked a dreadful greyish-white before, but recognizable. Now he was a complete stranger as she held his nose shut and sealed his mouth with hers, to try to bring him back from wherever he had gone.

Her own hope expanded as she felt his chest rise beneath her. But then, as she paused and counted silently, and tried again, and then again, she knew that it was her breath of life inside him, not his.

Keep trying, the St John's man had said—

The tweed-man touched her shoulder, and she saw that he was holding the Major's wrist as though he knew what he was doing. "There's still no pulse, nurse."

"The doctor's coming," said Sandra to no one in particular and everyone in general. "And he said he'd call for the ambulance."

Elizabeth looked down at Major Turnbull—at what had been Major Turnbull, but wasn't any more. The doctor and the ambulance could come now, but the Major would have no use for them. And, by the same token, she knew exactly what she must do, according to the rules.

"Hold his neck up again—and his back." These weren't the rules. And maybe she'd done everything wrong anyway, by the St John's man's rules. But she had to try once more, rules or no rules.

Again the sickeningly slack mouth, and the stubbly cheek, and the faint smell of after-shave. Father's rare evening peck-on-the-cheek had been brandy-flavoured, and old Major Birkenshawe's moustache always smelt of tobacco and whisky; and Paul's mouth, that one and only night—

She sat up, shaking with fear and distaste with herself.

"He's gone, poor devil," said someone. "It must have been his heart."

Her fear expanded almost into panic. No one with a heart condition passed R & D's medicals. And she was breaking the rules.

She picked up her bag and stood up. "I'll get a blanket," she said.

They were all staring at the Major. And who would want to question a Sister of Mercy after what she'd done already? "I'll get a blanket from my car," she repeated unnecessarily.

Then she was in the passage again, with the still-empty reception desk in front of her—and then she was outside, backing into the *Olde English* coaching inn yard, with David Audley still fumbling around to get their overnight bags out of the car.

"Put them back in, David."

"What?" He stretched, and stamped one leg. "What?"

So little time! "Put them back in." She seized the car-key from him and threw the nearest bag into the car. "Major Turnbull got here ahead of us. And he's dead."

He stared at her for only a fraction of a second, and then threw the bag in his hand into the car and turned away towards his side of the car without any change in his expression.

Get in—start car—reverse out—

"Not too fast," murmured Audley. "Turn right."

Not too fast—turn right—

Audley twisted in his seat. "You watch the front. I'll watch the back," he said.

VIII

THERE WAS NOTHING remotely menacing down the main street of Fordingwell: it was just a village street, nicer than most because the houses and little shops were set well back, a line of neatly-pollarded trees on one side and a scatter of parked cars on the other, with a few people going about their Fordingwell business.

"Take it easy, Elizabeth—not too fast," murmured Audley soothingly. "Down the hill and over the bridge. The speed limit ends there. You can put your foot down then."

Just ordinary people, they looked to be, left and right: butcher, baker, candlestick-maker—a knot of children, a young man chatting up his girl—a young motor-cyclist, black-helmeted, eyes on the girl, further down—a trio of men packing tools into a van outside a fine Georgian house locked in scaffolding—

Down the hill and over the bridge—but watch that motor-cyclist, just in case—

"Where are we going?"

No answer. Audley was intent on his wing-mirror.

Odd, how her palms were sweating on the wheel when she wasn't in the least hot. *"Young ladies do not sweat, Elizabeth. Nor do they perspire. If they do anything, they 'glow'."* But her palms had always sweated when she took her first look at exam papers, and she had always surreptitiously wiped them on her skirt under the desk.

Over the bridge. No sound of any motor-cycle, and the road up the hill beyond was Roman-straight and empty. And steep, too—*foot down*—in Fordingwell's coaching days, if this was the old main London road, they must have had an extra team of horses here in the winter, to haul the coaches up in the snow, and slow their descent, like on Shotover at Oxford —but her own horses were pulling her away now, leaving

Fordingwell, and the King's Arms, and Major Turnbull behind in their own shared forever.

"Where are we going?" Audley repeated the question. "At this moment I have not decided where we are going. But take the first side road to the left, anyway. And then maybe left again—south-south-east is the general idea, for the time being. Just use your bump of direction."

There would be a maze of little country roads ahead, because in England there always was. "Is there anything behind us?"

Audley fiddled with the mirror again. "Not as far as I can make out."

"There was a motor-cyclist . . . The maps are under your seat."

"Yes. But I think he was more interested in that pretty girl in the Laura Ashley dress."

They were over the brow of the hill. And, sure enough, there was a sign-post coming up. Funny that David had noticed that the girl had been pretty, when she hadn't. And funnier still that he had identified what she was wearing—David, of all people! Did Faith wear Laura Ashley dresses—or little Cathy? A bit old and a bit young, respectively, she would have thought. But they were all the rage, of course. But *funny*, all the same —*David, of all people!* Screamingly funny, even.

And now she could read the name on the signpost—and that was funny too—*Hell's Bottom 2*—and funnier still, again, that the road to *Hell's Bottom* wasn't as broad and wide as the road to hell ought to be, it was a narrow, pot-holed track. But she had better not start laughing, just in case she had hysterics, with everything being so funny.

She decided against *Hell's Bottom*. "You're sure it was a Laura Ashley dress, David?" she said instead.

He looked up from a map, which he had found, first at her, then in his mirror again, and then back at her. "How was he dead, Elizabeth?"

She wiped her sweaty palms on her skirt, one after another. "Heart attack, it looked like."

Audley stared at her for another moment, and then bent over his map again, studying it intently. "Along here, about a mile, on the left—'Lower Hindley', it should say on the sign.

157

And that'll put us on the Winchester road, sooner or later."

Her own wing mirror gave her a sudden long view back, of a reassuringly empty road. "We're going to Winchester, are we?" But she couldn't decide where she would feel safer: alone in this empty countryside, unprotected, or lost in a busy city, still naked.

"No." Then he shifted awkwardly. "Well . . ."

"What?" Another sign-post was silhouetted on the next rise. "Well what?" But then she understood. "You mean—you mean I'm supposed to be in charge. Is that it?" She snapped at him, although she had not intended to do so.

"No . . ." He bridled. "Or . . . yes, I suppose so."

It was ridiculous—Elizabeth Loftus pretending she was in charge of David Audley. It had always been . . . if not ridiculous, then *mischievous*, Latimer's strategy. But Latimer had never envisaged what had happened in the King's Arms, Fordingwell. Because what they both knew was that the odds against Major Turnbull having a heart attack to order at a rendezvous were even more ridiculous.

"Hah—*harumph!*" Audley cleared his throat. "You are . . . *absolutely* sure . . . that he was—that he *is*, that is to say . . . *dead*, Elizabeth?"

Elizabeth felt herself hardening as he forced his words out: they were all the bloody same—Paul and David, Father and Major Birkenshawe—all the same, the bloody same, when it came to their man's world: all the bloody, *bloody* same, notwithstanding all the evidence to the contrary, from Queen Boudicca to Mrs Thatcher.

Lower Hindley. Touch the brakes—*accelerate*—there was a little more loose gravel on the silly road than she'd bargained for, but her little beauty was equal to it any day—*any day!* "You're not scared, are you, David?"

He steadied himself. "Yes—just then, I was—" He reached down for the map, which had fallen off his knees "—but before that I was merely frightened half out of my wits. Because what I don't understand always frightens me—" The road twisted unexpectedly, and he rolled against her "—as it should do you equally, Elizabeth dear."

The road straightened—*Lower Hindley 5*—and Elizabeth

finally straightened herself out with it. Perhaps she should have been terrified—and ought to be frightened still. But there was a difference between being *terrified* and merely *horrified*, she decided: or, only briefly horrified, but then momentarily irresolute, faced with the unexpected. And then (which was now the exact opposite of *funny*, whatever the opposite might be)—*sickened*, maybe—?

Those teeth—those dreadful false teeth in her hand—slimy-hard! And that mockery-of-a-kiss, almost a French-kiss, against that toothless mouth, and those toothless gums—

But even that wasn't quite the truth. "I broke the rules back there, David. Doesn't it say, 'When a contact is compromised —'—what does it say? 'Run like hell', is it?" That was it, paraphrased. "You were a long time in the yard, getting the cases out. So I didn't know quite what to do." But there was still something in the back of her mind, which she couldn't reach.

Audley sniffed. "As it happens . . . I was stretching my legs, trying to get some feeling back into them." Sniff. "This isn't a very comfortable vehicle." He kicked out at the car irritably. "What did you do, for God's sake?"

What was it, that she couldn't reach? "He wasn't breathing —he had no pulse." Those lessons in the First Aid class, which the Headmistress had made compulsory for every mistress, obliterated everything for an instant. *"Whatever you do, don't give up"*, the St John's man had said. *"Not until the doctor comes."*

Audley turned towards her, but wordlessly.

"If you must know, David, I tried to revive him. Only I didn't try for very long, and you're supposed to keep trying. But then, by our rules, I shouldn't have tried at all. I should have left immediately, shouldn't I!"

There were times when Audley's ugliness became brutal, almost Neanderthal, and this was one of them. "I see. So you did the wrong thing both times—is that it?" He started fiddling with the wing-mirror again, but gave it up in favour of turning round. Not that he could see much that way. "Damn car! Can you see anything behind?"

"No."

"Neither can I. So we may be lucky. Or they may only have wanted Major Turnbull." He looked at her again. "So now you have to do the right thing, that's all."

He wasn't going to help her. "I want to report in, David." That was easy. "And I want protective back-up." That was prudent as well as according to the rules, even if poor Major Turnbull had only succumbed to natural causes: nobody could fault her for any of that.

"Fine. So we want a telephone, short of the new technology we ought to have. And a phone in a Police House would be ideal. But I doubt that Lower Hindley boasts a policeman of its own." He peered ahead. "Just keep going."

Just keep going, thought Elizabeth automatically. But then she thought *why Major Turnbull?*

"Why should anyone want to kill Major Turnbull?"

"God knows!" He smoothed the map on his knee. "But he went to the Pointe du Hoc. So maybe they picked him up there."

"Major Turnbull was researching Mrs Thomas's death, David. And you said that was above board—back in 1958—?"

"Uh-huh?" He couldn't deny the most obvious implication. "Meaning what?" There was an unnatural note to his voice. "Meaning I missed something, back in the deeps of time? Perhaps he did have a heart attack."

Elizabeth remembered what Paul had said about David Audley and Debrecen, when they came together. "You don't believe that, do you?"

"No," said Audley. "I can't say that I do."

"No." She felt suddenly outraged at the flatness of his reaction. "Neither do I."

Audley pointed ahead, to the left, without warning. "Over there, Elizabeth—pull in there."

"Over there" was a sudden line of flags-of-all-nations, waving over an assortment of used cars on the edge of the road, and a trio of petrol pumps set back on a forecourt beyond them, all of which had appeared from behind a small wood suddenly.

Elizabeth slowed automatically, on command, and steered towards the pumps. There was an ugly little kiosk behind them, and a ramshackle scatter of garage buildings beyond, with a combine harvester outside them as its main customer.

"Stop," ordered Audley.

Elizabeth glanced at her petrol gauge, and hated him. The needle was on low, and she ought to have thought of that herself.

"*Stop*, I said," snapped Audley, before they reached the pumps.

Elizabeth jammed her foot on the brake.

Audley sat there beside her silently, like an overpowering dummy, while a fat red-faced bald-headed man in greasy blue overalls stepped out of the garage door, wiping his hands on an oily rag, and stared at them questioningly for a moment. And then disappeared back inside the garage.

"Perhaps you're right," said Audley finally. "Perhaps I did miss something. Or anyway . . . if we have to make pictures, it's better to make bad pictures than good ones. I agree with that."

A knot of anger twisted inside Elizabeth. "Making pictures" was common departmental shorthand for footling hypotheses. But her picture of the Major on his back among strangers was no hypothesis. "I wasn't aware that I was making any pictures." She controlled her anger. "I was simply asking a question."

"Huh! This whole operation could be a picture." Audley tossed his head. "Just to show me making a whopping mistake back in '58. So now we're seeing the modern details drawn in, for good measure." He turned towards her. "A bit more colour here and there, and it'll be ready for the framer. And then Master Latimer can hang it behind his desk—and me with it."

She stared back at him. "Are you telling me that Major Turnbull could have been killed just to discredit you, David? And Major Parker before him? And Debrecen—?"

"If it was disinformation once, it could be disinformation again?" he completed her question. "That's certainly not beyond the bounds of ingenuity. There's a man on the other side, an old acquaintance of mine, who is undoubtedly capable of it. And if I was in his shoes I know exactly what I'd be doing next, Elizabeth." He smiled his ugliest death's-head smile at her. "But that can wait. Because the question is— what are *you* going to do next, love? After you've reported in?"

Elizabeth glanced towards the garage buildings. There would be a phone there, so she could report in easily enough, and get all the protection in the world, and all the good advice too. But none of that really answered his question.

The fat man came out of his doors again to stare at her once more.

"Would you rather have someone else alongside you, Elizabeth?" asked Audley gently. "You can send me packing quite easily, you know."

She watched the fat man. In a moment or two he would come across and ask her what her trouble was. And she couldn't begin to tell him. "Did you make a mistake, David —back in 1958?"

The fat man turned his head slightly, his eyes still on her, and spoke to someone inside the garage.

"Not so far as I know." He paused as the fat man disappeared again into the garage. "I suppose you could say Major Turnbull could be an end-product of someone's original error ... whatever that was. But after so many years I think it would be a little unfair to suggest as much. It's still 1984 which has killed Major Turnbull, Elizabeth—not 1958. So ... even if I made a mistake in 1958, we must not compound it by making another one now. That is what matters."

"Even if it ruins you, David?"

"Ruins me?" His voice came closer to her. "My dear Elizabeth—you've all got it quite wrong! You—and your Paul, doubtless—and most of all our esteemed Master Latimer, if you think that. The only thing that can ruin me is if I play fast and loose with you now, Elizabeth. What the hell do my antique follies matter? *Now* is what matters."

"We have to know why he died, David."

"Okay! But we already know what he was doing. So all we have to do is back-track along his route, for a start—eh? So we drop everything else, do we?"

The fat man had emerged again, but she turned to Audley as he did so, frowning. "But, David—"

"Exactly right, love! If we back-track, to find out what it was about Mrs Thomas that I missed, all those years ago, then we stop doing what we were planning to do. Is that what you want to do?"

That was it. Killing a field-man in his own country sounded all the alarms, but really solved nothing, because there were others to take his place. All it gained was time, if it drew maximum effort away from what mattered.

"Can I 'elp you, Miss—" The fat man leaned on the car, lowering himself with difficulty, his piggy-eyes travelling up leg and thigh and bosom until they reached her face, and registering inevitable disappointment then "—Miss?" She watched the eyes shift to Audley, uncomprehending as they took in the whole unlikely mixture: the hard-faced elderly gentleman with the plain woman in the sports car, engaged in a heart-to-heart exchange on his forecourt, maybe father-and-daughter, not bird-and-boyfriend as he had expected from the car.

"I'd like some petrol," she said.

"Right." He stood back. "You'll need the pumps for that."

"And a telephone?" Audley leant across her.

"No—" The fat man caught sight of the note in Audley's hand "—yes, there's one round the back, in the office."

Audley looked at her as the fat man walked towards the pumps. "Moment of truth, Miss Loftus."

Moment of truth, thought Elizabeth.

In fact, he had more or less told her to do what she had intended to do this morning. And that, oddly enough, was pretty much what the book said too: *plans should be adhered to unless compromised.* And since no one except David and she herself knew the plan, it could hardly be compromised yet. But it could be the wrong plan, nevertheless.

But the fat man had reached the pumps now.

"Very well, David."

"Very well?" His expression was made up of doubt and curiosity in equal parts.

"We'll go on as planned, to see your contact first. Then I

want to meet the famous Haddock Thomas as soon as possible. And I'll ask James Cable to look after the Major until we get back."

He relaxed. "We'll need transport. Let James look after that, too." He thought for a moment. "Tell him to lay on a plane at South Five, Elizabeth. Flight at six a.m.—Marseilles for Monaco. They'll fix the documentation and cover. You might suggest a little gambling party—the big spender can be me, and you can be my PA. And tell him to arrange a car and a driver—tell him to get Dale on to that." He smiled at her suddenly. "Decisions, decisions! But, for what it's worth, I agree with you, Elizabeth: going on is usually better than turning back."

But who was really making the decisions? she wondered, as she rolled the car forward the last few yards to where the fat man was fretting by his pumps.

After a few miles of his instructions, after they had reached the Salisbury road, and used it for another five miles and then left it for another labyrinth of minor roads, she felt able to draw on her account again.

"You're sure we haven't been followed, David?" She looked into her empty wing-mirror.

He shrugged. "We live in a technological age, my dear. So they may have bugged you somehow. And one day they'll probably have a satellite on your tail, I shouldn't wonder." He massaged his knees again. "But, for the time being, there are reasonable limits we can assume, as to their omniscience." He stretched his massaged legs in turn. "Meaning . . . anyone could have kept a tail on poor Turnbull, after he asked too many questions in Normandy. But they don't have the resources to follow everyone everywhere."

"Why did you abort Debrecen, David?"

"Good question!" He touched his wing-mirror idly, as though the previous question still echoed in his mind. "You know what I did—when old Fred asked me to draw up a list of Debrecen possibles, Elizabeth?"

She had to adjust her imagination, back twenty-six years,

to another David in another time. And she couldn't do it. "No, David?"

"I made a lot of money, actually—you turn right up here, by the church. I spent some at first—some of my own money, too . . . but I made a lot in the end—over there—see?" He pointed. "And ultimately I made a lot for General Franco too, when I rediscovered Spain." He nodded. "Maybe that's stretching it a bit . . . But I always like to think that I paved the way for the second British invasion, since Wellington." He nodded to himself. "Did you know, Elizabeth, that I had an ancestor killed at Salamanca, charging with poor Le Marchant?"

"What on earth are you talking about, David?"

"What?" One knee came up again. "Market research is what I'm talking about, love. I funded a friend of mine—half with Her Majesty's funds, half with my funds, I admit—to find out where the British took their holidays-abroad. And then I sold our research to the holiday-business—through my partner, who was the front-man for the enterprise . . . and he made a fortune too. Which was fair enough, because he did all the real work—he had a diploma in statistics, from Oxford . . . But, what we found out, between us, was where people went for their holidays in '58—places and dates and reasons. Although what *he* found out was in general, and what *I* found out was in particular. Because we quizzed some particular people about their colleagues—the ones I was interested in, but who hadn't filled in our innocent questionnaire. And some of 'em did fill in the forms, but not always correctly, as it turned out when we started cross-checking." He gave her a twisted smile. "It was a damnably weary business, I can tell you. But I got some sort of list in the end—not far now." He pointed. "Another mile or two, you turn right. Then there's a pond and a track among some trees on your left. Down the track, and tuck the car behind the trees—okay?"

He hadn't used the map since they'd left the Salisbury road. So, wherever they were going, he'd been there before, and not just once, thought Elizabeth. "So what happened then?"

"Then the real fun started, my dear. I left my pal to carry on the survey—it was good cover, if we had struck gold, if

165

anyone from the other side came sniffing around, looking for a rat. And by that time we were making honest money, too. I let him buy me out in the end." Audley chuckled suddenly. "All above board—paid Her Majesty back her share, plus interest—so whatever Master Latimer gets me for, it won't be for ancient peculation. But I made a bob or two all the same." He chuckled again. "And if I mentioned the name of our little company you might be surprised. Maybe I should have stayed in the business and told old Fred to find another genius."

"What happened, David?"

"I started to snoop, my dear. Eliminated the impossibles, snooped the possibles until it hurt. Then zeroed in on my short-short list."

"And that was where Dr Thomas came in?"

"More or less."

"And Sir Peter Barrie?"

"Him too." Audley nodded. "I gave him a damn good going-over."

"But you told him you weren't really after him." Elizabeth frowned.

"True." Audley rubbed his knee. "But sometimes I tell lies."

Sometimes? "Even though he'd already resigned from the service?"

"Uh-huh." He pointed ahead. "Your turning—"

"I can see it. Why did you give Sir Peter the treatment, David?"

Audley said nothing for a moment. "He wasn't 'Sir Peter' then."

Elizabeth looked for the pond. "Of course not. He was—a clerk in a shipping office, was it?"

"Yes . . . just a clerk in a shipping office. And I'm afraid that's the point, Elizabeth: he was just a clerk."

"But he was on your list all the same."

"Oh yes! He had been an assistant principal. Only he didn't really fancy the life—the civil service life. And it was a funny sort of period, the first half of the fifties, that life."

Pond—okay! She scanned the woods for their turning.

"How—funny?" There it was: a track between two holly bushes.

"Oh . . . hard to say, exactly—I was never a civil servant. But I'd guess the war had interrupted the pattern. A lot of odd types went in during the war. Some of 'em left at the end of it, but a lot stayed on—maybe over-promoted, too. Different tradition, as well. Like, your old-fashioned civil servant, he'd say 'Here's this piece of paper on my desk. But have we any legal powers to act in this matter? If not—why the devil is it on my desk?' But your war people—they felt that *everything* was the business of government. Different traditions made for a curious atmosphere. Tensions, too . . . And then there was Suez, of course. Stop here, Elizabeth."

The track had curved, so that the metalled road was lost in the trees behind them. Just ahead there were a couple of tiny cottages, hull-down behind their private hedges, over-shadowed by several giant beech trees. It was a very private place.

"I talked to his old boss—Peter Barrie's boss. He reckoned Barrie had let the side down by quitting, when he was lucky to be in the Service: 'I've seen bright young types like him before—the shine wears off 'em' . . . That was the typical over-promoted brigade talking. No wonder Barrie didn't hit it off with him!" Audley showed no sign of moving. Instead he turned towards her. "The truth is, my dear, at that moment Peter Barrie didn't have a friend in the world. And I already had a shrewd idea that it wasn't going to be so easy to dig up dirt on young men who hadn't actually *done* anything wicked. Except take their holidays at the wrong time. But he wasn't in any position to make waves, so I made him a test case, to see just how good I was at tracking—and bullying." He wrinkled his nose with distaste. "I found I was quite good. But I also found I didn't enjoy it much."

"But you cleared him."

"Oh sure! He had a perfect alibi. I mean . . . well, you remember what he said? He impressed half the waiters in Italy —they remembered his girl *and* his generosity, in that order. In fact, it was such a damn good alibi it was suspicious—who ever heard of an innocent man with a perfect alibi? So even though he wasn't really on the list any more—he'd quit the service and he was just a clerk to an egregious Greek—in spite of that I did my damnedest to break that alibi, just for the hell of it. And I checked him back to the cradle, too." The distasteful memory showed again. "But the rest you know: I couldn't break it, but I got on to the Haddock from it."

"And you cleared him, too. Was that another perfect alibi?"

Audley gave her a jaundiced look. "Not quite so perfect, maybe. He'd given out that he was visiting Romanesque churches in Burgundy. But actually he was shacking up with Barrie's girl, first in a hotel in Cannes, and then in a little cottage on the edge of the Vaucluse, at a place named St Servan—" He caught her expression "—St Servan? You know it?"

"How wasn't it perfect?"

"The alibi? St Servan *is* perfect . . . The alibi—" He shrugged slightly "—was an honest philanderer's one . . . or a lover's, let's say."

Elizabeth blinked questioningly at him.

"Ham-hmm . . ." He blinked back at her. "She was an uncommonly attractive young woman, was Delphi Marsh—Delphi *Thomas*. And it was . . . and still is . . . an idyllic spot, St Servan." Another shrug. "The sun, and the wine, and the smell of the wild herbs—lavender, and thyme, and rosemary—hah-hmmm—" He cleared his throat. "Lovers, Elizabeth—*lovers* . . . are not always in the habit of walking abroad, establishing perfect alibis for others to unravel. They often keep themselves to themselves. They—let's say they have other things to do, shall we?" He didn't shrug this time. But the effort of *not* shrugging was somehow mutually embarrassing. "Or . . . or, as I remember them from long ago . . . shall we say instead that Haddock Thomas didn't need to impress the fair Delphi by over-tipping the waiters? He was quite a man."

Elizabeth matched his not-shrugging effort with her not-letting-her-mouth-gape effort. Because what he was saying was itself impressive, and for a wildly different collection of reasons—reasons beyond his simple embarrassment at her pathetic inability to understand how *lovers* behaved among the wild herbs of Provence.

She forced herself to nod wisely. Because David Audley's famous memory of things long-past was nonetheless impressive (even though he'd had time, and reason enough, to refresh it recently).

"Uh-huh." He was glad to be able to press on. "So he couldn't account for his St Servan fortnight as exactly as Barrie could, for his Italian progress—which was more like a royal jaunt in Tudor times, with memories and largesse scattered behind it like confetti—do you see?"

What she saw was that Haddock Thomas—*Dr Caradog Thomas* more recently, and *Squadron Leader Thomas* formerly—must indeed have been impressive, to have been so much more certain of himself than Peter Barrie (or, anyway, more attractive, all those years ago). Because Sir Peter Barrie had been pretty goddamn impressive, and certain, and attractive just this morning.

"Yes, David—" But this time, as she tried to nod wisely again, she saw something else grimacing at her which took all the conviction from her voice.

"You do?" He caught her doubt, and threw it back at her angrily. "Do you? Do you, Elizabeth?"

That only made her more certain: he had already conceded the impossible, that he might have made a mistake—or even mistakes—all those years ago. But he had not yet admitted the slightest possibility that those mistakes had related to Haddock Thomas. Or, for that matter, to Sir Peter Barrie. He had cleared them both once, and innocent they both remained, notwithstanding the Pointe du Hoc and the King's Arms, Fordingwell.

"I see well enough." Her instinct was to hit back. But that would only betray her insight into his obstinate faith in himself. "Thomas's alibi stood up well enough, one way or another. And you found nothing else to suggest he was a Debrecen man —obviously."

"That is . . . correct, Elizabeth." He looked as disappointed as a boxer poised to parry a weak punch, with his own knock-out counter-punch ready, only to have the towel prematurely thrown into the ring.

"Yes." She mustn't smile—she must appear innocently

serious. And she had to get away from Haddock Thomas. "But you investigated other people—other names on the list—?"

"Oh yes. Yes . . ." He studied her speculatively for a long moment. "I worked over maybe two-thirds of the short-list before we consigned Debrecen to oblivion." He watched her narrowly.

"And—?"

He shrugged. "Cleared a couple. More or less."

"Including Sir Peter Barrie?"

"Three, then."

"More or less?"

"Didn't do them any good." He sniffed. "You put a question mark beside a name, and then rub it out. But the erasure still shows."

She began to see why he hadn't liked the job. "And—?"

"Ruined a couple more. More or less."

He had probably ruined Haddock Thomas. Or at least driven him out of the Civil Service, whatever he said to the contrary. But she didn't want to return to Thomas. "How?"

He thought for a moment. "They had two question marks." He looked at her. "Another one I killed. More or less."

Again, she remembered Paul's assessment of Audley plus Debrecen. "Killed, David?"

"Not personally." Audley showed her his hands. "Clean— see?"

There was, as always, a slight ink-stain on one of his fingers; the result (so Paul said) of his religious use of a leaky gold fountain-pen given to him by his wife as her first birthday present to him, years ago.

Audley considered his hands critically for another moment, then bunched them into fists on his lap. "He was the closest thing I had to success, actually. If that's what you'd call success." The fists tightened. "He probably was a traitor. Though whether he ever visited Debrecen is another matter." He looked at her. "I *leaned* on him . . . and he conveniently shot himself." He raised his shoulders slowly and eloquently. "Or maybe the KGB shot him—I was never quite sure. But if they did, it was very expertly done, anyway. *And* I didn't expect it." He gave her a dreadful smile. "Mistake Number One, possibly?"

One untimely death, plus Haddock Thomas's resignation: was that an emerging pattern? "Was that why the operation was aborted?"

"Partly that." He was studying the cottages ahead of them now: *cottages, idyllic, English,* as opposed to *cottage, idyllic, French,* near St Servan-les-Ruines, thought Elizabeth. "Not everyone I was bullying was as friendless as Peter Barrie. Haddock, for example—*he* had friends in several high places, rather surprisingly . . . You see, it wasn't popular, what I was doing —there were accusations of 'witch-hunting' . . . or, in the American vernacular, 'McCarthyism'—the Senator wasn't just history in those days, either."

She had clean forgotten about that. "This was happening in America, too . . . Of course!"

"Of course?" He came back to her quickly. "My dear Elizabeth, that was really the *chief* reason why we aborted . . . That is, apart from the fact that I was fed up—and Fred was worried about Research and Development getting a bad name . . . which was a lot more important than my being thoroughly pissed-off, in the final reckoning."

"It went wrong in America?"

"Wrong? Huh!" he emitted a growling noise. "It depends what you mean by 'wrong'—'Define your terms', I should say: maybe 'wrong' in '58 might mean 'right' in '84—eh?"

Irritation tightened her hands on the steering wheel, so that she suddenly became aware of them. They were no longer sweaty, merely disgustingly sticky. And she herself felt cold now, in the shadow of the trees, and tired and thirsty with it. Whereas he seemed altogether to have forgotten that he had been dying for a cup of tea an hour ago.

"The Yanks had three things going for them that we didn't have." He was lost in his own memory now. "They had the resources. And the man who was running their show was a real professional, much more experienced than I was . . ." He trailed off, memory engulfing him altogether.

Elizabeth dredged her memory. "And he enjoyed his work?"

"That's right." He focused on her. "I told you, didn't I?"

171

"You also said you didn't get on with him."

"An understatement. He disliked and mistrusted the English in general, and me in particular. He only worked with me because he hated traitors even more—he was a good hater. Old Scottish Presbyterian stock, out of Virginia from way back. They were always good haters."

Audley had done his homework on his hostile colleague, typically. "And you returned the compliment?"

"I didn't fancy him as a drinking crony. He didn't drink, anyway." He retreated behind more English understatement. "But more than that, I was a little scared of him, to be truthful."

The thought of Audley scared was itself a little frightening. And the more so because he was also quite notoriously a lover of America and all things American. "Why, David?"

"Huh! I was afraid I might turn up on his private Debrecen hit-list one day, for one thing. But I also didn't like his methods, they were a bit rough for my effete tastes—I suspect he regarded Senator McCarthy as a much misunderstood man. But he was damn smart, all the same."

"So what went wrong?"

"Hmmm . . ." He thought for a moment. "What we thought at the time was that he'd trodden too hard on too many toes —as I was doing—only much worse. And that was part of the truth: that he forced good men and true to gang up against him, because of the damage he was doing."

"And the other part?"

"Other *parts*, my dear . . . The other part we knew about was that when the good men got the dirt on him and he needed friends, we—if I may mix metaphors—we put the boot in. Because I convinced Fred that if he prospered in the CIA we could kiss goodbye to the Special Relationship, what there was left of it." He compressed his lips. "Mistake Number Two, in retrospect?"

Elizabeth waited for the third part of the truth.

Audley drew a slow breath. "What we think *now*—which we came to long afterwards, and much too late—is that *maybe* —just *maybe*—it was the KGB which fabricated the dirt on him . . . which was that he was taking bribes to discredit innocent liberals." Another breath. "Oh, it was all done neatly and painlessly, the way good men do bad deeds: he wasn't able to make a martyr of himself, or anything like that." He cocked a defensive eyebrow at her. "You understand?"

"Mmm ..." What she understood was that he was ashamed, but he wasn't actually going to admit it. "But David—"

"Yes?"

There was no way of putting it except baldly. And she was too tired to put it any other way. "If the KGB framed him ... that means Debrecen was genuine. Surely?"

"Oh no—it means no such thing." He had been ready for the question. "When you fish with a net, you don't just get what you're fishing for—you get all sorts of things. Just because we were fishing for one sort of traitor—a very rare and special sort, which maybe didn't even exist—it doesn't mean that we didn't catch anything else edible, which just happened to be swimming in the wrong place, at the wrong time."

Fish, thought Elizabeth.

And then *Haddock—*

> *Dance for your daddy, my little laddie!*
> *You shall have a Haddie*
> *When the boat comes in!*

Was Haddock one of those other fish, if not a Debrecen man?

"Come on, Elizabeth. Let's go and get some well-earned refreshment." Audley opened the car door before she could open her mouth, and she knew that he would avoid any question she put to him. She could only follow him—as she had been doing ever since their meeting in the foyer of the Xenophon Building. *Damn!*

And—*damn!*—her heels sank through leafmould into mud, threatening to unbalance her, if not to take her shoes off her feet. And—*damn again!*—she had no sensible country shoes in her overnight bag.

"David—" She grabbed the car for support as she tried to extricate herself from the mud "—David—"

He was busy stretching his long legs again and flexing his

shoulders on the other side of the car, free at last of it, just as he had done in the yard at the King's Arms. And then he stopped suddenly, and turned towards her with a new expression on his face, of quite idiotic pleasure, which matched the sun slanting over the cottages behind him rather than the beastliness of everything he had just been telling her.

"By the big holly tree—Holly Cottage," he jerked his head, still smiling foolishly. "Name of Willis—same as the cricketer, okay? I'll join you in a moment."

Her shoes were free, and her feet were still inside them. "Where are you going, David?"

"To have a look at the road." He nodded. "Just to make absolutely sure." He misread her expression. "Don't worry, Elizabeth. I promise you I'd never have brought us here, of all places, if I rated the risk a remote possibility." He shook his head. "Not here, Elizabeth."

What was so special about here—beyond their own safety?

"You take the cases." The smile came back. "I'll just check the road, to make assurance doubly sure—Holly Cottage, name of Willis—okay?"

"You take the cases"? She watched him retrace their route down the track for a few yards. Then he cut off into the trees confidently, as though he knew where he was going; which only confirmed her impression that he had been here before.

But that was David Audley, of course: having been somewhere before, and knowing someone there, was his stock-in-trade, acquired over the years. He had certainly been there before, in the foyer of the Xenophon Building, if not up to Sir Peter Barrie's holy of holies; and there had been that hail-fellow-well-met Egyptian general, who had been so old-world courteous and menacing at the same time—that was the world of David Audley, to the life-and-death of it.

Huh! And *"You take the cases"*—that was Audley too, she thought, as she hauled out the two overnight bags, and tucked her bag under her arm as best she could, and set out towards the holly tree.

At least, they weren't too heavy. And at least the beaten track, away from its verges, was firm enough. All she had to

174

do was avoid the puddles and the scatter of horse-manure along the way.

It was the biggest holly tree she had ever seen: holly was slow-growing—slower-growing than oak, was it? Or was it that people hacked at holly every year, for their Christmas decorations, to cut it back and diffuse its growth?

They had hacked back Debrecen, between them. But it had grown in spite of that—

She caught her heel in another soft patch, as she was gazing up at the topmost branches of the tree, and had to set the bags down in order to extricate herself again. Her shoes were muddy now—her best and newest Italian shoes, foolishly chosen this morning (God! Only this morning!) when she had dressed for London and Oliver St John Latimer, not for a muddy lane in the middle of nowhere and *bloody* David Audley—and now, as she straightened up again, a case in each hand, her handbag —her best Italian handbag, matching her muddy shoes—was trying to slip past her elbow—

The tiny sound caught her in the midst of an ungainly attempt to catch the bag between hip and elbow, and it was just sufficient to divert her attention: the bag escaped her, glancing off her knee to land in a pile of fresh horse-manure.

Elizabeth swore aloud that particular forbidden word which nevertheless described the handbag's fate exactly—and then found herself staring straight into the eyes of the little old man who had been watching her performance through a gap between the tree and the hedge.

For a moment they looked through each other with equal embarrassment. Then the little man peered past her down the lane, towards the Morgan.

Elizabeth put down the cases and rescued her handbag. Florentine leather ought to be equal to English horse-manure, she hoped. Then she looked at the little man again.

"If you sponge it, it should be all right," said the little man politely, in an educated voice at odds with his faded collarless shirt, which had been inexpertly patched in several places, and his old pair of army battledress trousers which were supported by even more ancient braces barred with rust-marks from their metal clips, as though they had supported the trousers of other men of different heights, or trousers of different lengths.

"Thank you." After the other word, her voice sounded incongruously demure in her ears.

He smiled at her. "If it's Mr Harvey you want—Andrew Harvey?—he lives in the other cottage, my dear." He pointed. "But you can leave your cases here, just inside my gate. I'll keep an eye on them, they'll be quite safe. Then Andrew can come and collect them." The blue eyes twinkled. "Mustn't have any more mishaps, eh?"

How old was he? wondered Elizabeth. When it came to the Ages of Man, there were really many more than Shakespeare's seven in these more complex and better-medicated times. Or, anyway, if this old man was a good ten years beyond her own dear old Major Birkenshawe—those parchment-folds of skin at his neck, and the mottling on the back of his hands, gave that away—his voice still had an edge to it, and that brightly twinkling eye was a long way from childishness.

"No—" It wasn't just the distant crashing in the under-growth, away behind her towards the car, which cut her off; it was the sudden look on the little old man's face, which lit up as though the sun had come out.

"Willy!" shouted Audley from behind her.

"Dear boy!" exclaimed the little old man happily.

IX

"DAVID, DEAR BOY!" The little old man ducked down from the gap in the hedge, to reappear behind his white-painted picket-gate on the other side of the tree. "What a pleasant surprise!"

"Don't talk daft, Willy." David's face bore the same foolishly beatific expression as the little man's. "I phoned you just this morning—remember?" He short-cutted across the grass towards them, oblivious of the horse-manure.

"Ah—" The little man flicked a glance at Elizabeth "—ah. But you are early, David. And that is a pleasant surprise, even though I have not had time to kill the fatted calf for you, consequently." He opened the gate, and held out both hands to Audley.

"Yes, I'm sorry." Audley took both the hands, then enfolded the little man in a bear-hug. "There was a slight hitch in our programme . . . so one of our engagements was cancelled."

"Not to worry, dear boy." Once released, the little man turned his attention instantly to Elizabeth again, catching her with her mouth open in astonishment. She had never before seen Audley embrace anyone, even his wife, let alone another man. "Now . . . just let me solve this young lady's problem. Now, my dear—"

"That's no young lady," Audley interrupted him. "Willy—meet Elizabeth Loftus. I told you I wouldn't be alone."

It was the little man's turn to register astonishment; which he did for several seconds, as he took in Elizabeth again—face and hair, Fink dress, muddy shoes and manured handbag. But where he had been smiling at her before, now he was frowning. "Indeed?" he said coldly.

Audley heaved a sigh. "Oh, for Christ's sake, Willy! Elizabeth and I are *colleagues*, and we are *working*—we are not

engaged in some illicit escapade behind Faith's back." Another
sigh. "Good God Almighty!"

Elizabeth watched the little old man's face break up from
hardening disapproval to such embarrassment as made her
instantly sorry for him. And, after all, he had at least done her
the back-handed compliment of assuming the worst; whereas
Audley, judging by his blasphemous reaction, couldn't even
see the funny side of it.

"Mr Willis—" She mustn't smile, and the fact that Audley
regarded the possibility with irritation made that easier "—
I'm sorry—I should have introduced myself straight away."

"Don't be sorry," snapped Audley. "Silly old bugger!"

Poor old Mr Willis struggled to get his face together again.
"Miss—ah—Loftus—*Loftus* . . . Mrs Loftus—?"

"Miss." Audley's brutal tone, coupled with the warmth of
his embrace and the look on his face when he'd got out of the
car, served only to emphasize his regard for the old man.
"Sometime senior scholar at LMH—and First Class Honours.
And a hockey Blue when Oxford beat Cambridge, as well as
everyone else . . . which is more than either of us can say,
when we played our little games." He had got the bit between
his teeth now. "Service rank . . . equivalent to assistant-
secretary in any appropriate ministry. But not my mistress at
the moment. Actually, more like my boss at this moment. So
treat her respectfully, Willy." As he turned to Elizabeth she
saw that this litany, or maybe the incongruity of its last items,
had restored his good humour. "Elizabeth, may I introduce
you to Mr William Willis, Master of Arts from your university,
sometime Commanding Officer of the Prince Regent's South
Downs Fusiliers and latterly of the Intelligence Corps, former
senior Latin master, Immingham School . . . and permanently
—*alas*—my godfather and guardian." He raised his hands
apologetically. "Which is presumably why he was so worried
about my morals and your marital status just now, the silly
old bugger." He turned back to his unfortunate godfather-
guardian. "Good God, Willy—as if I had the time, never mind
the inclination!"

"Miss Loftus." The litany had also given Mr Willis time to
get his act together again. "First—I was never a real 'I' Corps

wallah. And I only commanded a line battalion of infantry very briefly, until they decided I was too infirm of body, if not of purpose—a depleted battalion too—*audiet pugnas vitio parentum, rara iuventus.* And second, I am your colleague's—or your subordinate's—*former* godfather and legal guardian. I relinquished those daunting responsibilities long ago, on the occasions of his confirmation and twenty-first birthday respectively." He almost managed his original smile. "Before that, he was a sore trial to me."

"I can well imagine that, Mr Willis. He's a sore trial to me now."

"Ah . . . yes!" Honesty was allied with recent embarrassment. "You really must forgive me—" He held the gate open for her "—do please come in—let *him* bring the cases . . . which he should have been carrying in the first place, of course."

Elizabeth stepped carefully through the gateway, avoiding the vegetables which had fallen from Mr Willis's basket when Audley had bear-hugged him. "There really is nothing to forgive, Mr Willis."

"Oh, but there is!" He ignored Audley and the fallen potatoes and broad beans equally. "And it is not even as though it is entirely his fault, either. For he did say that he might bring someone—" He directed her along the side of the cottage, under a great cascade of clematis, alongside a bed thick with columbines and wallflowers "—it is I who am at fault."

"Silly old bugger!" repeated Audley, behind them.

"'Silly', unfortunately—'old', inevitably." Mr Willis pointed her past his back-door and his dustbin, towards the garden proper. "'Bugger', I reject. Shall we settle for 'fool'?"

The sitting-out side of the cottage, where thick thatch was lost in more spreading clematis, was ablaze with roses—old cottage roses competing with modern hybrids—round a tiny patio, and a lawn full of daisies to the exclusion of grass.

"Do sit down, Miss Loftus." He indicated a trio of elderly deck-chairs. "To continue my apology—but I see you are admiring my daisies."

It didn't sound like an apology, thought Elizabeth as she

lowered herself cautiously on to the faded canvas. "You have a lot of them, Mr Willis."

"I'm thirsty, Willy," complained Audley.

"A cup of tea, Miss Loftus?" The old man still ignored Audley. "Or . . . at this hour I sometimes treat myself to a glass of hock-and-Seltzer. I find it most refreshing."

Elizabeth smiled at him. "That would do very well, Mr Willis."

"Capital!" He lowered himself into the chair next to her, and then waved at Audley. "Well—don't just stand there, dear boy. Take the cases inside. The hock and the Seltzer is in the refrigerator, and the beer is where it always is. So *chop-chop!*" He bobbed his head at the lawn. "Yes . . . my daisies—they were there when I first came here, and I fought a great war with them, with one of those frightening selective weedkillers. But after a year or two they started to come back. And then one evening I was sitting here, planning another massacre . . . and I thought suddenly how beautiful they were, with their little rayed-sun faces, sacred to the Mother Goddess. So I went and put the weedkiller in the dustbin, and we're all perfectly happy now, living together." He watched her, but he wasn't smiling. "It's my age, you see."

What was he talking about now? She still had her smile pasted on her face, but although it suddenly felt out-of-place she didn't know what to do with it. "Your age?"

"That's right. I thought I heard a car—he did telephone me, and he did say he might have someone with him. And there you were . . . and there he *wasn't* . . . But also I come from a generation which does have difficulty in acclimatizing itself to the fullest implications of the sexual equality revolution. Which is why I jumped to that most unfortunate—indeed, unpardonable—*quite* unpardonable—assumption." He continued not to smile. "Simply, when he said why he was coming, I expected one of his wary young men. You must be acquainted with the type. Perfectly respectful, even respectable. But always looking around, not to say over their shoulders, but noting everything just in case. Which I know, because for a brief space of time at the end of the war, I had something to do with their breed. Or different breeds. I used to divide them into foxes, ferrets and hounds, for convenience's sake: different animal for different job . . . *Is it the hen-house you want raiding?* was what I used to say to myself. *Or something fierce to put down a hole?* Or is it *a hunt*, and the quarry has to be tracked and driven out of a field of kale or a briar-patch?" He studied her for a moment. "But you don't look like any of those, my dear young lady. In fact . . . in fact, if I didn't know better—or worse, perhaps . . . I *really* don't quite know what I'd make of you." The scrutiny continued, like the non-smile. "But no doubt that is part of your stock-in-trade."

Elizabeth became aware that she was still smiling. But there was an undoubted nuance of disapproval in what he had said, though of an entirely different sort from that in the look he had given her when he had taken her for the plainest playmate of all time. So perhaps she ought not to be smiling.

But the devil with that! He had served her with misunderstanding, and then good manners and the story of his daisy lawn, and with hock-and-Seltzer to come, only to give him time to study her at leisure. So she owed him nothing yet.

"Is that your complete apology? Or is there more?" She worked to improve her smile. "I am a vixen? Or—I don't know the term for a female ferret." He looked a bit like an elderly ferret himself, thin where he had once been wiry, but still sharp enough to catch the unwary. "But with hounds I suppose the word is 'bitch'?"

He sat up, and the canvas stretched dangerously under him. "My dear Miss Loftus!" He blinked at her, pretending embarrassment. And then looked at her sidelong. "Loftus . . . *Loftus* . . . Now, where did I read that name? Unusual name —" He compressed his lips and stared at his daisies. "*Loftus?*"

Audley appeared with a clink of glass and a somewhat disgruntled expression on his face. In turn, he handed them tall, cool glasses, and took one look at the third deck-chair and decided against it, ending up standing, looking down on them as from a great height. Elizabeth formed the impression that, after his initial pleasure in returning to a man whom he loved (and who returned that sentiment with interest), he was no longer quite so sure it had been a good idea.

He settled on her finally. "Well. What have you told him?"

The old man sat back. "Dear boy, she has hardly got a word in edgeways yet."

"I can well believe that." Audley buried his face in his beer.

"Loftus—*of course!*" Mr Willis turned back to her, his hock-and-Seltzer still untasted. "*The Times* obituary column! My favourite reading!" He beamed his delight at her. "When you get to my age you'll be just the same, you know."

"He knows he's still alive if he isn't in it," murmured Audley.

"That's not too far from the truth." Mr Willis nodded happily at Elizabeth. "In your fifties you worry when your contemporaries die. In your sixties and seventies you shake your head sadly, for the way of all flesh. But after that it's a cause for secret congratulation—*I am still here, in spite of everything*, you say to yourself . . . But—*Loftus*—"

"Elizabeth Loftus. Miss Loftus to you, Willy," said Audley.

"No, no—*Captain* Loftus, RN—and with that rare piece of purple ribbon, and that £10 per annum pension for valour —?" It wasn't really a question, because he had read her face. "Fought those German E-boats in the Channel—invalided out, and wrote history books?" His expression amended itself hurriedly. "Two or three years ago . . . he died?"

Three-and-a-half, corrected Elizabeth. Or three million? "He was my father, Mr Willis."

"There now!" He didn't try to disguise his old man's satisfaction with an undiminished memory. "It must be a great comfort to you, Miss Loftus—to have that cross, with its ribbon."

"She gave it to the Navy, Willy," said Audley, almost casually.

Audley knew that score, thought Elizabeth. But he didn't know it from her, because she had never added it up for him. And he wasn't flaunting his knowledge now to let her draw that conclusion, but only to put this difficult old man in his place. All she had to do was to hammer the point home.

"It wasn't my medal, Mr Willis," she said meekly.

"Ah . . ." He nodded, equally meekly. But that was how it always was in the presence of Father's VC: everyone was a push-over in its shadow, somehow. And the fact that she hadn't sold it to the highest bidder—with the fact that she neither wanted to keep it, nor needed to sell it, carefully hidden —was always to her credit. So now she must cash in on that.

"But we're here on business, I'm afraid, Mr Willis. Of which my father would have approved."

"Ah . . ." Something in him hardened unexpectedly. "But . . . you mustn't go on addressing me as 'Mr Willis', my dear. For then I must continue addressing *you* as 'Miss Loftus'." He sipped his hock-and-Seltzer. "I'm only 'Mr Willis' to boys and tradesmen—and then only to my face. Behind my back . . . well, in pre-war days I was always 'Willy'—sometimes even 'Little Willy', rudely." He nodded. "But in the war I became 'Wimpy' for 'J. Wellington Wimpy', because my brother-officers considered me somewhat loquacious. Which, compared with them, I was—since all of them were inarticulate, and some of them never spoke at all, so far as I remember. Except to order drinks from the mess waiters, anyway." He smiled at her again at last. "But David here belongs to the earlier period. So, for convenience's sake, if you joined him . . . then I might perhaps address you less formally? As 'Elizabeth'—greatly daring?"

"Greatly daring?" Audley echoed him derisively. "Huh! You can call her anything you like, just so you stop talking for a moment and start listening, Willy. Because we have some urgent questions for you."

The old man looked up at Audley with a strangely mixed expression on his face, of affectionate distaste. "Dear boy, *I know*—"

"I'm sure you don't—"

"Or I can *guess* well enough, more's the pity, from what you let slip on the telephone." Obstinacy joined the expression. "Knowing what I know about you . . . and about other matters."

"Other matters being Haddock Thomas."

"Other matters being other matters." Mr Willis came back to Elizabeth. "The decline of the nickname is a phenomenon I have observed in recent years. When I was a boy they were common. And in the army every 'White' was 'Chalky', or sometimes 'Blanco', and 'Millers' were almost invariably

'Dusty'. But now it does not seem to be the rule—I wonder why?"

"Haddock Thomas, Willy," said Audley.

"*Doctor* Thomas to you, dear boy. And to me," corrected Mr Willis. "Dr Thomas—yes? Or no, as the case may be?"

"You know him. You were both in that classical association of yours. You were on its committee together."

"That is factually correct. Although he was a grandee, and I was a humble member, far below the salt." The old man's face had changed: now it was blandly innocent. "He's well, I hope? He was younger than me, though grander. But even he must have retired from full-time teaching by now, surely?"

Audley considered his one-time guardian and godfather for a moment, then drank some beer, and then reconsidered him. "You're not going to be difficult, are you, Willy? Elizabeth wouldn't like that."

"I—difficult?" Mr Willis turned his innocence on her. "Why should I be difficult?"

Why indeed? wondered Elizabeth. "We do need to know about Dr Thomas rather badly—" She couldn't call him 'Willy': she couldn't call anyone *Willy* "—Mr Willis."

"Badly? *Rather* badly?" There was a glint of mischief in his eye. "Now, by that do you mean 'urgently'? Or is it a Freudian slip, and you need to know *badly* . . . in order to *do* badly?"

"Willy—"

"No!" The old man silenced Audley with a gesture, without taking his eyes off Elizabeth. "I will tell you a story, Miss Loftus. A little story?"

"So long as it is little," snapped Audley.

"Many years ago, Miss Loftus—more years than I care to number . . . but it was the year our 1st XV swept the board in the schools' rugger, *that* I do recall—many years ago, a ferret came to see me." He cocked his head at her. "A ferret —yes?"

Elizabeth nodded.

Mr Willis nodded back. "A frightened ferret, actually. But perhaps that was because he had a powerful letter of introduction with him, from a foxy type I'd known in the war—a foxy type which had metamorphosed into a hound—a wolfhound. Or a wolf—the leader of the pack, no less!"

"Willy—"

"The ferret wanted to know about a young man of my acquaintance. But at first he didn't show me his letter. Are you with me? So because I didn't trust him I demanded to know why I should give him more than the time of day, and that shortly—"

"It was 1957, Elizabeth," said Audley from above. "Sir Frederick Clinton was sniffing out my private life. Get on with it, Willy, for God's sake!"

"What?" The old man's voice cracked with irritation. "Well —now that you've *altogether* spoilt my story—have you got a letter, *Doctor* David Longsdon Audley?"

"Do I need a letter?" For the first time in Elizabeth's experience there was a note of something less than confidence in Audley's voice. "Don't you trust me?"

"No, I certainly do not, dear boy! I haven't trusted you since you were sixteen years old. I didn't trust you then, and I certainly do not trust you now."

"Why not?" Audley shook his head, almost as though bewildered.

"Why not? Well, if you don't know—?" Mr Willis stared up at him. "I hold you in my affection, and I have the highest regard for your abilities and intelligence, you know that—"

"Why not, Willy?"

"Because your ways are not my ways, and your gods are not my gods. Because we live on different planets. Because I will not make the same mistake as Marcus Aurelius did, David."

"Bugger Marcus Aurelius!" Audley's voice was harsh. "You spilt the beans about me to Fred Clinton's man. And Fred and I come from the same planet."

"But you have not got a letter, David," the old man spoke gently, almost regretfully. "Have you?"

"Who am I supposed to get a letter from? The Queen? Or the Prime Minister—"

"Certainly not *her*." Mr Willis shook his head. "I'm afraid there's no letter you could produce which would induce me to tell you anything I know about a good man . . . except that he *is* a good man . . . in case you are able somehow to twist it to your own purposes." He shook his head again. "You gave me time to think—you shouldn't have done that. But you did. And I have."

Elizabeth stared from one to the other, from the old man, gently regretful but utterly determined, to the big man, utterly nonplussed.

"I think there's something you should know, Mr Willis," she heard herself say.

"My dear young lady, I'm sure there's a lot I should know. But at my age one becomes resigned to the knowledge of one's ignorance."

"Dr Thomas was investigated many years ago," began Elizabeth.

He raised his eyebrows at her. "If that's what you want me to know, my dear, I'm afraid it is old intelligence. I heard that story many years ago. Not from Dr Thomas himself, but from another colleague. But perhaps you have a different version of the story?"

She must discount his gentle manner and his years, which were equally deceptive: he had had time to think, and he had deceived them both—not least probably at the start, by pretending to mistake her status, in order to gain more time in which to study her. But that was a game he could only play once with her. "I have the true story, if that's what you mean. Because Dr Thomas was cleared, Mr Willis. Is your story different from that?"

"I'll bet it is." Audley gazed around casually, at the cottage thatch, at the roses, at the daisy-lawn, and finally at Elizabeth. "He indulges himself with his liberal conscience. His is the generation of Our Gallant Russian Ally and smiling Uncle Joe Stalin, the great anti-fascist. And the heroic International Brigade in Spain before that."

"Dear boy, they *were* heroic—while you were hardly more than a snivelling child." The old man's voice was mild. "And we would both be dead most likely—maybe a year or two later, in some bloodbath somewhere other than Normandy, and less victorious—if our Gallant Allies hadn't fought Jerry all the way to Moscow and back."

186

"Very true, Willy. But they did not fight for *us*, you silly old bugger." Audley's voice had become equally mild, and weary with what must be an endless division of opinions between them, thought Elizabeth. "Nor even did they fight *beside* us, like *my* Gallant American Allies, whom you affect to despise with such hypocritical double-think." He toured the scenery again, and came back to Elizabeth once more. "You see, Elizabeth—as I was saying? *He* indulges his liberal conscience, and his tortured 1930s guilt complexes . . . and *we* hold the sky suspended above him—and for his peace-loving pupils, so that they can enjoy the same luxury—do you see?" He smiled hideously at her. "I should have remembered that. I should have got a letter from somewhere."

This would never do: they would tear themselves to pieces arguing old disagreements, to no possible purpose! So they had to be separated.

She drained her hock-and-Seltzer. "Get me another drink, David."

"A capital notion!" Mr Willis drained his glass, and offered it up for replenishment. "And your own glass, dear boy. And leave us to exchange great lies, and forget our course—eh, Miss Loftus?"

She waited until Audley had gone. "'Elizabeth' will do, Mr Willis."

He studied her again, and she knew that she was being re-measured, just as she had re-measured him. So she must allow for that.

"Let me guess, Mr Willis: your Dr Thomas was driven from the Government service back to teaching by security persecution, although he was pure as virgin snow—would that be close?" She had to hit him hard, he would expect nothing less.

He still measured her, playing for time. "And if it was?"

"It would be partly true, I think. But do you know who vetted him?"

That was news to him, her unspoken name. And it hurt him too, enough to dry up his reply.

"David did as he was told." The tactics of the hockey-field in a fast break-through applied now. "And he cleared him.

And then something else came up. So he was ordered to vet him again. And he obeyed his orders again—he didn't like it, but he did it." She prayed that Audley would take his time, with the hock and the Seltzer and the beer. "And he cleared him again." In other circumstances she would have given him a chance to react, but not now. "And that was in 1958. But now something else has come up—" Time hammered at her back, forcing her to play her highest cards by instinct, against her better judgement "—a man died recently, we think, because of it—" Once played, the cards made their own logic "—and do you know why we came here early—shall I tell you?"

Suddenly he looked older, and much more frail, so that for a moment she had scruples. Then she remembered Major Turnbull's false teeth, and her heart hardened because of that. "Now there's another man dead, Mr Willis. Someone I knew." She didn't know Major Turnbull at all. But Major Turnbull was nonetheless someone she knew—*"Grime has nothing whatsoever to do with coal-mining, Miss Loftus"*, he had said. So she knew him. "Do you know what I am, Mr Willis?"

He stared at her, still struck dumb against his nature. And she knew in that instant that Audley wasn't coming—that he wasn't stupid, so he trusted her just enough to take his time.

"I'm David's letter, Mr Willis, is what I am."

"His . . . letter?" That sparked him, out of his ancient memory of whatever Sir Frederick Clinton's letter-of-power had contained.

"In a way, yes." She mustn't blow it now. "I don't suppose you could tell me what Sir Frederick wrote, that made you change your mind all those years ago?"

He raised his eyebrows again. "Good gracious, no!" He opened his mouth to continue, then closed it tightly on unsaid words.

"No, of course." That must have been strong medicine of Sir Frederick's, she thought—to open his mouth, and then to close it like that. She smiled a hard little unsmiling smile at him deliberately. "He must have had something pretty good on you, though."

"My dear young lady—" He weakened almost comically

"—we all have our little secrets, which we would fain remain secret. Mine is safe, I'm glad to say, since I alone guard it now."

Elizabeth kept her nasty smile in place, and waited patiently.

He looked over his shoulder, shifting himself gingerly. But there was still no sign of Audley. "You said . . . you are David's letter?" He was putting two and two together nicely. "Then —I'm afraid it must be my old eyes, but I can't read what's written on you, my dear."

"No?" When he called her "Elizabeth" she would have won. "You're quite wrong about David, you know, Mr Willis. You shouldn't be worried about what he may do to your good Dr Thomas—he still believes that he made no mistake there." She nodded. "You should be worried *for* David. Because he's a softie, like you."

"He is?" He still wasn't quite convinced. "But you're not?"

Smile. "Since you like stories, Mr Willis—do you remember the one about young Prince Edward at the battle of Crecy?"

He goggled slightly. "He was the one who became the bloodthirsty Black Prince, was he?" He rubbed his chin with an audible rasp, reminding her unbearably of Father, who also hadn't shaved too closely in his old age. But then he pointed at her. "*Schoolmistress*—the car's wrong, and the clothes are wrong—but that's what I would have said, before I knew you better." Then he shook his head apologetically. "I'm sorry— Prince Edward of Crecy, you were saying—?"

Damn the man! "I'm here to win my spurs, Mr Willis. And my designed job is to get both of them—Dr Thomas *and* David. Because someone thinks Dr Thomas may be a traitor. And David . . . because he may have made a mistake, but he won't admit it." She would have liked to have spun it out, but there was a limit to the time Audley could give her. "But I'll settle for Thomas if you give me the chance."

He took only half-a-second to digest that. "How will my giving you Haddock Thomas help David? Always supposing that I can?"

But she was ready for that. "If he admits the possibility that he was wrong, then he's got a chance of turning the tables."

"And supposing he wasn't wrong?" His expression depressed her. "What then, Miss Loftus?"

"Then I shalln't win my spurs, shall I?" They were too far into truth for comfort now. Or was that the truth?

He seemed to sense her doubt. "Or you could just be telling me another story?"

"I could." There was no more time for finesse. "But if I'm not, then your good Dr Thomas has all the time in the world, but your wicked David hasn't. And there are two dead men who have no time at all—and you can ask David about them." She sat up in her deck-chair, feeling the canvas stretch dangerously under her. "David! Where are those drinks you were supposed to be getting? We're dying of thirst out here!"

"Coming!" Audley's voice reached them faintly from inside the cottage.

She challenged the old man with a look. "Well?"

"You're an evil young woman. And I have insufficient experience of evil women." He sat back. "Evil boys—yes ... Housemasters' wives—yes, to my cost ... And their daughters, latterly." He heaved a sigh. "But then, I must suppose that you are your father's daughter—if, as you say, he would have approved of what you are doing ..."

There was no reply to that: what Father might have thought of this was far beyond her imagination.

Clink of glasses—David Audley as the drinks-waiter was equally unimaginable. "Where have you been, David?"

He looked daggers at her, which she hoped were stage-weapons. "I have been carrying your bag up to the spare bedroom, Elizabeth. And, since there is but one spare bedroom, I have been searching for the Willis camp-bed—a relic of forgotten military campaigns, upon which I hope to snatch a few hours' sleep before long." He presented the tray to Mr Willis. "Because we must be up-and-away before dawn, Willy. So I hope you have a reliable alarm-clock."

"No problem, dear boy. Thank you. I shall ask the telephone to wake us all up." The old man looked up at Audley over his glass. "So you have not been altogether open and above-board with me, it would seem?"

"I haven't?" Audley lifted his tankard of beer off the tray, eyed the third deck-chair again, and then sank down on to the flagstones.

"Not that it surprises me." The statement was delivered to Elizabeth. "He was always a strange little boy, you know, Elizabeth. And an even stranger youth—gregarious enough on the surface, but solitary and secretive underneath. It was partly due to his upbringing, of course." He returned his gaze to Audley. "So, at all events, it is *you* who are in trouble, as much as—or perhaps rather than—Haddock Thomas?"

"Me?" Audley raised one shoulder. "Could be. But I look after myself perfectly well. So don't worry about that, Willy."

"Ah . . . now you must do better than that, if I am to help you. For Elizabeth here—she has been most persuasive. But not quite persuasive enough."

"Indeed?" Audley's face was set obstinately.

"Be reasonable, dear boy. Why should one superannuated pedagogue wish to spill the beans about another? Such an action requires the courtesy of an adequate explanation. You believed Haddock to be loyal after vetting twice long ago—correct?"

Audley didn't look at Elizabeth. "Yes."

"And you believe him to be loyal still?"

"Yes."

"In spite of evidence to the contrary?"

"There is no evidence to the contrary."

"But there have been . . . occurrences?"

Audley said nothing.

"What makes you so sure of Haddock?" The old man accepted his brief as devil's advocate.

Audley's lip twisted. "What makes *you* so sure of him, Willy —that we have to go through this rigmarole?"

"Hmm . . ." The old man gave Audley a flash of loving approval, which he extinguished instantly when he remembered Elizabeth. "So we both confide unshakably in our judgements—yours from long ago, mine of a somewhat newer vintage. So why should we fear? *Magna est veritas et praevalebit,* dear boy—*and Truth shall bear away the victory?*"

Audley sniffed. "If you believe that, then don't fight on my side, Willy." But then he shifted his position, bringing up his knees in front of him and clasping his arms across them in a quaintly youthful way which was quite uncharacteristic, but which Elizabeth found oddly touching. For this was how he might have faced the old man forty years ago or more. "My world isn't like that, Willy dear, you silly old bugger. And your world wasn't like that either, come to that . . . Besides which, the received wisdom in this case is that once upon a time I made a bad mistake somewhere down the line—do you understand?"

Mr Willis nodded. "We all do, dear boy—we all do." He didn't look at Elizabeth. "But you didn't make it with the Haddock—agreed?"

"Right. And nor did I make it with Sir Peter Barrie, who is the other candidate here." Audley flicked a glance at Elizabeth.

"Sir Peter—?" Mr Willis perked up.

"Doesn't matter." Audley shook his head. "The point is that I have the distinct feeling that I did make a mistake somewhere. I didn't think so at first, but now . . . now we've lost a man. And that makes it a First Division match, Willy, I'm afraid. Because the other side wouldn't have played so rough without damn good reason—" He frowned "—although I've been uneasy from the start, to be honest."

"Why?" The old man caught the frown.

"The original vetting wasn't just routine." Audley shook his head. "I can't tell you about that, Willy—sorry . . ." Another shake. "But the Other Side must have known how we'd react—how we couldn't let it go. Not after other things, just recently."

"'The Other Side' meaning the fellows with snow on their boots and red stars on their caps?" inquired Mr Willis gently. "The same chaps we ran up against at Balaclava and down the Valley of Death, when they were under different management?"

Audley's face screwed up. "Uh-huh. And I also can't help feeling that they must have known damn well that it would be me who would be sent down the Valley again. Because I was there last time. And they know about me, you see. They've even got a man over there who's an expert on me, who knows all my little secrets."

Elizabeth switched back to Mr Willis just in time to catch a curious flicker pass across his face. "*All* your little secrets, dear boy?"

"All except the ones you know, Willy, anyway—about me being a sullen and solitary youth, and putting my hand up Mrs Clarke's niece's skirt in the old barn, on those occasions when I wasn't being solitary." Audley rested his chin on his knees.

The old man waved a mottled hand irritably. "Don't be flippant, David. What do you *mean*?"

"What indeed!" Audley raised his head. "What I *mean* is . . . whether I was right or wrong about Haddock Thomas and Sir Peter Barrie back in '58, there is another interpretation of what I did then, which fits an altogether different scenario for it—one which will even do well enough if I was right, but much, much better if I just happened to be wrong." He raised his chin arrogantly. "Which I wasn't, as it happens. But who's to say that now, when old Fred's dead, and Brigadier Stocker—and my old tutor at Cambridge—among others? Because if Haddock is a traitor, then why not David Audley too?"

Old Mr Willis's jaw dropped slightly. "But that's daft, David."

Audley shrugged. "There's a man back in our office—a 'grandee', you would call him, Willy—a bloody basket-hanger I'd call him—who's gunning for me. But he doesn't matter, I can take him any day, with one hand tied behind my back and one foot stuck in a bucket. But if the KGB is setting me up now—if they're *siccing* me on like a hunting dog on to a motorway, after a real fox or an imaginary one—then *that* could be tricky."

Good God! thought Elizabeth: *This was something which not even Paul himself had thought of—although David himself had pointed at it already, when he'd said "If it was disinformation once, it can be disinformation again . . . There's a man on the other side . . . if I was in his shoes I know exactly what I'd be doing!"*

"I see." The old man eased himself forward, first to the edge of the deck-chair, then up and out of it. "Let me get you something, then."

193

Audley fumbled around for his glass. "That's very civil of you—"

"Not that!" Mr Willis shook his head at Elizabeth. "Carrying bags and looking for camp-beds, indeed! More likely, he's already had more than his fair share, surreptitiously . . ." He shuffled towards the cottage, still shaking his head.

Audley's eyes fixed on her over his beer as he drank. "And just what did you say to him . . . other than what he let slip?"

He didn't sound at all grateful, thought Elizabeth. "I asked him what was in Sir Frederick's letter."

"Huh! Old Fred must have had something juicy on him, to make him swallow his liberal conscience." He gazed up at the thatched roof, on which a flight of house-sparrows was dog-fighting noisily. "They first met during the retreat to Dunkirk, in which Willy's battalion was massacred and Fred acquired a mysterious DSO. And they never quite lost touch after that. In fact, I suspect Willy did a job or two for him later on. But he's never talked about it." His eyes came back to her. "And I'll bet he didn't tell you a damn thing, either."

"He said he had a little secret, actually."

"He did?" He watched the birds again. "I'll bet it wasn't so little! But when you've got a man's secret, you've got the man himself. 'If I told thee all was betrayed, what wouldst thou do?'—he knows his Kipling, does our Willy: he read me that when I was a boy. And now someone seems to be trying to tell me that, in a way . . . The only trouble being, I don't know what this particular secret of mine is." Once more he came back to her. "What else did he say?"

"He said his secret was safe now."

"Mmm . . ." He nodded. "It would be now that Fred's dead. Because Fred kept all his promises, right to the end. Lucky Willy!"

"And lucky David." The voice came from behind them: the old man had returned noiselessly. "Why lucky Willy, pray?"

Audley waited until the old man had seated himself. "Your little secret—your little sin . . . or your little *mistake*, anyway . . . it died with old Fred, presumably? Or did you miss that obituary?"

"No, dear boy. But it didn't say much about him, did it?"

"No." Audley shook his head. "But then it couldn't, could it? It could hardly say how he burnt the midnight oil all those years so that you could indulge your liberal conscience in safety, could it?" Audley paused. "Why 'lucky David'? I don't feel so lucky at the moment."

"Oh, but you are, dear boy, you are!" The old man searched for his glass on the flagstones, and then sipped from it. "Lucky in love—to have such a beautiful and understanding wife, and intelligent to boot . . . and a daughter who takes after her mother, not her father." He set down the glass carefully. "Lucky to be a round peg in a round hole—or whatever shape it is, it is your shape, at all events." He looked at Elizabeth. "Lucky in this instance too, to have so loyal and persuasive a colleague—undeservedly lucky there indeed, as in those other regards." He smiled at Elizabeth. "And he was lucky in war, also. For I vividly recall—all too vividly still!—having occasion to trace the route of his armoured regiment across the Norman *bocage*, shortly after its passage therein . . . Purely by chance, you understand, Elizabeth. For I had other fish to fry . . . But it was not difficult—it was well-marked with burnt-out tanks and the fresh graves of their occupants. So many, in fact, that I gave up stopping to check identities after a while, where there were identities, as the odds on finding his name shortened. For I wasn't so sure that he was so lucky then, you see." He switched to Audley suddenly. "Forty years to the day now, that would be, almost—eh, dear boy!"

And the Pointe du Hoc too, give or take a week or two, thought Elizabeth as she switched also.

Audley's face was a blank mask. "You said you were getting something, Willy. But I don't see anything. And I'm hearing nothing whatsoever of interest."

Mr Willis raised a mottled hand. "Season your impatience! *'Comes the deer to my singing—Comes the deer to my song'*—you remember that Red Indian poem we found, about the hunter lying in wait? You have sung your song, so now I have sung mine, over the telephone just a moment ago. And you are still most undeservedly lucky, because this deer is getting into his Jaguar car not far away—very close, indeed—and coming, because I have asked him to do so . . . And that he is even

195

here, in his little house across the hill, is further proof of your outrageous luck, when he could have been the other side of the country, in his new factory in the Cambridge Science Park. Although, I do admit that I did ask him to stay, after you telephoned me this morning."

"Who, Willy?" Audley interrupted him sharply.

"Wait and see. Meanwhile I shall use these unforgiving minutes to tell you what you don't know about Waltham School." He reached down for his glass, but raised his eyes to Elizabeth as his hand closed on it. "Or perhaps you do, eh?"

The eyes were sharp and bright, belying the rest of the face. "It's a very good school, I believe, Mr Willis."

"That's not the half of it, my dear." He let the hock-and-Seltzer moisten his lips. "Waltham is that rare perfect blend of pretension and common sense: it is that rare public school —or private *independent* school, in the modern jargon—in which any sensible child would like to be a pupil, or any fortunate teacher would like to be a master . . . or even an ancillary hanger-on—" He watched her carefully "—yes?"

If he was testing her then she might as well pass his test. "It does take girls in its sixth form though, doesn't it?"

"Only as an experiment." He twinkled with satisfaction. "But my spies tell me that the experiment is shortly to be abandoned, in any case. Does that please you?" He waited only long enough to accept her nod. "And to what do you attribute Waltham's excellence, eh?"

Enough was enough. "You tell me, Mr Willis. I'm not an educationist."

"Money, Elizabeth, money!" He slapped his knee, delighted with the outrageousness of his answer. "Enlightenment based on hard cash—the wickedly acceptable face of multi-national capitalism is its sure foundation." He challenged Audley in turn with this sudden departure from liberal conscience. "Did you know that, dear boy?"

If Audley knew it, he didn't show it. "I'm not an educationist either, Willy. I'm a heptagonal peg in a heptagonal hole— remember?"

The old man pointed at him. "Immingham is what you are —St Martin's School, Immingham: a very *minor* public school,

196

with much more pretension than common sense ... even though it did get you into Cambridge, David."

"We beat Waltham at rugger. And you taught there, Willy."

Mr Willis pointed at him. "We beat Waltham *because* I coached the 1st XV—and because the headmaster regarded rugby as a form of Christianity. And there is no disgrace in giving one's whole loyalty to a second-rate battalion." He gave Elizabeth an old-fashioned look. "Besides which, I doubt if Waltham would have taken a second-rate classics master, Elizabeth."

Audley had the agonized expression of a man who wanted to say something agreeable, but couldn't quite bring himself to do so.

"But at least those were the days when the classics still mattered, before Oxford and Cambridge had sold their birthright, and the pass with it." Mercifully, the old man was still staring at her. "You know what they used to say about a classical education, my dear?"

It was not the moment to recall her brief career as Fifth Form Latin mistress, acting, temporary, unpaid and only prepared one lesson ahead. "No, Mr Willis."

"Hah! It enables us to look down contemptuously on those who have not shared its advantages. And it also fits us for places of emolument not only in this world, but in that which is to come."

Elizabeth could no longer pretend she wasn't looking at Audley, because he was growling now.

"Take no note of him, Elizabeth," the old man pulled her back to him. "That is an apocryphal rendering of a remark allegedly made in a Good Friday sermon in Oxford Cathedral. And it is no longer true, alas—although it once was . . . except at Waltham School, perhaps. For there the classics still have status, thanks to the tradition established by the Haddock, who was senior classics master there for many years."

Audley had finished grinding his teeth. "You were talking about money, Willy, I thought?"

"Money *and* the classics, dear boy." Mr Willis was unabashed. "And eventually the Haddock."

Waltham was rich, Elizabeth remembered. In fact, it was

an envied by-word in the profession, both for its salaries and for its disdain of fund-raising appeals. "Money, Mr Willis?"

"There is a charitable trust, Elizabeth. The school was founded in the nineteenth century—Victorian buildings grafted on to the late Tudor mansion built with the stones of a Cistercian abbey. Added to in the thirties, rebuilt in the swinging sixties—and recently vastly extended to the design of Europe's most expensive architects' partnership, to win some international award or other. And all thanks—though not publicly—to PAM."

Audley breathed in. "PAM—Lord God!" he murmured. "Of course!"

"Pan-African Minerals," Mr Willis nodded. "Just a few Victorian businessmen, with a little venture capital, who speculated here and there—and elsewhere." Mr Willis cocked an eye at Audley. "Didn't they get into Mexican railways, too? And Malayan tin? And now they're into everything from hotels and holidays to car import franchises? They have certainly learnt to speak Japanese. Because one of Waltham's old boys —old *American* boys—was on General MacArthur's staff, looking the place over before the Korean War. Isn't that so?"

Audley said nothing.

"Well, whatever . . . PAM is huge now, and it has always poured money into the school. Its background hardly matters: what matters is that Waltham hands out scholarships like no other school, although it has always been very secretive about it. Just . . . the awards committee goes walkabout every year, and back come the pupils. Still mostly British . . . including *new* British, black, brown and yellow, incidentally . . . but also from the old African connection, now Nigerian, and Zambian, and Zimbabwian, and all the rest . . . But also Japanese and Hong Kong Chinese—and *Chinese* before long, I'd guess, the way things are going . . . But only first-class material. You can't *buy* into Waltham, no matter who your father is— eh?"

He had stopped because he was aware that they were both staring fixedly at him. And when neither of them spoke he stirred uneasily.

"Yes . . . well, you'll soon find out more, no doubt. I only know about the school—and what I know is fairly out-of-date, too."

"Go on, Willy," said Audley mildly. "This is all quite fascinating to non-educationists—eh, Elizabeth?"

Elizabeth didn't like his non-educational look, which was as though to rebuke her for not knowing any of this before, except that Waltham had seduced her scholarship girls into its sixth form.

But now Willy was getting the message too. "Otherwise it's a normal school." He shrugged too late. "The pupils are uniformed—not in wing-collars of course, just jacket-and-tie. Uniform is only to keep the parents happy. In Britain good schools have uniform—go to France or Germany, and it doesn't matter, but people expect it here. And out of class they wear their own kit—that was a Haddock-innovation."

He fell silent again, but they waited him out again.

"Academically . . . when I said 'first-class', I didn't quite mean that. The aim is to get the boys into good universities, but not just Oxbridge. It isn't a crammer's school, where the bright ones sit like cuckoos, with their mouths open, waiting to be fed. God knows, I've felt like a thrush sometimes, trying to fill the greedy little buggers!" He shook his head. "Waltham is said to go for character—the emphasis is on learning how to learn, and they pick for that ability." He stopped abruptly, staring from one to the other of them. "And, talking of cuckoos, I wish you wouldn't both sit there with your mouths open. Disagree—or agree . . . Or say you believe in comprehensive education, and I'm an elitist-fascist—or knock over a glass, or something."

Elizabeth looked at Audley, but didn't really need to: if Debrecen had ever been a place in which talent was processed early, then what about the actual talent-spotting, earlier than that? If Haddock Thomas had been a Debrecen-graduate, what better job could he have than talent-spotting? And in what better place than Waltham School? If the old Jesuit boast —*catch 'em young*—had any force—

"But we *are* cuckoos, Willy," said Audley smoothly. "So feed us some more worms, there's a good chap."

"Worms? Can of worms, more like!" Mr Willis looked around. "Where is the dratted man?"

"Worms, Willy." Audley pointed at his open mouth.

"Dear boy—" The old man's voice belied his words "—what else do you want? Religion?. Oddly enough, it's quite strong at Waltham in a real sense, because those who take part in it do so voluntarily. The school has a chaplain, but the Master isn't in orders. As a matter of fact, I believe he's a linguist with a Liverpool degree, if it's still the same man I met once. But the staff's very varied, at all events—and very well paid. And the selection process matches the pay. There was a joke, a few years back, about Waltham staff recruitment, in some educational magazine—or it may even have been in the *Times Ed Supp*—to the effect that, if you were short-listed, but didn't quite make it, you could always get a university fellowship or a job piloting the next American Moon-landing, as a consolation prize."

"And Haddock would have a hand in that, I take it?"

"Oh yes—Second Master at Waltham was never a bottle-washer's job, so the Master could go off junketing. The Master always led the school from the front—the Liverpool man was highly visible in the life of the place. And there was a *Third* Master who handled the time-table and the donkey-work. Second Master was big time—I told you the Haddock was a grandee. In fact, he was really *de facto* chairman of the staff selection board and the scholarship panel, and took it in turns with the Master to go trawling in foreign parts dear to PAM, and keeping up University contacts. Sort of foreign secretary to the Master's prime minister, you could say—" The old man caught himself in the mid-flow of his eloquence as he happened to glance from Audley to Elizabeth "—*hmmm!*"

"Go on, Willy." Audley had more successfully assumed an expression of guileless interest.

"Worms, did you say?" Mr Willis fixed his gaze on her. "And I said cuckoos. But snakes is what I'm thinking now! Or wolves—wolves pulling down old bulls for sport, maybe."

Elizabeth cursed her inexperience. "Nobody's pulling anyone down for sport, Mr Willis. I told you the way things were—and how they are. We are not concerned to establish anything other than the truth."

"The truth? Only the truth?" He dropped her almost contemptuously. "What I do not understand, David, is why you are wasting your time on Haddock, believing as you do. Could you not be better employed?"

"I could indeed, Willy," agreed Audley. "I have much better things to do—much better, and probably more pressing, and certainly more important things. From which I have been untimely ripp'd, Willy. However . . . as I was at pains to explain in words of one syllable . . . I think I am being set up, one way or another. And I think the basis for that setting-up *may* be some error I once made—not in regard to the snow-white Haddock—or in regard to his former friend. But I'm certainly not going to wait around for the trap to close. And Haddock is the only clue I've got at the moment."

"But he's no traitor, dear boy—not in a thousand years!"

"So he's been set up too, then." Audley's voice lifted defiantly. "And so clearing him—*clearing him for the third time, Willy* —could be reckoned as much my job now as it ever was, as well as saving my own valuable skin. Remember those rules you made? Bloody impossible rules—when I saw you after old Fred had recruited me in '57—remember?"

What rules? wondered Elizabeth, altogether frozen out of the exchange. And, when it came to the crunch, David Audley was a notorious rule-breaker.

But now there came another crunch, of tyres on the track on the other side of the privet hedge, accompanied by the opulent engine-noise of a much larger car than hers.

Audley stood up. "A Jaguar, Willy. Is this deer coming to your singing?"

"Ah!" The old man eased himself out of his deck-chair. "He took his time, but he is here at last." He peered over the hedge, but then looked down at Elizabeth suddenly, smiling his old-ferrety-smile. "A character-witness, I think you might call him. But then, if a man is innocent . . . A very tricky thing, innocence. Guilt is much more easily provable."

She watched him round the side of the cottage, and then turned to Audley. "I'm sorry, David."

"Sorry?" He wasn't listening to her.

"Haddock Thomas may be innocent. But he fits the De-brecen specification just as well at Waltham School as in the

Civil Service. Maybe even better." She mistrusted them both —the godson and the godfather. "Much more ingeniously, anyway."

"Yes." He was listening to her now. "Yes, he does."

It wasn't the answer she was expecting—so much so that it shut her mouth.

"Yes." When he smiled this dangerously sweet smile of his, he wasn't ugly. "You've done well, Elizabeth. I certainly wouldn't like to be caught between two such dreadful old men! But you did well."

"I did?" She hated the way he seemed able to read her, too.

"But you're quite wrong." The smile vanished. "The monsters on the Other Side are smart. But they're not that smart." He shook his head. "I made no mistake about Haddock Thomas and Peter Barrie. Not then and not now—may I swing for it if I'm wrong!"

Someone was coming. "So long as I don't swing with you, David." She observed him look past her, his face rearranging itself into its more usual expression of brutal neutrality.

The newcomer was a tall bespectacled young man, with fair hair and a ruddy complexion ravaged by acne. He took in Audley with a single glance, then his eyes focused on her legs for an instant before travelling inexorably upwards towards disappointment. It was a progression she had encountered many times before, to which she knew she ought to be inured.

"My dear Gavin—let me introduce you—" Mr Willis managed an extraordinary octogenarian skip round the young man "—Miss Elizabeth Loftus, daughter—*only* daughter, if my memory serves me right—of the late Captain Loftus VC, the distinguished naval historian."

"Miss Loftus." The young man hastened too late, as they all did, to take her hand. To cover up that disappointment he would treat her sympathetically, if he ran to form.

"Mr Gavin."

"Thatcher, actually, Miss Loftus—Gavin Thatcher." The ruined cheeks creased into a shy grin.

"But no relation to our other Sovereign Lady," said the old man. "That splendid woman!"

"Wimpy—you're a trouble-maker." The young man looked at Audley. "And you're the godson, sir? He's told me about you."

"Oh, yes?" Audley pretended to know an ally when he saw one as he extended his hand. "And you're from the Cambridge Science Park?"

"Watch yourself, Gavin!" snapped Mr Willis. "He's tricky."

Elizabeth stirred herself to intervene while she was still in credit. "Mr Thatcher—"

"*Doctor* Thatcher," Mr Willis corrected her. "And she's tricky too, Gavin. The female of the species, in fact."

For a moment the young man didn't know what to say, but could only blink at her. "Is that your car out there, Miss Loftus? The green Morgan?" He touched Audley with another look, but rejected him on the grounds of age and size. "How long did you have to wait for it?"

"I bought it second-hand." What was he after?

He frowned. "This year's model—the registration?"

"I bought it from an American serviceman, Dr Thatcher."

"With a right-hand drive?"

He was damnably observant, for a very young Jaguar driver. "He was posted unexpectedly to a place where there are no cars—left or right." She smiled at him. "I was lucky." She didn't want to antagonize him, but the old man had left her little to lose. "Were you one of Dr Thomas's pupils, Dr Gavin?"

Mr Willis sighed theatrically, and then circled round them to pick up the tray on which Audley had brought the drinks. "Hock or beer, Gavin?"

"Nothing, thank you." Dr Thatcher stared at her. "Why do you want to know, Miss Loftus?"

Mr Willis straightened up. "Gavin was the top classical scholar of his year. And a double-first thereafter . . . Compared with him you are an historical *plumber*, David—a hewer-of-wood and drawer-of-water, intellectually speaking. His involvement with the so-called high technology of the computer age stems purely from the Haddock's advice, allied to his latent skills. It seems that some classicists are quite surprisingly competent in computer skills—rather the same way some mathematicians are allegedly musical, if you scratch them

sufficiently. Is that not all common knowledge in high places?"
He looked questioningly at Audley.

Gavin Thatcher shook his head. "That's rubbish, of course,
Dr Audley."

"Rubbish that the Haddock didn't steer you to Business
School after Cambridge?" Mr Willis's voice was almost old-
maidish. "Rubbish that he didn't then tell you about—who's
that young fellow you introduced me to, your partner-in-crime
—? The ex-IBM Old Walthamite who had the idea for those
esoteric devices you are presently selling to the Americans?"

Gavin Thatcher shook his head again. "Who exactly do you
work for, Dr Audley? May one ask?"

"Does it matter?" Audley jerked his head towards the old
man. "If we're vouched for, does it matter?"

That wasn't the way to handle the top classical scholar of
his year, decided Elizabeth. "We work for the Government,
Dr Thatcher. In an indirect sort of way, which we can't
explain. But we're also working for you. And I hope we're
working for Dr Thomas most of all, as it happens." She risked
a glance at Mr Willis. "True, Mr Willis?"

"Good God, young woman—don't ask me!" Put on the
spot, Mr Willis squirmed uncomfortably. "I'm just a silly old
bugger!"

"Oh?" It wasn't what she'd hoped for. But she still had
something in the bank with this young man. "But you summoned Dr Thatcher to talk to us—about Dr Thomas, surely?"
She looked at the young man.

"Somewhat equivocally, Miss Loftus. If not mysteriously."
Because she was plain he didn't want to be cruel to her. "I
was planning to return to Cambridge this evening. But he
insisted that I must delay my departure, because of an urgent
matter involving Dr Thomas. What do you want to know?"

"Dr Thomas was the Second Master?" What did she want
to know, that he could tell her?

"Yes." Doubt began to overlay his surrender.

"I've never met him, you see." She must not give him time
to think. "What's he like?"

"Like?" He seemed momentarily astonished at her ignorance, to the extent that he flicked a glance at Mr Willis. "Well

... tall, thin, eloquent and short-sighted—you mean, what's he *like*—?"

"He played rugger rather well when he was young," murmured Mr Willis.

"Not in my time. He just taught the theory of the game."

"And the classics," murmured Audley, in a tone matching Mr Willis's.

"Yes—" Gavin Thatcher could sell his esoteric devices to the Americans, but he couldn't play Audley and Mr Willis and Miss Loftus simultaneously.

"Yes?" Elizabeth gave him the rest of her capital. "Greek and Latin? Tell me about that."

"Yes." He relaxed perceptibly: whatever doubts he still had, he couldn't relate them to Virgil's verse or Caesar's prose. "'*Gallia est omnis divisa in partes tres*'—or '*Hell! said the duchess*' —that's as near as damn-it what he said, in his first lesson, on my second day at Waltham. And he said all the best Latin was exact, and compact, and elegant, and Caesar's was as good as any, so we'd begin with him. And all we had to remember was that the Gallic Wars were like Cowboys and Indians—'How the West was won'."

He stopped, and Elizabeth hoped against hope that neither Audley nor Mr Willis, who both liked to hear the sound of their own voices, would say anything.

They didn't say anything.

Gavin Thatcher drew a deep breath. "I remember . . . '*Thus with the years seasons return, but not to me returns day or the sweet approach of ev'n or morn*'—with the emphasis on *day* . . . and '*Me only cruel immortality preserves*'—emphasis on *me only*, because the order of words is one of the glories of Latin verse, of course. Although Latin isn't in the same class as Greek."

Elizabeth didn't dare look at either of them: Gavin Thatcher was already out of her class, in that other world of gold, at which lesser mortals might just guess, but in which they could never travel.

"I remember quoting Catullus at him—'*Multas per gentes et multa per aequora vectus advenio*'—which we hadn't been told to read . . . And he gave me hell after that: he damn well concentrated on me!"

He wasn't trying to be arrogant, Elizabeth cautioned herself: he was only treating them as equals, after Mr Willis had dismissed Audley as a mere *historical plumber*—and David in his time had been a scholar!

This time there was no danger of them speaking.

"In Greek we read Xenophon—*'The Sea! The Sea!'*—and the Gospel according to St Mark, and the *Odyssey*. Greek was the real thing, of course—the big thing. Not just the language, which is more fun than Latin—more intricate—but the ideas, do you see?" He paused.

"The Gospel according to Haddock," Audley whispered to himself.

"The Gospel according to anyone worth his salt," murmured Mr Willis. "All the rest of history is a postscript, a mere postscript." He smiled at Audley. "You were wasting your time, dear boy. I told you so all those years ago, but you wouldn't listen." Then he sighed. "But the greatest wonder of all, to me, was that they actually paid me for teaching this glorious stuff!"

She didn't want them arguing again. "He taught you philosophy?"

"Not as such." Gavin Thatcher shook his head. "But that was pretty much what it was all about, somehow. The languages were ends in themselves, but also means to greater ends. Or *an* end—γνῶθι σεαυτόν—*know thyself*. 'Make what you can of that', Haddock used to say. 'Some people have learned a great deal from it.'" He frowned at her, suddenly embarrassed again. "Is this really what you want? What else do you want me to tell you?"

"What else did Haddock tell you?"

"Well . . ." The frown cleared ". . . he told me to join the school choir, for one thing."

"He's a Christian then?" Somehow it surprised her.

"No. Not really, I don't think—"

"He's a Welshman. Or his parents were Welsh." Mr Willis gestured vaguely. "The Welsh are forever singing. They don't seem able not to."

"They're forever playing rugger too," said Audley.

"He said the ways of God were far too strange for him, as

206

a matter of fact." Gavin Thatcher ignored him. "He always said he would have expected the Messiah to have started from —and improved on—*The Nicomachean Ethics*. And then, why didn't He ensure that His teaching was written down straight-away in Greek—or Latin—so the whole civilized world could understand it, instead of in Aramaic, or Syriac, or whatever? Which was like trying to spread the Good News in Cornish." He grinned at her. "But he never said any of that in front of the Chaplain. He liked Old Tank—we all did." He looked at his watch quickly, and then at Mr Willis. "I really do have to be going, Wimpy. I'm supposed to be seeing a chap in Cambridge after dinner, about some more venture-money. And it's a hell of a drive from here." He smiled apologetically at Elizabeth. "And I don't think I've been much help, either."

"He steered you into business, did he?" asked Audley. "He kept in touch, after you left the school?"

"That's par for the Waltham course, dear boy," said Mr Willis. "They have a good after-sales maintenance service for their products."

"The Master advised me, actually, Dr Audley. But Haddock opened a few doors for me." Gavin Thatcher bent down to put his glass on the tray. "And he did once give me one bit of priceless business advice."

"And what was that?"

The young man stared at Audley. "It was the last time I saw him while I was still at school, before I went up to Cambridge. He said that in my first term there would be the Freshers' Match in which rugby-playing newcomers would have a chance to show their ability."

Audley nodded. "I remember. Yes?"

"He said I was to forget what he'd taught me. On that occasion only I was to play for myself, and not for the team." He looked at Elizabeth. "The purpose of the Freshers' Match isn't victory for one side, or even a good game, you see, Miss Loftus. It's selection. And I was a wing-three-quarter then—do you know about games, Miss Loftus?"

"Gavin, dear boy—" Old Mr Willis levered himself to his feet again "—she has a hockey Blue, from a year in which her dark blue trounced your light blue."

"I beg your pardon, Miss Loftus." Only his complexion saved him from blushing. "Then you'll know that no one passes to the wing in such games, of course." He paused. "So Haddock said I must ask for my old position, as full-back. And then, when I got the ball in the open, I was to run with it. And if I had to kick it, I was to kick ahead, not into touch—and kick so high, and follow up so fast, that when the ball came down I would be there."

"And *that*, Miss Loftus, is the secret of making your first million before you attain your thirty-first year," said Mr Willis. "Right, Gavin?"

"You are an old *bastard*, Wimpy!" Gavin Thatcher's eyes ranged from Elizabeth to Audley and back. "Dr Audley—Miss Loftus—"

"'Silly old bugger' is the majority view. But come on, then—" the old man shepherded the younger one "—you must not drive too fast in that big car of yours, and kill yourself. Why do you not have a car like Elizabeth's? Or is it status? Will you have a Rolls-Royce next time?"

Elizabeth knew only that the young man was going, when she didn't want him to go. And the thought pushed her further than she would have gone if she had had more time. "You loved him, Dr Thatcher—Haddock?"

"Loved him?" The outrageous idea arrested him as he was ducking under the cascade of clematis at the corner of the cottage. "I was *terrified* of him half the time—and I hated him the other half. You just wait and see for yourself—" Whatever other truth he had to impart was lost as Mr Willis pushed him from behind, muttering almost incomprehensibly as he did so.

"'Loved him'! Stuff and nonsense!" The old man disappeared too.

Audley was looking down at her, almost sympathetically. "Well, Elizabeth?"

"Well—*what?*"

"Well, you're quite right: hate is akin to love. And you've now had Peter Barrie, and Willy . . . and that far-too-bright young devil, sucking his high-tech silver spoon, on Haddock Thomas—or *the* Haddock, as Willy insists on rendering him. So what have you got?"

"And I have you, also. But I have only the ones you wanted me to have, David."

"True—very true. But then you've got the man who vetted him in '58—vetted him *twice*. And you've got an ex-friend, who lost his girl to him. And you've had a colleague, and newer friend, neither of whom has nothing to gain or lose—one of whom cares more for me than him, whatever he may say . . . but who is not about to compromise his principles for me. Which is more than I can say for myself." He drew in a breath. "Because if I thought Haddock Thomas had screwed me back in '58, then I'd be screwing him now—vengeance plus self-preservation, Elizabeth: that's just about the most potent cocktail you can serve, believe me." He nodded. "To which now you've added an ex-pupil, my dear."

"But Haddock still appeared on the Debrecen List, David." Over the privet hedge the sound of the big Gavin Thatcher car interrupted her.

"If there ever was a Debrecen List." Audley's expression became ugly. "All I got on Haddock was *nothing*. And all you've got on Haddock is nothing, too."

"Including what Major Turnbull didn't give me?" She matched his ugliness with hers. "And Major Parker jumped off the Pointe du Hoc, did he? Nothing plus nothing, is that?" From ugliness to brutality was only a short step. "Or did you miss something?"

"If I did, then it was because he was too clever for me—and so was Peter Barrie. And they'll be much too clever for you now, if it's proof you're after—"

"Proof?" Old Mr Willis brushed past his clematis. "What sort of proof is that? Proof to sway an English jury, than which there is nothing more oblivious to proof? Or proof-*spirit*? In which case we can now drink something stronger than anything you have consumed so far. And I have a casserole in the oven. So are you going or staying now, dear boy?"

"I thought I smelt something in the kitchen. Staying, Willy. But going long before dawn, as I told you." Audley sat down again, rather wearily. "I'm getting too old for this sort of thing. And much too old to be reminded to know myself. It's far too late for that now."

Mr Willis sat down. "You haven't succeeded there yet, then?"

"Good God, no! I look at myself in the shaving-mirror each morning, to check for the tell-tale signs." He shook his head. "But when you see the signs, it's too late."

It worried her to see him like this. "What signs, David?"

He looked at her. "What you should be worrying about, Elizabeth, is what you're going to put in your report to your master, the sainted Oliver, after we have visited St Servan-les-Ruines tomorrow."

"About the sainted Haddock Thomas, whom everybody loves—including you, David?"

"Oh—not sainted, believe me." He shook his head again.

"Certainly not sainted!" Mr Willis echoed him.

"But everyone loves him."

"And he loves everyone." Mr Willis admired his daisies. "The boys—"

"And their mothers. And their sisters." Audley admired Mr Willis's daisies too. "And their aunts. Strictly out of term, of course. He was always careful that way. And his colleagues."

"And their wives." Mr Willis nodded agreement. "And their sisters."

Audley nodded. "Their colleagues' sisters. And the wives' sisters."

Elizabeth remembered the fair Delphi, Haddock Thomas's best friend's girl. "And their fiancées?"

"Them too," agreed Audley. "And you too, tomorrow. All grist to his mill, if it wore a skirt. He had a lot of love in him, as I recall."

"He enjoyed the occasional tipple, too. As *I* recall. And probably still does." The old man smiled reminiscently at his daisies, and then turned the smile to her. "There comes a time, my dear young lady, when one's . . . ah, one's *attraction* . . . to —*to*, not *for* . . . the fair sex declines. But I have never yet been rejected by the cork in a bottle—at least, not now that there are these mechanical openers which require no strength."

"So, you see, Elizabeth—" Audley abandoned the daisies "—*not* a saint, the Haddock."

"Just very careful," agreed Mr Willis. "Not to say *judicious*, in his sinning."

They were playing with her. "And a lover of the Classics, as well as an incomparable teacher. He loved to teach."

"That above all—" The old man turned to Audley "—David?"

"You think so?" Audley considered the proposition seriously for a moment. "I think . . . when I took him to the cleaners, and then hung him out to dry, back in '58 . . . whatever was to his hand at the time, that was what he loved best. He was just a natural-born great lover, I'd say."

"But not a traitor, David." The old man wasn't smiling.

"No evidence, Willy. Not then—so probably not now. But then, with the very good ones . . . the *very good ones*, Willy— not just the clever ones, or the lucky ones—the ones we've missed, because we missed something—or someone has missed something . . . because the very good ones are the ones Elizabeth and I are after . . . with *them*, Willy, evidence doesn't really come into it. With the very good ones, we don't have to say 'yes' or 'no', but just 'maybe'." He had flicked glances between them as he spoke, but now he was back with the old man. "And if 'maybe', then we have to take a closer look at your Gavin, to see just what sort of high-tech contracts—and *contacts*, too—he's into, which the Russians would also like to be into. And then maybe—it's a great word, 'maybe'—we'll just tip the word, so as he won't make his first million before he's thirty-one. Or his tenth million before he's thirty-five. *Maybe*, by the time we've finished with him, he'll go and teach Latin and Greek at Waltham—like Haddock Thomas did, even—?"

"David—" The old man's voice had the beginning of an outraged squeak in it.

"Are you going to make him a 'maybe', Elizabeth?" Audley cut him off. "With your two dead majors, you can hardly do anything else, unless you back your judgement as I did, back in '58. And as everyone now seems agreed that I made a mistake you can hardly do that, can you?"

She knew why he was so weary now; and it was not just

because he was old enough to be her father, and he'd had a hard day, which had included a dreadfully untimely death behind them only a couple of hours ago, which could only be natural against the odds; it was also because of something he'd just said—which was something he'd been saying all along, or hinting at off and on, which she'd never quite been able to grasp.

"What signs, David? In the mirror?" She was weary too: it had been a long day, since Paul had seen his tripod masts in the mists of this morning. But she could see them now, at last. "What signs?"

He nodded at the old man. "He's to blame."

"I am?" The accusation made Mr Willis forget his outrage. "How?"

Audley scowled at him. "'*Wer mit Ungeheuern kampft, mag zusehn, dass er nicht dabei zum Ungeheuer wird*'—don't you remember your 'know thyself' advice, you older *Ungeheuer?*" He switched the scowl to Elizabeth. "Trust him to spout Nietzsche at me, not Plato, or any of his other Greek hoplites! And this was back in '57, after I'd been recalled to the colours on his recommendation—his *bloody* recommendation, too!"

"A most misunderstood philosopher, Nietzsche." The old man's face became bland as he turned to her. "Do you not have the German language then, Elizabeth? And you an historian? I remember David arguing with me that all the best medieval history books were written in French and German, so Greek was really a waste of time, and he could keep up his Latin without taking any more exams."

"The hell with that!" exclaimed Audley. "Do we harry Haddock to an early grave? And do we persecute Peter Barrie, just in case, because he'll do just as well? And do we persecute everyone they've promoted or advanced, to make double sure, because we're not sure? Because that's the self-defence option now—yours and mine, Elizabeth."

What was an *Ungeheuer?* "You know I don't speak German, David."

"Just check your mirror. Or look for the horror that sits grinning on your pillow, in the small hours—it always shows up in the dark, no matter who is there beside you: 'he'—or 'she'—let's say 'we'—'we who fight monsters must take care, lest we become monsters too thereby'." He picked up his glass, and frowned at it because it was empty, and then looked at her. "You'll have to decide for yourself tomorrow, Elizabeth. But, speaking purely personally, I'm *buggered* if I'm going to become a monster—either for the sainted Oliver, or for the KGB."

X

"OVER THERE, ELIZABETH." Audley ignored the taxi-drivers. "The red Fiat—the fellow in the dark glasses."

"David—" But he was already stepping out, oblivious of the puddles.

The roar of an aircraft reversing the thrust of its engines drowned the rest of her appeal, but he turned back to her into the noise as it shrieked and then died away. "What?"

"Where's Richardson?" The sun came out from behind its cloud into a patch of Mediterranean-blue sky, flashing on every reflective surface and sharpening up every shadow with an alien clarity.

"What?" He squinted at her.

"Never mind." She fumbled in her bag for her own dark glasses, more for self-defence than appearance: she had composed herself for this encounter, but she should have known better that there was no armour against reality so far from home. "I'm coming."

He swung away, back on his original course, without a second look at her. And she had composed herself in-adequately for that too—Audley trailing her into the field, which he now plainly wasn't doing, so that her com-posure slipped, with no greater problem than to avoid the puddles.

But at least Audley knew the man, for he was shaking him warmly by the hand as she reached them.

"Miss Loftus—" The man swept the case (which Audley hadn't offered to carry; but she was getting used to that) out of her hand and into the open boot almost without looking at her "—into the back, please."

For a southern Frenchman, almost as swarthy as an Arab, the accent was startling Public School English, unsettling her further.

"You too, David." He looked around the car park quickly. "Let's get the hell out of here."

A nasty humiliating suspicion enveloped her as she did as she was told. "Captain Richardson?" The car slammed her back in her seat.

Richardson, Peter John, Captain (Royal Engineers), retired? She had decoded a dozen SGs from him in the last six months, each about the same unbreakably code-named subject, but all from Northern Italy.

"Richardson is me. But I left the captain behind twelve years ago, Miss Loftus." He swung the wheel. "I answer to 'Peter'."

He might answer to 'Peter', but he drove like a rush-hour Italian, thought Elizabeth. "What happened to Mr Dale—Peter?"

He continued to drive like a maniac, without bothering to answer.

"She said 'What happened to Mr Dale?', Peter," said Audley.

"I heard the first time. You're going to have to be quick this time, David. Otherwise you're going to be in trouble." Not-captain Richardson studied each of his mirrors in turn. "And I don't mind you being in trouble. But I do mind me being in trouble—in France. Because I've still got a clean slate here."

Audley settled back. "Just answer the lady, there's a good fellow. All they told us before take-off was that Dale wouldn't be meeting us and you would. But they didn't tell us why." He drew in a breath. "And the lady is in charge, not me."

"Is that so?" Richardson took a look at her in his mirror. "I'm sorry, Miss Loftus."

"Don't be." She watched Audley's fingers drum on his knee. "What about Mr Dale?"

"I have a message for you, actually. I'm to tell you the Major wasn't a natural event—whatever that means: the Major wasn't a natural event?"

Audley's fingers stopped drumming.

"Thank you." The steadiness of her voice surprised her. "And Mr Dale?"

"Probably safe, back in Paris by now." He looked at the clock. "Most likely asleep in his bed."

Elizabeth closed her eyes for a second. "Why did he leave?"

"He saw someone he knew, but not quite quickly enough. So he didn't reckon to his cover any more. And I just happened to draw the next-shortest straw, unfortunately."

"The French, you mean?" asked Audley quickly. "The DST?"

"Among others." Richardson's voice almost contemptuous. "His face is all too well-known in certain official circles, anyway—like yours, David, if I may say so."

"Ah! The French . . . Stupid of me, I agree, Peter." Audley recovered quickly. "I do rather have this damned blind spot about the French, Elizabeth. I've lived here twice—once when I was a mere boy, on exchange, before the war . . . and once for several very happy and frequently inebriated years later on, after Cambridge, as a tax exile. And, of course, I invaded them in '44—it is a really wonderful country to invade, with all the wine and women. So some of my very best friends are Frenchmen, and I do *rather* take them for granted . . . Which is stupid, Peter, I do agree."

And she had been stupid too, thought Elizabeth: the French had been on to the Pointe du Hoc, and they would surely have traced Major Parker back to St Servan after the Americans and the British had demonstrated their interest in him. And, as she had cause to know from even her limited experience, the DST was jealous of foreign intelligence intrusions.

"Stupid?" Richardson snorted. "Apart from your youthful indiscretions—about which I'm glad to say I know nothing . . . my God, David! You're a three-time loser anywhere. But *here* of all places!"

"Here?" Elizabeth glanced for a second at the dense holiday-traffic on the other side of the autoroute, heading south, and then at the sign pointing them northwards, past Avignon and Orange, to distant Lyons and faraway Paris. "Why here?"

Richardson reached down and threw a map back into her lap. "Don't you do any homework in London? Doesn't the Plateau d'Albion mean anything to you?"

216

She looked at him. "The Plateau—?"

"*Perfide* Albion is us, Miss Loftus," said Richardson. "The *Plateau d'Albion* is where the French have got their IRMBs siloed—plus one or two longer-range missiles now, I shouldn't wonder. Right, David?"

Audley took the map from her. "St Servan's in the sensitive radius?"

"What the hell d'you think? It may not be in the red radius, but it's for damn sure in the pink. And they may not be able to log every tourist who drives along the Nesque gorges, but they'll have logged every foreigner resident in the pink zone. And there are enough large hoof-prints around your Dr *Caradog* Thomas by now to make them decidedly twitchy, I'd guess—" Richardson leaned back "—unless you know something that I don't know, anyway—?"

Audley looked at her at last. "I think we maybe are in trouble, Elizabeth. Or . . . like the man says . . . we're going to have to be very quick, in and out."

"And *gone*," agreed Richardson. "If we can get away from St Servan in one piece, Dale's got a man in Avignon who can split you up. And then you can head for Belgium, not the nearest frontiers, which will be covered. Or you can throw yourselves in the embassy in Paris and shout 'Sanctuary! Sanctuary', like the Hunchback, and make it a diplomatic incident. Just so long as I'm back home in Italy, I don't give a damn!"

"It's that bad? Is it, Peter?"

The shoulders lifted. "Search me—this is not my territory. But Dale ran like a frightened rabbit. And he doesn't scare easily."

"Among others?" Elizabeth had been trying in vain to get a word in edgeways. "What others?"

"Yes," agreed Richardson. "He thought the Other Side was maybe savouring the tourist attractions of the Vaucluse. So that also helped to concentrate his mind."

"The KGB?" Audley notoriously hated departmental euphemisms.

The shoulders lifted again. "He wasn't sure. But he wasn't happy." Richardson rocked in his seat. "But don't get me wrong: he ran because he saw this DST heavyweight—not because of any damn Red."

It was all going wrong, thought Elizabeth. It had gone wrong in Fordingwell, before it had properly started. And now it was going wrong in France, before they had even reached St Servan-les-Ruines. And she couldn't even say that she hadn't been warned: Paul had seen his damn tripod masts looming out of the mist yesterday. Perhaps David Audley had seen them too—perhaps that was why he hadn't demanded to run the show, even.

"So you're in charge, here on the ground, Peter," said Audley mildly.

Richardson muttered something Italian. "In charge? Do me a favour, David! We're consultants, not the cloak-and-dagger brigade. I'm *supposed* to be in Milan at this moment—where are you supposed to be? What's Dale really supposed to be doing?" He tossed his head. "I'm sorry, Miss Loftus, but it's the truth: I'm not really *in charge* of anything—we don't have the resources for that sort of game. So Dale's got two watchers —a nice enough couple, husband-and-wife, and she's pretty as a picture—and they're such bloody *amateurs* that they might even get away with it, I don't know . . . But *amateurs*, all the same—and if I was properly in charge of a surveillance which attracted a personal appearance of Dr David Audley— and, saving your presence, David, your presence attracts trouble like a pile of butcher's offal attracts flies—then I'd need six people, at the very least. And they'd have to be good. And even if they were, I'd want them changed every three days." He began to accelerate past a line of lorries labouring northwards up a gradient. "In a high security zone, Miss Loftus, it's like the old Arab proverb: guests start to smell on the third day." He pushed the Fiat past the last lorry. "But now you are in charge. And I await your orders."

They were all the same, thought Elizabeth bitterly: the smell of trouble made them all take refuge in someone else's responsibility if they couldn't run for cover. "What did Dr Dale tell you about Dr Thomas? I assume he briefed you before he left?"

"Oh, yes—" He took another look at her, and met her dark glasses again with his own "—yes, he did that. But he didn't know quite what he was supposed to be doing, of course. Any more than I do."

"What did he say?" There was no point in sharing her own doubts with him: one of the things she had to learn fast was not to sympathise with other people's minor problems. She had given her youth to Father's every whim, anyway: so if ex-Captain Richardson didn't like his job he could complain to someone else later. If he should be so lucky.

"Not a lot, really." He didn't like not knowing, and he didn't like her much either—just as he didn't much go for Audley. In fact, he was probably adjusting *ugly bastard Audley* to *ugly bitch Loftus* at this moment.

"Tell me not-a-lot, then." It was really no different from teaching recalcitrant Third-Formers, who had to be driven before they could be led.

"He's an old man—an old dog retired to his kennel in the sun." He shrugged. "What is there to tell?"

"For Christ's sake, Peter!" exploded Audley. "Stop shitting us!"

"An old dog—okay." Audley's sudden anger calmed her even more. Because, if Haddock Thomas was an old dog, and Richardson was a dog in the prime of its life, then it must be hard on an old dog like Audley with a bitch like Elizabeth Loftus alongside him.

"An old dog, Mr Richardson?"

"Huh!" Audley growled as he subsided into his own kennel. "An old Cara*dog*, more like!"

"What?" Richardson made no sense of that.

"Dr Thomas, Mr Richardson," said Elizabeth.

"'Doc'—*M'sieur Doc*, to be exact—that's what the locals call him—" He massaged the steering wheel "—but that's funny, you know. Because Dale said it didn't have anything to do with him being *Doctor* Thomas—'*il est professeur*', is what they say, if you push them. Like, in Italy, we say *professore*, not *dottore*. So I don't know why he's 'M'sieur Doc'."

Audley grinned at her, with sudden pure wicked pleasure. "Had-*dock*, son of Cymbeline, or *Cunobelin*, King of the Brigantes and Enemy of Rome, before Queen Cartimandua handed him over to the Romans, Elizabeth—remember?''

Caractacus—Caradoc—Caradog—Craddock—Haddock . . . and finally *M'sieur Doc*, in his final metamorphosis, thought Elizabeth. "So what do the locals say about him, Mr Richardson?''

"Nothing to his shame, Miss Loftus.'' Richardson leaped over all Audley's nonsense to come to the point. "They think the world of the old devil, as a matter of fact.''

"Old devil?''

"I merely quote Andy Dale. The old boy first came there on his honeymoon, and he's owned the cottage for donkey's ages. It seems his wife died young, but he still used to come down every summer, and sometimes in the spring too. So he's pretty much part of the scenery. Goes every morning to get his bread and his two-day-old *Times*, and every evening for his drink with the lads—he likes his drink . . . Chats up the women—likes them too . . . Waves at the girls, and they wave back.'' Richardson paused. "In his younger days he did more than wave, apparently.''

Audley gave her an "I-told-you-so'' look.

"They think the world of him, anyway: 'the famous English professor'.''

"Does he have visitors?''

"He has lots of visitors. That is, apart from his local cronies who crack bottles with him regularly. It seems his old pupils call on him quite often. And there are parties of boys from his old school come in the summer. Usually half-a-dozen, plus a master. The boys camp out in his little garden. The word in the village is that they talk together in Latin and Greek, and he tells them tales of *Jules César* and his great wars in these parts.'' He stared at her in his mirror. "Real subversive stuff, eh?''

"Recent visitors?''

"No boys at the moment. There was an elderly American a week or so ago—'*un professeur Americain*', according to the locals, Dale says. Stayed one night at the *Vieille Auberge*. Name of Parker. Visited him in the evening. Left next morning.''

"Name of Parker?'' Audley shook his head at her. "It just doesn't make any sense, Elizabeth. Even if Parker was running scared—if he knew the CIA was on his heels—one side or the other—"

"The CIA?" Richardson gave a start. "Oh Christ, David! Not *them* too!"

"Does he have a phone?" snapped Audley.

"Yes, he does—*Christ*! David—us *and* the Other Side . . . *and* the Yanks! You'll never get away with it—"

"Parker could have phoned." Audley ignored Richardson. "They could have met somewhere safe perfectly easily. He didn't need to leave tracks a mile wide, Elizabeth—right to Haddock's door."

"Haddock?" Richardson waited in vain for an explanation. "I was going to suggest that we might just pass you off as another visiting professor, David. And if you go in and out like greased lightning, and get what you want from the old devil and then run like hell . . . But if the entire intelligence population of Western Europe has been sniffing round St Servan—no wonder Andy Dale abandoned ship!"

It was worse than that, thought Elizabeth. If they hadn't been on to Parker when he'd visited Haddock Thomas, the French would surely have been on to him after the Pointe du Hoc. So they were damn well bound to be in St Servan—she should have expected that even without Dale's confirmation. So they would be driving into a trap now.

Audley was looking at her. "Well, Elizabeth?"

"Our turn-off is about ten kilometres ahead," said Richardson. "But I can turn left, into Avignon, instead of right. And if there's anyone on our tail, they won't be expecting that. Or, even if they are, I can run them around and zip into the underground car park in the *piazza* by the papal palace—they'll have to be bloody good to follow us there before we can ditch this car and run. And Dale's man in Avignon will split us up and get us out from there." He shrugged. "I can come back to the car, if you like, and make like I'm waiting for you." He shrugged again. "If they made me at the airport then I haven't got anything to lose. And I haven't actually *done* anything . . . except chauffeur a three-time loser a few miles. So they'll just hold me for a day or two, and maybe lean on me a bit, and ask me for my name and number." Another shrug. "Or with any luck they'll just follow me back to the Italian frontier, and see me off the premises."

What should she do? wondered Elizabeth desperately.

"It's less than five kilometres now, actually," said Richardson. "And counting."

She wanted to ask Audley what to do. But if she did then she'd never be able to make a decision again without remembering that she hadn't measured up, this first time.

"They might not be following us, of course." Richardson thought aloud for her benefit. "They could be so sure of us that they're just waiting at St Servan. Or they may not be there at all—I don't want to influence you, Miss Loftus. Because they could be as incompetent as we are, even. Unlikely as it may seem."

That was dirty play. Because they both knew that the French might make big mistakes, usually for political reasons, but they seldom failed at this level, and particularly not where the Americans and the British were involved, who were soft targets.

"Harumph!" Audley emitted a strangulated sound, after having tried almost pathetically to keep silent. "Remember what Colonel Butler always says: '*Booger them! Thee do tha' owern thing, lass!'*"

Colonel Butler had certainly never said anything like that in her hearing, if it was a Lancashire accent which Audley was attempting to reproduce.

But the French motorway signs were coming up ahead—

Pride or prudence? Or *common sense?* Father believed that women had been fabricated from Adam's rib without any of those qualities—

Major Birkenshawe had said once, when she had come to say "Goodnight", although she had not been going to bed, because she had been typing one of Father's manuscripts at the time: "Come on, Loftus— you knew Jerry was going to hit you with his E-boats, that last time— because you'd got the Ultra decode—Liza, my dear! Off to bed? Just trying to get a straight answer from your father—eh, Loftus?"

And Father had said, without looking at her, as though she didn't exist, "My dear Birkenshawe—the Navy, unlike the Army, isn't hired to run away. It's hired to fight—Goodnight, Elizabeth—"

"Turn right, Mr Richardson. I have absolutely no desire to visit the underground car-park at Avignon. So let's go to St Servan."

Richardson drove, as he was told: signalled, slowed, drove . . . slowed again, signalled again, and finally accelerated without another word, letting his silence pronounce his disapproval.

Elizabeth stared out of the window, trying to see what she found herself looking at. She had always wanted to visit Provence: it was one of those places every schoolteacher ought to know, the land of van Gogh and Cézanne, and Madame de Sévigné, and Daudet and his mill, and *Tartarin de Tarascon*, and St Louis at Aigues-Mortes, and above all the monumental relics of the Romans. But in Father's time she had never travelled anywhere, and now she couldn't see anything at all —just a rich foreign countryside like a great busy market garden full of fiercely growing things glimpsed in gaps in cypress hedges and lattices of bamboo.

Why was nothing ever as it ought to be, not even freedom and power and adventure?

"Hah-hmm . . ." Audley cleared his throat, as though to attract her attention. "Quite right, Elizabeth. For the record."

She looked at him in surprise. "For the record?"

He smiled. "You didn't ask me for advice. You did your own thing. But, for the record, I am advising you nevertheless . . . to go on to St Servan." He tapped Richardson on the shoulder, somewhat urgently. "Got that, Peter Richardson? *'Dr Audley insisted—'*—got that?"

"Uh-huh." They burst out of a shadowy avenue of cypresses into open country at last, with hills ahead, and other hills behind misting into a heat haze. "'There is the enemy—there are the guns': if Captain Nolan comes back from the Valley of Death he will dutifully recall what Lord Lucan said to Lord Cardigan. Just so he comes back all in one piece is all he cares about now. But he will dutifully and gratefully recall every last word and syllable afterwards. If there is an afterwards."

Elizabeth still looked at Audley, trying hard not to feel affection for him. Because sentiment was always dangerous in this game, and with someone as devious as David it might well be dangerously misplaced, too. "Why, David?"

"I was going to ask you the same question, my dear. Why?"

"I asked first."

"But you're in charge. I am but a soldier-of-the-line— . . . Or, in these parts, a time-expired legionary cheated in his discharge."

"Then, if I'm in charge, I can pull rank on you, David."

Another smile. "And I recruited you, didn't I? So I have no one else to blame, except myself?" He also chuckled. "Fair enough!"

It wasn't fair enough: if they had played dirty with her, they'd played even dirtier with him. But it was a dirty game, and no one had forced him to play it. And she had other, dirtier doubts about him, anyway.

"I'm too old for this sort of thing. But, more than that— *much* more than that—I'm too busy: I have much more urgent and important things to do, than worry about some allegedly horrendous mistake I made, years ago—

> *The times have been,*
> *That, when the brains were out, the man would die,*
> *And there an end; but now they rise again,*
> *With twenty mortal murders on their crowns,*
> *And push us from our stools—*

"So now I must stop what I ought to be doing, and manoeuvre to protect my back from my enemies on my own side. And I can't blame them, that's the trouble. Because, in their shoes I might be doing just the same thing. Because there is something bloody queer about all this—I know that, if I know nothing else."

Audley fell silent and Peter Richardson drove furiously. And the orchards and almond-groves had fallen behind them: now there were vineyards, immaculately cultivated, with distant ruined castles on the low hills on either side of them. "What we're doing, Elizabeth, is running out of time. Because this whole affair revolves around time, I suspect. Because Parker didn't need to call on Haddock Thomas the way he did—he could have taken his time to set up that meeting. And why did he go over that cliff at the Pointe du Hoc? They could have taken him out *any* time—just as they could have taken out Haddock Thomas."

"And Major Turnbull?"

"Turnbull?" The car swerved slightly. "What's with old Brian at the moment? I heard Jack Butler had acquired him after he'd lost his cover. Is he in on this?"

"Mmm . . . ?" Audley pretended not to have heard the question properly. "What about him? Brian *alias* Turnbull?"

"Nothing. Difficult old sod." Richardson shook his head. "Remember me to him, though. And . . . just tell him it wasn't my fault, that business about his cover. But if he'd stayed where he was he'd have been on borrowed time—tell him that."

Thoughts jostled Elizabeth's mind, relevant and irrelevant. She had the other half of his name now, which she had never known, or even needed to know: the unimportant (and quite inappropriate) half. *Brian*—

"I'll do that. If I see him." What Richardson didn't need to know Audley wisely didn't tell him. "You wanted to know, Elizabeth—*why*, was it?"

If someone, somewhere, had wanted Major Turnbull dead, for whatever reason, then it would have been no problem putting a contract out on him: that didn't prove anything more than Richardson had already done, with that message of his. The fact of Fordingwell—the terminal event—was less important than its timing; which was what Audley had been saying.

"We have to go on, Elizabeth, because we don't have any choice in the matter. That's all." Audley leaned forward. "Would that be Bomb Disposal logic, from your Royal Engineers days, Captain Richardson?"

"Uh-huh." Richardson held the wheel tightly, letting the car drive itself along a Roman-straight road towards the hilltop ahead, which boasted a *tricolore* above its ruined tower. "But there were such things as anti-handling devices even in our day, designed to blow us up. So we didn't just hit it with a hammer because it wasn't actually ticking." He half-turned towards Audley. "And you seem to think your bomb is still ticking, if I heard you correctly?"

"My bomb?" Audley sniffed, and turned to Elizabeth. "There speaks a peace-time bomb disposal officer, my dear. When my old chemistry master was a bomb disposal officer in London in 1941 he always had half-a-dozen bombs—and a couple of land-mines—on the go, in the Blitz. He always used to say that it wasn't a question of *when* he'd be blown up, so much as *where*. In fact, the last time he came back he got the Head to set the Sixth Form scholarship class a variation on the old *Would you save the baby or the Elgin Marbles?* question: *Would you save a row of houses in the East End or the local sewage works?* And, I tell you, that really stretched us. Because we'd never seen a sewage works, let alone an East End house."

"So what was his answer?" Richardson fell into the trap.

"He never got round to telling us." Having caught his man, Audley returned happily to Elizabeth. "If I'm wrong about Haddock, it'll take you months to get any sort of lead. And if I'm not wrong it'll take you forever. But in the meanwhile I want to get back to a bomb of my own at Cheltenham, which could go up any minute. So let's hit this one with a bloody hammer . . . And if it goes off in our faces—if he laughs at us, and tells us that there isn't one damn thing we can do now . . . because there isn't one damn thing we *can* do—except maybe I can resign, and you can get a feather in your cap, if you want to wear a feather . . . *if* he laughs at us, that'll be something better than nothing."

"I don't want that sort of feather, David. But what if he doesn't laugh?"

"Oh, he'll laugh—old Haddock'll see the joke, whether it's on him or us. He won't have changed. Aged, maybe . . . but not changed." Audley nodded. "He should be just about ready for drinking now: aged in the wood." Another nod: he was excited, rather than pleased, at the prospect. "Besides which . . . if I don't quit—and I'm damned if I'm going to quit for Oliver St John Latimer—what can they do to me? The way things are at Cheltenham, they need me more than I need them right now." Another nod. But this time the excitement was smoothed by rather smug confidence. "So what can they do to me?"

"Oh, great! Bravo!" murmured Richardson. "Vintage patriotism, 1984: 'My country needs me—but it's paying less than the going rate'. But you're asking the wrong question, I suspect."

"And what is the right question?"

"You may well ask!" But Richardson didn't seem disposed to answer.

Audley waited, and Elizabeth decided to wait too.

The landscape was closing in on them again. There were more orchards now, as well as vineyards—peaches, or almonds maybe, or even olives, but something exotic, anyway; but, more strange than the *flora* (and there was no sign of any *fauna*, except Frenchmen in French vehicles, which made the road even more foreign), was the suddenly-jagged landscape.

"It's not worth looking, Miss Loftus."

"I beg your pardon?"

"Just because you can't see them, it doesn't mean they aren't there. Or, anyway, that they haven't got us covered. They're at St Servan, anyway."

"I was looking at the countryside, actually."

"Uh-huh?" Richardson drove in silence for a time. "Nice, isn't it? Myself, I don't like the French. But then my mother was Italian, so I suppose I'm biased. However . . . your Italian —he has his faults, but he wants to be a gentleman, even when he's picking your pocket, or cutting your throat. But your Frenchman—he's got style, but no one would ever accuse him of being a gentleman."

"Balderdash!" said Audley. "Poppycock!"

"Possibly," agreed Richardson equably. "But when it comes to self-interest—call it *La France*, if you like—he can be mean and smart, is what *I* mean."

"It isn't what he means at all, Elizabeth," said Audley. "Come to the point, *Pietro*."

"Okay. Have it your own way." Richardson shrugged. "The further we drive up this pretty road—and if those clouds weren't in the way you might just see Mont Ventoux, Miss Loftus—the further we drive up it, the queasier I feel."

Another shrug. "If we were just tourists . . . but no one's ever going to accuse *you* of being just a tourist, David . . . And if Andy Dale got just a whiff of KGB up there, at St Servan, before he glimpsed this French DST fellow . . . And now you say that it was the Yanks led you to this old boy in the first place—" Shrug "—God knows what he's done—*I* don't want to know, not now: I want to be able to say *Mein Gott! I voss only obeying orders: I voss only drivink ze car!*—just so we get in quickly, and then get out quickly. Will you at least do that?"

It was looking less and less like a good idea, and more and more like a stampeded amateurish error, thought Elizabeth. "We won't stay for lunch, Mr Richardson. All right?"

"I hope you won't, Miss Loftus—I hope you won't!"

"There's a two-star restaurant in St Servan," said Audley.

"La Vieille Auberge." Richardson nodded. "Have you ever been in a French slammer, Miss Loftus?"

"Shut up, Peter," said Audley. "Just drive."

"Onomatopoeic, Miss Loftus," said Richardson. "American slang for the sound of the prison door closing. And I'll bet there isn't a CIA man to be found in a thirty-mile radius of us now. Because they're not nearly as stupid as their allies like to think."

"Shut up, Peter," said Audley again. "Just drive."

Peter Richardson just drove.

"Have you been in the field long, Miss Loftus?" he said at length.

"Drive, Peter," said Audley.

She couldn't even concentrate properly on the countryside, after she found she couldn't think straight. Not even when she saw a strange field, and caught a stranger smell.

"Lavender," said Richardson obligingly. "Or a sort of lavender. What they grow is some sort of hybrid—the real stuff grows wild, higher up, with thyme and rosemary. I remember stopping off up here—oh, it must have been fifteen years ago —when I was driving my first girl down to Amalfi, to see

my mother's folks. We stopped off further north, though—
Buis-les-Baronnies, it was . . . It was okay then, because there
were no missiles on the Plateau d'Albion . . . Now, when I
come over, I keep to the autoroute, just to be on the safe side."

Eventually he stopped, quite deliberately.
"Phone-box here, just round the corner. Got to make a call."

Elizabeth sat in silence, until it became oppressive.
"Have I made a mistake, David?"
Audley stared down the village street, in which nothing
moved. "We all make mistakes. Maybe I made a mistake, a
long time ago. If I did, then maybe we've both made another
one now. Join the club."

Richardson came back.
"That's okay. He's just gone out on his terrace, to read his
morning paper. He'll have his coffee. And then some more
coffee. By the time we get there he'll be thinking about his first
drink." He let in the clutch.
"But I still don't think I made a mistake, Elizabeth," said
Audley.

Peter Richardson just drove, again.
There were hills now, and twisting valleys, up and down,
and through and around, with scrubland rising up here and
there above fertile fields, hinting at the wilder country of Peter
Richardson's real lavender. And—
*And that had been the country to which Haddock Thomas had taken
his beautiful scheming Delphi, long ago. And had he returned here to
die here, because this was where he had once been happy?*

And there were villages, set high up on one side, or low down
on another—low down, but still on promontories in their
valleys, each with its ruined medieval castle tower and its
church—each at once different from the last one, yet identical.

It was perched on the side of a ridge—a plateau, almost—
also just as different, but just the same—

"I'll go straight in, and drop you off outside his place. I can turn round at the top, somewhere . . . I have to come down a different way, but I'll sound the horn—one short, one long, one short—as I come by, underneath his terrace. Then I'll fill up the tank at the gas station, and I'll have a drink at the *auberge*—for an hour?" Richardson glanced over his shoulder at Audley. "Same signal—okay?"

Elizabeth cracked. "And if everything isn't all right?"

"Long-short-long . . . if I'm lucky." He signalled and slowed to leave the main road. "Dead silence if I'm not. Okay?"

Elizabeth craned her neck to try to take in the terrain of St Servan-les-Ruines, but too late, because of listening to Peter Richardson: the huddle of the village was already lost behind a screen of trees, and she had lost the shape of everything. But it was still so peaceful that the whole charade was utterly unreal, anyway.

"Here we go, then," said Richardson, in a voice so suddenly-serious, like a fighter pilot making his low-level run, that she was jolted from unreality to reality.

It was larger than it had seemed, on that first uninformed look, when it had been just another village: there was a street, and another street, with shops in it—even a shop with dresses in it, which no English village would ever have possessed; but then no English village she knew of still had a baker's shop— a butcher's shop—never mind a two-star *auberge*—

The Fiat swung sharply, through 180 degrees, under a cliff of ancient stonework, towards a tiny fortified gateway, under a cascade of flowers which reminded her insanely of old Mr Willis's cottage far away in soft green England, which was so near in time, but so desperately and helplessly far away in miles.

"Where are the ruins?" She heard her own voice almost with surprise, it was so sharp and confident.

"What ruins?" Richardson slowed to negotiate the gateway.

"St Servan-*les-ruines*?"

"Search me." He changed gear once he was through. "It all looks fairly ruined to me. I never thought to ask."

Just as unexpectedly as they had arrived in the village, they were unexpectedly out of it again, into an area of stunted holm oaks and scrubby vegetation, but with an equally sudden view of a fertile and well-cultivated valley below, bathed in hot sunshine.

Yet not quite out of it after all, maybe: the narrow road fell gently towards a final huddle of houses perched on a flat shelf in the hillside amid a cluster of shade-trees.

"Prepare to abandon ship," said Richardson. "Dale's people will have their eye on you from up there." He pointed up the hillside, to a modern house almost on the crest of the ridge, not unattractive, but sited with fine (and presumably French) disregard for an otherwise unspoilt landscape. "He was lucky to pick that up, it overlooks the old dog's kennel perfectly . . . They're supposed to be a honeymoon couple. But I won't tell you any more, just in case the worst comes to the worst." He twisted towards Elizabeth as he slowed down. "Honeymoon couples inspire a certain delicacy even in the worst and most nosey of people, Andy Dale reckoned, Miss Loftus. And they keep themselves to themselves."

Where had she heard that before, just recently—?

"Out," said Richardson, just as she remembered. And the remembrance of Haddock Thomas and his bride here all those years ago, and in the very year which mattered, was a cold and desolate thought, quite unwarmed by its irony.

But Audley was already out of the car, and had skipped round to open her door with uncharacteristic good manners.

"Good luck—" Richardson's glasses were black in the glare "—to us all, Miss Loftus."

The house was very old, and not very large though unnaturally high for its size, but sturdily restored up to the iron water-spouts under its pantile roof.

The car accelerated away, leaving Audley standing somewhat irresolute before the choice of a front door and the wrought-iron gate in a shoulder-high garden wall. Then he resolved his irresolution simply by peering over the wall on tip-toe, and choosing the gate for her.

There was a little shady garden, under a pergola of some

sort of vine, with all the light and colour concentrated on the edge of a terrace, where a man in a panama hat sat amidst a blaze of red flowers and scatter of books and newspaper pages, with a glass in his hand and a puff of blue-grey tobacco smoke above him.

But the gate had squeaked, and the man changed the picture as it fixed itself, turning towards her.

"Dr Thomas?"

"Hullo there—?"

Slow, gravelly voice, the sound filtered through many years and many bottles. But years of what else? wondered Elizabeth: just many years of *hic, haec, hoc*, and Caesar's *Gallic Wars*? Or many years of *treason*?

She felt Audley's large presence at her back, pushing her forward, overawing her from behind even in the shadow. And in that instant she steeled herself against disappointment. For, whatever he was, and whatever he had been, Haddock Thomas could only be an anti-climax in the flesh, innocent or guilty.

"Hullo there?" He peered towards them over his spectacles, which had slipped far down his nose.

Elizabeth advanced. Just for this brief moment she might be as beautiful as Helen of Troy for all he knew, and that wouldn't do at all.

"Dr Thomas?" She whipped off her dark glasses and entered a shaft of sunlight which cut through the canopy above.

"Yes." He placed his glass carefully on the table beside him, rose to his feet, and finally removed his panama. "Once upon a time, anyway."

The light had half-blinded her for an instant, but her next step took her into shadow again.

Nothing very special, indeed: neither horns nor halo, neither Caliban nor Hyperion in retirement. Just another old man.

"Forgive me, Dr Thomas." In that moment of half-blindness she had missed his first reaction to her. Now she saw only that he wanted to recognize her, from his gallery of wives and sisters of long ago, but couldn't do so. "Elizabeth Loftus, Dr Thomas." Just another old man: younger than old Mr Willis, but much taller and thinner, and sun-browned (sun-browned with perhaps a hint of dear Major Birkenshawe's whisky-flush,

232

maybe), leathery-tanned by age and sun and alcohol. "We haven't met."

"Until now." He smiled the correction at her, and pushed his spectacles up his nose with his index finger. And then smiled again, without embarrassment at what was in sharp focus at last.

"But *we* have met," said Audley from behind. "Back in the deeps of time, Haddock."

Haddock Thomas stared past her, frowning slightly, but only with the effort of memory, with no outward hint of any emotion. Yet then, if he wasn't what he had seemed all these years, he would be good, thought Elizabeth bleakly. Too good, in fact.

"Don't tell me, now." For the first time there was the very slightest hint of Welshness beneath the gravel. "My eyes are not what they were—" The eyes, faded china-blue, came back to Elizabeth "—too much staring into the sun, you see, Elizabeth Loftus. Long ago it was a matter of life-or-death to look into it—'The Hun in the Sun' behind you was very likely to be the last thing you ever saw, with no need to worry about old age. But from this terrace I have watched the sun over too many cloudless days, and the moon rise over starlit nights of dreams—Axel Munthe was right, he knew the price of sinning. But, of course, he also knew that the price was worth paying, for the sin. And that's one of the world's troubles today: the crass belief that we have a right to something for nothing. When, in fact, we have no *rights* at all—and even *nothing* is expensive. Indeed, *nothing* may prove to be the most expensive commodity of all—even more costly than the sun itself."

"He was always like this, Elizabeth," said Audley. "Or, perhaps not quite so philosophically pompous when he was younger. But quite bad enough, as I remember."

Haddock Thomas continued to look at her. "It's the voice, you see, Miss Loftus—Mrs Loftus—?"

"Miss, Dr Thomas." *She mustn't like him: they had all succumbed to him—his pupils, his equals, even his interrogator and the friend whose girl he had taken—they had all liked him.*

"Miss Loftus. The eye can be a great deceiver. Not merely in the present—not merely the picture which lies, or the quickness of the conjuror's hand—it deceives memory too. *Smell* is much better, perhaps best of all, so long as it lasts. But *sound* now . . . '*a tinkling piano in the next apartment*' and the cry of John Peel's hounds, and the leather on the willow . . ." He placed his cigar on an ash-tray beside his glass and then offered her his hand. "And now I believe they've proved that every voice has its print, as unique as every finger, Miss Loftus."

Audley loomed in the corner of her vision, in full sunlight.

"And David Audley?" He relinquished her hand and offered it to Audley. "'Dr Audley, I presume?' should I say?"

Audley said nothing for a moment, as the sound of a car, close but invisible, rose from below the terrace wall.

Beep-baaarp-beep!

"Haddock." The two men measured each other for changes. "It's been a long time. But you look well."

"A long time, indeed. So do you. Still doing the same job? Much higher up, though?"

"The same job, Haddock," said Audley gently. "I follow my destiny."

"Still on The Wall?" Haddock Thomas looked at Elizabeth. "I'm sorry, Miss Loftus. An old joke—a very old joke, indeed."

She mustn't let them patronize her. "But they say the old jokes are the best ones, Dr Thomas. May I share it?"

"I don't know that you will find it very amusing."

"An RAF joke?" She watched him. "Or a Civil Service joke, perhaps? Or a schoolboy joke? Give me a clue."

He measured her with a look. Actually, he had measured her already, but with an eye only on bust and waist, hip and leg, quite unashamedly. But this time the measurement was a different one. "It is a Kipling joke, Miss Loftus. A *Rudyard* Kipling joke." The Welsh was more pronounced. "Are you a reader of the great man's works?"

She dared not look at Audley. Paul always made outrageous fun of his obsessive weakness for Kipling, deliberately quoting back to him. But somehow she didn't think this was that kind of joke. "I read him when I was a child, Dr Thomas."

"But not afterwards? A pity! Much of his best work is for grown-ups. But then the English have a blind spot there.

Which is all part of their guilty misapprehension of their history, as well as of him. But no matter, eh?" He was looking at Audley now. "I told him—oh, it must have been almost before you were born, I told him—that he would never gain preferment in his line of business . . . Or, that when it was offered to him, he would not want it—like Kipling's Roman centurion . . . who was not a Roman at all, of course, for he had never seen Rome, nor known the heyday of Rome, but only lived with his legends and his illusions. But there! I told him he would gain no preferment, and receive no thanks, if he chose to serve on The Wall—the *Great* Wall—the wall which the Emperor Hadrian caused to be built, to keep out the dreadful barbarians, when he realized that the game couldn't be won." He smiled. "The same emperor, my dear, who knew how small and defenceless and ephemeral was his soul— '*Animula vagula blandula, hospes comesque corporis*' . . . But he would have none of it, for he knew the Roman's reply: '*I follow my destiny*', he said. And off he went!"

"*Harumph!*" grunted Audley. "One of the things you must understand about the Welsh, Elizabeth, is that they are greater liars than rugger players. For this is the advice I gave *him*, not the advice he gave me."

"Is that so?" Haddock Thomas glanced at Audley for a second. "Well, let's say that we gave each other the same advice, then? And I took his advice—but he did not take mine, eh?"

Given half a chance they would go on sparring like this forever, thought Elizabeth. But if Peter Richardson was right they did not have forever left.

"You had a visitor last week, Dr Thomas. An elderly American." She tried in vain to match Audley's casual tone. "Can you tell us about him?"

Haddock Thomas measured her again as he smoothed his thinning hair and replaced his panama. Then he shook a little brass bell which had been hidden on the table and gestured Elizabeth to an empty chair. "Yes . . . yes, I wondered about that." He smiled at her again. "After what David's said, I mustn't be a Welsh liar, must I?"

She sat down. And she caught him admiring her legs as she

crossed them carefully, the way she had been taught to do. "I beg your pardon—?"

He gestured towards Audley. "Get a chair, David . . . It wasn't really just his voice, Miss Loftus: he's been in the back of my mind for a week or so . . . when I can't honestly remember recalling him these last ten—or even twenty—years or more." He watched Audley retrieve another chair from the shadows under the vines. "But that's not true, either . . . It's more like never *quite* forgotten, but never *quite* remembered." He cocked his head at her. "One day you will discover how very protective memory is, my dear: it tries to dignify us as well as soothing our pain, so that we can believe that we are the masters of our fate . . . at least, if we are satisfied with the outcome, anyway—eh?" Once again he was watching. "Free will is always better than pre-destination, don't you think."

He was pushing her out of her depth, making her wonder how she had got here, to St Servan-les-Ruines, after all those years with Father.

"The American reminded you of David?" The memory of Father steeled her to the more important business in hand. "Major Parker?"

"Major Parker—" For one fraction-of-a-second he looked clear through her "—Major Parker!"

"Who saved your life?"

"Is that the story now?" Haddock Thomas looked past her. "Ah, Madame Sophie!"

A minuscule Frenchwoman deposited two glasses and another bottle on the table, swept away the half-full bottle with a hiss of disapproval, and was gone before Elizabeth could react.

Haddock Thomas shrugged at Elizabeth. "You didn't knock at the front door, so she hasn't looked you over—so she disapproves of you."

"But she'll finish the bottle herself, nevertheless?" said Audley.

"That may well be." Haddock Thomas pointed at Audley. "You know too much, David—about people. That is one of the things I remember about you now." He filled the three glasses, and presented one to Elizabeth. "And you know too much about *me*, I am thinking now, Miss Loftus. For a stranger."

"She knows far too little about you, my dear fellow," said Audley, reaching for a glass. "That is the whole trouble."

"The whole trouble?" Haddock Thomas looked at each of them in turn. "But whose trouble? Mine, would it be?"

"Ours, Dr Thomas," said Elizabeth. "Didn't Major Parker save you once? A long time ago?"

"A very long time ago." He nodded. "But you know his name nevertheless. And you know he was here—a very short time ago. Did he tell you that?"

"Did he save you?"

"He plucked me from the sea—yes. He and a spotty-faced youth in a helmet much too big for him. I could have kissed them both. Perhaps I did, I don't remember. Did Major Thaddeus Parker tell you that also?"

"He didn't tell us anything, Dr Thomas. He's dead."

"Dead? How—?" He looked at Audley suddenly. "Not my trouble, did you say?"

"I didn't say, as a matter of fact, Haddock." Audley sipped his wine. "Your trouble . . . perhaps. Mine—certainly."

Haddock Thomas said nothing for a moment, but simply stared at Audley. Then he started to say something, but stopped.

"Why did Major Parker come to see you, Dr Thomas?" asked Elizabeth.

"Why should he not?" Haddock Thomas still didn't look at her. "How did he die, Miss Loftus?"

"He was murdered, we think."

Again, Haddock Thomas didn't react immediately. Instead he took up his own glass and turned away from them both, looking out over the valley beneath, full-face into the sun, drinking slowly but steadily until the glass was nearly empty. Then he poured he last of it on the ground at his feet.

"They threw him over the cliff at the Pointe du Hoc, Haddock," said Audley brutally. "Just about where he climbed down that morning, before he rescued you. We think he may have had a rendezvous there. But it wasn't the one he was expecting."

237

The old man turned slowly back to Audley, ignoring Elizabeth. "So it's all starting again, is it, David? After all this time? Is that really possible, man?"

Elizabeth was tired of being ignored. "Perhaps not, Dr Thomas."

This time he did look at her.

"If it never ended, Dr Thomas—" She looked down Admiral Varney's nose at him "—why then, it has no reason to start again, has it?"

"Never ended." It wasn't a question, he merely repeated the words. And it wasn't hatred or anger in his eyes, let alone fear. But it might be distaste. Then he turned to Audley once more. "What do you think, David? Or what do you *believe*— which is better?"

"It doesn't matter what he believes." With a little practice she might catch an echo of Admiral Varney's voice, too. "If Major Parker was a traitor, Dr Thomas, *then what are you?* That is what matters."

This time he didn't look at her. "By damn, David! You've got a hard one here, and no mistake! Is this what it's like now? Or maybe the one our Ruddy wrote about—

"When you're wounded and left on Afghanistan's plains,
And the women come out to cut what remains—
One of them, maybe?" He set his glass on the table and filled it to the brim, and then picked it up and turned towards her. "And if I am a traitor too, Miss Loftus—what then? Will you cut up these remains?"

They were exactly where she had always feared they would be, once she had let herself be pushed too hard and too fast. But then, out of nowhere, she remembered Father. "Some people say youth is sweet, Dr Thomas." Her youth had not been sweet, that was what memory told her. "But I have observed that time running out is even more valuable when you are old. Is that so?"

He still wasn't frightened. But he showed his teeth when he smiled, for the first time, and she realized, also for the first time, that it wasn't only the memory of Father that was driving her.

"Is that some sort of threat, Miss Loftus?"

238

But she *had* seen those teeth before. And they were not like Father's at all, of course—Father's had been his own, because he never ate sweets or took sugar in his tea.

"Not a threat." She hadn't touched her wine. "This is my first job, 'in the field' as they say. Or 'first combat mission', for a Spitfire pilot, would that be?" She tipped her glass, and the wine slashed out like a pool of blood, engulfing the few drops he had spilt. "I sent a colleague out yesterday to inquire into your past." Some of the wine had splashed on her shoes, staining them indelibly, she noticed. "So now he's dead. Do you have any explanation for that, Dr Thomas?"

Haddock Thomas stared at her in astonishment. Then he looked at Audley—who was also staring at her. "Do you have an explanation, David?"

Audley turned his head slowly, without taking his eyes off her until he was almost facing the old man. "The received wisdom is that I made a mistake, Haddock. Long ago."

"A mistake?"

"About you." Audley paused. "Or if not you, then Peter Barrie, maybe."

"*Peter Barrie?* That's foolishness, man!"

"Yes. That's what Peter Barrie said—about you."

Haddock Thomas moistened his lips. "Have you any evidence?"

"Two dead men is what we have," said Elizabeth.

Audley shook his head. "Not a thing. But then, if I did make a mistake . . . then you're good. One of you—or both of you."

"And if you didn't make a mistake?"

Audley drew in a deep breath. "Let me make a picture for you, old comrade—if that's what you are—if I made a mistake." He drew in another breath. "Long ago . . . something went wrong on the Other Side—something *slipped*. So there had to be a salvage job, to save their inside man." Another breath. "If it was Peter, then they acted very quickly: he resigned, and became a nobody. There was no evidence against him—he just had to start again somewhere else. If it was you . . . if it was you, they were a bit slower. Or they decided to take more of a risk. But in the end they reckoned you'd never be altogether trusted. So you started again, too." Audley

239

shrugged. "You each did well, anyway. And in the way they wanted you to do well, like maggots in an apple."

Haddock Thomas sat back. "A maggot, am I? But—"

Audley raised a finger. "There's more. One of you—or both. Plus Delphi Marsh, of course."

The old man sat up. "Now, David—"

"She would have been your contact. Or your alibi. She complicated things very nicely at the time—moving from one of you to the other, as required. I spent a lot of time on her. Maybe she was my real mistake."

Haddock Thomas's jaw tightened. "Now, you can leave Delphi out of this, David. Make all the pictures you like of me, and of Peter. But leave her out of them."

"I'm afraid I can't. Because she comes in again, you see."

"Again? What?" The old man's hands tightened into bony fists on his lap. "How?"

"Our colleague who died yesterday was looking into Delphi's death, Haddock," said Audley gently. "He couldn't have found anything so quickly. But I think I know what he didn't have time to find, in any case." He switched to Elizabeth suddenly. "You see, Elizabeth, Mrs Delphi Thomas wasn't pregnant when she had her road accident. And that isn't a picture—that's a fact." He turned back to the old man. "Sorry, Haddock."

The old man shook his head. "No need to be sorry, man. We only invented that baby to make Peter angry, rather than sad. It was the least we could do for him, to make him hate us both."

"Was that it?" Audley cocked his head. "Well, indeed! And I always thought she trapped you with it! Now there's a turn-up for the book!"

"Not so clever, eh?" The old man wasn't smiling. "And is that your picture, then?" He frowned suddenly. "But then . . . if you believed *that* . . . then you can hardly believe your picture, David—?"

"Not a word of it." Audley sounded almost cheerful. "I spent a lot of time on you—all three of you. And I was in my prime then, not the doddering fool I am now. And now I've all the wisdom of hindsight to add."

"And what does hindsight add?"

"Well, for a start, if either you or Peter have been working for the Other Side these twenty–thirty years, you damn well haven't earned your keep. I had a devil's advocate run-down on you both, a couple of days back. And, in your very different ways you both qualify for the firing squad—but theirs, not ours, old comrade."

Elizabeth sat up. "You never told me that, David."

"You never asked, Elizabeth. And, besides, I wanted you to come to your own conclusion." He shrugged unapologetically.

"I see." Haddock Thomas poured himself another drink. "But then, again, I do not see at all."

"What don't you see?"

"I don't see why you are here—here to rake up a past which I have no desire to recall in this fashion."

"My dear Haddock, I do not want to be here." Audley sniffed, and held out his glass to be re-filled. "As a matter of fact, I was busy with something much more important than raking up your fairly innocent past."

"But two men are dead, nevertheless." Haddock Thomas turned to Elizabeth. "He talked about old times, Miss Loftus —Major Parker did. He said he had come back for the D-Day anniversary, and he thought he'd look me up. He had very little to say. But then we really didn't have anything in common."

"Least of all treason," murmured Audley.

"But now he is dead." The old man stared across his valley again, shading his eyes with his hand. "And your colleague is also dead. While investigating . . ." He trailed off. "And for those two reasons—not wholly inadequate reasons, I must now admit—for those two reasons you are here, David. In fact . . . in view of our shared past, you could really hardly avoid coming to see me—no matter that you believed me to be innocent. Perhaps that might even supply a greater compulsion —" He half-looked at Elizabeth "—rather than leave me to other tender mercies . . ." He returned his gaze to the distant hillside. "When the received wisdom (whatever that may entail . . . but 'received wisdom' is difficult to argue with, I agree!) —the *received wisdom* is that you made a mistake." He continued to stare across the valley, but fell silent now.

Elizabeth found herself wishing that she hadn't poured her drink on the ground. She was thirsty, and she had ruined her shoes. And for a moment she had also shown herself an Elizabeth Loftus who rather frightened her.

"But I didn't make a mistake," said Audley.

Elizabeth gave him a look of pure hatred, which she couldn't disguise.

"He's getting drunk again, you see, Elizabeth." Audley brushed aside her hatred. "He must have a liver like an old boot. I remember getting him drunk back in '58—very drunk . . . and it wasn't difficult even then."

"You didn't make a mistake," agreed Haddock Thomas. "But, whereas that is what you *believe*, it is what I *know*, you see, David. Marxism, with all its egregious little heresies, socialism included, has never attracted me."

"I know. You spent a whole night telling me, indirectly." Audley smiled at Elizabeth. "The uniting theme of all classical literature is the right and wrong uses of authority—Antigone telling Creon to go bowl his hoop, according to Sophocles, and also Augustus in *Res Gestae* . . . You made a great impression on me that night, Haddock. I just couldn't see you doing a Philby on us."

"No?" Haddock seemed to be fascinated by something far below and far away. "I'm flattered."

"You should be." Audley closed his eyes. "'*This amazing mental dimension, where nothing is barred, and the extent to which you can think is only limited by the limits of your own comprehension and imagination: it's like being let into the Universe itself—the whole atmosphere of the classics is of a boundless, expanding, gloriously fascinating, bloody marvellous universe—and let's throw our thoughts out there!*'"

"Did I say all that? Well, I must have been pissed, I agree!" The far-away horizon still engrossed the old man. "And you must have a bloody-marvellous memory, David."

"No. Just a tape-recorder under the table. We weren't so good with bugs then, but you didn't know the difference. And I played it again just the day before yesterday, to refresh my not-so-bloody-marvellous memory. We didn't have bugs, but we weren't wholly inefficient."

"But you have made a mistake, nevertheless." Haddock Thomas turned to Audley at last.

Audley opened his mouth, then closed it. "What did I do wrong?"

"Nothing *then*." Haddock Thomas looked sad. "But everything *now*, I suspect."

This time Audley's mouth remained open.

"You said you were busy doing something important. But you're not doing it *now*, are you?" Haddock opened his old hands on his lap in an eloquent gesture. "Could it be that they want you busy *here*, wasting your time and mine, simply so that you can't be busy *there*, David?"

Haddock Thomas turned back to Elizabeth. "I always used to tell my boys that the Latin language is simple and logical. And Greek is even better—more elegant, even. But if you look for complexities, you will only end up by deceiving yourself. So look for the simplicities, and all the nonsense will disappear."

Audley stood up. "Can I use your phone, Haddock?"

"My dear fellow, of course—"

The garden gate squeaked and clanged at their backs, cutting him off.

"Or perhaps not," said the old man, staring past them. "Because, unless I am very much mistaken, you are about to be taken into custody, David. In which case you will be here for some time, I'm afraid."

Elizabeth saw two things unforgettably, in the instant of disaster, which were all the more memorable for the difference between them.

The DST men who came through the gate were old Mr Willis's creatures: hounds who moved left and right, ready for anything while they made way for the huntsmen behind them who would make the arrest, if not the kill.

But they were moving, and Audley wasn't.

At least, he wasn't until he raised his glass to Haddock, without turning round.

"My mistake—this time, if not last time, Haddock." He sipped the wine. "But then, you got me into a lot of trouble then, too, I seem to remember." He took another sip.

"Oh, no!" Suddenly Haddock was very Welsh. "It wasn't me then, and it isn't me now. We all make our own mistakes in the end, David. We don't need any help from outsiders."

EPILOGUE:

Mistakes and Monsters

COLONEL BUTLER HAD an atavistic preference for handling difficult situations standing up, like any old red-coated infantryman facing cavalry. So when Audley finally arrived he had positioned himself by the window, away from the funk-hole of the Director's desk.

"Well, David?" For one last moment he pretended to admire the view across the Thames, which he considered vastly inferior to both his neat Surrey hedgerows and his native Lancashire dales.

"Jack." Audley sounded unabashed. But then he had never been an easily abashed man. "Good leave?"

"Curtailed leave." Neither did Audley look more crumpled —tie always carelessly knotted, good suit always creased— than he habitually did. "What the hell have you been doing?"

"Ah . . . now *latterly* I have been in the pokey, in a gentlemanly sort of way." Audley grinned disarmingly. "The French didn't treat us badly, actually—thanks to Peter Richardson getting off a call to Dale just before they swooped. It was all really more embarrassing than unpleasant."

"Oh yes?" Colonel Butler was not disarmed. "And is that how you would describe what happened to Brian Turnbull, David?"

The grin vanished and the shutters which Butler knew of old came down. "Yes. That was a bad scene, Jack. But not my fault."

Butler concealed his astonishment with some difficulty: he had not expected Audley, of all people, to weasel out of it like that. For tactical reasons, if not for moral ones, Audley had always been ready to take the blame in the past, even when it had not been properly his. "No?" He tested his incredulity casually.

"No, Jack." Audley shook his head.

247

Another tack, then. "Yes. That's what Oliver Latimer says."

"What?" Audley frowned. "*What?*"

"Latimer says you were only obeying orders. He has taken full responsibility for everything that has happened."

"Well—" There was a flicker of fire behind the shutters "—well, you can fuck that for a game of soldiers, Jack—for a start!"

"Indeed?" Torture would not have wrung that from Audley. But, as Butler had calculated, he was never going to let himself owe anything to Oliver St John Latimer. "But he did give you an order. Is that not so?"

"*Phooey!*" Audley gestured angrily. "I wouldn't have obeyed it if I hadn't wanted to." He tugged at his tie. "Christ, Jack —I was all ready to make a bust at Cheltenham . . . or almost ready, anyway. I could have gone to the DG—or the Joint Committee—*no trouble*! You know that as well as I do!"

"But you didn't." Butler controlled his own anger. "So your man in Cheltenham is probably in Moscow by now, with all those American transmissions in his head. *And* . . . we lost Brian Turnbull." He almost added *Who was one of my subalterns in Korea, under another name, in another time, damn you!* But there was nothing to be gained from that: the letter he had to write, to that elderly maiden aunt in Eastbourne who was all the next-of-kin Brian Turner had, was his business, not Audley's.

Audley was staring at him. "We would have lost Turnbull anyway, Jack. Even if I hadn't screwed things up. Or someone, if not him."

Now they were coming to it. "What do you mean?"

Audley took time to think. "You asked me what the hell I've been doing, Jack. And the answer is that I've been making the mistake I was supposed to make—no question about that. I let myself be taken, and they took me. And, at a guess, it was Panin."

"Panin?"

"Uh-huh. Old Nikolai's been laying for me for years—he knows me as well as I know him, from way back. You should remember, Jack. It was about the time we met again, long after the war, you and I. And he was one of Professor Kryzhanovsky's recruits too, so he'd know about the whole Debrecen nonsense without even having to look it up: he knows exactly how I tick—all he had to do was to wind me up. And killing people has never worried him, because he's a monster: he kills people selectively, like daisies in his lawn.''

Butler remembered Professor Nikolai Panin: that deceptively gentle face, slightly sheep-like with its badly-set broken nose; he had been . . . he had been a scholar once, not a psychologist—or archaeologist—?

"They wanted to get the Cheltenham man out, Jack. And I made another mistake there, because I didn't think he was on to me . . . Or, anyway, I didn't think he was going to run quite so quickly. But if I'd been there, in Cheltenham, I'd have maybe picked up the signs last week, when those American transmissions were coming through." Audley shook his head. "I don't know . . . *But they didn't know*—that's the point. So they wanted to get me out of there. But I'm just a bit too senior to have a convenient accident—" He cocked his head at Butler "—which would have resulted in a reciprocal sanction, maybe? Or something like?"

Butler said nothing. Audley might guess how the land lay there, but it was still beyond his certain competence.

"Okay." Audley accepted his silence. "But my guess is that, with what the Americans were doing to him, the man Parker was ready to run, so he was expendable. So Parker was to hand, and he was also one of their possibles from the alleged Debrecen List. And they must have known that he had a connection—an *innocent* connection—with Haddock Thomas, whom I had cleared back in '58. So they set Haddock up with Parker, and then killed Parker rather crudely, so as to set *me* up, Jack. Because they were pretty sure we'd react to the Debrecen List, after what happened to Latimer in America last year."

Butler thought about Elizabeth Loftus's Interim Report, which lay in his top drawer a few feet away, and understood what Audley had left unsaid there: the unanswered questions in the whole Debrecen affair had been festering in the files for a quarter of a century—that was an unacceptable truth of it.

"But the way it worked out—" Audley spread his hands

"—it worked out the way things always do: better than they'd planned in one way, and worse in another—"

Butler held his tongue with a shrewd idea of what must be coming.

"And you don't need to look so bloody innocent, Jack." Audley was too quick for him. "We both know that Oliver *Saint*-John Latimer has made himself a Debrecen-expert since last year. And maybe Nikolai Panin was relying on that—I wouldn't put it past him, by God! In which case he would have reckoned that the fat sod would be only too pleased to set me up—right?"

Colonel Butler knew he couldn't have that. "Oliver acted perfectly correctly, David. Apart from accepting all the responsibility."

"Oh, sure! Oliver's not *stupid*," agreed Audley. "He didn't pull *me* out of Cheltenham until Turnbull had sussed things out. And he put poor little Elizabeth in charge—" He held up his hand to cut Colonel Butler off "—because it looked like a good training . . . Don't tell me, Jack! I can just hear the sainted Oliver justifying himself." He sniffed contemptuously. "So what happened was that I was hooked—partly because I thought Latimer was after me, and partly because I suspected that I was about to be framed by the Other Side—the Other Side being Professor N. A. Panin . . . All of which pushed me into making a mistake at Cheltenham, I agree! But I was *hooked*, anyway: Oliver had to do what he did, and so I had to do what I did, not only to watch my back, but also to protect poor old Haddock. And Peter Barrie, too."

Butler thought of the other memo in his drawer, from Neville Macready, warning him away from Sir Peter Barrie of Xenophon Oil, whose peace of mind was not on any account to be disturbed by any persecution, pending the completion of the Egyptian talks. And, as always, Macready was extremely persuasive.

"But I didn't turn up on the Pointe du Hoc," continued Audley. "Poor old Turnbull did, instead. And although I did leave Cheltenham for a day or two, there was no guarantee that I wouldn't return there. So they had to do something to make sure of me." Audley's face became blank. "If Latimer had sent Elizabeth to the Pointe du Hoc it would have been her. But he sent Turnbull, so it was him. But once we'd lost someone in the field, whoever it was . . . Jack, I couldn't quit then."

They had been taken, thought Butler. It had been Latimer and Audley, but it might very well have been *Butler* and Audley. So the final and inescapable responsibility was his.

But then he thought: *why was Audley so relaxed, for God's sake?*

And then he thought: *it couldn't be because David was in the clear, technically (on Latimer's order), or even actually (because even a clever man couldn't be condemned officially for being not quite clever enough, in these labyrinthine circumstances—not so long as he was Director, anyway!).*

Audley's face broke up. "Sorry, Jack. I fucked it up—I know!" But then he gave Butler a sly look. "But all is not lost, actually."

The sly look accelerated Butler's post-mortem thoughts. He had already prepared himself for the Minister's anger, and Number 10's recriminations: the fact that GCHQ Cheltenham still wasn't secure would actually strengthen the Government's stand on hard vetting and de-unionization. So, when this particular defector surfaced in Moscow eventually, Research and Development would survive, if only because it would be politically convenient for it to continue to do its important duties, beyond the scope of normal intelligence. But that still left a fearsome problem unsolved which Audley had overlooked.

"And the Americans?" It was unfair, when the CIA had raised the hare in the first place. But the British had let the animal escape, and that was what mattered. "We've lost their transmissions, David."

The sly look remained. "They won't make waves this time. And you can thank Paul Mitchell for that, Jack."

Butler schooled his face. Putting David Audley and Paul Mitchell on anything together should have warned him that they would exceed their brief. "What have you done?"

"Nothing really." Audley trod the pattern of the carpet geometrically. "It was just . . . he was handling the signals traffic the fellow was receiving." He twisted at a right angle towards Butler. "And . . . we were monitoring it to see what he was particularly interested in, to get a back-bearing on it, to find out what they wanted to know—eh?"

Their eyes met briefly. "Yes?"

"Paul had this idea." Audley twisted again. "He cleared it with Latimer, and then he talked to the Americans. And—so —they adjusted some of their figures for him, on a one-off irrational deviation, to destroy the readings. Which means that in about a month's time the Russians will have some inexplicable decimal points. Nothing very serious at the moment . . . but it will become serious." He looked at Butler sidelong. "And then they'll begin to wonder whether I didn't leave Cheltenham deliberately, if we play our cards right— whether *their* Cheltenham man isn't really *our* Cheltenham man in drag, do you see?"

Butler saw.

"The choice is ours, strictly speaking," said Audley. "I didn't know he was going to run, as I say. So we can play it in a lot of different ways, for the time being. And, if you like —in fact, I'd recommend it—you can ask the Americans which way they want to play it. Because that way you can tell them you let him run—that you deliberately ordered me away from Cheltenham, to give them the choice . . . Only, you'll have to do that bloody quick, Jack. Otherwise they'll smell a rat."

What Butler thought was that Audley had covered himself, on both flanks and in the rear. In fact, both Oliver St John Latimer and David Audley had covered themselves, although in very different ways, even as they had made different mistakes. But that was mere professionalism. Except that there was still one complication, which could not be overlooked.

He could send Audley away, and think of it at leisure. But that was not the way he had once commanded his company in the best days of his life. So it was not something to be fudged now, as though it didn't matter. "Elizabeth Loftus, David."

Audley's mouth lifted, one-sided. "Dear Elizabeth—yes, Jack?"

He underrated her, thought Butler. In the last analysis women were still merely sex-objects for David Audley: he was a product of his class and his education, pickled in the aspic of time in spite of his intelligence, when neither Mitchell nor Cable would have made the same mistake. "She has submitted an interim report, David."

The corner of the mouth remained contemptuous. "That was her brief. And she's had a couple of days to think about it. So what?"

So Audley was about to learn something, thought Butler. And that must be a lesson for him, too. "She wants more time, to consult the record, David."

"I don't bloody wonder! She was rather pitched into the deep end, poor woman!" Audley was still innocent. "And with me, too. So she was a bit out of her depth, Jack."

There were times when cruelty was satisfying. "What do you think of her?"

Audley drew a magisterial sniff. "She'll do, Jack—she'll do." He nodded. "She doesn't panic in adversity. In fact, she's one tough lady . . . But, you must remember, she's my recommendation . . . for our obligatory female—" Much too late, he caught a hint of something hostile in the question. "What does she say, then?"

Being a little worried was always good for Audley. "She thinks we perhaps ought to re-open the Debrecen List, David."

"Oh?" Too late, Audley realized he was too late.

"She lists five possibilities." Butler recalled Elizabeth Loftus's report easily because it had been impeccably typed, although she had not had time to submit it to Mrs Harlin, never mind the computer. "But she discounts two of them as unlikely. She merely left them in the margin for me to bear in mind."

"Uh-huh? Which leaves three. One of which is the re-opening of the Debrecen List, presumably." Audley nodded, but then smiled. "Well, at least I convinced her about Haddock Thomas and Peter Barrie, anyway."

"No. Actually, you didn't." Butler savoured the change in Audley's expression. "She thinks we should take another look at the list. With Haddock Thomas and Barrie on the top of it. The two names she discounted are Latimer's and yours, David."

Audley stared at him for a moment. "Ah . . . Yes, I suppose you could say that we fit quite well, at that." He pursed his lips. "The right original date . . . and I did help to screw up the '58 inquiry. And Latimer put me in the right place to do it again this time. So that's fair enough, Jack. I'd go along with that, anyway."

"But she discounted you all the same."

"Ye-ess . . . monstrous decent of her." Audley was smiling again, but it was a different sort of smile. "So what does she know about the other two that I don't?"

"Nothing. She says she only knows what you want her to know. And you have a deep subconscious affinity with each of them."

"I like them both—if that's what she means, Jack."

"More than that. You see them both as alternative Audleys. People you might have been—the pure tycoon or the pure scholar-teacher, each a round peg which found its round hole. Which, of course, you never really have, thinks Miss Elizabeth Loftus."

Audley took another and longer moment to think about that. "And what does Colonel Jack Butler think?"

Typical Audley! "He thinks he'd like to know what Dr David Audley thinks. Which is what Dr David Audley is paid to do."

Audley nodded slowly. "He thinks she isn't stupid. '58—and '57 too—were years of decision for all three of us . . . Haddock and Peter Barrie and me. Each of us changed directions. But there's no disgrace in that—there *was* no disgrace."

"You don't regret it?"

Audley raised an eyebrow. "That's a funny question from you, Jack. You answer it for yourself before you ask me."

Wild horses would never tear the word *duty* out of David Audley, Butler realized: saluting the flag was a public action, but kissing it was a private one, not to be mentioned. And regrets didn't come into it.

"What matters is what I think of Haddock Thomas. And Peter Barrie, Jack." Audley spoke casually, almost lightly. "What I still think."

Butler nodded. "So you think I should not act on Miss Loftus's recommendations?"

"On the contrary. Indeed, if I were you I'd take up all five, just to be on the safe side." There was a glint in Audley's eye now. "With a sixth from me, of course."

Butler knew the glint. "Which is?"

"You must put Elizabeth Loftus in charge."

"Why her?"

Audley made a face. "Isn't she the obvious choice?"

"Why her, David?"

Audley looked into space for an instant, then concentrated on Butler with peculiar intentness. "Back in '58, before I started on the Debrecen List, I was on the way to becoming a pretty bloodthirsty character. I'm not at all sure that wasn't why old Fred Clinton put me on it—and kept my nose to the grindstone . . . to teach me that if there's no difference between them and us, then we might as well join 'em and have done with it." He held Butler's eye without blinking. "I came damn near to resigning. But in the end I decided to rejoin the human race, even if only as a part-time member."

Butler nodded slowly. "You want to cut Elizabeth Loftus down to size in the same way?"

"Not quite." Audley shook his head. "But there was a moment, back in France when we were pushing old Haddock, that Elizabeth began to enjoy what she was doing a bit too much. And she must have already had those recommendations of hers in the back of her mind by then. Which is fair enough . . . except that we just could have another little monster in the making, I'm thinking." He shrugged. "Maybe that was what old Fred thought, back in '58—I don't know. And maybe she'll prove me wrong, I don't know that, either." He grinned suddenly. "Although I do, actually. Because I was in my prime back in '58—I didn't make mistakes then, like now, Jack . . . But, either way, she'll know what she is, monster or not, when she's finished with Haddock Thomas. And when he's finished with her."